PRAISE FOR *BAD JUJU*

"Chandler's writing is casual, but strong—without pretense. The pace is swift and constant . . . building up to an explosive ending. Hot and thick, the atmosphere reeks of earth, blood, and decay. The astringent air carries with it a sense of malevolence and resentment. No matter where you look, no matter how shallow you breathe, this town will touch you. Outstanding! Randy Chandler is horror's best kept secret! Buy it immediately, and discover the genre as it should be." —Kelly Tomblin, *Horror-Web*

"*Bad Juju* was one of the good ones. I climbed into that sucker and couldn't get out. It was a real Venus Flytrap of a novel, absolutely compelling . . . I love old-school horror when it's done right, and Randy Chandler did this absolutely right. I'd recommend *Bad Juju* without a single reservation [to] folks who dig old-time horror." —Steve Vernon, author of *Devil Tree*

"A full-bore, take-no-prisoners, one-man mission to once and forever completely upend & recontextualize the hallowed traditions of the Southern Gothic." —t. Winter-Damon, co-author of *Duet for the Devil*

"A high octane read . . . scary as hell." —Walt Hicks, author of *The Deathgrip Collection*

"Reading *Bad Juju* is like being bitten by scorpions again and again and again, then asking for more because it felt so damned good." —T. M. Wright, author of *Bone Soup*

"This is a brilliant book, and ranks right up there with James A Moore's *Serenity Falls* as my favourite town under siege by evil novels of all time." —Ginger Nuts of Horror

ALSO BY RANDY CHANDLER

NOVELS AND COLLECTIONS:
Daemon of the Dark Wood
Devils, Death & Dark Wonders
Dime Detective
Duet for the Devil (with t. winter-damon)
Hellz Bellz
Angel Steel

EDITOR:
Stiff Things: The Splatterporn Anthology
Red Room Magazine
Year's Best Hardcore Horror

BAD JUJU

RANDY CHANDLER

RED ROOM PRESS

WWW.REDROOMPRESS.COM

First Red Room Press Trade Paperback Edition, March 2018

Cover and interior by Inkubus Design www.inkubusdesign.com

ISBN 978-1-936964-09-3

Visit Red Room Press on the web at: redroompress.com
facebook.com/redroompress
twitter.com/redroombooks

WWW.REDROOMPRESS.COM

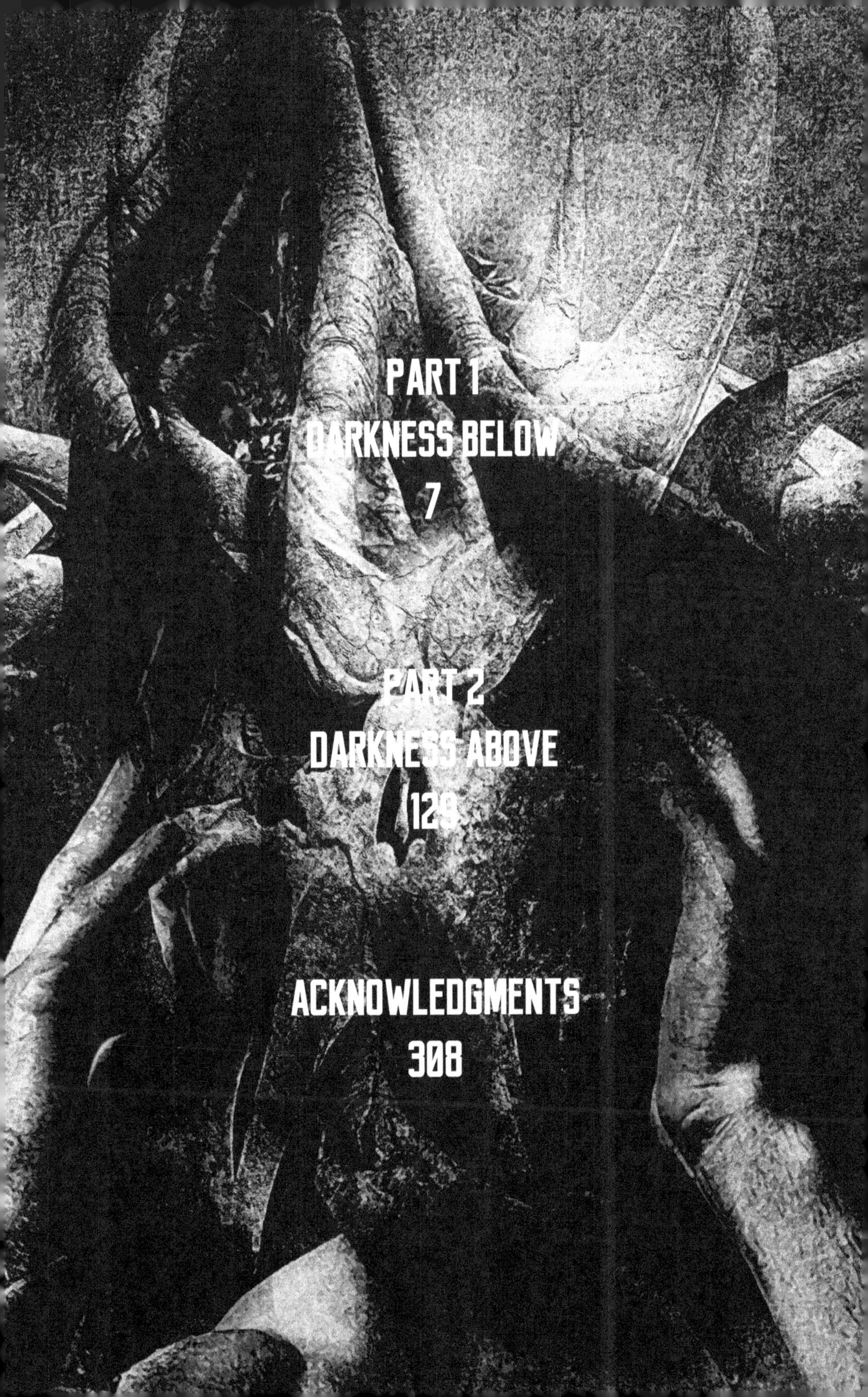

PART 1
DARKNESS
BELOW

CHAPTER 1
RATS

T hey left Skeeter's truck parked just off the red-dirt woodland road and tromped onto the desolate landscape of rubbish and waste, woebegone junk evacuated from the bowels of town and left out here in the elements to rust and decay.

Skeeter carried his rifle across his shoulders and behind his neck like a weightless barbell, his wrists propped over the horizontal weapon and his bent arms hanging like misshapen V's.

Joe Rob toted his rifle in the crook of his arm, its muzzle angled toward the ground.

"You hold that thing like you're escorting it to the prom," said Skeeter. "A regular country gentleman."

Joe Rob shot him a cool glance, then said, "The way you got yours up on your shoulders, you look like you're wearing a yoke. Damn yokel."

Skeeter rolled his eyes beneath the bill of his ball cap, then stopped and looked up at the late-summer sky as if he were reading something there.

"*What?*" said Joe Rob, stopping beside him.

"Storm's coming."

"Oh. So now you're the yokel weatherman." Joe Rob grinned at his own wordplay.

Skeeter shook his head, unsmiling. "I'm serious. See the way those clouds are piling up? Won't be long before they're thunderheads."

"Then I reckon we'll just have to nail some rats *before* we get struck by lightning."

"I thought rats were night feeders," said Skeeter. "*Nocturnal* sons-o'-bitches."

"Well, they are. But there's so damn many of 'em out here now, there's bound to be some early risers looking to get a jump on the competition. Chief Keller says he's never seen anything like it."

"'A plague of rats'," Skeeter said in booming imitation of Vinewood's new police chief.

"Damn, son, you sound like one of them radio preachers. I ain't shitting you. You could be pulling down some serious bucks with that act."

"Nope. I'm thinking it'd be cool to be a submariner aboard a nuclear submarine."

"What about your old man? I thought he wanted you to take over the family business."

"I tell you what, bud. No way am I ever gonna be a mortician. I don't care what he says."

"Make good money, though."

Skeeter barked a hollow laugh. "There ain't enough money in the world for me to make my living sucking the guts out of dead people. I'll just wait and inherit my share of the family fortune when the dad croaks."

"Man, that's cold. And anyway, I thought you wanted to be a relief pitcher for the Atlanta Braves," Joe Rob needled his friend.

"That was last year. You gotta keep up, Joe Rob. That was high-school shit. We're all grown up now. Men of the world. This is the part where we put away childish things."

"I notice you're still wearing your senior ring." Joe Rob wiped sweat from his forehead with the back of his hand. "And I still say it's cold, talking about your old man like that."

"Hey, everybody dies," Skeeter proclaimed. "Sooner or later we all end up in extremis."

"In what?"

"*In extremis.* It means deader than a fucking doornail, the way my old man uses it. He never uses the word 'dead.' He'll say, 'I got two *in extremis.* Don't wait dinner for me.' Like that. Undertakers don't ever say 'dead.' That's the first thing they teach 'em in mortician school."

Joe Rob shook his head, then swatted at a troublesome gnat in front of his face. Skeeter pulled his rifle off his shoulders, rested it against the side of his leg while he dug a tin of tobacco from his jeans pocket and stuck a healthy pinch of Skoal in his mouth.

They resumed their trek through the city dump, weaving their way through the clutter of old refrigerators, washing machines, deep freezers, ratty pieces of furniture, a baby carriage with a broken wheel, plastic trash bags stuffed with unseen debris, and various unidentifiable hunks of junk. A water-stained commode sat upright amid the other refuse.

"Somebody threw away a perfectly good shitter," Skeeter observed.

"Must be the throne for the king of the dump."

"Well, if you need to take a dump while you're here, there you go."

"Oh shit," said Joe Rob.

"Be my guest," Skeeter guffawed.

"No, I mean oh shit, there's Odell Porch." He nodded his head in the direction of the woods on the other side of the barren landfill. "What the hell's he doing here?"

"Seeing as how he's carrying a rifle, I'd say he's here to shoot rats. Or us."

"Scary dude," Joe Rob said, lowering his voice. "Crazy as hell."

"And mean as a pit bull. Let's get the hell outta here. Ain't no rats anyhow."

"Just that big one with the fucking deer rifle."

"Ten-four."

"Shit, he's waving at us."

"Walk away. Pretend you don't see him." Skeeter's voice took on a raw edge, the way it always did when he was scared.

"Too late."

A sudden chill made Joe Rob shudder in spite of the afternoon's muggy heat. He knew then that they shouldn't be here in the middle of this scabbed-over wound in the earth. The junkyard artifacts were somehow endowed with bad mojo. And Odell Porch was the Mojo Man himself. The Mad Prince of the Realm, come to punish trespassers.

"What-chew pussies doing here?" Odell challenged. He strode toward them, holding his rifle at port-arms and building up a good head of steam.

"Nothing," Skeeter said at the same time Joe Rob said, "Hunting rats."

Decked out in faded cammies and combat boots, Odell Porch looked like a soldier in some rag-tag Third-world army. He wore a red bandanna as a headband. A dark stubble of beard shaded the lower half of his sun-burned face. With a wolfish grin, he said, "Take more than them little .22 pop guns to nail these varmints. Check this shit."

He reached into the gunnysack slung over his left shoulder and pulled out a dead rat the size of a house cat. "Izzat a rat, or what?" he said as he dangled the rodent by its tail, giving them a good look at his blood-matted trophy.

"Jeez," said Skeeter, "that's the biggest rat I've ever seen."

Joe Rob wanted to ask Odell why he was collecting his kills in the gun-nysack, but thought better of it and decided not to. He didn't want to know what the man was going to do with his dead rats. If only half of what he'd heard about the Porch clan was true, it wouldn't be much of a stretch to imagine Odell's family sitting down to a Sunday dinner of fried rat, collard greens and sweet potatoes.

"Damn right it is," Odell said, dropping the rat back into the sack. "You girls best high-tail it outta here and leave these varmints to a real shooter."

He slapped his rifle for emphasis.

Thunder rumbled in the distance, and Skeeter warily eyed the darkening western sky.

Joe Rob said, "Yeah, we were just leaving. Storm's coming."

"Right," said Skeeter.

"Hey," Odell said with an odd glint in his eyes, "you're the undertaker's son, ain't cha."

"Yeah?" Skeeter nervously adjusted his ball cap, then rubbed his nose and touched the bill of his cap again, reminding Joe Rob of the ritualistic behavior most pitchers go through before hurling the ball at home plate.

"Reckon you seen some sights at your old man's shop, huh?" Odell fingered his nostril, dug something out and flicked it into the air.

"Not really," Skeeter answered.

"Bullshit, you ain't. You mean to tell me you ain't never snuck no looks at dead pussy?"

Odell put his hand on Skeeter's shoulder and dug in his fingers until Skeeter winced in pain.

"Don't bullshit me, boy," Odell warned.

Joe Rob thought he smelled booze on Odell's breath. The Porch clan, it was said, came from a long line of moonshiners and horse thieves, and over the course of the last century Odell's forefathers had done their part in earning Graves County, Georgia, the nickname "Bloody Graves," according to local legend and lore. Seeing Odell Porch at close range, Joe Rob didn't doubt that the man was descended from ruthless outlaws.

"Tell me," commanded Odell, keeping Skeeter in his rough grasp.

"Ow! Okay, okay. I did sneak a look at Judy Moody after she was killed in that wreck," Skeeter confessed.

"How'd she look?" Odell's leer became a 'possum's grin.

"I don't know," Skeeter stammered, "she looked . . . dead. You know. But still pretty. She wasn't too messed up on the outside. She died of internal injuries."

"You saw her snatch?"

Skeeter hung his head and mumbled something.

"Speak up, boy."

"Yeah, I saw it."

Odell laughed and slapped Skeeter's shoulder. "I know you did, Mr. Undertaker's Son. And I bet you done a lot you ain't telling."

"We gotta go," Joe Rob said in an attempt to rescue his friend from the clutches of Odell Porch. "Before the storm catches us."

As if on cue, a burst of thunder shook the earth. When the thunder rumbled itself out, another sound came to the fore: a girlish scream, or more accurately, a *whoop*.

"Damn me," said Odell. "Looky there."

Joe Rob and Skeeter turned in unison and looked where Odell was pointing his rifle. A wraith-like figure in a long, white gown was sliding down the shallow embankment at the edge of the woods. She whooped again before coming to a stop at the bottom of the rocky incline. Then she started sobbing as she buried her face in her hands.

Odell jogged toward her, with Joe Rob and Skeeter at his heels.

Hearing their approach, she looked up. Tears rolled down her cheeks as she gave them a wide-eyed appraisal.

"Are you all right?" asked Joe Rob.

Her eyes darted about wildly.

Realizing that the sight of three strangers with guns was probably not a reassuring sight to the young woman, Joe Rob said, "We're not going to hurt you."

She suddenly scrambled to her bare feet and made a dash for the woods, but Odell grabbed her wrist and held her in place. "Whoa there, honey," he said. "Take 'er easy now."

That's when Joe Rob saw the plastic wristband on her captive wrist, the kind they gave hospital patients. Odell saw it too, and said, "You ran away from the loony bin, didn't cha?"

The loony bin was the private psychiatric hospital located just outside the city limits of Vinewood, three miles south of the dump.

"Hell, I run away from there myself once," Odell boasted.

Joe Rob and Skeeter both had heard rumors that Odell had been committed to Browner Psychiatric Hospital after his early discharge from the Marine Corps, and here was Odell himself confirming it as the truth.

Still holding her arm, Odell asked, "So where you running to?" He bent her arm so he could read her wristband. "Jessica A. Lowell."

She shrugged, eyes downcast. Her auburn hair was a mass of Medusa-like tangles, and her milky complexion was flushed red with the day's heat.

"Why did you run?" Skeeter asked her. He scratched his ankle with the toe of his opposite boot.

She looked at Skeeter, then spoke for the first time. "It knew I was there."

"*What* knew you were there?" Skeeter queried.

"The dark thing," she said softly. She glanced about, furtive and fearful.

Odell grinned, his eyes fixed on the bosom of her thin nightgown. "Well don't you worry, little lady. We won't tell it you're here. No ma'am. You jest let Odell take care of you."

Joe Rob knew at once what Odell had in mind for the girl. No way could he let that happen. "I'm Joe Rob Campbell," he said, "and this is Skeeter Partain. We can give you a ride to wherever you want to go. That's Skeeter's truck over there."

Odell scowled at Joe Rob. "You boys be on your way," he said. "She needs a grown-up to help her. Get on, now. Respect your fuckin' elders."

Skeeter started toward his truck. Joe Rob stood his ground; he was not prepared to leave the girl in Odell's dubious custody.

Maintaining his hold on Jessica Lowell's wrist, Odell raised his rifle in a one-handed grip and pointed it at Joe Rob's chest. "I ain't telling you again, boy," he said.

Joe Rob looked into Odell's eyes and saw the cold-blooded stare of a snake, poised and ready to strike. Reluctantly, he turned and trailed Skeeter to his truck.

"This is fucked," he said to Skeeter, who was already behind the wheel. "You know what he's gonna do to her."

"I know better than to go against that crazy sumbitch," said Skeeter, sticking the key in the ignition. "I ain't ready to die."

The sun made a brief appearance through a small break in the dark clouds. Joe Rob looked back across the dump and saw Odell leading the girl into the long shadows of the moss-hung trees. He cursed and slammed his fist on the hood of the truck. Then the storm clouds swallowed up the sun again.

"Come on, man," Skeeter pleaded. "Get in the truck. That chick's nuts anyway. She don't even know what's going on."

Joe Rob was about to explain to his friend how that was exactly the point—that the girl didn't know how to protect herself—when he heard the scream. Not a whoop this time, but an honest-to-God shriek of terror. "God damn it," he said quietly, then worked the bolt of his rifle, snapping a .22 long hollow-point cartridge into the rifle's firing chamber. "I'm going to get her."

"You're crazy!" Skeeter snatched the cap off his head and slapped it against the truck's dash.

"May be." Holding his rifle in a high port-arms, Joe Rob started jogging back toward the dump and the woods beyond. Odell be damned, he thought as he leapt over a crumpled cardboard box of decomposing paperbacks, I'm not letting him have her. No fucking way.

When he reached the edge of the woods, Joe Rob slowed to stealthy walk, his eyes searching the underbrush for Odell and the girl. A white blur caught his eye.

There she was, lying on her back at the foot of a tall pine, her white gown riding up above her knees as she tried to back-pedal away from Odell, who was standing over her, unfastening his camouflage pants. His gunnysack of dead rats was on the ground near his feet. Surging wind filled the moss-bearded trees.

"I got what you need, little honey," Odell cooed to her. "It'll settle you right down. Better'n any medicine they give you at that fuckin' loony bin."

Joe Rob pushed through a tangle of brush and raised his rifle. "No," he said.

Odell hunched his shoulders and turned around to face him. His lips twisted into a smile, but there was no mirth in his cold eyes. "Ain't no sloppy seconds today. You best git yer ass outta here."

"Leave her alone," Joe Rob said, his voice quivering as much with fear as with anger.

Odell seemed to notice for the first time that Joe Rob's rifle was pointing at him. Then he glanced at his own rifle propped against the trunk of a small birch, obviously calculating his chances of reaching it before catching a .22 slug with his flesh. "You stupid li'l peckerwood," he hissed like a viper. "You throw down on me, you hafta die. No two ways about it."

Jessica Lowell hugged her bare knees and began rocking herself, whispering some bizarre incantation.

"Just go, God damn you," Joe Rob said. "And leave your gun."

"Cain't do that." Odell casually hitched up his pants and buttoned them.

Joe Rob raised his aim from Odell's chest to his snake-eyed face. "I mean it," he warned.

The first drops of rain began to fall, pattering softly on the pine straw. Joe Rob shuddered with some unrecognized emotion.

Odell suddenly pointed his finger at the girl rocking on the ground. "Take a good look at her," he said. "See what yer about to die for and ast yerself if she's worth it."

Then Joe Rob made his mistake. He took his eyes off Odell Porch and glanced at Jessica Lowell. Later he would wonder if things might have turned out differently if he had not taken his eyes from Odell—though of course he would never really know.

In the brief instant he looked away, Odell drew the hunting knife from its sheath at the small of his back and sprang at him.

Joe Rob instinctively stepped back from his attacker, startled by the gunshot that rang out. A third eye opened in Odell's forehead and began weeping red tears as he staggered about like a bumbling drunk determined to stay on his feet.

Then Odell's eyes rolled up in their sockets and he toppled to the ground. The dark eye in his forehead remained open, leaking blood.

"Oh Lord," Joe Rob moaned. "I shot him."

Jessica A. Lowell began to giggle. Her giggling became cackling laughter. The hollow laughter of the mad.

"It doesn't want *me*," she tittered. "It wants *him*."

She raised her arm and pointed her finger at Joe Rob Campbell.

*   *   *

Skeeter hated his best friend at that miserable moment. Didn't Joe Rob see the position he was putting him in? What the hell was he supposed to do? Sit here and wait while Joe Rob went and got himself killed? Drive off and leave him to go against Odell Porch? Yeah, just drive the fuck away.

He put his hand on the key, hesitated, then cranked the engine. The old green Chevy pickup roared to life, rumbling and shaking like a harnessed beast impatient to be given free rein.

Skeeter shouted a curse, then turned off the ignition. Fuming, he hopped out of the cab of the truck, grabbed his rifle and went after Joe Rob.

He heard the gunshot as he approached the woods. Fear spawned a metallic taste in his mouth. His heart thumped wildly in his thin chest. But he pushed on into the woods. He was pretty sure that the sharp report had come from Joe Rob's .22, rather than Odell's .30-.06. Joe Rob must've fired a warning shot to show Odell he meant business. He was like that, Joe Rob was; whenever he got his hackles up and his mind set on something, nothing could turn him away. He was one stubborn son of a bitch then.

Skeeter tripped over an unseen root and stumbled onto a scene he would never forget. The girl was pointing her finger at Joe Rob, and Joe Rob was standing over the sprawled body of Odell Porch. Just below Odell's headband a neat hole had been punched into the center of his forehead.

"It wants *him*," the girl repeated maniacally.

"Jesus Christ!" Skeeter blurted. "You *shot him*."

"I didn't mean to," Joe Rob said meekly. "He came at me with a knife. I . . . it just went off. Oh Lord. I think he's dead."

"Check his pulse."

"You do it. I can't touch him." Joe Rob dropped his rifle and sank to his knees. "I'm sick."

"Dead head," Jessica Lowell said, then lapsed into another fit of inappropriate laughter.

"Shut up, God damn you!" Skeeter shouted at her. "This is all your fault. Crazy ass bitch."

She covered her mouth and laughed into her hands like a misbehaving child.

Skeeter knelt down by Odell and touched his fingers to Odell's neck. "His heart ain't beating. He's dead, no shit."

Joe Rob retched, then spewed a foul gush of vomit onto the ground.

Skeeter backed away from the corpse, then moved away from Joe Rob when he caught a whiff of his puke. "What the fuck do we do now? Huh? I told you not to come back."

Joe Rob wiped his mouth and nose with the back of his hand, then turned his face skyward to catch the rain. He coughed, spat, then said, "We go to Chief Keller. Tell him what happened. It was self-defense. He had a fucking knife."

Skeeter shook his head. "Think about it, man. The law might let you off, but the Porch clan will kill you. You think they'll care what the law says? No fucking way. Old man Porch and his boys will come after you and keep on coming till you're dead. You *know* what they'll do to you. They're *Porches*, man. They ain't hardly human. Remember Monroe Shockley. Everybody knows they killed him, but nobody could ever prove it. Be the same with you."

Joe Rob nodded acknowledgment as he sat back on his haunches. "Then what do we do?"

"We bury him deep in the woods where nobody will find him. If anybody asks, we'll say we never saw him."

"What about her?" Joe Rob nodded at the girl who had thankfully gone silent.

"She's crazy as a loon. Who's gonna listen to her?"

"Yeah, but what if she comes out of it and tells what she saw?"

"Jesus, Joe Rob, *look* at her. You think she's all of a sudden gonna go sane? It don't work that way. She probably won't remember any of this. She's probably on so much medication right now that this is nothing but a bad dream to her."

"It's a bad dream all right," Joe Rob said woefully. "Lord almighty."

"Well, whadaya say? It's your ass on the line. Do we bury him or go to the cops?"

Joe Rob rubbed his face with both hands. Then he looked at Odell's corpse. "We bury him."

"Damn right."

"What do we do with her?"

"Nothing. We leave her here, just like we never saw her. They'll find her eventually and take her back to the nuthouse."

"I don't know, man," Joe Rob said. "Something could happen to her. I mean, she's not safe out here. In her condition."

"Hey, we're not responsible for her. She ran away. That's got nothing to do with us."

"But . . ."

Skeeter squatted down beside his friend and put his hand on Joe Rob's shoulder. "Listen. If we bury the body, that makes me as guilty as you. An accessory to the fucking crime. That gives me a say in this. And I say we leave her. Think about it. If we take her back to the hospital, they'll want to know where we found her. Hell, she could say we tried to rape her. We don't want any connection to her, don't you get it?"

"But I told her our names," Joe Rob whispered.

Skeeter thought about this a moment, then turned to the girl and said, "Hey. Do you know my name?"

If she heard him, she gave no sign. She had resumed her rocking motion and seemed to have folded in on herself, withdrawing deeper into her madness.

"See? Nothing to worry about. Now let's get it in gear before somebody comes along and sees us."

*   *   *

Joe Rob looked at her, loathing her and wishing he'd never laid eyes on her. He got to his feet and wiped his mouth on the shoulder of his shirt. He tried his best to clear the fog of unreality from his head, but his thoughts remained jumbled. Logic failed him. He had to rely on his friend to guide him now. "Where can we bury him?"

"Out past the wolf's den. On the other side of that little creek. Nobody would have any reason to go digging there."

"Yeah. Okay."

"Wait here," Skeeter told him. "I'll pull my truck up as close as I can."

He watched Skeeter jog off through the rain, keeping his back to the man he had just killed, fancifully wishing the corpse would just disappear while he wasn't looking.

The cooling rainfall felt clean and good, but he knew there would be nothing to wash away his sin. He had taken a human life and nothing could change that fact. His finger had twitched and a man had died.

It was so easy—too easy—to kill a man.

I had to do it, he told himself. Odell would've gutted me with his knife if I hadn't shot him. Sure as hell he would've. I didn't even think about pulling the trigger. It was like it pulled itself, or maybe it was that part of me that wanted to survive that did it. Can that be a sin? No. I did nothing wrong.

His ruminations were interrupted by the approach of Skeeter's truck. As he neared the edge of the woods, Skeeter swung the truck around and backed right up to the outermost trees, then he hopped out of the cab to let down the gate of the truck bed. The gate dropped with a metallic bang.

Joe Rob glanced at the girl to see if she would react at all to Skeeter's return. Her long hair was plastered to her head by the rainfall, and her teeth were chattering, but the same vacant expression remained on her face. She was in the world, but obviously not *of* it. Joe Rob's heart went out to her but slammed into the stone wall of her withdrawal. A terrible sadness settled in the center of his chest. He fought the urge to cry, to bawl like a baby.

"Let's get the sumbitch in the truck," said Skeeter.

"Maybe we should wait till dark," Joe Rob suggested.

"No, we need to get this done. Now."

Skeeter bent over Odell's corpse and pulled his headband down so that it covered the bullet hole in his forehead. "Maybe that will keep his brains and shit from leaking on my truck."

"Jesus, man."

"You get his feet. I got his head."

Joe Rob bent to the task and grabbed Odell's ankles. "Christ, I think he shit his pants."

"'Course he did. That's what happens when you die. Everything lets go. Dying's dirty business."

They carried the body through the underbrush and got it to the back of the truck.

"On three," said Skeeter as he began to swing his end of the suspended corpse like a lumpy bag of potatoes. "One . . . two . . . three!"

They let go and Odell was momentarily airborne, then he flopped onto the truck bed with a hollow thump. Skeeter covered the bed with a canvas tarp and secured it with multicolored bungee cords.

"All right," he said. "Let's get the hell outta here."

"Wait. We forgot his gun."

"Damn. Good thinking. His rat bag too."

They went back for the rifle and the gunnysack.

The girl was gone.

"Where the hell did she go?" Joe Rob looked around for some sign of her departure.

"Who cares? Forget her." Skeeter snatched up Odell's rifle. "Better this way. Now you don't have to feel bad about leaving her. She left us."

Joe Rob picked up the gunnysack. "Yeah. Good point."

The rain was slacking off when they got back to the truck and tossed Odell's rat bag and rifle under the tarp.

"Your shovel still in the back?" Joe Rob asked as they climbed into the pickup and simultaneously slammed their doors.

"Yeah. Pickaxe too." Skeeter cranked the engine. "Ground's pretty soft where we'll plant him. We can have him in the ground in no time. Then forget this whole fucking mess."

"I wish it was that easy. I'll never forget this shit, man. No fucking way."

Skeeter drove across the landfill, winding his way through an obstacle course of junk piles and broken appliances. The truck skidded over a slick patch of mud, then bumped over a shallow gully and emerged onto the red hardpack of Nebula Road.

"Shit, there's a car," Skeeter said as he turned on the headlights against the premature dusk.

Joe Rob leaned forward and peered ahead through the windshield.

A black Firebird with tinted windows was coming down the road toward them.

"Who is it?"

"How the fuck should I know?" Skeeter said. "Shit, shit, shit."

"I've never seen that car before. It's probably not somebody who'll know your truck."

The Firebird blew past them. It was an older model, flat black with a coat of primer.

Skeeter's eyes went to the rearview mirror and watched the black car slow, then turn into the mouth of the landfill. "It's turning at the dump. Ah fuck! That's not good."

"No shit."

"Maybe it's Odell's ride," Skeeter offered. "We didn't see his truck, ya know."

"Nah, don't say that."

"You think he hiked all the way from the Bottom to shoot rats?"

"He could've. It's only five or six miles."

"Not fucking likely. That's his ride. One of his brothers coming to pick him up. And he saw my fucking truck. God damn!"

"You don't know that," Joe Rob protested. "And if we don't recognize the car, the driver probably won't know your truck."

"All he's gotta do is ask around." Skeeter slipped into his imitation redneck voice: "'Old green Chevy with a confederate flag on the front bumper? Sounds like Skeeter Partain, the undertaker's son.'"

"Fuck it. Once we bury the body, nobody can prove anything. No point worrying about it now."

Skeeter floored the accelerator, wanting to put as much distance between them and the scene of the crime and the Firebird as possible.

Joe Rob turned in the seat to keep vigil through the rear window. He half expected the car to give chase. He exhaled a sigh of relief when they turned off Nebula Road and onto the smaller rutted road leading to the wolf's den. The woods thickened and the trail finally played out in a swampy thicket less than a mile from their destination.

They jumped out of the truck and removed the canvas tarp, then Skeeter said, "You're the weightlifter. You carry Odell and I'll get the rest of the shit."

Joe Rob gave no argument. It was his kill; he should be the one to carry the body. He pulled Odell to the edge of the truck bed, bent down and pulled the corpse onto his shoulder in a fireman's carry. Skeeter hooked the gunnysack of rats over his own shoulder, grabbed the shovel, the pickaxe and Odell's rifle, then followed Joe Rob up the path leading to the wolf's den.

Breathless with exertion, Joe Rob said, "I'm gonna have to bathe in the creek to get this shit smell off me."

"Good idea." Skeeter anxiously glanced over his shoulder to make sure no one was following them.

They trudged past the small outcropping of rock that formed the little cave-like structure they called the wolf's den, waded across the narrow creek and stopped in the middle of a small clearing twenty or so yards deeper into the woods.

Joe Rob bent over and dumped the corpse off his shoulder. Skeeter was already testing the ground with the shovel. "Ground's pretty soft," he said. "Let's get her dug."

"You sure you wanna do this, man? It's not to late to go to the cops."

Skeeter thrust the pickaxe into Joe Rob's hands. "Shut up and dig. We go to the cops, we're both dead and you know it."

Joe Rob lost himself in the digging; his only thought was of making a hole in the earth. The rain ended, and all that was left of the summer storm was an occasional flash of distant lightning in the eastern sky. It was full dark by the time they had fashioned a shallow grave in the ground, and Skeeter went back to the truck to get his flashlight.

Standing there, alone in the dark woods, Joe Rob was suddenly afraid. He spooked himself with the idea that Odell Porch was going to get up and shamble toward him like one of those zombies in *Night of the Living Dead*.

"Skeeter?" he called. "Hurry up with that flashlight! I can't see shit."

What the hell could be taking him so long? The truck wasn't that far away.

He tightened his grip on the pickaxe, thinking irrationally that if Odell did get up and come after him, he would bury the sharp point of the axe in Odell's skull.

Then he saw the light bobbing toward him through the trees.

"Stop yelling," Skeeter called in a loud whisper.

Joe Rob could've hugged and kissed him just then. They had been best friends since the eighth grade, bled their wrists in a blood-brother ritual, graduated high school together, and now here they were playing out an incredible scene that was—as Joe Rob saw it—nothing less than an ultimate test of their friendship. And Skeeter was passing the test with colors flying, God bless him.

Skeeter held the light while Joe Rob rolled the corpse into the grave.

"Rest in peace, you crazy fuck," Skeeter said.

Joe Rob tossed in Odell's rifle, then picked up the gunnysack and dropped it on top of Odell's face. They took turns shoveling the sodden dirt into the shallow grave, and when they were done, they spread pine straw and dead leaves over the newly turned soil.

"Listen, man," Skeeter said. "None of this ever happened. We don't breathe a word of it to any-fucking-body. No matter what."

"No matter what," Joe Rob agreed.

"Blood brother's oath." Skeeter arched his brows.

"Damn straight. Blood oath."

Standing over the hidden grave, they touched their scarred wrists together, then shook hands to seal the vow.

Then Skeeter summed it up for them: "All we did was bury some rats."

Joe Rob nodded, wishing he could believe it.

CHAPTER 2
A BAD PATCH

"You look damn good for a dead man," Luke Chaney said to the corpse. He laid his hand on the open casket. "Happy trails, old friend."

He turned and walked softly out of the flower-filled viewing room, made his way down the carpeted hallway and emerged on the front porch of Partain Funeral Home. He squinted against the brightness of the day.

"Hello, Luke," said James Partain, who had posted himself at the top of the porch steps like a somber, dark-suited doorman.

A small cluster of friends and relatives of the late Calvin Hull huddled at the far corner of the wrap-around porch, talking in muted tones.

"James," Luke said with a curt nod.

"We don't see much of you these days. What have you been doing with yourself?"

Luke shrugged. "This and that."

"Enjoying your retirement?" Partain's deep-set eyes twinkled in his otherwise expressionless face.

"I'm getting used to it." Luke stuck his hands in his pockets. "You did a good job on old Calvin. All made up like a movie star. He would've liked that."

"I did, didn't I," Partain said, speaking softly in spite of his obvious enthusiasm. "Took ten years off him. It helped, of course, that he had strong features to begin with. Then it's just a matter of bringing out those features with subtle touches of makeup, shading the flaws. I studied art before I went into mortuary sciences."

"Is that right? I guess that explains it. You're a regular Rembrandt for dead folks."

Partain winced. "I see you haven't lost your irreverent sense of humor."

"But I'm dead serious," Luke quipped.

"Please, Luke." Partain showed him the palm of his hand. "I would appreciate it if you would be a little more sensitive in your comments. The bereaved don't like to hear the D-word."

"The D-word?" Luke was beginning to enjoy himself. He didn't like funeral homes, and he didn't much care for James Partain.

"Yes. D-e-a-d," he spelled it out. "You used it twice in a matter of seconds."

"Did I?"

Luke glanced at the huddle of mourners, then leaned close to Partain, cupped his hand to the side of his mouth and whispered, "You don't suppose they think he's only sleeping, do you?"

James Partain scowled.

"You take care, now, James," Luke said and slapped him lightly on the shoulder.

Luke sauntered down the porch steps and jaywalked across 2nd Street. He briefly considered dropping in at the redbrick police station, but decided against it at the last minute. He wasn't in the mood for chit-chat with his former colleagues, so he bypassed the station house, crossed the alley and cut through the narrow passageway between Howell's Five And Dime and Grubb's Hardware; he stepped from the shadowed alley onto sun-baked Main Street.

The sinkhole that had killed Calvin Hull was roped off with yellow "Caution!" tape, and through-traffic was blocked by yellow-and-black saw horses affixed with battery-operated flashers.

He crossed Main, skirting the killer hole, and went into City Drugs. The air-conditioned coolness and the amiable smell of food cooking on the grill behind the lunch counter welcomed him.

Doc Taggert was in the back, filling a prescription for a woman Luke didn't recognize. Of course George Taggert was a pharmacist, not a physician, but most everyone called him Doc or Doctor; it was one of many harmless small-town traditions. Luke had never called him anything else. George Taggert *was* Doc.

He waved at Doc, then pointed at an unoccupied booth opposite the lunch counter. Doc nodded assent from his little alcove of shelves stocked with all manner of pill bottles. Luke slid into the booth and ordered iced coffee for himself and hot black coffee for Doc. Betty Lee the veteran waitress was too busy to share her latest tidbits of gossip with Luke, so she shared a wink and a waggle of her long-nailed fingers.

"I was beginning to think you'd dropped off the face of the earth," Doc said with a smile half hidden by his big white brush of a moustache. He sat opposite Luke and folded his hands on the tabletop.

"Like Calvin? No, I'm still here."

"Hell of a thing," Doc said soberly. "Makes you think."

"Yeah."

"It could've been any one of us. But it just happened to be Calvin on that very spot when the earth fell out from under him. Jesus, can you imagine what that must've been like? Tooling along Main Street in your new car, then *boom*. The street falls away and the earth swallows you up."

Luke shrugged his thick shoulders.

"Dr. Jackson said it was his heart that killed him. His back was broken in two places, but he would've survived that. It was the shock that got him."

"Calvin was damn lucky."

"*Lucky?*" Doc's bushy brows arched upward.

"Yeah. Lucky he didn't have to spend his remaining years in a wheel chair, collecting his shit and piss in plastic bags. His heart knew his time was up."

"I didn't know you were such a fatalist, Luke."

"I don't know about that. But when your number's up, that's it. End of story."

Doc took another sip of coffee, then smoothed his moustache with his thumb and index finger. "You in town for the funeral?"

"Nah. I don't do funerals any more. I just came to pay my last respects to Calvin. And to see how you were doing."

"I'm doing fine. It's you I'm worried about."

"Me? What are you talking about?"

"I know you, Luke. You can't bullshit me, so don't even try. Ever since you turned in your badge, you've practically been a hermit. This is the first time I've seen you in . . . I don't know how long."

He waited for Luke to respond. When he didn't, Doc said, "This is about Monroe Shockley, isn't it. And Fate Porch."

Luke shook his head in a noncommittal gesture.

"You did the best you could," Doc went on. "Even the state cops said there was just no hard evidence. Fate Porch and his boys got away with murder and there's nothing you or anybody else can do about it. But you just can't turn it loose, can you? You resigned because of it, but you didn't stop with quitting your job. No, you quit the whole damn community. Just up and removed yourself from the whole shebang. Turned your back on everything you stood for and walked away. So, you tell me, Luke. Did it make you feel any better? Has your self-exile worked for you?"

"You talk real pretty, Doc," Luke said with a humorless grin. "But you got it wrong. Fate Porch ain't off my hook just yet."

"Lord *God*, but you're one mule-headed son of a bitch. Is that plain enough for you? You're the stubbornest old fart in the whole damn county."

"You make that sound like a bad thing."

"What? You couldn't get the goods on him as police chief, so you're going after him as a private citizen? What's wrong with this picture, Luke?"

"You tell me, Doc."

Doc sighed. "That's just the trouble. Nobody can tell you anything. Nobody ever could. Everything's got to be your way. I swear, Luke, I don't know why I waste my time trying to talk sense to you."

"We go at things a different way, that's all it is."

"No. That's *not* all it is. You've not been the same since Jenny died. You've got—"

"There's no need to get into that," Luke said with a cold edge of warning in his voice.

"All right. But you know it's true. And then when Shockley was murdered, you did your dead level best to hang it on Porch and his boys, but you couldn't do it. *Nobody* could. But being you, you couldn't live with that. So you resigned. I'm sure you saw it as a question of honor. You failed to do your job so the honorable thing to do was resign. But you know what? I don't think it was honor at all. I think it was all about your pride. You're a prideful man, Luke. Don't tell me you're not. You couldn't feel proud about the way the Shockley case turned out, so you turned in your badge."

Luke downed a big slug of his iced coffee. "Not bad for a pill pusher. But you're making it more complicated than it is. We all get a bad patch to hoe now and then, and the only thing to do is put your back into it and work your way out."

"But when you're fifty years old, your back ain't what it used to be. A man has to know when to give up on a particularly bad patch and go on to new ground."

A cute blonde barely out of her teens approached their booth hesitantly. The nametag on her blue smock said her name was Missy. "Uh, Doc?" she said softly. "Phone call. It's Dr. Jackson's office."

Doc slid out of the booth and told Luke he'd be right back.

Luke downed the rest of his drink, left a couple of worn dollars on the table, and departed. He knew Doc was only trying to be helpful, but some of his remarks had cut a little too close to the bone, and Luke had no intention of getting into a superheated debate with his old friend.

He stepped out into the street, ducked under the yellow tape and stood at the edge of the sinkhole where a big chunk of pavement had broken and collapsed a good twenty feet into the pit. He stared at the slab of asphalt lying slantwise at the bottom of the hole.

"You ever seen the like?" someone behind him said.

He turned, and there was Corny Weehunt, his face scrunched up in a moronic look of awe. It had been said that Corny was next in line for the unofficial position of town idiot, right behind Otis Dellums, but Luke knew better.

"I's here when they hauled his car outer there," Corny said with considerable pride. "Shoulda seen it, Chief. Ol' Mr. Calvin was dead where he sat."

"I'm thankful I didn't have to see it, Cornelius," Luke said.

Weehunt looked puzzled by this, then shook it off like a dog shedding water, and proceeded to describe how they had winched the death car out of the hole. "Folks is worried now the whole town might be swallowed up." He pointed a bony finger down at the slab of Main Street slanting into the deep pit. "Lookit that. Like a road to Hell, sho nuff."

Luke nodded absently, looking into the sinkhole. He thought: Now *there's* a bad patch.

*   *   *

He stopped at Suggs' Supermarket to do his biweekly grocery shopping. He loaded his rickety shopping cart with meat, fresh produce, dog food and the usual staples. As he roamed the aisles, he was haunted by memories of his dead wife Jenny. She had done most of their shopping, but sometimes she would persuade him to tag along, telling him that his company made it special for her, "like our first year of marriage when we had so much time together." Such simple pleasures had meant the world to her, and Luke had not been one to deny her those pleasures, though grocery shopping had always seemed like a boring chore to him. And now, two years after her death, he somehow felt he was shopping for her rather than for himself. He could almost feel her presence, more so here than at the home they had shared for so long. She had died of complications following a routine hysterectomy. The last time he had seen her alive was just before they rolled her into surgery. She had looked at him with wet eyes full of sadness and apologized for failing to bear him a child. "Hush now," he told her. "I don't care about that. It's too dangerous for you to be pregnant again. I don't want to lose you." And she squeezed his hand and smiled through her tears. "I love you, Luke Chaney."

Then she was gone, and he was alone, except for the faithful companionship of his dog. To evade the wrenching grief, he tried to lose himself in his job, but the crime rate in a town the size of Vinewood made that almost impossible, so he finally stopped running from his grief and let it overtake him. He got drunk, he ranted to the Heavens and even cursed God, but the anguish didn't abate until he let himself cry. He cried his heart out for the better part of a moonless night, and awoke the next day with an unexpected feeling of serenity. He still missed Jenny fiercely but he knew then he could manage the pain; he could live with it.

A year later Monroe Shockley was murdered—dismembered and be-headed in the stand of pines behind his farmhouse. The head was never found. Luke worked the case like a dog worrying a slippery bone. He threw himself full-bore into the investigation and became convinced that Fate Porch was responsible for the killing, but there wasn't even enough circumstantial evidence to bring charges against Porch and his ruffian offspring. Fate's hot-blooded boy Odell had started the whole mess by shooting Shockley's favorite hunting dog, and the situation quickly developed into a full-blown feud. With less than two miles of woods separating the warring homesteads, it was inevitable that the feud would escalate to new levels of violence and end badly. When Fate Porch's hound wandered onto Shockley's property and began rooting in his wife's flower garden, Shockley cut the hound down with a shotgun blast and dumped the carcass in Fate's front yard.

A week later Monroe Shockley was dead.

Luke was heading for the checkout when he remembered he needed onions. He went back to the produce section and saw Skeeter Partain restocking bananas.

"Hey, Skeeter," he said.

The boy nearly jumped out of his skin, dropping a bunch of bananas on the floor and bumping his knee on the display table.

"Didn't mean to sneak up on you," Luke said by way of apology.

"I guess my mind was somewhere else," said Skeeter, picking up the dropped fruit. He wore a blue apron over his green-and-white-striped uniform shirt.

"I know the feeling. So how do you like working produce?"

"It's all right, I guess. Till I get something better. I'm thinking about joining the Navy."

"Is that right?" Luke saw that the young man's hands were trembling and that he avoided making eye contact. "You all right? You seem kind of twitchy."

"Yes sir, I'm fine. Had a rough night is all."

"Had a few of those myself. Well, you take care, Skeeter."

"You too, Chief Chaney. *Mister* Chaney, I mean."

Luke picked up a bag of onions, then pushed his cart to the checkout. Midge Harmon flirted with him as she scanned his items, but he didn't rise to take her sugarcoated bait. He paid his tab, loaded the groceries in the back of his truck and drove home.

When he pulled up in front of his house, Hondo came bounding off the front porch to greet him. The big dog was a bundle of wagging tail and happy whining as he twined about his master's feet.

"Watch it, boy," Luke said sternly. "You trying to trip me? Come on and help me get this stuff to the house. I might have a butcher bone for you, if you behave yourself."

After he put the groceries away, he poured himself a glass of iced tea and sat sipping it in the front porch rocker. Hondo was stretched out at his feet, chewing bits of raw meat from the fresh bone Luke had given him.

"It's a hot one, old boy," he said.

Hondo responded with a guttural groan as he gnawed his prize.

"Couldn't've said it better myself." He reached down and ruffled the fur about the white German Shepard's ears. Then he set his glass down, closed his eyes and settled back to wait for nightfall—and for another surreptitious reconnaissance mission into Porch territory.

CHAPTER 3
DAY AND NIGHT

J oe Rob saw it coming. There was no way he could stop it—even if he'd wanted to, which he didn't. The bastard had been riding him all week, picking at him for no good reason, and he'd had enough.

He called himself Ho Down, bragging that "the hos stand in line to get down on my long black snake," but his real name was Curtis and he was a wise-ass troublemaker who was always lipping off to anyone within striking distance. A Def Jam badass Mac Daddy—whatever the hell that was. And to make matters worse, the guy thought he was some sort of slice-and-dice comedian, a black Don Rickles, and the cleverest guy on God's blue earth.

He had started in on Joe Rob first thing that morning while they were bouncing around in the back of the pickup, on the way to the construction site. There were six of them in the truck, four blacks and two whites. Joe Rob was sitting with his spine against the back of the cab, watching the two-lane blacktop unwind behind them.

"Hey, Blow Job," the wannabe comedian shouted at Joe Rob from his perch on the wheel housing. "You look like shit. You up all night chokin' the chicken?"

No, you asshole, I was up all night because every time I shut my eyes I saw the face of a dead man looking at me with his evil middle eye. So don't fuck with me or I just might have to kill you too.

"Leave the man alone," said Johnson, the oldest and blackest of the six laborers. "He ain't said nothin' to you."

But Joe Rob found himself almost wishing the loudmouth boogie would keep it up so he would have a reason to wail on his black ass. *Push me just a little more and see what happens*, his eyes told Ho Down. Something dark and venomous stirred in his belly, a coiling, slithering rage. A long black snake of a different—and more dangerous—kind. Joe Rob had never thought of himself as racist but the way he was feeling toward Ho Do made him wonder if his thinking had been wrong all along.

30

Ho Down must've glimpsed that reptilian darkness in Joe Rob's eyes, for a look of uncertainty appeared on his mud-brown face and he backed off in uncharacteristic silence. He had nothing more to say to Joe Rob until lunch break, his ill-chosen words a sharp stick poking the snake of wrath.

"Blow Job's off his feed today," he said. "Whasamatter, boy? Grandma wouldn't give ya no pussy last night?"

Joe Rob was sitting on a piece of plyboard, downing the last of his Gatorade when Ho Down said the words. He tossed the plastic bottle aside, stood up, walked over and picked up a stray two-by-four. Like a batter in the on-deck circle, he tested the heft of the board, then made straight for his tormenter, cocking the two-by-four over his shoulder.

"Hey, wait now," said Ho Down, stepping backward. "You ain't—"

Joe Rob swung the sturdy board, twisting at the waist and driving the impromptu bat right at Ho Down's head.

Ho Down stumbled, trying to get out of the way of the board, but it caught him on the shoulder and sent him sprawling over a wheelbarrow and to the muddy ground.

The other men looked up from their brown-bag lunches, surprise etched in their sweaty faces.

Joe Rob cocked the board again and slammed it into the downed man's back.

Ho Down hollered out in pain.

Johnson moved quickly for a man of his immense size. He seized the board with one hand and threw a powerful arm around Joe Rob's head. "Easy now, son," he said softly in Joe Rob's ear. "That's enough."

Joe Rob relaxed in Johnson's headlock. He felt strangely secure there in the crook of the man's massive arm. Secure in the knowledge that he couldn't kill anybody as long as he was swaddled like a fussy baby in a blanket of dark muscle.

"You cool?" Johnson whispered, his deep voice a soothing rumble.

"Yeah," he answered.

Johnson released him.

Ho Down was writhing on the ground, cursing and moaning that his arm was broken.

"Uh-oh, here come the boss man," Johnson said.

Mr. Threadgill planted himself in front of Joe Rob and stood there with his hands on his hips. "You know my rule, boy. You fight, you walk. I want you off my site. We'll mail you your last paycheck."

Joe Rob nodded. He picked up his tool belt and slung it over his shoulder.

Mr. Threadgill turned his attention to Ho Down. "Stop your crying, boy. You ain't bad hurt."

"He tried to *kill* me. Crazy muthafucka." Ho Down got to his feet, nursing his injured shoulder.

"You can press charges if you want to," Mr. Threadgill told him. "But you do that on your own time."

Joe Rob walked away, leaving his job behind, and started along the blacktop for home. The blistering sun made mirages on the road ahead: dark ghosts dancing on shimmering black pools. There was no breath of wind. A bead of sweat rolled down his ass crack.

"I wanted to kill him," he said as if explaining it to himself. "I'm almost sorry I didn't."

＊　＊　＊

The mystery car cruised past the supermarket parking lot as Skeeter was climbing into his truck. The same primer-black Firebird with tinted windows and no visible driver. *It was waiting for me,* he thought. *They're onto us.*

His hands shook as he started the engine.

All the way home he monitored the rearview mirror to see if he was being followed, but he saw no further sign of the mystery car. He parked in the shade of the big maple tree, unlocked the door to the small cinderblock building behind his parents' house and entered his living quarters. It was a one-room affair with fireplace and a tiny bathroom with a tiny toilet and a shower the size of a phone booth; he'd been living there since his graduation from high school. For Skeeter the place represented a step toward independence and a move away from his father's stifling authority. He could come and go as he pleased as long as he obeyed his old man's three basic rules: No booze, no drugs, and no girls on the premises.

He wanted to call Joe Rob and alert him to the fact that the Firebird had been circling the parking lot like a shark circling its prey, but Joe Rob wouldn't be home from work until after six, so Skeeter had an hour to kill. He turned on the stereo and tuned it to his favorite country music station, then hooked a can of soda from the refrigerator and flopped onto the lower tier of the bunk bed and downed half the drink before stopping to catch his breath. He cut loose with a satisfying belch. The window-unit air conditioner labored loudly, and Skeeter closed his eyes, hoping to catch a few z's, but the specter of the mystery car would not let him rest.

It was out there somewhere, circling, spiraling closer and closer . . . .

32

The phone jarred him from his anxious thoughts.

He snatched it up. "Hello?"

Silence.

"Hello!"

"Hey, asshole. Guess what."

"What the fuck, man? You off early?"

Joe Rob said, "I got canned."

"You got *fired*? For real?"

"Yep. I lit into that Ho Down motherfucker with a two-by-four. Thread-gill gave me the axe."

"No shit. Man, that sucks."

"That sonofabitch asked for it. You shoulda heard him crying and moaning. It was great."

Skeeter took a ragged breath, then said, "Yeah, well I got some news that ain't so great. That black Firebird was cruising the parking lot when I got off work."

"You shittin' me?"

"I wouldn't shit you. You're my favorite turd."

Neither of them laughed at the tired old joke.

"That's not good," said Joe Rob.

"What the fuck do we do about it? I mean, we gotta do *something*. Right?"

"We've got to find out who it is. Then we'll figure out what to do."

"Hell, it's one of *them*. One of Odell's brothers. You know it is."

"Could be."

"We're screwed, man."

"Chill out, Skeeter. This is no time to panic. We'll think of something."

"Yeah. Right. Meanwhile they're right on my ass."

"I'm coming over. You just sit tight."

Before Skeeter could say anything more, Joe Rob hung up.

A throbbing headache was blooming behind Skeeter's eyes. He left his cool lair, walked across the back yard and entered the house through the back door. His mother was at the stove, stirring a pot of boiling cabbage. The smell gave him a sick feeling in the pit of his stomach and seemed to make his headache worse.

"Hi, Mom," he said, massaging his forehead.

"Hey, honey. Your father's going to be late for dinner, but if you're hungry, you can go ahead and eat. It'll be ready in about ten minutes."

"Nah, I'm not hungry. I just want some aspirin for this headache. I'll eat later."

"You sure?" She picked up her cigarette from the ashtray by the stove and drew smoke into her lungs.

"Yeah. If I ate now I'd probably puke."

"Hard day at work?" She brushed a clump of graying hair from her face. Her cheeks were flushed from the heat of her cooking.

"Pretty busy," he said as he opened a pantry door over the stove and found the bottle of aspirin next to the spices. "Dad get a body?"

"Yes. Some poor girl got herself snake-bit. She was a runaway from Browner's. John Robertson found her out on Nebula Road. By the time he got her to the hospital, it was too late. It's so sad."

"Jeez." Skeeter fumbled with the bottle of aspirin. When he popped off the childproof cap, the bottled slipped out of his hand and a handful of white tablets spilled out on the counter. "Shit."

"Language," she scolded.

"Sorry."

She gave him a glass of water. He tossed three tablets into his mouth and washed them down with a big gulp.

"The girl's family lives in Vidalia," she went on, "but they wanted your father to go ahead and prepare her, then take her home in the morning."

"What kind of snake was it?" He leaned against the kitchen counter, feeling suddenly light-headed.

"I don't think they know for sure. John Robertson said it was probably a rattler." She crushed out the cigarette in the butt-filled ashtray, then she placed her fingers to his forehead. "You don't look so good. I hope you're not coming down with something. Summer colds are the hardest to shake. No fever though."

"It's just a headache. I'm all right."

"You should go lie down a while." She turned down the flame under the big pot of roiling cabbage leaves. The bubbling, spitting drone of the boiling water was almost hypnotic.

"I'll be okay. Joe Rob's coming over."

"Well, you boys stay out of trouble, you hear?"

"Yes ma'am."

He went out the back door, wondering if he should tell Joe Rob about the girl or if he should pretend ignorance of the fact of her death—at least for the time being. He needed his friend to be clear-headed, not distracted by any guilt he might feel over Jessica Lowell's death. He wasn't sure he should tell him, but he was sure of one thing: They were in deep shit and had to find a way out of it before things really got out of hand.

Driving across town to Skeeter's, Joe Rob cranked up the volume of the CD player. The throbbing bass and shrieking guitar of Metallica's "Ride The Lightning" reawakened the black serpent in his belly, and he found himself hoping for a confrontation with the driver of the Firebird—whoever the son of a bitch was. *Fuck with me, I'll fuck you up bad. I guaran-fucking-tee ya.*

He remembered something his father had taught him the same day the old man instructed him in the essentials of street-fighting and basic-training hand-to-hand combat: "Yea though I walk through the valley of the shadow of death, I shall fear no evil, for I'm the meanest motherfucker in the valley." It was the dog soldier's creed Dad had learned in Vietnam, and it applied to street fighting, as well as armed combat. "When the shit starts flying," he had said, "you've got to bring smoke and fire, without hesitation. You hesitate, you're dead." Unlike most vets Joe Rob heard about, his father didn't mind talking about the war. In fact, the old man seemed to love talking about it, especially when he had a few drinks under his belt. Except for a hellhole called Devil's Valley. "That place lived up to its name, I shit you not," Dad had explained. "It was hell on earth. I wouldn't have been surprised to see the Devil Himself in that fucking valley. That's what the troops called it. Devil's Fucking Valley. Some really bad shit happened there." And that was all he would say about Devil's Valley. But Joe Rob still remembered the haunted look in his father's eyes whenever the old man said those words. *Devil's Fucking Valley.* It wasn't the look of the meanest motherfucker in the valley, that was for sure.

Fuck that, Joe Rob thought as he banged his hand on the wheel in time to the music. *Anybody fucks with me, I'll send 'em to Devil's Fucking Valley. Like I did Odell.*

*   *   *

Full dark settled over the countryside. The leaves of the pecan tree in Luke's front yard shifted restlessly against the rising wind, and the fine wire mesh of the screen door whispered windy prognostications of coming rain.

Luke stood on the porch, his gym bag hanging from his shoulder and his exposed skin slathered with insect repellent. He stank to high heaven, but the noxious fumes would keep the South Georgia vampire mosquitoes from feasting on his blood. He looked up at the sky and watched the quarter moon disappear behind scudding clouds.

Sitting nobly at his feet, Hondo rolled out his tongue and licked Luke's hand, then whined in protest as he tasted the harsh chemical of the repellent.

"No, you can't come with me, old boy," Luke said. "Where I'm going they like to shoot your kind."

Luke stepped off the porch, and the dog tagged along expectantly.

"Stay," he said sternly.

Hondo sat obediently on his haunches.

"Good boy."

As he was about to climb into his pickup, a splash of light illumined the gravel driveway in front of his two-story house. The headlights of a small car snaked up the driveway and painted him in amber.

"Who the hell can this be?" he muttered.

Behind him, Hondo went on alert, his ears at attention and his tail slapping the ground in anticipation.

Tires crunching gravel, the car rolled to a stop beside Luke's truck. The driver's door swung open and a petite woman in white shorts and a powder-blue T-shirt stepped out.

"Well, hello there, Shorty," Luke said, smiling. "This is sure a surprise."

"Call me that again and I'll kick your shin," she said, smiling back at him.

"Sorry. Miss Tyler."

"*Ree*, dammit."

"Ree Dammit." He grinned.

"Same old Luke," she said, trying not to laugh. "Always trying to get my goat."

"I didn't even know you had a goat, Shorty."

She kicked his shin.

Hondo wagged his entire body between them, wanting to join the playful fun.

"Okay, okay. Truce. Is this a social call or are you here just to abuse me?"

"I brought you a peach cobbler. Not that you deserve it."

"Best cobbler in the county," he declared. "But you're right. I don't deserve it."

She turned back to her Toyota and reached in for the covered casserole dish of peach cobbler. Luke caught himself admiring the fit of her tight shorts on her shapely rear.

"Come on in the house," he invited, averting his eyes. "I'll make a pot of coffee to go with it."

"I don't want to intrude. You look like you're going somewhere." She nodded at the gym bag slung from his shoulder.

"Nah. Not really." He put the bag in his truck and walked with his guest toward the front door.

"It's dark as sin out here in the boondocks," she observed. "I like it."

As they mounted the porch steps, she sniffed at him. "Is that a new cologne or are you working pest control now?"

"Mosquito repellent. Those suckers love me."

"'Cause you taste so sweet, no doubt. Ha."

"You're a pistol, Ree."

"Don't let my size fool you," she advised. "I'm a cannon when I have to be."

"I know it. I always said you were the loose cannon on the town council." He escorted her into the roomy kitchen. "Have a seat."

She pulled out a chair and sat at the kitchen table while he loaded the coffee brewer and got it going. It wheezed and gurgled like the death rattle of a terminal emphysema patient, but it made great-tasting coffee.

Luke sat across the table from her and watched as she spooned generous portions of cobbler into their bowls. Ree was ten years younger than he was, and she wore her forty years very well. Few women become more attractive in their middle years, but Ree was one who had improved with age—like fine wine or gourmet cheese.

"You look deep in thought," she said as she set his bowl in front of him.

"I was just thinking about wine and cheese," he said.

She shot him a puzzled look.

"How some women get better with a little age on them," he said.

"If that was supposed to be a compliment, it wasn't a very good one. You should never call attention to a lady's age, Luke."

"But—"

"And you sure as heck shouldn't liken her to cheese. Wine maybe, but definitely not cheese."

"But I—"

"Cheese is curdled milk. It brings to mind mold and rats. And nowadays even flatulence—as in 'cut the cheese.'"

"Hold on, Shorty, I—"

She kicked his shin under the table. "I told you not to call me that."

He held up his hands in surrender. "I was just trying to say you look damn good. You get better looking every time I see you. There. Is that okay? Jesus."

"Why, thank you Luke. That's sweet of you to say. But I'd appreciate it if you wouldn't blaspheme."

He shook his head in defeat. "I can't win with you."

"Not if you don't get in the game." She winked a twinkling blue eye.

"What's that supposed to mean?"

"You know what I mean. You've been on the sidelines a long time now. Maybe it's time to strap on the pads and get back on the field."

"I love it when you talk dirty," he said, struggling to keep a straight face.

She kicked at his leg again, but this time he moved it out of the line of fire. She laughed.

He shoveled a spoonful of cobbler in his mouth. "Umm, this is delicious."

"Thank you. It won me a blue ribbon at the county fair."

The conversation lagged as they ate. Then Luke got up and poured two cups of coffee.

"You quit coming to church," she said, dabbing a napkin to her lips.

"It's been a while," he admitted.

"You should come back. It would do you good. You need to get out more."

He took a sip of steaming coffee. "Me and the Lord don't have much use for each other these days."

"I think I know how you feel. After Ben died, I was so angry with God I didn't set foot in church for weeks. Ben was a good man, too young to be taken from me that way. A loving God wouldn't allow such a thing. That's how I was thinking at the time. But I got over it. Maybe it's just taking you longer to get over losing Jenny. It's all right to be angry with God. He can take it."

"I'm not mad at God. I can't be mad at something I don't believe in."

"Oh, Luke," she said with unaffected sadness.

"Let's change the subject," he said. "I try to steer clear of discussing religion and politics."

"All right. I really didn't come here to preach to you anyway. I came because I miss seeing you. And because I thought maybe I could twist your arm enough to get you to have dinner with me sometime."

He studied her over the rim of his cup. "You mean like a date?"

"Yes, I guess I do. We're both widowed. And Vinewood's not exactly running over with hot prospects, if you know what I mean. I like you, Luke. I'm . . . attracted to you. And I think you kind of like me too. Am I wrong?"

"No, you're not wrong."

"Well, there you go." She smiled in obvious relief. "And you know I'm a good cook."

"I know you're a fine woman." He paused, measuring his next words. "But I'm not sure I'm ready for that sort of relationship. It wouldn't be fair to you for me to get into it and then find out I couldn't handle it. That could make for bad feelings between us, and I wouldn't want that."

Ree reached across the table and placed her hand over his. "I appreciate that, Luke. But believe me, I can take care of myself. I'm a big girl—even if I am short. Will you at least think about it? About us?"

"I think about you more than you know," he said. He turned his hand over and held her hand in his palm. "My mama taught me never to turn down a good home-cooked meal when the cook is a woman of good stock."

"Your mama was a wise woman. How about tomorrow night? I hate to seem too eager, but I don't want to give you time to change your mind."

"Tomorrow night's good."

She squeezed his hand, smiling warmly. "All right then. Six o'clock. I'll cook you up something special."

They finished their cobbler and sat sipping coffee, shyly smiling at each other like enamored school kids. Then she filled him in on the latest town gossip and he listened politely, though with little interest.

She pulled a small brown paper bag from her purse. "Do you mind if I smoke a cigarette?"

"Go right ahead. I didn't know you smoked."

She took a pack of cigarettes from the bag, fished one out and stuck it between her lips. She fired it with a disposable lighter, then blew a stream of smoke toward the ceiling. "I've quit more times than I could count. But I just can't seem to give them up. You have an ashtray?"

He got up, opened a drawer under the kitchen counter and found a souvenir ashtray from St. Augustine, Florida. He set it in front of her. "Jenny used to smoke, but she quit the last time she got pregnant."

"I didn't know that."

"She didn't do it much in public. Smokers were getting a bad rap even then."

"Don't I know it. Ben smoked like a chimney. A three-pack-a-day man. Probably why he had his heart attack."

"You always carry your smokes in the little brown bag?"

She tittered. "Like an alcoholic brown-bagging his bottle, I know. But see, I'm going to quit smoking. That's my motto. I've been saying it for years. And to that end, I never buy them by the carton. Just a pack or two at the time. And I won't buy a cigarette case or a permanent lighter, because that would be admitting that I can't give them up. My smoking is just temporary. Get it? It's just one of those quirky little games people play with themselves, I guess. I *intend* to quit someday. But you know that old saying. 'The road to hell . . .'"

"' . . . is paved with good intentions.' Right. But if there's a hell, I don't think you'll end up there for smoking tobacco. If that's your biggest vice, I don't reckon you need to worry."

"You're probably right. I do enjoy my cigs. Life is short and the Lord can call us away anytime. I suppose I should enjoy it while I still can." She knitted her brow. "I don't guess you heard about that poor gal who ran away from the mental hospital and got bit by a snake."

"No."

"She died in the emergency room before they could give her the antivenom or whatever they call it."

"Antivenin. Anybody I know?"

"No. A young girl from Vidalia. Prominent family. They'll likely sue Browner's for letting her run off. At least that's the talk around town. Bad news spreads like kudzu vines in Vinewood, you know."

"Don't you know any good news?"

She grinned. "The best news is that you've accepted my invitation to dinner. I imagine *that* news flash will be all over town in a day or two. Can't you just imagine what they'll say about us?"

She ground out her cigarette in the St. Augustine ashtray. "Well, I better head home. If I keep on talking your ears off, you won't want to come for dinner."

She rinsed their bowls and left them to soak in the sink, then he walked her to her car.

An owl hooted in the woods behind the house. The moon peeked through a break in the clouds.

"I'm glad you stopped by," Luke said. "And thanks again for the cobbler."

"There's plenty more good home-cooking where that came from. I'm liable to fatten you up some." She rose up on her toes and hugged him, then whispered in his ear. "Do me one favor. Don't wear that insect repellent tomorrow night."

He chuckled. "I won't."

"'Night, Luke."

"G'night. Watch out for deer on the drive home."

He watched her drive off, wondering if he'd made a mistake in accepting her invitation. When her taillights winked out of sight, he pushed the matter from his mind so he could focus on his primary objective.

He climbed into his pickup and took the back roads to the bottomland where the Porch farmhouse stood at the edge of fields gone fallow. He parked in a stand of pine trees at the edge of a pasture, slung the gym bag from his shoulder and began the two-mile trek to his target.

* * *

"I knew we shouldn't've left her," Joe Rob said. He was sitting on the hearth of the cold fireplace, his hands clasped tightly as he absently did an isometric biceps exercise. Skeeter was on the top bunk, his legs dangling over the side, feet jittering nervously in the air.

"Don't," Skeeter said. "I don't wanna have to listen to you beat yourself up over what we shoulda done. Besides, this is a good thing. Bad for her, but good for you. The only eyewitness is dead."

"You sure it's the same girl?"

"Who else could it be? How many nuthouse runaways you think there coulda been on Nebula Road yesterday?"

"I need to see her," Joe Rob said.

"*Why?*"

He shrugged. "I just do. I have to see for myself."

"Shit, man, we—"

"You've got a key. We wait till your old man comes home, then we go to the funeral home and check her out."

"Fuck that, Joe Rob. I ain't worried about her. I'm worried about the sonofabitch in the Firebird. And so should you be. Fuckin' corpse can't hurt us."

"I told you, we'll deal with that when the time comes."

"Yeah? How? What're we gonna do? We can't do anything without making ourselves look guilty." He shrugged. "Maybe the best thing to do is ignore it. Act normal. *Innocent.* If anybody asks if we saw Odell, we say no. Nobody can prove different. Odell's people know he's missing, but unless they find his body, that's *all* they'll know for sure. There ain't no way they'll find the body. And we sure as hell ain't gonna tell 'em where to dig."

Joe Rob narrowed his dark eyes and gave Skeeter a warning look. "Unless they grab your ass and beat it out of you."

"Jeez, you think they would?"

"If they thought you knew something? Hell yeah." Joe Rob lifted the tail of his black T-shirt and drew a pistol from the waist of his jeans. "That's why I brought you this."

"Your stepdad's forty-five?"

"*My* forty-five. It's the only thing the bastard left me that's worth having. That and the trust fund, but I can't touch that till I'm twenty-one. And by then there won't be much left, 'cause my grandmother gets a monthly allowance of three hundred bucks for my care and feeding."

He flipped the pearl-handled automatic around and offered it butt-first to Skeeter.

"I can't take that, man."

"Hell, I ain't giving it to you. I'm just letting you use it till this whole thing blows over. Go on, take it. It's got a full clip. Keep it in your truck. If somebody tries to fuck with you, that oughta be enough to discourage 'em."

Skeeter reluctantly accepted it. "Thanks."

"Now let's see if your old man's home yet."

*　*　*

They went up the back stairs and entered through the rear door of the funeral home. They knew Skeeter's dad was home eating supper. As soon as they were inside, the acrid smell of embalming fluid hit them full-force. The prep room was in the rear of the building, and the odor of the formaldehyde always seemed to collect there in the stairwell on the first floor. The waxy scent of industrial-strength deodorizer added a sickening sweetness to the unpleasant bouquet.

Joe Rob had seen bodies in the prep room before and had even once been allowed to watch Skeeter's father aspirate the contents of a body's abdominal cavity with a powerful suction device and witness the entire embalming procedure. He'd been fascinated by the spectacle, but the experience left him with a grim outlook on life and death and humanity. "We're all just big skin-bags of blood and stinking guts," he had said to Skeeter afterwards. "That's what life boils down to." Skeeter had responded with "Duh," in confirmation of what had been obvious to him for years, as the undertaker's son.

The most disturbing sight Joe Rob had seen in the prep room was the body of a middle-aged man, post-autopsy. The opened and emptied chest cavity with the ribcage split down the middle had looked like the hull of an Indian canoe. The top of the skull had been removed with an electric saw and was wired back in place like a beanie cap. Skeeter's dad had peeled the dead man's scalp and face away from the skull and then stretched it tightly back into place like an obscene mask. Sometimes when Joe Rob looked at himself in a mirror, he would imagine his face being peeled away from the bones of his grinning skull.

Skeeter flipped a light switch and the back hallway leapt from darkness into somber light. He jerked his thumb at the closed door marked PRIVATE. "Go ahead," he said. "She's in there."

"Aren't you coming?"

"I don't want to see her. This is your thing, not mine."

"I don't want to go in there by myself," said Joe Rob. "Come on, man."

"She's *dead*. She can't hurt you."

"I know that. I just don't want to be in there alone with her. Humor me. All right?"

Skeeter sighed. "All right. You want me to hold your frigging hand?"

"Fuck you, man. I'll go by myself."

"Don't be an asshole." Skeeter turned the doorknob and flung open the door. It banged against the inner wall. The light from the hallway reached into the cold, darkened room and made gloomy shadows.

"You trying to wake the dead?" Joe Rob whispered. He meant the comment to be humorous, but the would-be joke fell flat and died a humorless death.

"There she is," Skeeter said, waving a finger at the sheet-draped body on the stainless-steel table in the center of the room. "Do what you gotta do."

Joe Rob stepped lightly across the tile floor as if afraid a heavy tread would disturb the corpse's rest. He stood beside the table and Skeeter came to stand beside him. At the foot of the table was a porcelain sink where the blood and other bodily fluids drained during the exsanguination/aspiration process. The blood, Joe Rob recalled, was forced out of the body by the infusion of embalming fluid—a neat and tidy procedure compared to the vacuuming of the belly's foul-smelling contents with the sharp-pointed stainless-steel tube attached to a thin vacuum hose. He felt a little queasy just remembering the way Mr. Partain had pierced the belly of Silas Turner with the aspirator and moved it around inside the gut of the corpse until all the stinking fluids had been vacuumed out and emptied into the sink.

Joe Rob broke out in a cold sweat. He was about to tell Skeeter that he had changed his mind, that he didn't want to see the body of Jessica A. Lowell, when Skeeter reached down and peeled the sheet away from the naked corpse.

With a sharp intake of breath, Joe Rob took a step away from the dead girl. Her skin was waxy and incredibly white. The small mounds of her breasts were peaked with puckered nipples of bluish purple, and the auburn thatch of pubic hair was slightly darker than the hair of her head. Her neck was propped on the rubber neck rest, her arms resting by her sides. Her face was frozen in an expression Joe Rob could only think of as peaceful. Without the grimacing and bizarre facial machinations of psychotic agitation, she was actually pretty—and more youthful-looking. Twenty-two or-three.

"Nice body," Skeeter said. "Too bad she was nuts."

"Too bad she's dead."

"Yeah, that too. Let's find where the snake bit her."

Skeeter bent close to the body and began looking for fang marks. He checked her legs and ankles first. "There," he said, pointing to the discolored area of flesh just above her right ankle. "That's where it got her. Can't really see the holes, but that dark patch there is where the poison started killing off her cells. Necrosis."

"Got her here too," Joe Rob said, pointing out the same discoloration on the edge of her right hand. "Probably a defensive wound."

"Yeah. That's pretty good, Sherlock. And after it bit her, she panicked and started running and that sped the poison through her system. She was fucked from the get-go."

"Never had a chance."

"Seen enough?" asked Skeeter.

"Yeah. Just . . . give me a minute alone with her."

"Jeez, make up your mind will ya? Hey, man, you ain't into necrophilia are you?"

"What's that?"

"Corpse fucking."

"Fuck you, no. Just leave us alone."

"All right. Just don't get all weirded out." Skeeter turned toward the door. "And cover her up when you're done."

When Skeeter was out in the hallway, Joe Rob touched the dead woman's forehead, then stroked her hair. "I'm sorry," he whispered. "I only wanted to help you. I didn't know . . . ."

His voice broke in a single sob. He withdrew his hand from her hair, pulled the sheet over her, then walked away, turning out the light as he left the room.

"Feel better now?" asked Skeeter. He was leaning against the wall beneath a painting of a covered bridge.

"Not really." He wiped the corner of his eye.

Skeeter shrugged. "Life's a bitch."

"And then you die."

Skeeter switched off the hall lights and moved toward the back door. Joe Rob followed blindly through the inky darkness, anxious now to be gone from this death-haunted place. The thick carpet muffled their footsteps, but the old hardwood floor creaked and groaned with their passage. The place seemed alive with ghostly murmurs.

Then the back door opened to the sultry night, and Joe Rob felt as though he couldn't get out of the suffocating, creaking building fast enough. He hurried past Skeeter, bumping him into the doorframe, and stepped outside. He took several deep breaths to clear the formaldehyde fumes from his lungs.

"What the hell's wrong with you?" demanded Skeeter.

"Nothing. I just had to get outta there. Place was choking me."

"You're losing it, man." Skeeter shut and locked the back door.

They clattered down the back stairs and piled into Skeeter's truck, which was parked on the gravel drive in front of the shut-up garage housing the two hearses. After three attempts, the pickup's engine finally turned over and rumbled to life.

"Gotta get this thing tuned up," Skeeter said. "Needs a new set of points bad."

"Whadaya think she meant by 'the dark thing'?"

"What?"

"The girl. Jessica. That shit she was saying about 'the dark thing.' Remember? First she said it knew where she was. But after I shot Odell she said it didn't want her. It wanted *me*."

"Jesus, J.R. The bitch was loony-tunes. Forget that shit. It don't mean nothing."

"I don't know, man. I almost believed her. I mean, sure she was crazy, but the way she said it, it was *real*."

"Yeah, you're losing it."

"She pointed her finger at me and I swear I could almost feel it. Like she was . . . directing it to me."

"Feel what?"

"The dark thing! What the fuck ya think?"

"I think whatever she had must've been contagious, and you caught a bad case of it." Skeeter grinned to let him know he was joking. "Keep talking like that, *you'll* end up in the nuthouse."

Joe Rob slumped in his seat as Skeeter slammed the truck in gear and sped off, tires kicking up gravel.

"She spooked you," Skeeter said. "That's what it is. You were already freaked out from shooting Odell, so when she laid that crazy shit on you, it stuck. You just gotta shake it off."

"I don't know. Maybe you're right."

"Fucking-A I'm right. What else could it be?"

Joe Rob stared ahead through the windshield at nothing as they wheeled onto 2nd Street and zoomed past the police station.

"Hey, Joe Rob?"

"What?"

"I got your dark thing hanging," said Skeeter, grabbing the crotch of his jeans.

Joe Rob tried to laugh, but what came out was a garbled croak.

CHAPTER 4
NIGHT VISION

Luke set his gym bag on the stump of a felled oak tree, unfolded his canvas-and-wood camp chair and sat down. The night sky was thick with clouds, and the only light came from the windows of the two-story farmhouse on the edge of scrubby bottomland, twenty yards away. A hot breeze soughed through the stand of scrub pine at his back and rustled the foliage in the thicket in front of him.

He opened the bag, took out the shotgun microphone and mounted it on its stand on top of the stump, then put on the headset. He got out his night vision goggles and strapped the futuristic facemask in place over his face. He activated both systems. First he adjusted the eyepiece diopters, then he turned up the volume of the shotgun mike as he shifted its aim toward one of the open windows of the Porch house. In his earpiece he heard the tinny sound of television voices. He avoided looking at the lighted windows; he scoped out the darkness in front of the house where the two pickup trucks were parked, then he swept the gloomy space between the house and the barn. The goggles returned good visuals, tinted an eerie green. Satisfied that no one was skulking about outside, he switched off the goggles and listened to the sounds.

He had purchased the equipment through the Internet. The Russian-made goggles had cost him five hundred bucks, and the shotgun mike had set him back two hundred. The way he figured it, the high-tech spy equipment would prove to be a good investment if it helped him finally nail Fate Porch and his boys for the murder of Monroe Shockley. As it was, his snooping had already provided enough evidence to have Bill Keller arrest Luther Porch for dealing marijuana, but a drug bust was not what he wanted. He would take them down for murder and nothing less.

Sheet lightning flashed in the distance. Lightning without thunder. Frogs and noisy insects sang their night songs. Luke swatted at a mosquito buzzing around his ear. He wondered what Doc would think if he knew he had been coming out here with his spy stuff three or four nights a week for the last month. *He would think I was obsessed, trying to fill a deep personal emptiness with my unauthorized surveillance. He'd probably say something like, "You're Captain Ahab and Fate Porch is your Moby Dick." And he would probably be right. But it won't seem so crazy if I get that son of a bitch on the business end of my harpoon.*

He glanced at his watch: 9:25 P.M.

Luke had learned a lot about the individual members of the Porch clan during his night watches. He knew that in five minutes or so, Fate and his mother, Agnes Porch, would come out to sit on the front porch, unless the old lady was under the weather, in which case Fate would settle himself in the cane rocker and enjoy the cooling evening in solitude like a low-rent Lord of the Manor. As often as not, his youngest boy, Cowboy, would join him on the porch if there was nothing good on TV. Cowboy's given name was Lem, but his family called him Cowboy because he always wore a Western-style hat on his shaved head and a pistol on his hip. He fancied himself a quick-draw artist and was forever practicing his "greased lightning" draw. On rare occasions, Odell would plunk his narrow butt in a front porch rocker and chew the fat with Paw. The elder son Luther was usually off somewhere in his muscle car, most likely cruising the neighboring town of Vidalia for easy women, as he considered himself a pussy hound. It was Luther who did most of the dope dealing, but sometimes he would take Cowboy along to ride shotgun, particularly if he expected trouble, or if he just wanted a show of shooting-iron force. Cowboy was the most unstable one of the bunch, with a hair-trigger temper and a voracious appetite for attention. Luke suspected that any break in the case would come from Cowboy's loose lips.

Right on schedule, Fate came out on the front porch and sat in his rocker. He fired up his pipe and commenced to rock to and fro, the chair creaking beneath the weight of his big frame.

Five minutes later, Cowboy emerged from the house and sat on the porch rail. He pushed up the front brim of his hat. "When's Luther coming back, Diddy?"

Luke adjusted the aim of the shotgun mike, pointing it at the space between father and son.

"I 'spect he'll be home directly," Fate said.

"Reckon what he's found out?"

"Have to wait and see." Fate's voice was edged with irritation.

"You think them boys done something to Odell?"

"Goddamn it, boy. Stop pestering me. Ain't you got nothing better to do?"

"I'm just worried about him is all. Ain't like Odell to just go off like that and not tell nobody."

Fate puffed his pipe and looked around as if he'd heard something close by.

"Gramaw says she fears the worst. She says all the signs are real bad."

Fate grunted. "She says a lot of things. That don't make it so."

"But she read the bones. And they ain't hardly ever wrong."

"Maw's feeling poorly. Hell, she's old as dirt. I wouldn't put too much stock in what she reads in them chicken bones. Nor her tea leaves. Now Luther's looking into it, and he'll find out what there is to find out. So you just forget about Maw's talk of omens and such. Ain't none of that gonna tell us what happened to Odell."

"Okay, Diddy. I'm just worried is all." Cowboy jumped down from the rail, spun around toward the front yard and drew his pistol. "Tell you what, though. If we find out them boys done something to Odell, I'm gonna put so much lead in 'em, it'll take a Mack truck to haul off their bodies."

"You ain't gonna do nothing unless I tell you to. Don't you forget that, Cowboy."

"No, sir. I won't." He spun the pistol on his finger, then holstered it with his usual flair for showmanship.

Luke's full attention was riveted on the two men, and he was hanging on their every word. Odell was obviously missing, and the Porch clan suspected "them boys" of having something to do with his disappearance. Whoever the "boys" were, this was certainly an interesting development. He considered the possibility of catching the Porch men in the act of committing new crimes, then cautioned himself not to count chickens before eggs were laid.

From inside the house, the old lady called out for Cowboy.

"Coming, Gramaw," Cowboy yelled. He went inside, the screen door slamming shut behind him.

A few minutes later, Luke heard the rumble of an approaching vehicle. He looked to his right and focused his attention on the driveway leading from the dirt road to the house. A moment later a Firebird came speeding up the driveway and stopped in front of the house. Luther Porch hopped out of the car and bounded up the front steps.

"Well?" Fate said.

"It's the undertaker's boy," Luther said. "I know where he lives, where he works and who he hangs out with."

"Partain's boy?"

"Yes sir. That's the one. Works at the grocery store."

Luke thought, *Skeeter Partain? What the hell's he got to do with Odell?*

Fate said something that was garbled, and Luke inched forward, moving the shotgun mike closer.

". . . not sure who he is," Luther was saying, "but I know what he drives. Be easy to find out. I'm pretty sure he was the same one was with him at the dump."

Fate sucked on his pipe, then said, "I 'spect he'll tell us anything we want to know."

Cowboy came charging out onto the porch. "Big brother! You nail the sumbitch?"

"I know where to find him," said Luther.

The old lady called again from inside.

Fate stood up. "Let's go tell Maw, so she'll stop that damn yelling."

They went inside. Luke moved, working his way around to the rear of the house where Gramaw's second-story bedroom window was opened to the night air. He stopped, crouched by the corner of the smokehouse and aimed the mike up at the old lady's window. All he could hear was the drone of muffled voices. Finally, one voice rose shrilly above the others, and Luke heard it clearly. The old lady said, "I had a vision, by God. And the hand of darkness was upon him and the darkness took him down."

Then a man's voice, probably Fate's, responded incoherently.

Then the old woman once more, shouting: "*'Vengeance is mine,' saith the Lord.*"

*   *   *

Luke packed his gear in his gym bag and hiked back to his truck. He drove home, wondering how Skeeter Partain might be connected to the apparent disappearance of Odell Porch. The boy had seemed awfully jumpy when Luke spoke with him in the produce department earlier in the day. Was that a coincidence, or was Skeeter on pins and needles because of some run-in with Odell? Or because he was hiding something? Some guilty knowledge? But knowledge of *what*? Luke couldn't fathom it; he needed more information before he could piece together a reasonable scenario. And to get it, he would have to prime Skeeter's pump and get him talking.

It was 9:55 PM now. A little late for a social call on a young man he hardly knew, but given the fact that Skeeter Partain was under the dangerous scrutiny of Fate and his boys, Luke knew he had to see Skeeter tonight, if he could find him. He wasn't sure, but he thought Skeeter still lived with his parents on Maple Circle.

At 10:26, Luke rang the doorbell of James Partain's brick home. James came to the door in Bermuda shorts and an Izod shirt, but somehow the man still managed to look like an undertaker.

"Evening, James," Luke said. "Is Skeeter home?"

"Skeeter? What do you want with Skeeter?" Partain looked puzzled.

"I just need to talk to him a minute."

"Has he . . . I . . . I know this isn't a police matter, since you're no longer a policeman. What's this about, Luke?"

"It's nothing you need to worry about. I just want to talk to him. Privately."

"I think he's out back. He's bunking in the little house in the back yard. Come on, I'll show you the way."

Luke followed Partain through the house and out the back door.

"The light's on and his truck's here, so he should be inside," Partain said. "He's not in any kind of trouble, is he, Luke?"

"No. It's nothing like that," Luke answered, though he knew he was twisting the truth. Skeeter most likely *was* in trouble of some kind, but until Luke could learn more, there was no point in alarming James with what, at this point, was only conjecture.

"Well, I'll leave you to it," James said. "But I don't mind telling you, this mysterious visit has me curious."

Luke said, "Don't worry, James. It's just something Skeeter might be able to help me with. It's no big deal. Really."

James Partain walked back to his house, and Luke knocked on the door of Skeeter's cinder-block abode. The muffled voices inside fell silent. Skeeter opened the door. A look of surprise came into his face when he saw Luke.

"Hey, Skeeter. Mind if I come in?"

"Uh, no, no. Come on in." Skeeter glanced nervously over his shoulder at the Campbell boy, Joe Rob, who was sitting at a card table, a can of soda at his elbow.

Luke stepped inside. "Evening, Joe Rob."

Joe Rob nodded, but said nothing. He took a sip from his can of cola and averted his eyes.

"You're wondering what the hell I'm doing here," said Luke, pulling up a metal folding chair and sitting at the card table. "So I'll tell you straight out. I have reason to believe Fate Porch and his boys have taken an unhealthy interest in you, Skeeter. Maybe in you too, Joe Rob."

Luke watched both of them for a reaction.

Skeeter's eyes got big and his jaw dropped.

Joe Rob's face seemed to darken with sullen anger.

"What makes you think so?" asked Skeeter, sitting on the lower berth of the bunk bed.

"Well, I can't really say right now. But the point is, they've been watching you. And they seem to think you might know something about Odell. Turns out he's missing."

"Why would I know anything about that?" Skeeter's voice shook as he spoke.

"I was hoping you could tell me," Luke said.

"I don't have anything to do with Odell . . . or any of 'em. They're bad news."

"Yes, they are. Which is exactly why you need to tell me the truth. This could be a dangerous situation for you. If you tell me what's going on, I can probably help you with whatever it is."

Skeeter looked askance at Joe Rob. Joe Rob sat stone-faced, arms crossed over his chest.

Skeeter said, "I don't *know* anything. Nothing's going on that I know of."

Luke drummed his fingers on the rickety card table. He looked at Skeeter. He drummed harder, louder, building to a nerve-wracking crescendo, capped off by banging the shank of his palm on the table. Skeeter winced. Joe Rob stared at him through the narrow slits of his eyes. "Listen, boys," Luke said, taking an ominous tone. "This is not a game you want to be playing. These people will chew you up and shit you out the other end if they even *think* you crossed them. That I promise you."

Joe Rob uncrossed his arms. "We don't know what the hell you're talking about, *Mister* Chaney."

Luke pursed his lips, nodding. "How's your grandmother, Joe Rob?"

He shrugged, momentarily caught off guard by Luke's sudden change of tack. "Okay, I guess."

"Give her my regards." Luke stood up. Looked at Skeeter. "You come to your senses, give me a call. I'm in the book. But don't wait too long. I don't figure you've got that much time before the manure hits the blower."

He walked toward the door, then turned and added, "And then it'll be too late."

CHAPTER 5
SNATCH

"How the hell can he know anything?" Skeeter fumed. He was pacing a semi-circle about the card table.

Joe Rob sat in brooding silence, watching his friend's tiger-like pacing.

"I mean, he's not a cop anymore, but that don't mean shit. He *knows*. I don't know how he knows, but he does."

Joe Rob said, "He knows those assholes are scoping you out. We already knew that. So what?"

"But how does he know that much? This is fucked up, man."

"Cool it, will ya? Don't get your bowels in an uproar."

Skeeter flopped into the chair that Luke Chaney had, only moments ago, vacated. He tried to calm himself. "All right. There's no way he could know what happened to Odell. But he knows he's missing and that those Porch cretins are dogging me." He cracked his knuckles to keep his hands from fidgeting. "He wants to help us. Maybe we should let him."

"He can't help us. He ain't even a cop, not anymore."

"No, but if we told him what happened, and that the reason we didn't go to the police was because we were afraid that the Porches would kill us—"

"Fuck that! We already agreed, man. Took a blood oath that we'd never tell. No matter what."

"Yeah, but—"

"'But' my ass. You break a blood oath, I'll have to fuck you up."

"*What?*" Skeeter couldn't believe what he'd just heard.

"That's what happens when you break the oath. You know that."

"What's wrong with you, man? You're actually *threatening* me? Your blood brother?"

"That's the rule."

"Bullshit. That's no fucking rule. You just made that up."

"Guess we need fresh blood." Joe Rob reached across the table and seized

Skeeter's wrist and pinned his hand to the table. He pulled a pocketknife from his jeans and flicked the blade open with one hand, then swiped the cutting edge across Skeeter's wrist. Blood filled the gash.

With a yelp of surprise, Skeeter yanked his hand free.

Joe Rob made a similar cut in his own wrist, then laid his hand palm-up on the card table. "Come on, do it. Touch cuts."

"Jeez, you *are* fucking nuts."

"Do it, Goddammit! I'm not playing." Joe Rob pointed the tip of his knife at Skeeter.

"Fuck you, Joe Rob. Go ahead. Gut me with that fucking pig sticker. I don't give a shit. Go ahead, you fucking psycho. Do it. That'll solve everything, won't it?"

Joe Rob came out of his chair, upended the card table and tossed it aside, then poked the knife against Skeeter's belly.

Skeeter didn't back down. Nose to nose, they glared at each other for an interminable moment of frozen time.

Then Joe Rob stepped back, almost casually, folded the blade and jammed the knife back in his jeans pocket. "I should've known you'd wimp out on me," he sneered. "Fucking pussy. I'll handle this shit by myself."

Joe Rob walked out and slammed the door.

The slam reverberated with terrible finality in the echo chamber that was Skeeter's skull. He knew for the first time in his life what it meant to be truly alone.

And it terrified him.

* * *

He woke with a start, his heart racing as if to flee some imminent threat. He sat up in his bunk and looked around. Moonlight at the curtained window seeped in around the edges and gave the darkened room a faint illumination of cold, silvery light.

Skeeter listened closely to the night, hearing nothing but the humming rattle of the air-conditioner that washed him with frigid air and the background murmuring of insects. The hair at the nape of his neck was drenched in sweat.

Must've been dreaming. Dreamed I heard something and woke myself up.

He glanced at the red numerals of the digital clock on top of the old filing cabinet that served as his bedside table.

1:15 AM.

Shit.

Gotta sleep.

A knot of fear twisted tighter in his abdomen. A dull pressure behind his eyes signaled an oncoming headache.

He flopped back onto his damp pillow and kicked off the bed sheet.

Relax.

Sleep.

But don't dream.

His attempt at self-hypnotic relaxation failed to induce sleep. His mind churning with unbidden images of violence and blood, he fell into a moonlit limbo somewhere between wakefulness and sleep—a netherworld with shadowy figures skulking at its edges, the skulkers armed with knives and guns.

Gotta piss.

He drags himself from bed and stumbles into the tiny bathroom. Takes his semi-erect penis in hand and aims it at the thighs of the dead girl . . .

Dreaming . . .

. . . that I got up to piss.

He came fully awake, dragged himself out of bed and made his way to the tiny bathroom where he *did* begin to empty his bladder. He shivered as the stream of urine splashed into the bowl's water and he sighed with relief as the aching pressure of his full bladder dissipated. "Ahhh . . ."

The piss seemed to go on forever, as did the accompanying pleasure of release.

Pissing like a racehorse. "Uhnnn . . ."

Then the stream became a trickle, the trickle became a dribble, and Skeeter shook the last few drops from the tip of his penis, slipped it back into the folds of his boxer shorts and headed back to bed.

As soon as he came out of the bathroom, a shifting shadow seized him. A hand covered his mouth, muffling his startled cry, and something sharp and cool pricked the soft flesh of his throat.

"Make a sound and I'll make you bleed," whispered a rasping voice.

Joe Rob?

Another shadow fell upon him and forced him to his knees, then onto his back. The scent of sweat-soured clothing and rancid armpit odor sickened him.

Not Joe Rob. Jesus . . .

The second shadow did something that made a sharp tearing sound, then slapped something thin and sticky across Skeeter's lips.

Duct tape. Oh shit, it's . . . .

They rolled him onto his belly.

. . . Odell's brothers.

And tied his hands behind his back with scratchy rope. The two shadows yanked him to his feet and hustled him out the door and into the night.

The strong musk of their combined body odors nearly made him gag.

As they forced him into the yawning trunk of the black Firebird, Skeeter wished with all his being that this was just a dream.

CHAPTER 6
INSOMNIA

Luke came awake, thinking—hoping—it was time to get up. He rolled onto his side and looked at the clock. 1:33 in the damn morning. He groaned, knowing he would not be able to get back to sleep and that he would spend the next few torturous hours trying in vain to clock some decent rest time. He had been plagued by these early-morning awakenings for several months now, and none of the sleep remedies he'd tried had done any good. His circadian rhythms were far out of whack, and he was now a full-fledged insomniac, never getting more than three straight hours of restful sleep a night. He was building up an unhealthy sleep deficit that was certain to exact a cruel toll in the coming days and weeks. He got through most days by building up enough momentum to keep him going till nightfall, but it was becoming harder and harder to get up to speed, and he was becoming more lethargic, more zombie-like, with each passing night and subsequent day. When he could, he would grab a catnap after lunch, and that usually helped recharge his internal batteries, but over all, the quality of his day-to-day existence was deteriorating, his mental outlook dimmed and distorted by the effects of prolonged sleep deprivation.

He had tried Melatonin, Valerian root, Benadryl, and chamomile tea, but none of these prevented his middle-of-the-night awakenings. Then he tried several prescription drugs, and one of them seemed to help for a couple of nights, but then it lost its effectiveness, and his abnormal sleep pattern reasserted itself with a vengeance. Three or four shots of hard liquor just prior to bedtime seemed to be most effective in getting him through the night, but the ensuing hangover and headache made booze an unacceptable sleep aid.

So he was cursed with insomnia, and had to make the best of it any way he could. To that end, he relied on his obsession with the Porch clan to provide the impetus to get through his zombie days. Each new day was another opportunity to turn up the crucial bit of evidence that would bring

Fate and his boys to justice. So far, this motivation had worked pretty well; yet he couldn't help but wonder if his obsession was somehow connected to—perhaps even responsible for—his insomnia. He wondered, too, why he never dreamed anymore—or if he did dream, why the dreams remained unremembered.

Luke took another look at the clock. Five minutes had past since his last time check. Maybe he should get rid of the goddamn clock.

"Goddamn," he said, tossing his pillow across the room. "Might as well get your ass up."

He rolled out of bed and went into the bathroom to take a leak. Pausing in front of the mirror, he studied his reflection, noting the blood-shot eyes and the purplish bags hanging beneath them. *Starting to look like an old man. Shit. What's next? Prostate trouble?*

He emptied his bladder, then padded through the dark house and downstairs to the kitchen, where he opened the fridge, squinting against the glaring light from the recessed bulb, and poured himself a small glass of milk. He drank it down, rinsed the glass and set it on the counter next to the coffee maker. He wanted coffee—could almost smell it brewing—but nixed the idea. Coffee now would kill any chance he had of getting back to sleep.

He decided to go back to bed and try to read himself to sleep. If he could drop off for even half an hour, he would be grateful upon awakening. And if he couldn't—reading would distract his mind from its nagging worries concerning Skeeter Partain and Fate Porch's boys. Before turning in for the night, Luke had called Chief Keller at home and asked Keller to instruct the night patrol to make frequent drive-bys of the Partain house. Keller, who had taken over as chief upon Luke's retirement from the force, was glad to oblige, but had naturally wanted to know the reason for the drive-bys. Luke had responded, "Just trust me on this, Bill. I think the Partain boy might've run afoul of the Porch boys. If he has, it could mean trouble." Keller, bless his loyal heart, hadn't questioned Luke further.

But Luke knew that having a squad car make frequent passes by Partain's house was not a sufficient safeguard against any devilish moves of the Porches. Fate and his sons had proven themselves more than proficient at eluding the lumbering reach of the arm of the law.

He fluffed up his pillow, then settled back to read Howard Bahr's *The Black Flower*. The trouble was, he became so engrossed in the beautifully written novel of the Civil War that he wasn't the least bit sleepy. He forced himself to shut the book, making a mental note to find a duller book to use as a sleep aid.

Another glance at the cursed clock. 2:16.

He turned off the light and tried to will his body into a state of deep relaxation. His muscles responded, but his mind was too busy making random associations and chattering to itself to allow sleep to overtake him.

At 2:30, he gave up and crawled out of bed.

He sat a the kitchen table, waiting for the coffee to brew, and he pictured Ree Tyler sitting across the table, where she had sat last night, looking finer than any woman should to a man in his fifties. He massaged his temples, wondering if he should break his date with her. Something was obviously brewing between the Porches and Skeeter Partain, so now was not the time to take a night off from his surveillance of his long-time quarry. On the other hand, he *wanted* to spend time with Ree, wanted to be in the company of a good-hearted woman. *Would making love to her cure my insomnia?* He flushed at the thought. He wasn't sure he still knew how to seduce a woman. Did insomnia affect a man's sexual prowess? *What if I can't get it up?*

The coffeemaker made its last asthmatic gurgles, signaling that the brew was ready. He poured himself a large mug and held it to his face, savoring the heady, steaming aroma, then slurped a mouthful.

Ah, life's simple pleasures.

A fresh pot of coffee.

The love of a fine woman.

A good night of sleep.

"Shit," he whispered. "I've got work to do."

Promises to keep, and miles to go before I sleep.

The lines of poetry memorized years ago in high school decided him. He would call Ree later today and ask for a rain-check on the dinner invitation. Tonight he would keep his vigil on the Porch farmhouse.

CHAPTER 7
THE BAD PLACE

Joe Rob Campbell climbed the cement stairs to the back door that opened into his room in his grandmother's house. He slipped quietly inside, not wishing to wake his dead mother's mother. Grandma was a sweet old lady, but she asked too many questions. Where were you so late? Who were you with? You weren't drinking, were you? You know how people love to gossip, don't you?

Tonight he was in no mood for an interrogation. He just wanted to crash and sleep away the darkness. He wanted to turn off the loop of violent images running endlessly through his mind. He didn't want to think about the way Death seemed to follow him, first taking his mother and stepfather in an auto accident, then taking his grandfather a mere six months after Joe Rob had moved in with his grandparents. It almost seemed as if Death had finally overtaken him and claimed him as its instrument with the killing of Odell Porch.

He stripped off his clothes, and fell into bed. He was asleep as soon as his head hit the pillow.

Odell was there, waiting for him, opening his third eye and using it to peer into Joe Rob's soul. Odell was not alone. The psycho woman was with him, pointing her finger at Joe Rob in venomous accusation. Snakes twined about her naked shoulders and dangled from the tangles of her hair. Her breasts were nippled with the segmented hard-shell rattles from diamondbacks' tails, and the rattles quivered now, clattering like tiny maracas, sounding their sibilant warnings. But this back-from-the dead Medusa only made him laugh. She couldn't turn him to stone. He had already hardened his heart and turned himself to stone from the inside out. His harsh laughter shattered her like delicate crystal, the fallen shards reflecting light from a ghost moon. Odell's bullet-hole eye looked too deeply into Joe Rob's soul and was forever blinded by the limitless darkness. And Joe Rob was at last left alone.

He slept the sleep of the dead.

Skeeter woke to a nightmare. A nightmare of pain and humiliation. A nightmare that wasn't a nightmare at all, because this was really happening. He was trussed up and hanging by a thick chain in the loft of an abandoned barn. The smell of the rusty chain and the copper-like scent of his own blood formed a pungent bouquet that filled him with terror.

Though he was alone now, Skeeter knew they would be back.

They're going to kill me.

It had started in earnest the minute the lid opened and the two Porch ruffians hustled him out of the Firebird's trunk. The dilapidated farmhouse and the sun-bleached-to-gray barn loomed like dreamscape structures in the ghostly moonlight, and Skeeter knew at once where they'd brought him. This was the Bad Place, the old farmhouse everybody in town said was haunted by the farmer who had killed his wife and kids with an axe, then hanged himself in the barn loft. And just then Skeeter believed it was so. The very ground was infected with evil.

They pushed him into the barn and made him climb the ladder to the barn loft—no easy task with his hands tied behind his back. He slipped twice, barking his shins on the ladder.

On the third try he made it to the top and fell face down on a pile of rotten hay. His captors came up behind him and lifted him to his knees. Someone lit a lantern.

"You know who we are, boy?" said the one in the cowboy hat, resting his hand on the butt of the pistol he wore on his hip.

Skeeter shook his head: no.

The man cuffed him on the ear with the back of his hand. "You're lying. You don't wanna lie to us, ya dumb piece of shit. You know who we are?"

Skeeter nodded.

"That's right," said the man in the hat. "We're Odell's brothers."

The other brother stepped forward and seized Skeeter's chin in his rough hand. "And you're gone tell us about Odell. We know you were out at the dump the day he disappeared, so we think you can tell us where he's at. Take that tape off his mouth, Cowboy."

Cowboy reached down and snatched off the duct tape, ripping Skeeter's lips raw and making him yowl at the pain.

"Scream all you want to," Cowboy said. "Ain't nobody gonna hear you."

The other brother—Skeeter couldn't think of his name—moved behind him and Skeeter heard the clinking rattle of chain links.

Cowboy grinned and said, "Luther here's gonna hang you up on this chain so we can work on you real good. Then you'll tell us what we wanna know."

"I don't know anything!" Skeeter blurted. "I swear. We were at the dump but we didn't see your brother. I swear to God."

"Bullshit," Cowboy said with a sneer. "He's lying, Luther."

"We went to shoot rats," Skeeter told them. "If Odell was there, he must've left before we got there. We never saw him."

"Oh, he was there all right," said Luther, passing the thick chain around Skeeter's torso and under his armpits. "And he didn't leave on his own. He woulda waited for us to pick him up. He sure as hell wouldn'ta walked all the way home. He was a mite crazy but he was more lazy than crazy, least when it comes to walkin' anywhere."

Luther hooked the chain behind Skeeter's back, and all of a sudden Skeeter was hoisted off the loft floor, suspended by the hanging chain. He began to twist and turn slowly in the air, his bare feet feeling strange with nothing solid beneath them.

"So," said Luther as he secured the free end of the chain to a big rusty nail hammered into the wall.

"So," said Cowboy, taking up his brother's refrain, "you're gonna tell us. Where's our brother?"

Skeeter looked into their faces and saw their resemblance to Odell. The close-set eyes, the thick jowls, the cruel twist of the lower lip, pinned-back ears, the muddy complexion: these were the earmarks of the Porch genes. He licked his dry lips, then said, "I don't know *where* he is. I'm telling ya, I *don't know.*"

With no warning, Luther punched him in the gut. The air *whuffed* out of him and he began to swing back and forth from the force of the blow. Nausea bloomed deep in his belly, rose up his throat and filled his mouth with acidic saliva.

A hunting knife appeared in Luther's thick fist and he jabbed the tip of the blade at Skeeter's belly. Skeeter drew in his stomach but the sharp steel punctured the soft flesh just to the right of his navel and he cried out in pain.

Luther Porch sneered with obvious contempt. "Got ourselves a real pussy, li'l brother. Just a little stick and he's already bellyachin'. What's he gone do when I really start cuttin'?"

"Shit his britches and scream like a girl." Cowboy was bouncing on his heels, anxious to get in on the fun. "Lemme cut his balls off, Luther. Then he'll really scream like a girl."

"I ain't sure he's got any balls. Let's check him out."

Luther reached up and grabbed the waistband of Skeeter's boxer shorts. Skeeter kicked at Luther's arm, cracking his toes against the man's elbow. Luther ignored the blow and yanked the cotton shorts down to Skeeter's ankles.

"Well, I'll be damned," Luther said with a laugh. "I never seen such a little-bitty dick. Ain't hardly worth the trouble of cuttin' it off."

"Still hurt like a bitch, though," Cowboy said. "That's what counts. Lemme hold your knife. I can take his sack off with one little whack. Bet he'll talk to us then."

"Wait now," Luther said. "I reckon he should have a say in this. Tell me, boy. You rather lose your dick or your balls? Hmm?"

"Please," cried Skeeter, "don't cut me. I'll tell you everything. I will. I promise."

"But we ain't even hurt you yet." Luther said. "I don't reckon your tongue's loosened up enough to tell us everything. See, we don't wanna hear no bullshit. We hear any bullshit, you're gonna hurt so bad you'll be beggin' us to kill you." Luther punctuated his comment with the knife, opening a deep gash in Skeeter's left thigh.

Skeeter didn't scream this time. He clenched his teeth and grunted at the pain. Tears filled his eyes and snot ran from his nose. "It wasn't me," he blurted. "It was Joe Rob. *He* killed him."

"Sonofabitch," Cowboy spat.

"Killed Odell?" Luther's beady eyes went stone cold. His face became a mask of lifeless flesh.

"Yeah. It was an accident. I swear. Odell was gonna rape this girl. A runaway from the nuthouse. Joe Rob tried to stop him and Odell went at him with a knife and the gun just went off. He didn't mean to shoot him. It just happened."

"Goddamn," Cowboy said as he began pacing about the barn loft. "Goddamn motherfuckin' sonofabitch, they killed him. He's *dead*, Luther. How we gonna tell Paw?" Then he stopped pacing, drew his pistol and jammed the muzzle into Skeeter's stomach. "I'm gonna blow your fuckin' guts out!"

"No," Luther warned as he seized the wrist of his brother's gun-hand and pulled it away. "Not yet. Calm your ass down."

"Did you hear what he just said?" Cowboy was incredulous.

"I heard, goddammit. Now back off."

Skeeter already regretted his blurted words. But now that he'd said them, he had to convince these heathens that their brother's death really had been an accident—that Joe Rob hadn't meant to kill him. Otherwise, they would surely kill Joe Rob and it would be Skeeter's fault.

"Where's my brother?" Luther asked in a voice that was eerily calm and even.

"We buried him out past the wolf's den. You know where that is, right?"

"Who's this Joe Rob motherfucker?" Luther's words came out through gritted teeth, and Skeeter sensed that the man was holding back a whirlwind of raging violence. Cowboy paced back and forth, twirling his pistol on his index finger.

"Joe Rob Campbell. He's my best friend. That's how I know he didn't mean to kill him. Joe Rob's not—"

"He the one drives that old piece-of-shit Mustang?"

"Yeah, that's him."

"Where is he right now?"

"He's . . . he's probably home in bed."

"Where's home, dipshit?"

"That big brick house on the corner of West Main and Fifth Avenue? That's his grandmother's house. He lives with her." Skeeter glanced at Cowboy, who continued to pace, mumbling to himself.

Luther continued his questioning. All business now. No more playing with his prey. "If it was an accident, why didn't you go to the cops?"

"We were going to, but . . . we were afraid you guys wouldn't believe it was an accident. Or wouldn't care and would kill us anyway."

"Smart boy." Luther sheathed his hunting knife, and Skeeter breathed a small sigh of relief. "And this girl you said Odell was gonna fuck. What about her?"

"She's dead. Rattler bit her. She's at my dad's funeral home."

"Let's go get that sumbitch, Luther," said Cowboy. "He's dead and don't know it."

"He's dead all right," Luther said. "But first we got to tell Diddy. He calls the shots."

Oh Jesus, I've killed Joe Rob. Skeeter's physical pain was supplanted by his guilty anguish. He had ratted out his best friend, broken a blood oath, and if he was allowed to live, he would have to live with his cowardly betrayal till the end of his days. "But it was an accident," he told his captors. "Joe Rob didn't mean to kill your brother. You don't have to kill him."

"You don't know shit," Luther said with a feral snarl. "You open your mouth again, I'll cut your fuckin' tongue out."

"Ort to cut it out anyway," Cowboy said. "I need to hurt somebody. And this sumbitch was there when Odell died. He's got to pay."

"Not till he takes us to where they buried him. He's gonna dig him up, then he's gonna die."

"You hear that, you sorry piece o' shit?" Cowboy grinned maniacally at Skeeter. "That hole you dug for our brother's gonna be your own fuckin' grave."

Luther picked up the lantern. "Let's go wake up Diddy."

"He's gonna be so pissed, ain't no tellin' what he's liable to do. Maybe I should wait here and make sure this motherfucker don't go nowhere."

"He ain't goin' nowhere. You think he can break that damn chain?"

"No, but what if somebody comes along and—"

"Nobody's coming out here in the middle of the night. This place is haunted, don't you know?"

"Yeah." Cowboy grinned and gave Skeeter a push. The chain creaked against the wooden rafter as Skeeter swung back and forth over the barn-loft floor. "Hang loose, motherfucker. We'll be back real soon."

The Porch brothers descended the ladder, leaving Skeeter in darkness and deep despair. When he heard their car drive off, he began to cry, sobbing at first, then blubbering like a heartbroken baby. He cried for himself and for his best friend. He wept for Odell Porch and for Jessica A. Lowell.

And when he was all cried out, he began to pray.

CHAPTER 8
FATE

Fate Porch sat at the kitchen table, sipping home-brewed whiskey and smoking his pipe. The home brew burned his throat going down, but it took away the dry bite of his smoking tobacco, and it gave him a pleasant buzz that took some of the edge off his anxiety. He was worried about Odell, but he wasn't ready to believe his mother's grim prophecy of the boy's death. The old lady's prognostications usually turned out to be right, but she wasn't infallible. She had the *sight*, but she was old and her mind wasn't as sharp as it used to be. Anybody could throw the bones, but it took someone with true second sight to read them properly, and if Maw's mind was dulled by her years, then her interpretation could be wrong. Fate was banking on her being wrong; he just wasn't ready to accept that one of his sons could be dead, cut down in his prime. But if Odell *was* dead—if some son of a bitch had killed him—then there would be hell to pay and nothing else for it. And Fate would personally see the killer delivered into the hands of Old Scratch.

He got up to stretch his bones and get the kinks out of his back, then he went out on the front porch in hopes of seeing the boys drive up, but they didn't. Not yet. He stuck his hands in the deep pockets of his overalls and rocked on his heels. In a rare moment of self-reflection, he admitted to himself that his age and his poor health were catching up with him and that his oldest boy Luther would have to take over soon as head of the family. Sooner than Luther knew. Because Fate had cancer. He could feel it eating away his insides, and Maw had confirmed it with her sight. Fate didn't hold with doctors, so medical treatment was not an option. As his name implied, he was a fatalist; if he was meant to die of cancer, then so be it. No doctor's scalpel was going to change his fate.

He was confident that Luther was ready to take the reins of familial leadership and that their relatives in Vidalia and Statesboro would give the boy the same respect they had given him. Luther had inherited Fate's iron will and coldly calculating mind, and he surely would need those attributes to keep Cowboy and their more slovenly cousins in line. Luther had been toughened by their hardscrabble existence and had come to understand that life could crush a man of weak will in the blink of an eye. Fate had given his eldest son plenty of bare-knuckled instruction, beating him mercilessly when it was called for, but never to the point of breaking his spirit. That was the main thing. You could beat a man down to his knees, but you had to leave him a shred of dignity if you expected him to get up again on his own two feet. Luther knew what it meant to take a beating, but there was no quit in the boy. The only way to keep him down was to kill him. And if you killed a Porch, you were as good as dead, because the family motto was *blood for blood*. Fate's own father had shotgunned two revenuers who had shot and killed Fate's uncle during a raid on his moonshine still. "It all boils down to two things, son," Fate's father had told him on his sixteenth birthday. "Blood and honor. *Family* blood and *family* honor. Ain't no bloodshed too much if it's shed in defense of that honor. Cain't nobody else do it for you either. Not the cops, not the government, not Jesus Christ Hisself. It's all up to you and yours." Fate had learned his lessons well, and so had Luther in his turn. And if Maw was right about Odell being dead, then Fate was going to let Luther call his own shots in settling the matter. It was his time.

Headlights coming up the driveway pulled Fate from his ruminations. Now he would learn the fate of his middle son, Odell. And Lord help anyone who might have harmed the boy. He stepped off the porch and went out to meet the boys as they were climbing out of Luther's car.

"It's bad, Diddy," Cowboy told him as he slammed the passenger door and spat on the ground. "Real bad."

"Not so loud," Fate said in a loud whisper. "You'll wake your gramaw."

Luther eased his door shut. "The Partain boy says his friend killed Odell. Shot him and buried him out past the wolf's den."

"Oh Lord," Fate moaned. His throat clenched and the cancer made itself known in a stab of sharp pain. A wave of dizziness washed over him and little spots of light appeared in front of his eyes.

"You all right, Diddy?" Luther asked.

"Yeah. Just a dizzy spell. You believe the boy?"

"We got him hung up in the old Jenkins barn. Gave him a little taste of my knife and he broke. No way he's lying, the little pussy."

Cowboy said, "You want us to go get the sumbitch, right? The pecker-wood that killed Odell?"

"Joe Rob Campbell," Luther said. "Lives in that brick house on the corner of West Main and Fifth Avenue."

"What do you think, Luther?" Fate tried to see his oldest son's eyes in the darkness.

"Well, the first thing to do is get Odell's body," said Luther. "Take the little peckerwood with us and make him dig it up."

Fate nodded. "Then what?"

"Cut Partain's throat and bury him right there. Even if he didn't pull the trigger on Odell, he was there. Can't leave him alive no how 'cause he could go to the cops."

"And the Campbell boy?"

"Seeing as how he lives in the middle of town, we'll have to be real careful. We go drag his ass out of bed, take him out in the woods and kill him. Unless you wanna kill him yourself."

Fate rubbed his stubbled chin, contemplating Luther's plan. "No, I won't kill him. I'll let you have that pleasure."

"What about me?" Cowboy chimed in. "He was my brother too. I want a shot at the little bastard."

"Luther's calling the shots," Fate said.

"Damn, Diddy, why—"

"Hush up, boy," Fate warned Cowboy. "Don't make me go upside your head."

Luther wasted no time in taking up the mantle of leadership. "We'll take my car. Get a couple of shovels out of the barn, Cowboy. I'll get a blanket for Odell. You coming with us, Diddy?"

"Bet your ass I am." Fate swallowed the pain in the back of his throat and ignored the foul taste emanating from the cancer that was slowly eating his life away.

The front porch light came on, and his mother appeared behind the screen door. "Fate?" she called. "It come to me how to get the one you want."

"What, Maw?"

"Come to me in a dream," she said. Unlike her rail-thin body, her voice was deep and strong. "You must take off the ring finger of the one you have and send it to the one you want. He'll come to you if you do that."

"God . . . dang it," Cowboy said, modifying his curse so his father wouldn't smack him for taking the Lord's name in vain. "Gramaw's spooky, ain't she? How you reckon she does it?"

"You hear me, son?" the old lady called.

"I hear."

"She already knows about Odell, don't she?" Luther whispered.

Fate nodded. "She knows. She knew before any of us."

"What's she talking about, take off the ring finger?"

"The Partain boy. He wearing a ring?"

"Hell, I don't know" Luther shrugged. "He might be."

"He's got a school ring," Cowboy said. "I seen it. It's one of them Blue Devil rings. Like the football team? I had dibbs on it."

"That's what she's talking about," Fate said. "Send the finger with the ring still on it to the son of a bitch who killed Odell. We'll send a note with it, saying if you wanna see your friend alive, do what we say."

"Oh, yeah, I get it," Cowboy said.

"But what if he goes to the cops?" Luther asked.

"Your gramaw says it'll bring him to us," said Fate. "He won't go to the police."

"We ain't gonna stick the finger in the mail, are we?" Cowboy said.

"Hell no," Luther said. "We'll deliver it our own selves. Get the bolt cutters. We'll take off the sumbitch's finger with a clean cut."

Fate was nearly overcome with fatherly pride. He reckoned he had raised his boys right. After he was dead and gone, Luther and Cowboy would see to it that the family honor was upheld, come hell or high water.

And he had an inkling that there would be plenty of hell coming their way.

CHAPTER 9
NIGHT WATCH

Cornelius Weehunt stood on the rim of the sinkhole and gazed down into the thick darkness. He didn't like standing this close to the hellish pit, and it scared the bejesus out of him, but *somebody* had to keep watch until it was filled in and paved over. Nobody else was doing it, so Corny had taken the task upon himself. Sure, it was a thankless job, standing here in the middle of the night with Main Street deserted and creepy. Nobody would come up to him later, shake his hand, pat him on the back or give him a medal for it, but he didn't care about that. All he cared about was making sure nothing evil came out of there to plague his town. And if something did rise up from hell's depths, *he* would be the one to raise the alarm. He remembered a story from his childhood about a little boy who stuck his finger in a dyke to hold back a deadly flood, and he likened himself to that heroic little boy. That story was one of very few he could remember since his accident ten years ago. He had fallen off a ladder while painting a house and landed on his head. The doctor said he was lucky to survive the fall, what with his head injury and all. It had hurt his brain, the doctor said. Hurt it bad. Killed off a little part of it. He would never be like he was before the accident. His memory was full of holes. He sometimes lost whole days, and try as he might, he couldn't remember where he'd been or what he'd done on those lost days. And that wasn't all. Sometimes he would fly into a rage for no good reason and smash up things, yell and curse. Once he'd even attacked his best and only true friend, Otis Dellums. Otis had been eating Vienna sausages out of a can and Corny had jumped up and kicked poor Otis in the mouth, busting his lip and knocking out a tooth. He still felt real bad about that, but good old Otis didn't hold a grudge. Otis was retarded. But he had a good heart, and when he smiled at you, it made you feel warm all the way down to your feet. People said Corny was retarded too, but he knew that wasn't true. It was just that part of his brain was dead. And evidently it wasn't one of the real important parts. If it was, he wouldn't be standing here now at the edge of the sinkhole in the middle of the night, watching over things for the whole town of Vinewood, would he? Heck no. Corny Weehunt was smart enough to know what it meant to be a good citizen. And seeing as how nobody else was out here but him, he figured he was some ways better than all those people snug in their beds on this sultry night. He was like those old railroad signalmen his father had told him about, solitary men manning their lonesome outposts in the dark of night, dedicated to their work and giving up warm beds to make sure the trains ran safely over the tracks. Corny was sure his father would've been proud of him for keeping this night watch.

"Ain't no flies on Cornelius Weehunt," he said aloud. "Just these damn skeeters." He slapped his ear where a mosquito was buzzing. He didn't think he got him, but the slap made his ear ring so loud that he couldn't hear the skeeter anymore.

But he could hear Whisperer. He could hear Whisperer just fine, though he sometimes wished he couldn't. It wasn't that Corny didn't like the company of the whispery voice that often spoke to him; it was more that he didn't always like or even understand the things Whisperer whispered to him in that rasping, hissing voice that reminded him of insect wings buzzing inside his head. If asked, Corny couldn't have said if the voice was male or female, but of course nobody ever asked because Corny never told anyone about Whisperer. He figured that people would say he was crazy if they found out about the voice inside his skull and that Doctor Jackson might even want to put him back in that mental hospital if he knew about Whisperer. And Whisperer wouldn't like that at all. The last thing Corny wanted was to make Whisperer mad. Bad things happened when Whisperer got mad. Really bad things. Like the time the voice had told him to shoplift that bone-handle hunting knife from the Economy Hardware Store. Corny knew stealing was wrong, though he *did* like that knife a lot and wouldn't have minded owning it and wearing it on his belt. That was the time he had refused to obey Whisperer and had talked back, saying, "Stealing's wrong. It's against the law and I ain't gone do it." Old Man Jones had given him a queer look and come out from behind the counter to stand right behind Corny. "Who you talking to, Corny?" Jones asked. Corny said, "Nobody. Just myself." And Jones said, "You ain't thinking of stealing something, are you?" "No, sir," Corny said. And Old Man Jones said, "Better go on now if you ain't fixing to buy something." Then the bad thing happened. In a slithery voice Whisperer told—*commanded*—Corny to pick up that bone-handle knife, slip it out of its leather sheath and point it right at Old Man Jones' big potbelly, which was exactly what Corny did. That incident had landed Corny in jail, but Chief Chaney let him out after Corny promised that he would stay out of the hardware store. Luke Chaney was a good man who understood Corny's special problems. The chief knew Corny was not a bad man. But even Chief Chaney wouldn't have understood about Whisperer. And Chaney wasn't Chief anymore. Besides, Corny knew in his gut that Whisperer didn't want him to ever tell anybody about Whisperer. And if he ever did spill the beans, Whisperer would make him suffer for it.

Now, as he stood at the edge of the killing hole, swaying a little in a rising wind, Corny cocked his head and tried to hear what Whisperer was saying. The hissing words were garbled but he could make out the urgent tone in the voice. Whisperer was telling him something of great importance, but he couldn't quite make out the words. "Damnation," Corny whispered back. "Tell me plain."

But the whispering stopped suddenly, the way insects sometimes stop their chittering when something hungry threatens them. *Something hungry*, Whisperer hissed. And the darkness down in the hole thickened like cold gravy and he backed away, his heart thumping hard in his thin chest and making his ribs tingle. The street lights of Main Street flickered and dimmed, painting the storefronts and the street with a sickly light, reminding him of old, old photographs, black & white but yellowed to brown with age. It was then that Corny knew the darkness itself was hungry. He had no idea what the dark could be hungry *for*, but he sensed that whatever it was, it couldn't be good, and that it—the dark—was very, very dangerous.

He turned away and loped down the street, putting as much distance as he could between himself and the hole of congealing darkness.

CHAPTER 10
RIDE OUT THE NIGHT

Luke slipped into his jeans, threw on a T-shirt and jammed his feet into his boots, then stepped outside, his boot heels tapping a hollow tattoo on the front porch and rousing Hondo from his watchdog's slumber.

"You stay, boy," he said. Hondo yawned and watched him with sleepy eyes as he walked to his truck, climbed in and started the motor. Since he couldn't sleep, he had decided to ride out the night. He would cruise the streets of Vinewood and the outlying roads, swing by the Partain home on Maple Circle, then drive by the Bottom to make sure Fate and his boys weren't up to any middle-of-the-night mischief.

As he drove by the high school, he saw the police cruiser prowling the parking lot beside the brick gym. He pulled off the road and flashed his lights at the cruiser, then stopped beside the blue-&-white. Craig Hemphill rolled down his window and said, "Hey, Luke. What're you doing out this time of night?"

"Couldn't sleep," Luke told him. "Everything quiet?"

"Quiet as a tomb," Hemphill said. "Like always."

"You checked on the Partain place?"

"Yes, sir. As ordered. Nothing doing there."

"Chief Keller tell you trouble might be brewing between the Porch boys and the Partain kid?"

"Sure did. You know what it's about?" Hemphill scratched at his wide chin.

"Nah. Just that something might be up."

The young officer nodded. "You miss it, don't you, Luke? The job?"

Luke smiled. "Only on nights like this when I can't sleep."

"Shoot, only time I can't sleep's when I'm pulling the graveyard shift. I'm so sleepy now I can hardly keep my eyes open."

"Enjoy it while you can. Things change when you get older."

"Hell, Chief, you ain't that old."

Luke gave him a two-finger salute. "Old enough to know better," he said, then drove away.

He drove across town and slowed down as he passed by the Partain house, then circled the block and stopped behind the little cinderblock building that was Skeeter's living quarters. The boy's truck was parked on the dirt driveway, and the pillbox building's windows were dark. There was nothing to suggest that Skeeter was not safe inside, snoring the night away in his bunk. Luke sat there a full minute, his truck's engine idling with a deep rumble. Then he cut the engine, grabbed a flashlight from the glove box, got out and crept to the window. He clicked on the light and aimed the beam through the small opening between the flimsy curtains. From his vantage point he could see the foot of the bunk bed, but his field of vision was too limited for him to determine whether the bed was occupied.

In the near distance a dog barked, setting off a mounting chorus of canine barks and howls all across the neighborhood. Cursing silently, Luke hastened back to his truck. He didn't want to be caught skulking about in the dark. Some homeowners would shoot first and ask questions later. He didn't know if James Partain owned a gun, but this was not the time to find out. He started the engine and drove off down the tree-lined street.

He cruised past The American Legion building and Ree Tyler's house just outside the city limits. He imagined Ree curled up in bed, sleeping peacefully. Sleeping in the nude. He imagined himself lying beside her, smelling her perfume, snuggling against her warm flesh. He immediately felt a twinge of guilt for indulging in such lascivious thoughts. He chastised himself for being unfaithful to the memory of his dead wife. What would Jenny think if she could somehow look down on him, see into his heart and mind and know of his lustful feelings for Ree Tyler? Would she release him from his vows and wish him well? Or would she regard him with the intense jealousy she had occasionally exhibited when she was alive? He accelerated and drove south toward the Bottom and the Porch farmhouse, trying to push the idea of a jealous ghost from his mind.

He turned off the blacktop and drove up the rutted dirt road until the darkened farmhouse came into view. Fate's Ford pickup and the old Cadillac were parked in front of the house, but the used Firebird Luther had recently acquired was nowhere in sight. Was Luther conducting some nocturnal drug deal? Was he shacking up with a girlfriend? Or was he closing in on Skeeter Partain and Joe Rob Campbell? Of course there was another possibility, one that Luke had to consider: It was possible that Odell had shown up and was inside the dark house, safe in his own bed—nixing any potential trouble between the Porches and the two "townie" boys, Skeeter and Joe Rob. Luke couldn't imagine what Skeeter and Joe Rob might've done to arouse the ire and suspicions of Fate and his sons. Odell Porch was a bully and a hothead, not the sort of man two boys fresh out of high school would wish to tangle with or go against. Joe Rob was a scrapper, a former high-school football star, but he was a babe in the woods compared to ex-Marine Odell; and Skeeter was a scrawny scrub of a young man, not at all athletic. If they had a run-in with Odell, it almost certainly would've been unintentional.

Luke turned around and drove back to town. As he was cruising down Main Street, someone shambled in front of his truck, and he slammed on the brakes to keep from hitting the startled man.

"Corny?" Luke shouted. "What the hell's wrong with you? I could've killed you."

Cornelius Weehunt staggered backward and fell on his ass.

Luke hopped out of the truck and helped Corny to his feet.

"Sorry, Chief Chaney," Corny said, dusting off his rump. "I . . . I thought something was chasing me."

"Chasing you? Who's chasing you?"

Corny looked around and pointed in the direction of the sinkhole in the middle of the street. "I thought something was fixin' to come out of that dang hole and get me."

"I don't see anything now? Do you?"

"No, sir. But honest to God, I thought I did."

"What are you doing out here in the middle of the night?"

Corny looked down at the asphalt, mumbling to himself.

"What's that?" Luke pressed him.

"I's just keeping watch, you know, on the hole."

"Watching for what?"

"I don't rightly know. Something just told me I ort to do it. That's all."

"Well, get in the truck and I'll drive you home."

"Yessir."

Luke drove Corny Weehunt to the boarding house on Poplar Street and let him out. "Don't wake folks up when you go inside," he told the child-like man of thirty years. "And don't be telling anybody you saw something coming out of that hole. You hear me?"

"Yessir, I hear." Corny gave him a furtive glance, then got out of the truck, slunk up the sidewalk and slipped inside the front door.

Luke smiled to himself and shook his head. "Poor bastard," he said.

Before driving home, Luke cruised by the brick house on the corner of West Main and Fifth Avenue. Joe Rob Campbell's '67 Mustang was parked behind the house. "Four A.M. and all's well," he said, then added, "I hope."

CHAPTER 11
GRAVEDIGGER'S SORROW

Skeeter raised his chin from his chest and watched the shadow-shapes come up the ladder to the barn loft. A flame flared, a lantern was lit, and he saw the wizened face of Fate Porch in the lantern's light. Skeeter had promised himself that he would not humiliate himself further by begging for mercy. Whatever the bastards had in store for him, he would confront it like a man. But when he saw Fate Porch, his hopes rose and he thought he might have a chance of survival if he could appeal to the elder man's maturity and seasoned reasoning. Maybe the man wasn't the monster everyone said he was.

"Mr. Porch," Skeeter blurted, "it was an accident, I swear. I didn't shoot nobody. I—"

"Shut your yap, boy," Fate Porch said. Skeeter saw the hurt in the man's sad eyes, and his hopes sank. "Get him down," Fate told his sons.

Luther unhooked the other end of the chain and Skeeter dropped to the loft floor, tumbling forward on his face.

"Stand up, you pussy," Cowboy snarled. "Told ya he was a pussy, Diddy."

Skeeter struggled to his feet, his hands still bound behind his back. Someone pushed him toward the top of the ladder and he stumbled forward, lost his balance and almost took a header over the edge of the loft, but a yank on the chain snatched him back.

"Goddamn, he's a worthless peckerwood, ain't he!"

"Lower him with the chain," said Fate. "And don't drop him."

"Set your ass down there, boy," Luther said. "Right on the edge."

Skeeter sat on the edge of the barn loft with his legs dangling. Someone pulled the chain tight behind him, then shoved him over the side. The chain bit into his armpits as he was lowered to the ground. Then the chain came rattling down on his head and shoulders, knocking him to the dirt floor of the barn. Dirt and debris stuck to his sweat-streaked face.

I'm in hell, Skeeter thought. *I'm not dead yet, but I'm already in fucking hell.*

They walked him outside and deposited him in the trunk of the Firebird, then slammed the lid on him. A moment later, the car was in motion and Skeeter was bouncing around in the darkness of enclosed space that smelled of exhaust fumes and tire rubber. He sobbed softly to himself.

The bumpy ride seemed to go on forever. Skeeter wondered if the driver had gotten lost on the way to the wolf's den, but then the ride was over and the trunk was opened, a flashlight's beam blinding him.

"Get his ass out," someone said. And rough hands grabbed him and hauled him out of the trunk. His head hit the trunk's lid and he grunted in pain. Cowboy untied his hands.

"All right, boy," said Fate Porch, handing him a flashlight, "take us to where you buried my son."

"Yes, sir," Skeeter said. Barefoot and wearing only boxer shorts, he led them through the trees and underbrush, shining the light ahead. Shadows danced around the nimbus of light. An owl hooted somewhere nearby, and Skeeter half-remembered an old homily that said something about an owl's hoot presaging death. Out here in the dark woods, with the Porch men behind him, it was easy to believe that the owl was singing of his own impending death. He led them across the little creek and to the place of Odell's unceremonious burial. "Here," he said, stopping and pointing the light at the clumps of pine straw and dead leaves on the ground. "That's where we buried him."

Luther took the flashlight and thrust a shovel into Skeeter's trembling hands. "Start digging, motherfucker."

He used the blade of the shovel to scrape the leaves and pine straw off the freshly turned soil, then started digging. The ground was soft, the digging easier than the last time. Though he was near physical and emotional exhaustion, the digging had a calming effect on him. He was able to ignore the stinging knife wounds in his leg and belly and concentrated on nothing but the act of digging.

Luther lit the kerosene lantern and set it on the ground. Fate sat on a log and lit his pipe, its pungent smoke drifting languidly in the lantern light. Cowboy practiced his quick-draw, pointing his pistol at Skeeter and saying, "Pow," at the end of each draw.

"Stop that, son," Fate told Cowboy. "Don't wanna shoot him on accident."

"I ain't gonna shoot him," said Cowboy, indignant. "Not till you say to."

Skeeter worked the shovel, sweating profusely and trying to ignore the spoken words of his captors, but there was no blocking out the reality of his situation. He was digging his own grave. His life on this earth was close to its end.

The hole deepened and the pile of shoveled dirt grew. Skeeter was dripping sweat. He was tired, light-headed, and his palms were blistered, the blisters already ruptured and burning. His mouth was dry, his lips cracked, and he was thirstier than he'd ever been. But still he dug on through the pain.

Then he noticed the stink. The stench of Odell's rotting corpse. The next shovelful came away and revealed the camouflage-splash of Odell's clothing.

"There he is, Diddy," said Cowboy, pointing his pistol into the hole.

"Damn, I smell him," Luther said, then turned away and retched.

Fate stood up, looked down at Skeeter and said, "You be careful now. I don't want Odell tore up with that shovel."

"No, sir," Skeeter said, clearing dirt away from Odell's head. He uncovered the gunnysack containing the dead rat and tossed it out of the hole. Cowboy immediately snatched it up and pulled the rat out by its tail. "God almighty, you buried my brother with a goddamn rat?!" Cowboy sputtered.

The shovel's blade nicked the dirty, discolored flesh of the corpse's cheek. Skeeter cursed under his breath, then leaned the shovel against the wall of the grave, dropped to his knees and began to dig with his hands. The stench made him gag, so he held his breath as he dug dog-style. The bandana headband came into view. Skeeter was careful not to expose the bullet hole beneath the bandana. He was afraid that if they saw the bullet hole, they would kill him on the spot. It didn't make good sense, but it seemed imperative to keep the bullet hole hidden as long as he could; it was the only way he could think of to postpone his death—even if only by a few minutes.

"They buried him with a *rat*, Diddy," Cowboy ranted. "That's . . . that's sacrilegious as hell. Let me kill the sumbitch now."

"No," Fate said sharply. "You know the plan. Settle down now."

Plan? Why do they need a plan to kill me? Must be something about Joe Rob. Why can't they just go get him like the got me? Don't need much of a plan for that. They're crazy, that's why. Crazy mean. Crazy as shithouse rats. Hadn't been for rats, I wouldn't even be in this fucking mess. Joe Rob's fucking fault. His idea to go to the dump and shoot rats. "Goddamn Joe Rob," he muttered.

"What's that, boy?" asked Fate Porch.

"Nothing."

"Come on out there now," the man said. "My boys will take care of their brother."

Skeeter got off his knees, stood up and tried to work the kinks out of his cramping legs. His head swam on woozy waves and he thought he was going to pass out and topple over on top of the corpse. He steadied his legs and braced his hands against the dirt walls of the shallow grave. He tried to climb out of the hole but couldn't gain purchase on the ground above him.

"Get him outta there," Fate told his boys.

Luther and Cowboy reached down, grabbed Skeeter's arms and hauled him out.

"Tie his hands and feet," said Fate, "then get Odell outta there."

The brothers tied Skeeter's hands behind his back, then bound his ankles tightly together and left him lying facedown on the ground. While Luther and Cowboy went about the dirty business of getting their dead brother out of the grave, Fate Porch demanded a full account of the killing from Skeeter. Skeeter told him the whole sad story, placing particular emphasis on the fact the he (Skeeter) wasn't actually present when the shooting occurred.

After a long silence, Fate said, "So if y'all had left when Odell told you to, he'd still be alive and we wouldn't be here now."

Skeeter lifted his cheek form the damp ground and said, "Yes, sir. But Odell woulda raped the girl. We . . . Joe Rob couldn't let that happen."

"Don't matter now," said Fate. "Girl's dead and so's Odell. Now you and your hero friend have to die and that'll be the end of it. All on account of a crazy woman who got herself snakebit anyhow. Sad state of affairs, ain't it?"

Skeeter didn't bother to reply. He knew now that nothing he might say could change his fate. He and Joe Rob were as good as dead.

* * *

They took him back to the rundown barn behind the abandoned farmhouse and hung him up in the barn loft again. But this time, they left his hands untied.

Cowboy took Skeeter's left hand and made a show of closely examining the class ring on Skeeter's third finger. "That's a nice ring," Cowboy said. "I coulda had me one, 'cept I had to quit school and go to work. You wouldn't know about that, would you? Being the son of a rich undertaker and all."

"I work," Skeeter said, then immediately wondered why he bothered to argue with the crazy cretin in the cowboy hat.

"Yeah, but you don't have to. You just work for extra spending money. Right?"

Luther walked toward him with long-handled bolt-cutters in his hand, and Skeeter realized what was about to happen. He tried to jerk his hand out of Cowboy's grasp, but Cowboy held firm.

"Hold him still," said Luther.

Fate Porch stood with his arms folded across his chest, watching impassively.

"No! Please . . ." begged Skeeter.

Luther held up the scissor blades of the bolt-cutters and Cowboy stuck Skeeter's ring finger in the steel V. Skeeter tried to pull his finger out of the biting vise, but Cowboy's grip was too strong.

"Jesus Christ," Skeeter blurted, "if you want my ring, just take it. You don't have to cut off my finger!"

"It ain't for us, dipshit," Cowboy said, his breath foul in Skeeter's face. "It's for your asshole buddy. The sumbitch that shot Odell."

"Hold him still, dammit," Luther told his brother. Then he scissored the handles together.

Skeeter's finger came off with a loud snap, and a ragged scream ripped itself from his throat. His whole body jerked, swinging a little on the chain. Unable to cope with the pain and the horror, his mind escaped into a netherworld of semi-consciousness.

CHAPTER 12
HARLOT

Joe Rob's erection woke him. He was lying on his belly, his stiff penis so engorged with blood that it throbbed more with pain than with dream-inspired lust. He rolled onto his back, took his cock in his hand and gave it a few good strokes, but nixed the idea of finishing off the chore. His bladder was uncomfortably full, so he rolled out of bed and went into the adjoining bathroom to take an urgent leak. His "piss-hard" in hand, he pushed his stiff prick down in low aim so he wouldn't piss on the toilet tank or the wall, then cut loose with a strong stream of concentrated urine. By the time he was done, his cock had shrunk to half its full-alert size, but his free-floating lust had not abated. His thoughts turned to Charlotte Claymore, the town whore. He had paid a visit to Charlotte the Harlot the night of his graduation, but that transaction had been anything but satisfying; he'd shot his wad on her bare belly before he'd had a chance to sheath himself and slip inside her. To her credit, Charlotte hadn't belittled his premature expenditure; she had caressed his head and whispered sweetly into his ear, telling him it was nothing to be ashamed of and that it happened all the time with horny young studs like him. She kept his fifty dollars and sent him on his way, sadder and maybe a little wiser in the ways of women of the world.

He shook the last drops from his cock, went to the sink and washed his face in cold water, brushed his teeth with strong mouthwash, and then got dressed and slipped down the back steps to his waiting Mustang. He backed out of the driveway, then drove up Main Street to the Quick-Stop Mini-Mart for a cup of coffee and a couple of donuts. He ate in his car, taking in the sunrise and listening to a Stevie Ray Vaughan disc. The Texas guitar player had been a favorite of Joe Rob's father, and Joe Rob had grown up idolizing Stevie Ray and memorizing the hottest licks of the blues man's nimble style. Now Vaughan was dead, and Joe Rob's dad was long gone, but Vaughan's music still touched Joe Rob in a way no other music ever did.

Every time he listened to Stevie Ray's songs, he felt a connection with his father—even though he had no idea where in the world the old man was. Billy Joe Campbell had been a talented musician with a jones for booze and dope. Joe Rob often wondered how things would've been if his father's addiction hadn't ruined his music career and his marriage. The old man had been a hell of a guitar player. Not as good as Stevie Ray, but who was? Of course, if Joe Rob's mom hadn't divorced Billy Joe and married a successful businessman, then Joe Rob wouldn't have inherited the money in his trust fund. What the hell? It did no good now to imagine how things might have been. His father was gone, and whether the old man was picking up gigs in Nashville or L.A., or panhandling spare change for cheap wine, Joe Rob didn't expect to see Billy Joe ever again. And if somehow his father were to show up, he didn't know if he would cold-cock the junkie for deserting him or hug him for caring enough to come back. Fuck it. Water under the bridge.

He drained the last of the coffee, crushed the empty Styrofoam cup in his hand and tossed it out the window, then drove across town to Charlotte the Harlot's seedy little house on Sixth Street. He parked behind her old VW beetle, walked up to the door and rang the bell. She came to the door in a threadbare housecoat. Her bottle-blonde hair was a nest of teased tangles, and her smeared eye make-up gave her a raccoonish look. She fixed him with angry eyes and said, "What the hell do you want this early in the morning?"

"Uh, you know. The usual." He stuck his hands in his pockets.

"Listen, stud, I don't keep fucking banker's hours. Come back tonight and maybe I'll take your money." She tried to shut the door on him, but he stopped it with his foot.

"Hey! You want me to call the cops?" Her face twisted into an angry caricature of itself, and she looked older than Joe Rob had thought she was. Seeing her now, he figured she was pushing forty.

"You won't call the cops," he said. "You're a fucking whore."

"Fuck you, sonny boy. The cops are my best customers. Move your goddamn foot."

"Come on, Charlotte," he softened his approach. "I'll give you a hundred bucks. Please?"

She gave him a studied look, then pulled the door open. "In advance," she said. "And as soon as you're done, you leave."

"Deal," he said, and stepped inside. He smelled stale cigarette smoke, perfume that reminded him of insecticide, and the day-old scent of Italian cooking, heavy with garlic and grease.

She led him into the bedroom, waved him to the Queen-size bed, then went into the bathroom and shut the door. He sat on the bed and pulled off his boots and socks. He heard water running and splashing in the bathroom, then he heard the woman gargle and spit. The toilet flushed, and Charlotte came out of the bathroom as he was pulling off his jeans.

She had discarded the housecoat and was wearing a short nightgown of diaphanous black and a skimpy pair of black panties. "Cash up front," she said, sashaying toward the bed.

Joe Rob took out his wallet, peeled off two fifties, then slapped the bills down on the nightstand. "There you go," he said.

She nodded. "You've been here before?" she asked.

"What, you don't remember me?" He put a hand over his heart. "I'm hurt."

"Yeah, yeah. I remember you. You're the football hero. Right? The fastest man on the field—or off." She flashed a sly smile.

"Hey, so I was a little too quick. Made your job easy, didn't it? You didn't even have to work for your money."

"Listen, honey, I earn every blessed cent."

"Right." He caught a whiff of her mouthwash and grinned up at her. "I think you'll have to work a little harder this time."

"Yeah?" She sat on the edge of the bed and reached inside his boxer shorts. "Let's see what you got."

"Hey, your hands are cold."

She pulled his semi-erect penis out through the opening and gave it a firm squeeze, looking closely at its tip.

"What're you doing?"

"Health check," she said. "Rubbers break, and I sure don't need a dose of the clap. Okay, you're clean. How do you want it?"

He stroked his chin as if giving the question serious consideration, then said, "Down and dirty. You can start with your mouth. Then we'll go from there."

Charlotte narrowed her eyes. "All right. House rules. You don't come in my mouth. I don't do anal, and I ain't into rough stuff. If you do something I don't like, I tell you to stop and you damn well better stop. If you don't, I've got a razor close by and I'll cut you. Got it?"

"Yes, ma'am. But what if I happen to like being cut?" He flashed her a wicked smile.

"If that's your trip, you can take your money and get out right now. I don't do that sick shit."

"Take it easy, Charlotte. I was just pulling your leg."

"Okay. Let's do it. I've got a hair appointment." She was clearly bored, but Joe Rob figured she just wasn't a morning person and that he was lucky she was willing to haul his ashes during her off hours.

"Wait. How about some music to set the mood? Last time you had music."

She reached over to the radio on the nightstand and clicked it on. A country & western song was playing, some chick singing through her nose.

"I don't like country," he said.

"That's Lee Ann Womack. Everybody likes her."

"If she was here, I'd probably fuck her, but I don't want to hear her sing, okay? Find some rock 'n' roll. Heavy metal would hit the right spot."

She scowled and turned the dial until she found a soft-Rock oldie. An Elton John classic. "There. That good enough for you?"

"That's fag music. Hell, just turn it off. We'll make our own music."

"Okay, stud. It's your dime."

"Dime my ass."

"You know? I liked you better when you were half drunk. You're a real pain in the ass, sober."

That one hit him wrong and the black snake writhed in his belly. He grabbed a handful of her hair and pulled her head down to his crotch. "Suck it, cunt. Or I'll give you a real pain in the ass."

Charlotte muttered something that was muffled by his crotch. She stiffened her neck and tried to resist, but he knotted her hair in his hand and kept the pressure on the back of her head. She gave up her resistance and took his cock in her mouth and sucked until it was rock-hard. Then she used her tongue on the sensitive underside of his penis, whipping his lust right up to the edge of eruption. He came close to shooting his wad in her mouth just because she'd told him not to, but backed off and withdrew at the last second. This time he was going to fuck her like a man, not like some fumbling punk-ass kid.

He stood, pushed down his shorts, then lifted her gown off over her head. Her full breasts fell into view, drooping onto the paunch of her belly. He rolled her onto her stomach, pulled her panties off and lowered himself onto the twin pillows of her buttocks, his cock falling into the soft crevice.

"Not in the ass," she warned him. Was there a note of fear in her voice?

Taking his cock in his hand, he dragged its swollen head along the crack of her ass, pausing at the puckered entrance to her asshole, then pushing on down to the lips of her pussy.

"Not without a condom, Goddammit," she told him. "There." She pointed a manicured finger at the little goldfish bowl filled with packs of Trojans on the nightstand by the radio. "Fuck that," he said. "For a hundred bucks, I want to feel what I'm fucking."

"No! Get off me, you bastard!" She bucked beneath him. He held her down and tried to force himself inside her, but she was too dry. He spat on his fingers and lubricated her with his saliva. "I'll have you arrested for rape," she threatened.

"You took my money. This ain't rape." He repositioned the head of his cock, then thrust his hips hard. With a pleasant burn of friction, his cock slipped inside her, and he rammed in to the hilt. "I'll kill you, you punk!" she shouted. "You're fucking dead!"

He grabbed another handful of her hair as if he were holding the reins of a horse, and pumped her with a vengeance. Riding bareback. He slapped her fleshy hip. "Yee hah!"

"Stop it! Please stop! You'll make me pregnant."

"No I won't," he said, panting with exertion. "Your ass is mine." And he pulled out of her vagina and jammed the head of his slick penis into her anus. She grunted. He thrust harder, forcing his rigid length deeper into the tight orifice. "I told you . . . I like it . . . down and dirty," he said. "Dark and nasty."

Charlotte began to whimper, but Joe Rob was oblivious to her whining protestations. He was riding a wave of dark power, and that wave was about to crest and break in a thundering crash of brutal lust.

He exploded inside her dark passage, burying himself deep and howling with release. When he was done, he rolled off her pillowing ass and collapsed onto his back. The room fell out of focus. He floated on receding waves, returning to calmer seas. The black snake in his belly was sated.

Charlotte sat up and slapped him hard across the face. "You sonofabitch!" She slapped him again. "Fucking bastard!" Again she slapped him.

Laughing, he grabbed her wrist and held it immobile. "Chill out, Charlotte. It's over. And I didn't knock you up. Unless you're gonna have shit babies."

"You white trash motherfucker," she hissed in his face. "I'll put a contract out on your sorry ass. I know a guy who'll kill you for a hundred bucks. You stupid shit. The same hundred you paid to fuck me up the ass is gonna pay for your killing."

Joe Rob cackled. "He'll have to stand in line, darling. You ain't the only one who wants me dead."

"Get out. Get your fucking clothes and get out of my house."

He let go of her wrist, stood up and got dressed. "You know what, Charlotte? You need to find another line of work. You're whoring days are over. Fucking your worn-out pussy is like trying to fuck an elephant. Your asshole is the only thing you got going for you. And every Tom, Dick and Harry's got one."

She reached under a pillow and pulled out a straight razor. She flicked it open and slashed at his face. He jerked his head back but the blade caught his cheek and opened a small gash just below his left eye. He drove his fist into her belly, and she doubled over and dropped to her knees, gasping for breath. He took the razor from her hand, pulled her head back and held the blade to her throat. Blood from his cheek dripped onto the knuckles of his razor hand. As he was about to rake the blade across her jugular, he saw Charlotte laid out on the gurney in the autopsy room of Partain Funeral Home, and pulled the blade away. He bent down, slid the razor's blade under his boot and snapped it off.

"You're lucky I didn't kill you, darlin'," he said. "You don't want to push your luck with me again."

*   *   *

As he drove home, he wondered what the hell had possessed him to treat poor Charlotte the way he had. He had never been violent with females before. It just wasn't his way. He was one of the good guys. Good guys didn't ass-fuck a woman against her will. Good guys probably didn't ass-fuck at all. What the hell was *that* about? But he knew the answer. *The dark thing.* Jessica A. Lowell was right. The dark thing wanted him. The dark thing had wanted him to hurt Charlotte the Harlot, to humiliate her. Degrade her. So he had. And he enjoyed it. That old black snake had come out and fucked her up the ass. Like the serpent in the Garden of Eden, the snake was demonic. Hell, it was Satanic. It had tempted him into darkness and he had yielded to the temptation. And it all started with the runaway from the nuthouse. It was as if she had passed it on to him, like a disease. *Infected* him with darkness. Then he had killed Odell and the dark thing *owned* him.

"Shit," he said to himself. "This is bullshit. I'm as crazy as Psycho Girl was if I believe this bullshit." The whore had mocked him and it pissed him off. That was all. *But I held the razor to her throat and almost killed her. I wanted to kill her.*

"Fuck it," he said and turned up the volume. Stevie Ray was singing about a Texas flood. He sang along, trying to drown out his dark thoughts. He felt good. He'd had his ashes hauled and things were looking brighter. He was a man. A man who could handle anything life might throw at him. Even those low-life Porch motherfuckers.

He pulled into his driveway, hopped out of the car, and bounded up the back steps.

And froze when he saw the white bloodstained envelope leaning against the back door.

"What the fuck is this?" He picked it up and felt something lumpy inside. His heart started pounding on his eardrums as he tore open the envelope.

"Jesus Christ," he said when he saw the severed finger still wearing the VHS class ring. The smiling Blue Devil face engraved in the setting gave him a lascivious wink. His own fingers trembled as he pulled the folded notepaper from the envelope and unfolded it.

Be at the old railroad trestle at noon
Or we cut off his head.

He didn't have to pull the ring off the dead finger and check the initials engraved inside the gold band to know that the finger was Skeeter's; the knobby knuckle and the dirt embedded under the nail from Skeeter's daily handling of produce left little doubt. The bastards had him, and he had told them who killed Odell, so now they were using Skeeter to lure Joe Rob into their hands. The old railroad trestle was out in the boondocks. A good place for an ambush.

Joe Rob glanced off to his left at the patch of woods, suspecting that the person who had left the note was out there watching him, making sure he got the bloody message. Yes, someone was out there all right. He could feel the eyes on him. Weren't they afraid he would immediately go to the police with this? How dumb could they be?

The black slithery thing coiled around the base of his spine began to twine upward, sliding over vertebrae and inching toward his brain. Joe Rob flashed a cold smile at the unseen watcher in the woods, relishing the thought of a shootout with those pig-fucking Porch bastards. Now was the time to be a man. The killing of Odell had been a reflex, almost accidental. He would kill the rest of them with murderous intent. And savor every bloody moment.

CHAPTER 13
A HEADS-UP AND A TAKE-DOWN

Luke was on his front porch, listening to the late-morning wind sough through the leaves of the pecan tree in the front yard and wondering if he should pay a visit to Fate Porch when the phone rang. He had just pulled off his boot to get at an itch between his toes, so he hobbled on one boot into the house to answer the phone on the third ring.

"Hello."

"Just thought I'd let you know," said the familiar voice, "I'm gonna do what you never could. I'm gonna take down the Porches."

"Joe Rob?"

"I don't have a choice. They got Skeeter and say they'll cut off his head if I don't show."

"Slow down, son," Luke said. "What—"

"But they got a big surprise coming," Joe Rob went on. "I'm gonna kill 'em all and let God sort 'em out."

"Wait now. Tell me where—"

The line went dead.

"Shit," Luke said. He depressed the switch hook, then punched the number that used to be his. Chief Keller answered in his smooth baritone.

"Bill, this is Luke. I just got a call from Joe Rob Campbell. He said the Porches have Skeeter Partain and that they're going to cut off Skeeter's head if he—Joe Rob—doesn't show up."

"What? Run that by me again?"

Luke went through it again, adding that Joe Rob said he was going to kill them all. "He hung up before I could find out where all this is supposed to happen. Or when."

"Damn, Luke. You sure this ain't some kinda prank?"

"No, this is the real deal. I talked to the boys last night but they wouldn't tell me what the hell was going between them and the Porches. Whatever it is, it's about to come to a head."

"Hang on a minute," Keller said. Luke heard muffled voices in the background, then Keller came back on the line. "Kirby just told me Mrs. Partain just now called in to report Skeeter missing. Said he didn't show up for work this morning and she has no idea where he is. His truck's still there at the house. And she found a gun in his room that she's never seen before."

"How you want to handle it, Bill?" asked Luke.

"I guess I better send a car to the Campbell house. Have 'em pick up Joe Rob if they can find him. I'll run out to the Bottom myself, see if I can get anything out of Fate."

"If they're using Skeeter as bait to draw Joe Rob, it's not likely they'd want him to come to their place. They'd want to get him out in the boondocks somewhere, some place isolated."

"Yeah, but where? There's hundreds of places like that."

"Damned if I know," said Luke. "But if you've got any hunches, now's the time to start playing 'em."

"What're you gonna do?"

"Start cruising and hope I get some hunches of my own."

"You still got that police-band in your truck?"

"Yeah. I'll call it in if I luck out and find these crazies."

"Do that, Luke. But remember, you ain't the police anymore. Don't you go getting in the middle of anything."

"Roger that." Luke hung up, retrieved his boot and slipped it on, then strapped on his gun belt, checked the load of his .38 and snugged it in the holster. He got his scattergun from the closet, then jogged to his truck and drove off in search of the impending shootout.

*   *   *

Joe Rob dropped the receiver in its cradle after his call to ex-Chief Chaney, then put on his tan hunting jacket to cover his small arsenal of weapons. His grandfather's .45 semi-automatic was stuck in the waist of his jeans, and on his right hip he wore his own .357 Magnum in a custom-made holster, slung low for maximum speed of the draw. Sheathed on his left hip was his father's old survival knife.

He bounded down the back steps and went into the basement to cut down the barrel of his Remington double-barrel .12 gage with a hacksaw. With the twin barrels shortened, he could hide the shotgun under his hunting jacket. It would be effective only at close range, but he intended to get as close as possible to the redneck bastards. Close enough to see their guts blown out of their bellies and splattered to Kingdom Come.

He checked his jacket's pockets one last time to make sure the extra ammo was there, then walked casually to his Mustang and got behind the wheel. He cranked the engine, gunned it a few times just to feel the throbbing of the engine, then he backed out of the drive and rode up Main Street to the Economy Hardware Store. He figured he still had a few minutes before Chaney's old cop buddies would be looking for him, so he parked in front of the store and went inside to buy a canister of pepper spray. He didn't really expect he'd have an opportunity to use it, but he thought it best to have it as a last defense, just in case. Going into battle outgunned, he would need every available advantage. He figured his main advantage was going to be surprise. He was counting it. He was going to hit them hard and fast, with overwhelming force. And he wasn't going to stop until they were all dead or he was.

It was going to be a killer show.

*   *   *

Corny Weehunt moved up Main Street in a shambling run, the partially detached sole of one shoe flapping against the sidewalk as he raced toward big hole in the middle of the street. A dump truck loaded with dirt was backing up to the hole, and several shopkeepers had come outside to watch the late-morning spectacle. A few pedestrians paused to see the first load of dirt deposited in the hole. Corny hobbled up to the edge of the sinkhole just as the truck prepared to release its full load of reddish-brown dirt into the hole's gaping mouth. He clapped his hands together and grinned, looking around for someone with whom he might share his excitement. He was relieved that he wouldn't have to spend any more nights watching the hole for any evil thing that might want to come out of there and do bad things to his town. But as he watched the dirt slide and tumble into the pit, Whisperer commenced a whispering that was so loud that Corny was afraid other people might even hear it. *RUN . . . RUN . . . RUN . . .*

There was no mistaking the urgency of Whisperer's warning. Corny turned away from the hole and ran down the middle of Main Street, past the saw-horse roadblock and into the path of a red car turning into a parking space in front of the Post Office. He threw out his hands just before he collided with the car's left front fender, and the impact snapped his right wrist and bounced him backward onto the asphalt. He sat there, dazed and in pain, clasping his injured wrist with the armpit of his opposite arm. The driver popped out of his car and looked down with a horrified expression at Cornelius. Corny knew the man's face but he couldn't put a name to the man with the splotchy red face and the big belly straining his red suspenders. Then the street shuddered beneath him and the storefronts rattled and a great cracking sound thundered up and down Main Street. The red-faced man was looking aghast at something behind Corny, and Corny turned and saw the dump truck dropping out of sight as if swallowed up by the street itself. A cloud of dust billowed up from the spot where the truck went down, and Corny knew then why Whisperer had urged him to run. The sinkhole had opened its mouth wider to claim another victim. And it was still hungry.

*   *   *

Joe Rob was coming out of the Economy Hardware Store when the dump truck fell into the hole. Like everyone else on the street, he froze, momentarily stunned by the violent collapse of another part of the street. No one moved until the hollow rumbling sound and the earth tremors ceased, then people went scurrying, some toward the hole, others away from it. Joe Rob's first impulse was to run to the sinkhole to see what had happened to the driver of the truck and to help get the man out of there, if possible, but he remembered his mission and jogged to his Mustang, anxious to get off the street before the cops showed up. He cranked the engine, backed out of the parking space and peeled rubber down Main Street, thinking: *The whole damn town's going down.*

He didn't notice the chopped Chevy that picked up his tail when he turned off West Main and headed out Route 47, nor could he see the leering grin of the Chevy's driver who turned to his companions and said, *"That's the muthafucka right there. I'm gonna fuck his shit up."*

CHAPTER 14
VISIONS

Agnes Porch sat in front of the mirror, brushing out her waist-length white hair. She usually wore it braided and pinned in crown-like circles on top of her head, but whenever she consulted the oracle, she would first take down her hair and brush out the braided crimps. She wasn't sure how it worked, but she was convinced that wearing her hair straight and natural augmented her visionary powers and increased the likelihood that her second sight would be true—that it would cut through the darkness and confusion to illuminate the true patterns hidden behind and beneath everyday reality. Once she had tried to explain *the sight* to her son, but that had been like trying to explain the workings of the telephone to a chimpanzee. Fate just couldn't grasp it, not because he was a stupid man—he wasn't—but because his mind wasn't wired for thinking in abstractions. And his sons were just as concrete as he was, chips off the old blockhead—except for Odell. If he'd lived, Odell might've been able to develop his natural gift for seeing into the otherworld and divining the future. *The sight* might've saved him if he'd been able to tamp down his meanness long enough to get his mind around that natural gift. But life had conspired against the boy. The Marine Corps had taught him new ways to use his meanness, and those head-shrinking doctors at Browner's had tried to destroy his gift with drugs and psychodoodle, making Odell think the voices in his head were a sign of insanity. *Hereditary psychosis.* That's what those quacks were getting at. Damn fools.

She put down the brush and gazed hard into the mirror, studying the features of the old hag who looked back at her. Ninety-two years old, and just as ornery and full of spit as she'd been at thirty. It didn't seem possible that she could be that old. But when she thought back over the decades of her life that spanned most of the last century—from the Roaring Twenties, through two world wars and on into the new Millennium—she *knew* she had the right to look like the old hag in the mirror. In fact, it was a true wonder that she wasn't already dead, given the hard life she and her family had always had to live.

I'm a Porch and a Porch always has a hard row to hoe, and the kind of enemies who want to put you six feet under, then piss on your grave. Always on the wrong side of the law, pursued by self-righteous lawmen more corrupt than any Porch ever dreamed of being.

Like the sheriff who gunned down my daddy for stealing horses.

And the crooked judge who hanged my uncle for no good reason.

Sure, we done some wicked things in our time, but never to nobody who didn't deserve it. It's a hard life and a body has to live hard to survive. And make no apologies for it.

She slipped on a stained apron and went outside to the chicken run, caught one of the less spry chickens and wrung its neck. Then she took the dead chicken into the barn, sat down at her ritual chopping block and gutted the fowl with a carving knife, stringing out its bloody innards and spreading them out on the scarred wood. She took a sip of muscadine wine, spit three times in three directions, then said the incantation learned long ago from a Creole conjure woman in Louisiana's bayou country.

Then she cleared her mind and began to read the entrails.

Patterns began to form on the bloody chopping block. She bent closer, peering hard through her bifocals and moving her palms in circular motions inches above the chicken guts to draw forth the visions that would speak to her inner eye—the eye blessed with *the sight*.

Her breath caught in her throat and she moaned as the patterns coalesced, forming mental pictures that chilled her old bones. She saw rats gnawing raw flesh. Daggers aimed at beating hearts. And a black wolf leaping from liquid darkness, its teeth already wet with blood.

The signs were all bad, even worse than the ones that had showed her Odell's violent death.

But the entrails had more to show her.

She wanted to rake the guts off the wood with the carving knife's blade before they showed her their worst, but she stayed strong, stiffened her spine and watched in horror as the darkness at the periphery of the vision thickened, writhing, slithering, encircling everything. The black serpent devouring its own tail and eclipsing all with unrelenting darkness.

Outside the barn a crow cawed. Insects sang in the summer heat. A fly lighted on a strand of the chicken's intestines. Agnes closed her burning eyes and let the sights she'd seen in the entrails resonate inside her skull, humming along the shallow convolutions of her brain until they were translated by her inner eye—the eye that never blinked, no matter how horrible the sights it beheld. Faces surfaced in oily blackness. The face of the boy who had killed Odell. The faces of Cowboy and Luther. The face of Fate, haggard and contorted with pain. The face of the boy whose finger had been removed. Remaining below the inky surface was the face of a man she couldn't identify. The dark liquid bubbled into a rolling boil, each bursting bubble resounding with the psychic pop of a gunshot.

And in those dark bubbles she saw the grinning face of Death.

She opened her eyes and pushed up from the chopping block, standing on weary legs. "Oh, Lord," she mewled, "I done wrong by them boys. I never should've . . ."

But I couldn't see it all then. I was only trying to help them get Odell's killer. I didn't see the Dark Angel riding that boy's shoulders.

It's too late now.

Nothing can stop it.

Agnes walked on stiff knees to the barn door and pushed it open, grunting with the effort. She looked out at the bright morning sky. The cumulus clouds were thick and tall, the weather changing. She could feel it in her aching joints. She looked at Fate's truck parked in the dappled shade of spindly pines.

Too late, unless I can drive that truck.

CHAPTER 15
RADIO TRAFFIC

As he gunned his truck down Nebula Road, Luke tried not to let his growing sense of futility get the best of him, but the truth was, he had no idea where Joe Rob was supposed to meet the Porch men. He didn't even know *when* the meet was supposed to happen. All he knew was that Joe Rob had said, *They got Skeeter and say they'll cut off his head if I don't show. Why*, Luke wondered, *would Fate Porch take such drastic action as kidnapping Skeeter in the first place?* If he wanted Joe Rob, why didn't he just snatch him too, rather than use Skeeter as an instrument of coercion? It was a reckless scheme, and reckless was one thing Fate Porch was not. Maybe Fate was not in on it. Maybe his boys were acting on their own. That could explain the recklessness, but Luke doubted that Fate's boys would undertake such action without consulting the old man. If they did, there would be hell to pay when Fate found out. Based on everything he knew about the Porches, Luke knew that Fate had to be running this show. Something had happened to Odell, and Fate was holding Skeeter and Joe Rob responsible. And with Joe Rob being so willing to shoot it out with the Porches, he must feel that he has nothing to lose. Had he killed Odell? Luke could think of no other explanation for this desperate situation. But if Joe Rob actually believed he could go against the Porches and best them in a shootout, the boy was in for a rude and deadly awakening. Joe Rob had been a fearless running back on the football field, bowling over defenders rather than run around them, but he was out of his league with the Porches.

The police-band radio spit the crackling voice of Chief Keller, interrupting Luke's rambling train of thought. "Chieftain, what's your location? Over." Chieftain had been Luke's call sign when he was still chief and Keller insisted that he keep it.

"Nebula Road, westbound," he responded.

"Roger, Chieftain. Be advised, I'm approaching the Bottom. All quiet so far."

"Ten-four, Unit One. Watch yourself, Chief."

"Roger that."

Luke had been monitoring the radio traffic, so he knew that Craig Hemphill was cruising the back roads east of town and Alvin Snow was covering the north sector. The only other officer on duty was Roy Crane, who was back at the station with Holly Stimson, the full-time dispatcher. For a town the size of Vinewood, with its population of five thousand, this was a full complement of on-duty cops, and with Luke acting as an auxiliary officer, manpower was bolstered by 25%. Nevertheless, Luke knew that wasn't enough. They were searching for a needle in a hay field, and time was running out.

Holly Stimson's all-business voice came over of the radio. "All units, all units, we have an emergency situation on Main Street. The sinkhole just took down a dump truck."

"Say again, Holly," Keller responded.

"Another piece of Main Street fell into the hole. The dump-truck driver is apparently injured."

"Jumping Jesus," said Keller.

Luke winced at the new chief's improper radio procedure.

"I'm on the way, Holly," said the chief. "Alvin, you and Roy proceed to the scene. Luke, I've got to handle this. Looks like we're drilling a dry hole anyway. Call in if you find anything."

"Roger, One." Luke sighed in frustration. He was on his own. The Lone Ranger without a badge.

With Keller on his way back to town, Luke decided to drive out to the Bottom and pay a visit to the Porch homestead himself. If none of the menfolk were there, he knew that Agnes Porch would be. From his surreptitious eavesdropping he also knew the old lady wielded considerable power in the family because of her supposed gift of second sight, and that Fate was superstitious enough to have faith in his mother's visions. From the conversations Luke had overheard, he deduced that the old lady's belief system was a patchwork of Christianity and backwoods hoodoo, the latter probably acquired during the years she lived in Louisiana. She was also something of a busybody, keeping close tabs on the activities of Fate and his boys. If the family business included nefarious dealings with Joe Rob and Skeeter, she would most likely know something about it, but whether Luke could wheedle any useful information from her, he had great doubt. At the moment, he figured it was his best shot.

If he found Fate at home, Luke was prepared to confront him with Joe

Rob's allegation that the Porches had threatened to cut off Skeeter's head. Of course, Fate would deny that any such threat was made, but it would put the bastard on notice that the police were on to him and might cause him to call off any plan for violent action. On the other hand, if they had kidnapped Skeeter Partain, they couldn't very well let him go without facing felony charges. The witness would have to be eliminated. The way the Porches played things out, Skeeter's life was forfeit. And like Monroe Shockley's head, his body might never be found.

Luke glanced at his watch. It was a quarter to eleven. He pushed the speedometer up to 70, the truck's tires humming over the blacktop as he whipped past cornfields, cotton fields, cow pastures and wooded flatlands. The sun was in and out of the clouds, and the air was already oppressively hot, promising another afternoon scorcher.

Luke's last face-to-face encounter with Fate Porch still haunted him. He had been executing a search warrant during the course of his investigation of Monroe Shockley's murder. While his six-man team searched Fate's farmhouse and property for physical evidence that could link him to the killing and decapitation of Shockley, Fate returned in his pickup from a trip into town and accosted Luke on the front porch.

"What the hell you think you're doing, Chaney?" Fate demanded, his face an angry crimson beneath his white stubble of beard.

Luke handed him the search warrant and said, "My job. I know you murdered Monroe Shockley and I'm going to nail it to you, one way or another."

Fate exploded with forced laughter. "What you think, I got his head hid under my bed? Or a murder weapon stashed in the closet? You're a sorry excuse for a lawman, Chaney. All you're doing here is making a goddamn fool of yourself. Folks in town's already laughing at you behind your back. I hear they already looking for a new chief. And you think tearing up my house is gonna help your case? I think you're digging your own grave."

"Are you threatening me?" Luke asked, biting back his anger.

"*Hell* no. I got no cause to threaten you. I'm just gonna sit back and watch you do yourself in. And I tell you what's the truth. I'm gonna enjoy every goddamn minute of it."

Luke could still hear the echo of those raspy words, and they rankled and stung now more than they did then. *Maybe Porch was right when he called me a sorry excuse for a lawman. But I'm not a lawman anymore, and I'm not done with him yet. Not by a long shot.*

As he drove down the gravel road to the farmhouse, Luke saw Fate's

Ford pickup off to the side, its front end resting against a tall magnolia tree. He pulled up beside the Ford and saw Agnes Porch slumped against the steering wheel, her long white hair hanging like a bright shroud over her thin shoulders.

He jumped out of his truck, threw opened the Ford's door and said, "Miz Porch? Are you all right?"

The old woman raised her head from the wheel, looked at him through the cracked lens of her bifocals and mumbled, ". . . reaper."

"Ma'am?"

Her gray eyes seemed to be swimming in a sea of wrinkled flesh. "All dead," she said.

"Who's all dead?" he asked, a sinking feeling in his belly.

Agnes Porch looked down at her hands as if trying to read something in them, though they were empty. "I was going . . ."

"Going where, Miz Porch?"

"To stop it." She began to rub her fingers with her thumbs, the parchment-like skin making dry whispers. "They don't know."

"To stop *what*?" Luke put his hand on her bony shoulder.

"It's too dark," she moaned. "Can't see."

"Where's your son? Where's Fate?"

"Fate? Fate!" she called. "You come back here!"

Luke sighed in frustration. "Don't move, Miz Porch. I'm going to call for an ambulance." He went to his truck, grabbed the handset, called the station and told Holly Stimson to send an ambulance. Then he went back to the old lady's side and tried to assess the extent of her injuries, but she was too disoriented to give reliable feedback. There was a knot on her forehead where her head must've struck the steering wheel, but he could see no other signs of external injuries. He knew there was a possibility of internal injuries, especially for a brittle-boned woman in her nineties, so he didn't try to move her from the seat of Fate's truck. He would leave that to the EMS crew.

"Help's on the way," he told her. "They'll take you to the hospital and make sure you're okay."

If she understood, she gave no indication. She continued to mumble to herself. Luke talked to her, hoping to break through her confusion and find out where the old woman without a driver's license had been going when she crashed into the tree. If he could find that out, he might be able to stop a bloodbath—if it wasn't already too late.

CHAPTER 16
ROAD SHOW

Joe Rob was on his way to Cedar Cove Trailer Park to score some coke from Candyman when the carload of blacks cut in front of him at the four-way stop five miles west of town. With just over an hour to kill before his appointed rendezvous at the old railroad trestle, he had decided that snorting some blow would make him battle-ready and give him an extra edge on the enemy.

And if Candyman was holding some speed, he would cop some of that too. When the shooting started, he wanted to be a supercharged balls-to-the-wall instrument of aggression. An invincible warrior. A berserker driven by bloodlust.

He smiled when he saw Ho Down hop out of the car with a baseball bat in his hands. "Just what I need," he said to himself. "A tune-up for the Big Show."

Joe Rob killed the Mustang's engine and stepped out to meet Ho Down and his three pals.

Holding up the bat with one hand, Ho Down said, "This my lucky day, Blow Job. I'm gonna hit a home run off your head."

A fat guy with a crowbar and a bushy Afro climbed out of the back seat and stood beside Ho Down. He held the crowbar down by his right leg. He was sweating profusely and Joe Rob read uncertainty in his eyes.

"Then Fro here gonna get in some licks just 'cause he don't like white folks," Ho Down added. "Right, Fro?"

Fro nodded. The other two young men leaned against the Chevy to watch the fun. One of them had a nasty smirk on his face. The other was smoking a cigarette and blowing smoke rings.

"You dead, muthafucka," Ho Down said as he gripped the bat with both hands and raised it over his right shoulder.

Joe Rob opened his hunting jacket with his left hand and pulled the .45 from the waist of his jeans with his right. He raised the pistol and pointed it at Ho Down's face. "Looks like you just struck out, asshole," he said, grinning.

Ho Down dropped the bat and backed up, "Hey, man, we just fuckin' wit-cha. That's all. Ain't no need to go busting no caps. Tell him, Fro. We just playin'. Right?"

The uncertainty in Fro's eyes had already changed to wide-eyed fright. He backed into one of his car-leaning pals, the one whose smirk had turned into a grimace. "Yeh, yeh, that's right," Fro agreed.

Joe Rob shifted his aim to Fro, pointing the muzzle at his belly. "Know what a .45 slug would do to your gut?"

"Don't wanna know," he said. His milk-chocolate skin was turning several shades lighter.

"It would pretty much turn your guts to chunky soup and make an even bigger hole as it blew out your back. That's if it didn't hit your spine. If *that* happened, you probably wouldn't feel too much pain while you were waiting to die."

"You ain't gotta shoot me, man," stammered Fro. "We just wanted to scare ya, that's all."

"Tell you what," Joe Rob said. "You do what I tell you and I won't shoot you. How's that?"

"Yeah, okay. What you want me to do?"

The older-looking man standing in front of the Chevy's rear fender said, "Shee-it, he ain't gone shoot nobody."

Joe Rob turned slightly and fired the gun. The slug went between Shee-it Man's lower legs and exploded the rear tire. The Chevy's rear-end sank on the flat.

"Goddamn!" Shee-it Man yelled.

"Next one draws blood," said Joe Rob. "You want it to be yours?"

"No suh," he answered, looking down at his legs.

"All right, Fro," Joe Rob said, waving the .45 in his direction. "Here's what I want you to do. Get a good grip on that crowbar and break Ho Down's legs."

"What?"

"Do it now. If you don't, I'll shoot you."

"You serious?"

"I'll count to three. Oh, and Ho Down? If you try to run I'll shoot *you*."

"Fuck, man, this is fucked up," Ho Down protested. "Why you—"

"One . . ." Joe Rob pointed the pistol back at Fro's belly.

Fro said, "Sorry, man, I ain't got no choice." Then he cocked the crowbar behind his shoulder . . .

"Two . . ."

. . . and swung it in a short arc that was more of a golf swing than a batter's cut.

The iron bar smacked into the side of Ho Down's lower leg, knocking it out from under him and toppling him to the grassy shoulder of the road. He screamed and gripped his injured leg with both hands, rocking on his bowed spine.

"Now do the other leg," Joe Rob ordered.

"Aw, man," said Fro, even as he positioned himself for the next hit with the crowbar.

"No! Please!" bellowed Ho Down, letting go of his injured leg and trying to crawl out of range of the next swing.

"Do it," warned Joe Rob.

Fro took aim and delivered the second blow, catching Ho Down across the shin of his left leg. They all heard the sharp crack and knew the leg was broken. Ho Down screamed and thrashed his upper body on the ground. Tears streamed down his dark cheeks. "Gotdammuthafuckinsonofabitch," he yelled.

His three companions looked with pained expressions at their suffering friend, all casting wary glances at Joe Rob.

Joe Rob waved his pistol at them and said, "Next time you boys think about fucking with somebody like me, remember this broke-leg piece of shit here."

Then he stuck the pistol in his jeans, climbed into the Mustang and peeled off down the blacktop. "Dumb motherfuckers," he said, then turned up his music and proceeded to the trailer park.

*   *   *

The ambulance lady told Corny his wrist wasn't broken. Just sprained, she said. She was pretty, and Corny had sprouted a fat hard-on while she was touching his sore wrist. He couldn't keep his eyes off her big tits sticking out behind her white shirt with the EMS patch on the shoulder and the nametag over the right tit that said her name was Jones. He wondered what her first name was but he was afraid to ask her. He wanted to get away from her before she noticed the way his stiff dick was pushing up the crotch of his overalls. "Put some ice on it when you get home," she said. He hoped she meant his wrist. She gave him a smile and went over to the edge of the hole to stand by her male partner who was watching the firemen trying to get the dump-truck driver out of his truck and out of the hole. They were talking to the driver so he wasn't dead. The policemen were there too, trying to keep everybody away from the sinkhole. Corny didn't want to get any closer to that hole. He'd already heard people say the hole might get even bigger, might even swallow up some of the stores next. He was close enough to hear the new chief arguing with Mr. Peters, the boss of the town council. Mr. Peters' face turned red he was so angry.

"This is on your head," Mr. Peters was saying to Chief Keller. "You're in charge of public safety. That idiot you call an expert doesn't know his ass from . . . from a hole in the ground. All he did was shine a light down there and say that was it, it wouldn't get any bigger. Well, I talked to an engineering geologist and he said we need to hire a crew to do extensive drilling down there to find out how big the damn thing is. Christ, there could be a whole series of caverns underground. I just hope to God there aren't any lawsuits because of your mishandling of this. We're going to have to spend a lot of money on a consulting firm to get this thing properly explored and filled in. We can't afford lawyers to fight lawsuits."

The chief was getting mad too. Corny could tell by the way the vein in his temple was standing out and throbbing like a hard-on. "Sanders is a geologist. I thought he knew what he was talking about."

"For Christ's sake, Keller. Sanders is a high school teacher who majored in geology. Now, until we find out how extensive this damn thing is, I want you to block all of Main Street to vehicular traffic and advise pedestrians that they will be shopping here at their own risk. It's going to hurt the merchants, but public safety has to come first."

Corny didn't understand all the big words Mr. Peters used, but he understood that there might be a lot of caves down there under Main Street, and maybe under some of the stores too. That was a scary thought. That was about as scary as that weird dark he'd seen moving around down in the hole. Corny wished he knew what it was that lived down there in those hidden caverns, moving around like a blobby black ghost. Whisperer knew something was down there, but Whisperer hadn't told him what it was. Maybe Whisperer didn't know what it was. Corny's hard-on went away as he watched the fire/rescue team haul the truck driver up on a metal basket-looking thing. The sexy ambulance lady and her partner loaded the driver in the ambulance and zoomed him off to the hospital, Christmas-colored lights flashing and siren whooping. Corny wandered back to the boarding house to put ice on his sore wrist, his mind teeming with dark images of haunted underground caverns and sexy women with big tits.

CHAPTER 17
SHIT-STORM WARNING

Skeeter was sucking wind, pretending it was water. The air in the barn loft was getting hotter by the minute as the sun headed toward its zenith, and Skeeter was already dehydrated, hanging from the rusty chain like a slab of raw meat. The stub of his severed finger throbbed, but it had stopped bleeding when Luther cauterized the wound with a cigarette lighter with its flame turned up as high as it would go. Except for a couple of bats hanging upside down from a rafter above him, he was alone. He supposed the Porch men were out there somewhere, waiting for Joe Rob to show up so they could kill them both. Skeeter wished they'd hurry up and get it over with; death would mean an end to his suffering.

Picturing his body laid out on his father's embalming table, he passed into a state of delirium. The bats began whispering to each other, mocking the weak human hanging below them. He looked up and saw that the bats had human faces. One of them looked like Odell, the other like Cowboy.

"Go on and kill me," he told them. "I don't give a shit."

*   *   *

Candyman greeted him with a grin. He was shirtless and his beer belly hung over his jeans, making him look like he was nine months pregnant. "Whass up, man?"

"Hope your water don't break while I'm here," Joe Rob said as he stepped inside the cracker-box trailer.

"What?"

"Nothing. Let me do a few lines of coke, man. And I need some speed if you got any."

"Got some white crosses from Mexico. Pop three or four tabs and it'll get you up to speed, heh heh."

Joe Rob dealt a fifty from his wallet and slapped it on the counter separating the kitchen area from the living room. A bleached blonde head rose up from the couch and a set of bleary brown eyes drank him in. "Hey, Joe Rob," said Candyman's porky wife, Marilyn. "How's it hanging?" She flashed him a lascivious smile. The TV was tuned to cartoons.

"Long and low," he said.

"Goddamn, you got a one-track mind," said Candy. "Fucking nympho." He went down the narrow hallway and disappeared into the bedroom.

"Come sit down," Marilyn said, sitting up and patting the empty space beside her. "These toons are a trip. This is the one where Daffy gets dynamite stuck up his ass."

"That's all right. I'll stand."

"Why you wearing a jacket in this heat?" she asked.

Joe Rob chuckled. "Haven't you heard? There's a shit storm coming."

"Tell me about it," she giggled, then turned her attention back to the flickering screen.

Candyman came back with a leather pouch of illegal goodies and laid out four lines of coke on the counter. He offered Joe Rob a cut-down plastic straw, and Joe Rob took it and snorted two lines. Pinching his nose, he handed the straw to Candy, who stuck it in his nostril and bent down to snort up the remaining two lines of powder.

"Hey, don't I get any?" asked Marilyn, bouncing up from the couch, her pendulous breasts jiggling behind her tight T-shirt like water-filled balloons. "You guys . . ."

"You already had enough," her husband said. "Do any more, you'll be humping the fridge."

"Fuck you, Rodney. Don't be such a prick."

He rolled his eyes. "See what I have to put up with? Don't ever get married, man. You'll fucking regret it."

"Eat shit," she said, then cranked up the TV's volume with the remote. The familiar sounds of cartoon violence filled the tiny trailer, rattling the wafer-thin walls and bringing a grimace to Candyman's jowly face.

"Give me the speed," Joe Rob said.

Candy pulled a plastic pill bottle from the leather pouch and shook out four tabs that looked a lot like aspirin. "Here you go. This will rev your ass up real good."

Joe Rob tossed them into his mouth and washed them down with tap water.

Scratching his hairy belly, Candy said, "You're kinda antsy already, man. What's up?"

"Nothing. I got to shoot some people is all."

"What the fuck're you talking about?"

"Remember the Gunfight at the O.K. Corral?"

"Shit yeah, I seen that movie a hundred times. What about it?"

"It's gonna be like me against the Clanton gang. Without Doc Holiday or the Earp brothers backing me up."

"What the hell you been smoking, Joe Rob. You ain't making no sense."

"Nothing. I'm just yanking your chain."

Candy lit a Marlboro Red and squinted through the smoke. "What's with the hunting jacket? It's ninety degrees already. And it sure ain't hunting season."

Joe Rob glanced around for a clock. Didn't see one. "What time is it?"

Candy walked over to the electric stove and looked at the built-in clock. "Eleven-thirty."

"Hunting season opens in half an hour."

"What—? Marilyn, turn that shit down, will ya? I can't hear myself think."

"That ain't nothing new," she said, thumbing a button on the remote to cut the volume.

The coke was kicking in good now, and Joe Rob grinned at his fat friend. "That's some kick-ass blow. When the speed kicks in, I'll be good to go. Got a beer?"

"In the fridge. Help yourself."

Joe Rob snagged a can of brew from the over-stuffed fridge, popped the top and took a big gulp. "Time to go. Thanks for the shit, man. If you never see me again, have a good life." He walked over to the couch, bent down and kissed the top of Marilyn's head. "Take it easy, pretty woman."

She craned her head back so she could see him. "I'll take it any way I can get it. You know me."

Joe Rob shook Candyman's hand, then went out the door, cranked up his Mustang and drove off.

"What the hell was that about?" Marilyn asked her husband.

"Damned if I know. I think he might be going to shoot some people."

"*What?*"

"He was strapped. Had a couple of pistols under his jacket."

"Who's he gone shoot?" She was on her knees, facing him and leaning her breasts over the back of the couch.

Candy said, "I don't know. Don't ask so damn many questions."

"Fuck you."

"All right." He grinned and grabbed his crotch.

She jumped up and followed him to the bedroom.

A stick of dynamite blew Daffy Duck into space.

*   *   *

Fate Porch leaned his stiff back against the side of the barn, took a pull from his flask of homebrew and winced as it burned the back of his throat. He glanced at his watch again. Twenty till twelve. Soon he would know if Maw was right about the Campbell boy. He still couldn't see how the boy would show up at the trestle without going to the cops, all the while knowing he was going to die if he did show up. Why show up at all? Was he that loyal to his friend? Could he possibly believe that he could come riding in like some picture-show hero and save his friend? Against me and my boys? Kid would have to be crazy to believe that. Or have a death wish. Maybe he felt some guilt for killing Odell. Probably it was an accident, like the other boy said. Too bad we can't just let it go and forget it, but that ain't our way. Family blood was spilled and there has to be restitution. The law wouldn't do nothing but give the boy a suspended sentence for manslaughter, if even that. Might say it was self-defense and make him out a hero for trying to save the girl from being raped and paint poor Odell as a depraved maniac with a history of mental illness. Folks in town love to sully the Porch name. Hell, us Porches are the boogiemen of Graves County. Modern-day outlaws. Well, damn them all to hell. We take care of our own. That's all we're doing here. That's why them two boys got to die. Paw would say the same thing if he was still alive.

Fate checked the load of his pump shotgun again, then lit his pipe.

Quarter to noon. Luther and Cowboy would be hiding in the woods by the trestle now, waiting for the Campbell boy to show up and see the note nailed to the trestle. The note would send him here to the old barn, and the boys would make sure no cops were following Campbell. Any cops show up, and Luther would call on the cell phone, and Fate would put the Partain boy in the back of the truck and haul ass before any cops got here.

Fate reached in his pocket and pulled out Cowboy's cell phone. Handy little gadgets they were. But not worth what it costs to use them. Still, it was amazing what you could do these days with all these electronic gizmos. And all that talk about the Internet. Fate didn't understand why anybody would spend hours in front of a computer screen looking at something that wasn't even real. The way Luther explained it to him, the Internet was a bunch of "sites" that didn't even exist in the real world. It was all out there in space but didn't really occupy space. The whole thing was crazy.

The little plastic phone chirped in his hand. He pushed the button and held it to his ear.

"Diddy?" It was Luther speaking in a loud whisper.

"Yeah."

"He's here. Looks like he's alone. He's reading the note now."

"All right. You know what to do. Wait a few minutes after he leaves to make sure nobody's following him, then get over here quick."

"We will. Okay, he's getting back in his car. We'll see you in a few minutes, Diddy."

Fate dropped the little phone in his pocket, then went inside the barn, the shotgun cradled in his arms. "Looks like Maw was right again," he said to himself. "The Lord surely favors the old lady."

*   *   *

Joe Rob wadded up the hand-printed note and stuffed it in his pocket and looked up at the creosote-scented crossbeams of the old trestle supporting track where trains no longer ran. "Go strait to the old Jenkins house," the note said. Dumb bastard couldn't spell for shit.

So it was going to be the Jenkins place. The haunted farmhouse. The Bad Place, as some called it.

He got back in the car and scratched off, rear tires kicking up gouts of red clay. He wasn't surprised that they weren't here at the old trestle. This would be their fail-safe spot, the place where they would see if he was alone or not. He stuck his hand out the window and waved, knowing that at least one of them was watching him from the woods.

The amphetamine was coming on strong now, having been kick-started by the cocaine already buzzing through his system. His heart was goose-stepping to the helter-skelter cadence of a heavy-metal march, and he was sweating like a hooker in a hot church. He punched up some vintage Stevie Ray and gunned the Mustang down the dirt road, heading for the old Jenkins place. His fingers did a double-time dance on the steering wheel. A nervous tic set his left eye jumping. Sweat rolled down his sides from his armpits. He turned the air-conditioner full-blast to keep from suffocating in the hunting jacket. Fear was fighting for a foothold in his electrified mind, but with the alchemical aid of the speed/coke euphoria, he transformed the fear into a warrior's pre-combat fury. He chanted the slogan his father had learned in Nam: "Kill 'em all and let God sort 'em out."

The black snake stirred in his belly, coiling into a tight ball of cold mystic muscle. Joe Rob's stomach fluttered. He had the sudden urge to take a shit, but he clenched his sphincter until the urge went away. The image of Charlotte the Harlot's round ass popped into his mind, and he got a killer hard-on as he recalled the delicious anal assault.

"Fuck 'em all!" he shouted. "They can't touch me."

He was two miles from his destination.

He was totally psyched for combat.

*   *   *

Luke was pacing beside the truck, watching for the ambulance and keeping tabs on the dazed old lady behind the wheel. Where the hell was the ambulance? It should've been here by now.

The noon sun was beating down on him, cooking the top of his head where his hair was thinning. He grabbed his ball cap from his pickup and put it on. Agnes Porch looked at him and said something he didn't catch, but her eyes seemed more focused. Was she coming around?

"What's that, Miz Porch?"

"Get my boys."

He draped an arm over the open passenger door and leaned close to her face. "Where are they?"

She blinked several times, then said, "Out at the Jenkins place."

"The Jenkins place. Are you sure that's where they are?"

"Yes. I'm sure. Hurry."

"Yes ma'am. I'm on the way. You just stay right here and wait for the ambulance."

He hopped into his truck, revved the engine and tore off down the gravel driveway and wheeled onto the dirt road. The old Jenkins farm was a good five miles away. If he floored it all the way, he could be there in ten minutes tops.

He got on the radio and called in his destination. Dispatcher Holly Stimson acknowledged.

"Advise all units," Luke said. "A possible ten-niner at the Jenkins farmhouse."

"Roger, Chieftain," said Holly. Then she breached protocol herself by adding, "Luke, you be careful out there."

CHAPTER 18
GUARDIAN ANGEL

Ree Tyler was about to lock up Tyler Antiques and go to lunch across the street at The Vinewood Cafe when the spirit materialized in the darkened mirror of an antebellum vanity. Framed by dark brown wood, the ghostly entity beckoned to her with softly glowing fingers, and she stepped closer.

"Beau," she whispered, her breath catching in her throat. Her guardian angel had shown himself to her two previous times, always in the same mirror, but this time his features were more distinct, his handsome face more defined in the murky glass. Her heartbeat made her breasts quiver, and deep in her belly there was an involuntary contraction of muscle. "I thought you'd left me."

I won't leave you. His lips didn't move when he spoke, but she clearly heard his deep melodious voice in her head.

She resisted the urge to touch the mirror. "You know about Luke Chaney?" she asked, somehow knowing why Beau was here. "That I'm seeing him tonight?"

Of course I know.

"Well?" Unbidden sexual tension charged the air. Ree found it difficult to catch her breath.

Darkness is gathering. You must be wary, lest it touch you.

"Be wary of Luke? He's a good man. I *know* he is."

The darkness may gather him, and you, if you get too close.

"I don't understand," she told him. "Are you saying I shouldn't see him?"

No, you must follow your heart.

She nodded, though she wasn't sure she understood what he was telling her. Beau's impatience made him quick to anger, and she didn't want him angry with her, so she didn't press him to explain further.

His image in the glass wavered. The reflection of the shop's opposite wall showed through his dark topcoat and his chalky face blurred. His voice remained strong. *The darkness rises like water. There is one who would open the floodgate.*

"What should I do? This is all . . . beyond me."

Give up tobacco.

A blush warmed her face. "That's it? Stop smoking?"

A slight smile appeared in the fog of Beau's face, then he was gone.

Ree touched her fingertips to the mirror. The glass was warm. She blew out a big breath that inadvertently fogged a spot on the mirror. She turned away, wanting a cigarette. From her previous encounters with Beau, she knew he had an odd sense of humor and that he liked to speak in riddles. Was his give-up-tobacco line a joke or was it his way of telling her there was nothing she could do about an impending flood of darkness? She didn't know.

Her stomach growled. She hung the Out To Lunch sign on the shop's door and walked across the street to the cafe. She didn't take her cigarettes.

Beau had first appeared to her after the death of her husband, when she was spiraling down into a suicidal depression. Zoned out on tranquilizers Dr. Jackson had prescribed for her, Ree had been remarkably unruffled when the apparition appeared in the antique vanity mirror. She giggled and said, "You're a ghost. A good-looking ghost." The ghost scowled. She said, "If you're trying to scare me, it ain't working." Then his voice was inside her skull, a sonorous voice wrapped in a deep Southern accent, and he told her his name was Beau and that he had come to save her from herself. He said he had known her in a previous life and that they had been lovers. A sucker for a romantic story, she asked for details, but all he said was that he had died in the War of Northern Aggression and that she had died the death of a lonely widow. Then he told her that her husband had crossed over and that he was happy, though he missed her very much. Beau instructed her to stop taking the medicine and to climb out of the pit of self-pity and get on with her life.

She had chalked up the encounter to drug-induced hallucination and stopped downing the tranks. Her Christian upbringing didn't exactly allow for reincarnation, but she was nevertheless intrigued by the romantic notion of a ghostly lover from a past life appearing to save her from her suicidal depression. It wasn't until Beau's disembodied voice saved her from stepping in front of a speeding car that she really started to believe that he was her guardian angel. Now she had no doubt, and she had successfully integrated the concept of reincarnation with her Christian beliefs.

Ree sat at a corner table and ordered a BLT on wheat and a glass of iced tea. She was oblivious to the other diners around her as she tried to make sense of Beau's warning that darkness was gathering. Until he had appeared in the mirror, she had been almost giddy with anticipation of her date tonight with Luke. It was to be her first real date since the death of her husband, but now she didn't know if she should go through with it. Beau had advised her to follow her heart, and her heart was set on being with Luke.

By the time the waitress brought her order, Ree had decided to keep her date with Luke and to be wary of anything suggestive of dark forces at work. What else could she do?

She took a bite of her thick sandwich. The juice from the slice of tomato dribbled down her chin. The fried bacon and crisp lettuce were unusually delicious, and she savored the first bite as she dabbed her chin with a napkin. She gazed dreamily out the window. It was a beautiful day, and the promise of a romantic night had her fairly tingling with anticipation. Nowhere did she see any evidence of dark forces at work.

Then she heard the young couple in the booth behind her talking about the sinkhole on Main Street, the man giving his eyewitness account of a dump truck falling into the expanding hole. "I couldn't believe it," the man said. "The street just fell out from under it and the damn truck dropped straight down, out of sight."

A chill slithered up Ree's back.

The sunlit day suddenly darkened.

*　*　*

"*Skeeter?*" called the familiar voice.

He lifted his chin off his bare chest and looked around. As far as he could see, he was still alone in the barn loft.

"*Skeeter!*"

"Grandma?" he croaked, his voice abrading his dry throat.

But how could it be his grandmother? She had died two years ago.

"*You're in big trouble, young man.*"

He giggled. "No shit, Grandma. Tell me about it."

The light outside dimmed as the sun went behind a cloud, darkening the interior of the barn. Skeeter glanced over the edge of the loft and saw a hazy shaft of eerie light floating just above the floor of the barn. Within the glowing shaft he thought he could see his grandmother's round face and white hair.

"*Come down from there this minute.*"

"I can't," he said. "I'm chained up. You have to help me."

"Do it directly, son."

Then he saw a flesh-and-blood figure step out of the shadows, and his grandmother's apparition disappeared. Shotgun cradled in his arms, Fate Porch looked up at him and said, "Hush up, boy. It'll all be over directly."

"Thank God," Skeeter mumbled, then shut his eyes.

He thought he smelled Grandma's apple cobbler baking in the oven. He knew he felt the heat.

* * *

Charlotte Claymore popped another Advil and washed it down with straight vodka. The burning in her anus had subsided some, but not completely. She'd had anal intercourse before, and it hadn't been that bad, but this time it had been against her will and she was still furious at the pushy little motherfucker, Joe Rob Campbell. No, little was the wrong word. If he'd been little, it wouldn't have hurt some goddamn much. *I should've whacked off his pecker with the razor, that's what I should've done.*

She picked up the phone and tried Carl again. This time he answered.

"Where the hell ya been?" she demanded.

"Hey, baby, what's wrong?" Carl asked.

"I just got fucked up the ass, that's what's wrong."

"What?"

"You heard me. I was fucking raped up the rear."

"One of your johns?"

"Yeah. A crazy fuck, Joe Rob Campbell. The high school football jock."

"What the hell you doing turning tricks this early?"

"He paid extra. Listen, Carl. He held a razor to my throat. I thought I was dead."

"Son of a bitch!"

"I want this guy dead. You hear me? You're supposed to be my protector."

"Not over the phone, goddammit."

"You know somebody, right?"

"Sit tight, baby. I'll be right there."

"Sit tight, my ass."

Carl laughed. Charlotte slammed the phone down. She poured herself another shot of vodka, then lit a cigarette. Carl could be a heartless bastard sometimes, but he knew people who would do anything you wanted done, if the price was right. He had once told her he had a man killed for ripping him off on a dope deal. A hundred bucks for the hit.

She tossed back the booze, sucked on her smoke, and smiled to herself. It would be worth a hundred bucks to make that butt-fucking bastard dead. Sure as hell it would.

* * *

As he sailed over the blacktop, Luke Chaney took the Rossi .357 Magnum from the glove box and checked the cylinder. Five shells were snugly in place, the hammer resting on the empty slot. The checkered rubber grip was a perfect fit for his big hand. It was more powerful and therefore more reassuring than the .38 holstered on his hip. He sighted down the two-inch blue-steel barrel and shuddered. He hoped he wouldn't have to use it, that he would be able to defuse the situation by virtue of his experience as an officer of the law, but he knew the chances of such a peaceful resolution were slim to none. The Porches had no respect for the law, and Joe Rob was obviously unstable and probably desperate to save his friend. Desperation in a testosterone-swamped youth was a dangerous thing. In short, this was not a situation a former guardian of the peace could enter waving a white flag. He had to be prepared to use deadly force—something he had never had to do as a cop.

He hoped he would be equal to the task.

* * *

Chief Keller responded immediately to his dispatcher's call. He left his junior officers to handle the situation on Main Street and sped off with emergency lights flashing, en route to the old Jenkins farm outside of town. Still stinging from the tongue-lashing Peters had given him, he saw the possible ten-niner as a way to redeem himself in the eyes of the head councilman. But he had mixed feelings about Luke's involvement in this powder-keg situation; having the former chief on the scene was a definite plus, so long as Luke's long-standing zeal to nail Fate Porch didn't make things worse.

He keyed his mike and raised Luke on the radio. "Chieftain, this is Unit One. What's your twenty?"

"Two miles east of target," Luke responded.

"I'm on the way. Wait for backup if you can."

"Roger, One. If I can."

"Shit," Keller said to himself. He knew in his gut what lay ahead. There was no way around it. The inevitable shit was about to hit the fucking fan. The devil's due was going to be paid in blood. "Shit!"

CHAPTER 19
PLAYING HERO

Joe Rob drove up to the sun-bleached barn and stopped ten yards in front of it. Its wide doorless mouth yawned in shadow. The noon air was close, windless. He killed the Mustang's engine, and the growling guitar riff of Stevie Ray's "Cold Shot" died with a haunting echo. The farmhouse was twenty-some-odd yards to his right, its paneless windows like eyeless sockets and its sagging porch like the limp tongue of a dead animal.

He sat stone still behind the wheel, his eyes searching for the enemy. The only living thing he saw was a crow perched on the apex of the barn's roof. With the sawed-off shotgun hidden under his hunting jacket, he stepped out of the car and stood behind the meager cover of the driver's door.

"Here I am!" he shouted. The echo of his voice was hollow and eerily forlorn.

The crow launched itself off the roof and beat its wings against the glaring sky.

"Skeeter! I'm here, man!" Joe Rob hollered. "Where the fuck are you?"

No response.

"Come on, you cocksuckers! Don't be shy. You want me? Here I am!"

Above, in the tall rectangular opening of the barn loft, a man came forward from the shadowy interior and into the bright light of the midday sun. Fate Porch aimed a shotgun down at Joe Rob and said, "Get away from the car."

Joe Rob stood his ground. "Where's my friend?"

"He's here," Porch said.

"Let him go, then you and me will settle up."

"That ain't how it works, boy. If you want him, you'll have to kill me and my boys to get him."

"Is that right?" Joe Rob smiled. "Well, send 'em on out and let's get to it, old man. I already killed that crazy fuck Odell. I might as well send the rest of you assholes to hell too. Well? Where are they?"

"Yonder they come." Fate Porch nodded at the dirt road in the distance behind Joe Rob.

Joe Rob glanced over his shoulder and saw the black Firebird speeding up the rutted, weed-choked drive from the road, then he looked back up at Fate Porch and at the shotgun barrel pointing down at him, its muzzle looking amazingly big, almost like one of those megaphone-muzzled blunderbusses of olden times. He knew it was some devious trick of his perception, probably perpetrated by the coke-and-speed cocktail he'd snarfed up at Candyman's trailer. It wasn't fear. He knew no fear. Even with the Firebird coming up on his flank and with the shotgun drawn down on him from above in the rectangular evil eye of the barn, he wasn't afraid. He *knew* he was in control of the situation. He was the one calling the shots. The pigskin was in his hands and he was going to ram it down their throats. His best runs on the gridiron had started with this same on-top-of-the-game feeling. Sometimes you just *knew* you were headed for paydirt and that nothing could stop you. This was one of those times. But something else had been thrown into the mix. Something he didn't stop to analyze, but noted only in passing. It was as if some switch in his brain had been flipped and the world all at once went weird. Everything within his field of vision was suddenly glazed with an aura of darkness. A halo of dark light surrounded Fate Porch's big head. The blunderbuss muzzle of his shotgun also glowed with that same black light. He looked back at the approaching Firebird. Its flat-black primer-coated body had a dark halo of its own. Then, unbidden, a black light went on in Joe Rob's skull and he nodded and said, "Ah, dark things."

And he knew it was time to light it up.

He said, "You fucked up, old man. You should never divide your forces like that." He took a step backward and brought the sawed-off double-barrel Remington out from under his jacket, easily clearing the top of the door with it, and fired both barrels at the old man, who fired his shotgun at the same time. Joe Rob had never been kicked by a mule, but when the butt of the sawed-off recoiled into his shoulder because he had rushed the shot before firmly bracing the weapon there, he had a damn good idea what a mule's kick would feel like. It hurt like hell, but it also felt good having that much power at your command.

The blast of Fate's buckshot shattered the half-mast window of driver's door and blew out the side mirror, and Joe Rob felt a rough tug on the left sleeve of his jacket. He dropped the sawed-off and drew the .45 from his belt. The surprised old man had fallen back into the loft. Joe Rob didn't know how bad the old fart was hit, but he knew both barrels couldn't have missed him completely. With Fate out of the picture, at least temporarily, Joe Rob was free to turn his full attention to the two fucks in the Firebird.

*   *   *

"He shot Diddy!" Cowboy hollered. "Goddammit, Luther!"

Luther jammed on the brakes and the Firebird fishtailed to a halt behind the Mustang. "Shoot him," Luther barked as he swung his door open and grabbed the Desert Eagle Magnum off the dash. But before he had a chance to get out of the car, the Campbell boy aimed and fired his pistol at Luther's head. The windshield exploded and a hail of glass blew into Luther's face, momentarily blinding him. Splinters of glass set his face on fire with biting pain.

Cowboy fell out of the car, knocking his hat off against the edge of the door. In a full-blown rage and desperate to get Campbell in his gunsights, he jacked himself off the ground and waved his gun in the general direction of the Mustang in front of him. But he didn't see his target. He glanced over at Luther, who was sitting, stunned, behind the wheel, his face studded with bloody fragments of glass. "Luther!" he yelled.

A second pistol shot punched through the passenger door and zinged past Cowboy's left arm. Then he saw Campbell standing in front of the Firebird, holding his pistol with both hands and lining up a shot at his head. Cowboy ducked, accidentally discharging his gun and sending a round uselessly into the ground. He crouched behind the door, afraid to raise his head. "This is fucked," he gasped. "Luther! Get up. Shoot the sumbitch."

Luther had a hand to his face, tentatively touching the shards of glass embedded in his flesh. He looked around at Cowboy. His eyes were the eyes of a stunned cow, dazed and stupid.

"Luther! Move! He's killin' us."

Luther blinked his eyes several times, then seemed to regain his senses. He raised his Desert Eagle and fired wildly through the shattered windshield. Three quick shots. But at least he was shooting.

Cowboy scrambled on his hands and knees to the rear of the Firebird, then rose to a crouch with his gun pointing forward. He saw Campbell drawing a bead on his brother, leaning against the Mustang, his arm stretched across the roof and his pistol propped and steady. If he got this shot off, Luther was sure as hell dead.

Cowboy straightened up and fired at Campbell's head. *Pop, pop, pop.* He rushed the shots but they were enough to spoil the sumbitch's kill-shot and make him duck behind his car. *Now we got him.*

"See where he is?" Cowboy asked his brother.

Luther nodded, then finally got his ass in gear and slipped out of the car, staying low and handling his .357 like he knew what to do with it.

"Let's get him," snarled Cowboy, thinking to himself that he sounded just like Elvis when he said it. Now this was more like it. This was how it was supposed to be. The sumbitch was going to die in the dirt, shot full of holes and shitting his britches.

*   *   *

Fate sat up cradling his shotgun, then hugged it to his chest. Its stock was slick with blood. He looked down at his belly. His overalls were drenched with blood, and his abdomen throbbed with fiery pain.

The little bastard had caught him off guard when he came out with a shotgun of his own and fired without hesitation. Twin barrels booming. Hit low. But probably not torn up too bad. Good thing there was enough distance to scatter the shot and soften the hit. More than a hundred pellets of lead at close range could damn near cut a man in half.

Pistol shots outside. Breaking glass. Cowboy yelling.

"Goddamn," Fate muttered. "Hope them boys can handle that peckerwood."

He tried to get up, but his legs wouldn't cooperate and he fell on his ass. Using the shotgun as a crutch, he tried again, this time making it to his feet. His gut hurt like twelve kinds of hell, but he managed to stay upright. He glanced over at the Partain boy hanging from the rusty chain. The kid's eyes were open but Fate got the idea the boy wasn't seeing much of anything. The boy looked addle-brained for sure.

Fate hobbled over to the loft's doorway and looked out, squinting against the bright sun. Down on the ground the gun battle was not over. The Campbell boy was crouched down in front of his car, his gun hand propped on the hood. His shaved head glaring in the sunlight, Cowboy was coming out from behind the Firebird, swaggering like John Wayne, and Luther was sliding out of the driver's seat, his gun at the ready.

"Let's get him," Cowboy said, striding big as you please into the line of fire. Couldn't he see the boy had him in his sights?

"Watch out, Lem!" Fate yelled, using his son's given name because it was shorter and quicker than shouting Cowboy.

Cowboy shot his gaze up at Fate, then froze with his gun still out there at the end of his outstretched arm. Fate tried to bring his shotgun up to get a shot off at Campbell, but when he lifted it off the loft floor, his legs collapsed with the loss of support and he went down again, cursing.

Two shots echoed outside. Then another. And another.

"Lord God," Fate said through clenched teeth as he crawled to the glaring opening to look down, desperate to see if Cowboy had been shot.

*   *   *

When the skinhead walked into the sightline of his .45 semi-automatic, Joe Rob grinned and squeezed off two shots that slammed squarely into the guy's upper chest and the skinhead flew backward, his mouth open in a silent scream and his eyes bugging out of his skull.

A second later the other Porch brother, coming around on Joe Rob's right and crouching behind the Mustang's rear bumper, snapped off a shot that zinged past his right ear. Joe Rob dove for the ground and rolled to his left, then sprang to his feet by the right front fender, putting the Mustang between himself and the remaining shooter. Another shot blew a hole in the passenger-door's window, spiderwebbing the glass around the hole.

Joe Rob hit the deck. Lying flat on his belly and holding his gun straight out in front of him, he watched and waited for Luther to move out from behind the left rear tire. A .45 slug to the ankle would surely bring the guy down and set him up for a killing body-shot or a headshot. But the guy had the same idea. He also went to ground, and fired under the car as soon as he saw Joe Rob. The round ripped into the Mustang's chassis just inches in front of Joe Rob's head. Joe Rob got off a shot almost simultaneously, and the left rear tire went flat with a whistling groan. Luther rolled out of sight behind the rim of the deflated steel-belted radial.

Joe Rob couldn't see him, but he heard his feet pounding the ground and he knew the bastard was on the move, running away from the Mustang. He pushed up from the ground and stood. He saw the top of Luther's head over the roof of the Firebird and he fired at it and missed. Luther returned fire. Three shots, one pinging off the Mustang's roof and the other two hitting nothing but air. The guy couldn't shoot for shit.

Staying low and leaning his back against the side of his car, Joe Rob switched the .45 to his left hand and pulled his .357 with his right. He popped up and fired the Magnum, putting two slugs through the remnants of the Firebird's windshield and another through the window of the passenger door. He didn't know which shot did the trick, but one of them clearly did, because Luther let out a yowl as he spun around and went down behind the Firebird's rear bumper.

Joe Rob ran. With the explosive speed that had made him a remarkable ball carrier on the football field, he sprinted past the two cars and cut right with both pistols raised and ready to shoot. It was a near ninety-degree cut his old coach would have been proud of. Out of the corner of his eye he saw a pickup truck coming up the drive, but he ignored it and locked his eyes on Luther Porch, who was on his back, bleeding from his left shoulder and waving his pistol around in an erratic attempt to draw a bead on Joe Rob.

Luther fired just as Joe Rob dug in his heels and stopped on a dime and a quarter. It was a wild-ass shot, not even close.

The driver of the pickup started blowing his damn horn in staccato toots. Joe Rob leveled both his pistols on Luther Porch and cut loose, pumping four, five, six shots into the son of a bitch. Luther's body stopped twitching on the fifth shot. The sixth and final shot demolished his right eye and went on to do untold damage to his brain.

The pickup lurched to a stop and Luke Chaney jumped out of the cab with a pistol in his hand.

Joe Rob brought his two guns around and aimed them at Chaney's chest.

*   *   *

"God-Almighty-shit-fire," Fate Porch said. Whether he was actually addressing the Lord and daring Him to shit fire, he couldn't have said, though he was surely angry enough now to call the Lord out and tempt His infernal wrath. What kind of God would make a man witness the killing of his sons? The last of his seed.

It had happened so fast, he hardly knew what he was seeing. His eyesight was failing and his belly was aching and bleeding to beat the band, but he saw enough to know his boys were all gone. That Campbell boy was a demon from hell, no two ways about that. And all Fate could do was watch because the demon was out of shotgun range.

He got to his feet, ignoring his pain, and hobbled over to the ladder at the edge of the loft. He looked at the boy hanging on the chain and considered pumping his belly full of buckshot, but decided not to because the noise would tip his hand. All that mattered now was getting close enough to Campbell to unload this shotgun on him. And on whoever it was that rode up in the truck with horn a' blowing. Looked like Luke Chaney's truck. Fate hoped it was. He'd wanted to kill that self-righteous son of a bitch for a long damn time.

He dropped his shotgun to the barn floor and started climbing down the ladder. It was slow going, but he made it without falling off. He picked up the shotgun and walked, bent over with belly pain, toward the doorway. He had no qualms about dying now. It was better this way than waiting for the cancer to take him. And now that all his sons were gone, he had nothing to live for. There was Maw, but her time was about up, too. She could spend her last days on the government dole in some Old Folks' Home if the Porches in Vidalia didn't take her in. *Just let me live long enough to kill this here demon. That's all I ask.*

Fate jacked a shell into the chamber, then straightened up and walked out of the barn, holding the shotgun down by his right leg and out of sight. His head was swimming rough seas and darkness was crowding his vision, but he willed himself onward and walked a crooked line toward the spot where Luke Chaney and the Campbell boy were squared off and pointing pistols at one another.

I don't care if they shoot each other, so long as I get to finish 'em off. A close-range shotgun blast to their faces will suit me just fine. Mighty goddamn fine.

*   *   *

Luke was aiming his Rossi .357 at Joe Rob Campbell's chest and looking hard into the boy's eyes, trying to read Joe Rob's next move. The boy was pointing two pistols at him like some Wild West gunslinger, and his eyes seemed to glow with dark fire. He had just gunned down two men and he looked like he wanted to go for more.

"Easy now, Joe Rob," Luke said, trying to keep the tremble out of his voice. "It's over. You got 'em."

Joe Rob didn't speak. He didn't drop his two-fisted aim. His lips were curled back in a grimace that might have been a wicked grin.

"Let your guns down," Luke said in a voice that was soft yet firm. "I'm not your enemy."

Some of the wildness seemed to go out of his eyes, but his gunhands didn't waver. The muzzles were still trained on Luke's chest.

"Come on, son. I can't have you pointing those guns at me. Talk to me."

Finally Joe Rob spoke. He licked his lips and said, "You ain't the law."

"No, I'm not. You're not either." Now was not the time to explain that he was an auxiliary officer.

"But you'll try to hold me till the cops come, won't you?"

"I can help you," Luke told him. "But you have to tell me what happened. Where's Skeeter?"

"They said he's in the barn."

"Then we have to go get him."

"Old Man Porch is in there too. He's hit but I don't think I killed him. He tried to shoot me. He's got a shotgun."

"Self defense, sounds like," Luke said, wanting to put the boy at ease as best he could. "Okay, now listen to me. I want you to put those pistols away and wait here while I go see what's up in the barn."

"Skeeter might be dead already," Joe Rob said without emotion. "I don't know. They already cut off his finger."

"He needs medical attention. I can call for help on my radio. But I can't do anything as long as you keep pointing those guns at me. You hear? The longer we stand here like this, the worse it is for Skeeter. "

"I ain't giving up my guns."

Luke decided the best he could do to end this standoff was to bargain with the boy. He would worry about getting the guns away from him after he'd seen what the situation was in the barn. For now, he just had to be sure Joe Rob wasn't going to shoot him. "I ain't asking you to," he said. "I just want you to stop pointing 'em at me, that's all. I have to go see about Skeeter and Porch, but I can't do that with you drawn down on me. Chief Keller's on his way here and I don't want you to get in a shootout with him either. That's why you got to put them guns away. Okay?"

Over Joe Rob's shoulder Luke saw Fate Porch coming out of the barn. The crotch of his denim overalls glistened with blood, and he was unsteady on his feet as he plodded toward them. Luke looked away from the old man, not wanting his eyes to alert Joe Rob that Porch was approaching. The situation was already volatile, to say the least, and he didn't know how Joe Rob would react to Fate's lame, determined approach, though he had the feeling that the boy would gun down the old man without hesitation. The way he'd shot Luther full of holes . . .

Luke shivered in the heat of the day. Fate was getting close. Any second now Joe Rob would hear his shuffling feet and turn around and see him. Luke knew he had to take charge of the situation, and quickly, but he didn't know how to do it without setting off more gunplay.

Porch was less than ten yards away now.

Joe Rob's pistols were still aimed at Luke's chest.

And Luke had no more time for figuring out what the hell to do.

Without further deliberation, he acted. He relinquished his aim, letting his gunhand hang by his leg and said, "Wait here," then walked past Joe Rob, wanting to put himself between the boy and the old man. He could only hope Joe Rob wouldn't shoot him in the back in his zeal to shoot Fate Porch.

Out of the corner of his eye, Luke saw Joe Rob turning to see where he was going. That was the bad news. The good was that the boy had let his aim drop some, so that his guns were no longer trained on Luke's torso.

"Hold up, Fate," Luke said to the wounded old man. "Stop right there."

Fate didn't stop right away. He took two, three more pained steps, then brought up a shotgun from behind the baggy leg of his overalls and pointed it at Luke's belly. The old man's face was scrunched up in a look of hate, but the look in his eyes was one of serenity—as if he thought he'd just said his last goodbyes to the world. It was the look in his eyes that scared the living hell out of Luke and told him the old man was going to squeeze the shotgun's trigger and give him a bellyful of buckshot.

"Son of a bitch," Joe Rob said when he saw Porch.

"No!" Luke shouted as he raised his pistol. He fired. *Pop. Pop-pop.* Three .357 rounds blew into Fate's chest, picking him up off the ground and knocking him backward. The shotgun separated from him and he landed on his back, raising a little puff of dust. He lifted his head and looked around like a man just waking up in a strange place, trying to get his bearings, then he gave Luke a nod of his head, closed his eyes and let his head back down.

Luke turned back to Joe Rob and said, "Stay back." Then he knelt beside Porch and touched his fingers to the bleeding man's neck. No pulse. "He's gone," Luke said.

He stood up. "You okay?"

Joe Rob nodded. He was no longer pointing his pistols at Luke.

"Let's go see about Skeeter."

* * *

In fact, Joe Rob was a long way from okay, but there was no way he could explain what he was feeling to Chaney. He couldn't explain it to himself. The sunlit world had taken on an extra dimension of blushing darkness, every visible thing haloed with dark luminescence and pulsing with otherworldly energy that was nevertheless in this world—whether by accident or by design, *who knew?* Not Joe Rob. Nor did he care. It didn't matter now. Nothing did. If he raised his guns and shot Luke Chaney in the back . . . so what? Chaney had a dark halo, too. Dead or alive, that halo would remain. It was *really there.* It was a little like the time he and Skeeter had dropped acid and tripped all night and half the next day, seeing all kinds of strange sights and shit floating in the air like purplish electricity. Once the shit kicked in, all you could do was hold on and ride it out to wherever it wanted to take you. And that was all he could do now: *Go where the shit takes you.*

He hop-skipped and caught up with Chaney. "Can you see that dark shit?"

Chaney looked at him sideways. "What?"

"Nothing," he said. "Never mind."

"This was a damn foolish thing you did, son," Chaney said as they entered the barn. "You're lucky you're not dead."

Joe Rob hawked a laugh. "Wasn't luck. I knew I could take 'em."

"Why the hell didn't you go to the police?"

"They would've killed Skeeter. They were watching me. Those two back there followed me here. Way I see it, I had no choice."

Chaney grudgingly nodded. He looked down at the floor of the barn and saw the blood trail Fate Porch had left on his way to his death. Then he called out: "Skeeter!"

Joe Rob looked up at the barn loft and said, "I think he's up there. That's where the old man was when he took a shot at me."

Chaney went straight to the ladder and scaled it. Joe Rob holstered his .357 and stuck the .45 in his belt and followed him up.

Wearing nothing but his boxer shorts, Skeeter was hanging from a rafter by a thick, rusty chain. His eyes were closed, his chin resting on his skinny chest. There was a nasty-looking gash in his side and a stab wound in his thigh, both encrusted with dried blood. The stump of his ring finger was blackened like a link of sausage left too long on a grill.

Chaney patted Skeeter's knee and called his name again. Skeeter's eyelids fluttered, then opened. There was no recognition in his eyes.

"Unhook that chain," Chaney said.

Chaney wrapped his arms around Skeeter's hips, taking the weight off the chain, and Joe Rob unhooked it. Chaney lowered Skeeter to the floor of the loft and put him in a sitting position.

"Skeeter," said Chaney. "It's all over. You're safe now. You hear me?"

Skeeter nodded. Joe Rob saw the dark halo around Skeeter's head flare up like a circle of fire atop a gas stove. "We got 'em, buddy," he said. "We killed those motherfuckers dead."

Chaney said, "Shut up, goddammit."

"Well, we did. He needs to know it. Look what they did to 'im."

"Can you stand up?" Chaney asked Skeeter.

Still dazed by the trauma inflicted upon him by the Porches, Skeeter nevertheless got to his feet and swayed precariously, but managed to keep his balance. The far-away look in his eyes was beginning to fade.

"Okay," said Chaney. "I'm gonna carry you down the ladder, then we'll get you to the hospital." He bent down and draped Skeeter over his shoulder in a fireman's carry, then took him down the ladder.

Joe Rob followed. When he heard the siren in the distance, he saw himself handcuffed in the back of a police car, on his way to jail. *No fucking way. I'm not going to jail.*

After Chaney put Skeeter in the cab of his pickup, Joe Rob drew his .45 and pointed it at Chaney. "Sorry, man, but I can't go to jail. I got to take your guns."

Chaney sighed and shook his head. "Don't do this, Joe Rob. This won't help your case."

"Got no choice. You can't hold me. You're not a cop anymore. I gotta borrow your truck. My car's got a flat and I ain't got time to change a damn tire." He reached out and yanked the pistol from Chaney's holster and tossed it into the back of the truck, then he pulled the pistol stuck in Chaney's belt and did the same with it. "Get Skeeter out and wait for the cops."

He saw that Chaney had left his key in the ignition. The wailing whoop of the approaching siren was getting too damn close. He had to get the hell out of there if he was going to avoid a gun battle with Chief Keller. Not that he didn't think he could take him; he just didn't want to have to shoot a cop. But he would if he had to. "Move it!" he told Chaney.

The police-band radio in the truck crackled to life. Keller's voice came out tinny and punctuated with static, nearly drowned out by the sound of the siren. "Chieftain, this is One. What's the situation? Luke, talk to me, dammit. What's going on?"

"Tell him everything's under control," Joe Rob told Chaney. "Tell him he can slow down."

Chaney reached past Skeeter's knees, picked up the handset and said, "One, this is Chieftain. Everything's under control. Slow down before you kill yourself. I'll explain when you get here. Out."

Skeeter looked at Joe Rob and said, "The fuck're you doin'?"

"Gotta book, man. They wanna take me to jail for this shit."

"They were gonna kills us," Skeeter said, a wounded look in his face. "You didn't do nothing wrong. They can't put you in jail."

"He's right, Joe Rob," said Chaney. "You acted in self-defense. You'll have to give a statement, explain exactly what happened, why you did what you did. I don't see that they've got any reason to jail you."

"I killed Odell Porch, too," he said. "Shot him in the head."

"He went at you with a knife!" Skeeter raised his voice. "He was gonna rape that girl! I was *there*."

125

"Come on, son," said Chaney. "Use your head. You take my truck at gunpoint, that's armed robbery. You *will* do serious jail-time for that."

Skeeter said, "That's right, man. Don't be stupid. You got this knocked. Hell, you're a goddamn hero."

Joe Rob looked at Skeeter, then at Luke Chaney. Their halos were starting to fade a little. "Y'all don't understand," he said. "I *liked* it. I enjoyed killing those sons-o'-bitches. I wish I could do it again. I don't think that's how a hero's s'pose to feel."

"You did what you thought you had to," Chaney said. "It was a combat situation. You can sort out your feelings about it later. But right now, you need to give me your guns. Chief Keller's gonna be here in about sixty seconds."

"Do it, brother," Skeeter urged him. "Give it up. It'll be okay."

Joe Rob saw the squad car coming up the weedy drive with its rack of emergency lights flashing. A tingle of excitement ran through his chest and his finger tightened on the trigger. The sudden urge to start pumping lead into the police car was nearly overpowering, but he reined himself in, flipped the pistol around and handed it to Chaney. "Fuck it," he said. "I'll play hero."

PART 2
DARKNESS
ABOVE

CHAPTER 20
END OF DAY

Cornelius Weehunt sank his teeth into the meat and tore a big chunk off the bone. The meat was tender, juicy. The juice dribbled down his chin. He wiped it away with the back of his hand and took another bite before he swallowed the first.

"Corny, mind your manners now," Aunt Mattie scolded from the head of the long table. Her thick glasses made her eyes look too big even for her chubby cheeks and sagging jowls. "Slow down and enjoy your food."

Kirby Cone grinned over his tea glass and said, "Where's the fire?"

Mr. Jones wiped his thin lips, adjusted his false teeth and said, "Got a hot date, Corny?"

The other boarders at the table laughed, but Corny didn't see what was so funny. He wasn't supposed to talk with food in his mouth, so he shook his head: Heck-no-I-don't-have-a-date-and-you-know-it. He put down his chicken leg and wiped his greasy fingers on his napkin so his glass of tea wouldn't slip through his fingers when he picked it up for a big lemon-tangy gulp.

"Best fried chicken in town, Miz Weehunt," said Lois Long. She was the handsome widow who didn't live at the boarding house but came every Friday for the fried-chicken supper and because—according to Aunt Mattie—she had eyes for Rufus Tilley, the book writer from Atlanta who spent all day tapping on his keyboard and only came out of his room when it was time to eat. He was a tall, thin man with a bushy salt-and-pepper moustache and blue eyes that seemed to drink in everything around him. He never said much, but Corny had the idea that the man knew most everything about everybody. Corny didn't like it when the man turned those blue eyes on him. He was afraid Rufus Tilley might see that he was hiding a secret. It wouldn't do to have him find out about Whisperer. Whisperer wouldn't like that at all.

Forks and knifes clinked and rattled against china plates, ice cubes tinkled in sweating glasses, men stifled belches, and the conversation around the long table rose and fell in volume, sputtered and finally died of boredom. Most of the boarders were men—retired and widowed—with little to say, and little of what they did say interested Corny. Usually it was stuff about the weather, politics, or what they did or used to do for a living. Still, this was Corny's favorite time of day. He liked the homey feeling it gave him, sitting at his special place at the table, breaking bread with people who were almost like family, and being looked after by Aunt Mattie who *was* family. It all reminded him of the way things used to be when he was a kid, back in the old days, way before his fall from the ladder that injured his brain and made everything before the accident seem like a dream—or like somebody else's life. Back when he had a momma and a daddy who bragged about how smart he was every time he brought home his report card with A's in every subject. Aunt Mattie said he was still smart, but that his brain just couldn't handle his smarts the way it used to. She said it was sort of like a radio without a good antenna—it couldn't pick up signals very well and there was a lot of static. Corny didn't think it was like that at all. He was smarter than folks thought, even though parts of his brain were dead, and now he could pick up signals people with normal brains couldn't. *He* could hear Whisperer, but nobody else could. And Whisperer was smarter than all of them. Whisperer knew things nobody else knew and whispered them to Corny. Whisperer knew he wasn't a dummy. Whisperer wouldn't waste time talking to a dummy.

John Henry Jackson came late to the supper table, mopping his brow with a handkerchief and apologizing for being late. He pulled out his chair and sat down next to Lois Long. "Y'all hear about the trouble out at the old Jenkins place?" he asked. He didn't wait for an answer. He said, "There was a big shootout. Fate Porch and his boys are all dead. Boy fresh out of high school killed 'em. Joe Rob Campbell. Dolly Chambers' grandboy, used to be a football hero. Luke Chaney was there too, but I'm not sure what his part was."

"Where'd you hear that?" asked Kirby Cone.

"Barber shop."

"Good Lord, John Henry," said Cone. "You know you can't believe half of what you hear there."

"No, it's true," insisted John Henry Jackson. "Buck heard it from Mr. Peters himself."

"Jake Peters?" Aunt Mattie asked.

"That's right. There was something about a kidnapping, but Buck wasn't sure about the details. Something about the Partain boy, Skeeter. Had his finger cut off. He's in the hospital."

"Good Lord!" Kirby Cone repeated. "Whole town's going to hell. First Main Street caves in, and now this?"

"Vinewood used to be such a quiet little town," Mr. Jones offered, crossing his knife and fork on the edge of his plate, as he always did when he was done eating.

"Well, I can't say I'm sorry to hear them Porch men are dead," said Mr. Jackson. "They were sorry white trash, mean as snakes. I'm sure they had it coming."

Aunt Mattie put her napkin in her plate and said, "Wonder what's going to become of Agnes Porch now? She's too old and poorly to live by herself."

"She's got relatives in Vidalia," said Mr. Jackson. "The way I hear it, she's no saint either. Some folks say she's the meanest one of the bunch, what with all her mumbo-jumbo and spooky doings."

The book writer perked up and actually spoke: "How's that?"

"Oh, some people believe she's some kind of witch," said Aunt Mattie. "A hoodoo queen or something. I never put much stock in all that."

"My Betty, God rest her sweet soul, went to her one time," said Mr. Jones. "And the old lady cured her arthritis. God as my witness." He put his hand over his heart. "She has the sight, too. She sees things. She knew things about Betty she couldn't have known any other way."

"Interesting," said Rufus Tilley the writer, stroking his mustache the way you'd stroke a pet. Corny wondered what kind of book the man wrote on every doggone day.

"I wouldn't want to get on that old lady's bad side," Mr. Jones said. "No sir-ree."

"Superstitious nonsense," proclaimed Mr. Jackson.

Mr. Jones shook his head. "Don't be too sure, John Henry. Agnes Porch is an unusual old woman. She lived a long time in Louisiana, and that's voodoo country, sure enough."

Corny could no longer contain himself. He blurted out the question that had been bubbling in his skull like water on the boil. "Does she make little dolls and stick pins in 'em?"

Mr. Jones chuckled. "I don't know, Cornelius. I wouldn't be a bit surprised."

"Shame on you, Mr. Jones," Aunt Mattie scolded. "Don't tell him that. He has enough bad dreams already."

Corny didn't hear what came after that. All he could hear was Whisperer's harsh voice deep inside his head, getting louder and louder—so loud he was afraid everybody at the table might hear it. He pushed away from the table, the chair legs scraping the floor with a noisy *uurk*, jumped up and ran out of the dinning room with Whisperer fairly shouting: *Hoodoo . . . Hoodoo . . . Hoodoo . . .*

* * *

Agnes Porch couldn't eat. The nurse told her she had to eat something, and Agnes told her to go away and leave her alone.

She hated hospitals.

She didn't trust doctors.

And she wanted to go home.

She used the remote to turn off the aggravating television, and stared at the ceiling. Without her glasses, the ceiling was a big, white blur, but that was all right. She didn't want things in sharp focus just now. Better to have things blurred and out of focus. Better not to feel the pain of her loss. They hadn't told her yet, probably thinking she was too weak for the truth, but she knew. No egg-sucking doctor or crooked cop had to tell her that her son and grandsons were dead. She had *seen* it while she was in the ambulance. She had seen their spirits departing their bodies. She *knew* their souls were not at rest. They were mired in syrupy darkness, caught fast and bogged down. She didn't know if she could help them, but she knew she had to try. She couldn't do anything as long as she was laid up in this hospital bed. She had to get herself home. Then she could try to set things right—as right as they could be. A heavy debt was owed, and she would do everything within her power to see it paid in full.

She shut her eyes and willed herself to rest. She would have to be strong for the task ahead. The required rituals would have to be performed without mistake.

The need for vengeance burned in her heart like a thousand suns. When the time was right, she would have it.

* * *

Three rooms down the hospital corridor from the dim room where Agnes Porch gathered her spiritual forces, Skeeter Partain was cranking up his motorized bed so he could have a better view of the TV bolted to the wall just below the ceiling. The stub of his missing finger was sporting a fat bandage, and the knife wounds in his abdomen and thigh were covered with rectangular patches of medicated gauze and surgical tape. His blue and white hospital gown was draped over the bed's metal side-rails and he was naked except for his clean boxer shorts. The gown had irritated the raw places under his arms where the rusty chain had bruised and chafed him, so he had pulled it off before the nurse started the IV of D5W solution his doctor had ordered as treatment for dehydration. "You'd be amazed at how much body fluid you can lose when you're hung up in a barn loft on a hot day in South Georgia," Dr. Sims had told him. But Skeeter wasn't amazed at all; he'd *been there*, for shit's sake, and he knew it had been more than just the heat draining him of his bodily fluids. He'd been sweating out of fear. The old saying, "Don't sweat the small stuff" hadn't applied today. He'd sweated for his frigging life.

His mother breezed into the room with a can of Pepsi from the vending machine. "Here you are, honey," she said after she'd popped the top for him. "Don't drink it too fast."

"Thanks, Mom," he said, turning the cold can up and taking a long pull of cola. He belched, then smiled. "Ahh, that's good. You call Dad?"

"Yes. He's talking to Mookie Vedders. Your father's going to make sure Joe Rob has the best lawyer in the county."

"That's Mookie Vedders," Skeeter agreed. "Do they think he'll be charged with . . . anything?"

"I don't know. That's what they're discussing now. I don't see why they would, though. I mean, my God, Joe Rob saved your life. He's a brave young man."

"He's my blood brother. He did what blood brothers are supposed to do. I just wish I could have killed those assholes myself."

She patted his hand. "I know how you must feel, but you're lucky things worked out the way they did. Taking a human life is . . . must be something you never get over. A terrible thing to have to live with."

"After what they did to me? And what they were going to *do* to me? They were going to cut off my damn head, like they did to Mr. Shockley. I sure as hell wouldn't lose any sleep over killing *them*."

"Well, it's all over now. It's best you try not to even think about all this."

"Mom? Are you sure Joe Rob's not in jail? I mean, don't worry about upsetting me. I just want to know the truth."

"Your father said he's still talking to the county investigator. Mookie Vedders will be there to take care of him. Mookie's not going to let them put him in jail. Not that I think they would even want to. The whole county knows what kind of people the Porches were. And Joe Rob's a good boy. From good stock. He's a hero in my book."

Skeeter nodded, then took another swallow of cola. Joe Rob was indeed a hero. But he was something else, too. Something Skeeter couldn't yet put a name to, but he'd had a close-up look at whatever it was, and it had scared the hell out of him. What if that psycho girl had been right? What if her "dark thing" *had* wanted Joe Rob?

And what if it now had him?

*　*　*

Luke poured himself a cup of hours-old coffee and sat on the edge of Chief Keller's desk. Keller was bent over his desk blotter, still struggling with the required paperwork generated by the multiple shootings, assault and kidnapping. Keller glanced up at Luke, rolled his eyes and said, "I got to hand it to you, Luke. You played this thing just right. You had the pleasure of shooting the son of a bitch and I get to do the damn paperwork."

"Necessary evil," said Luke, taking a sip of the black brew.

"Unnecessary bullshit. Half of it, at least."

Luke shrugged. He had already given his statement to Brian Batty, the acting homicide investigator for the county. Batty was a competent professional, and he had treated Luke as a brother lawman, though Luke was officially retired. Keller had explained that Luke had been acting as an auxiliary officer at his request, due to the temporary manpower shortage caused by the emergency situation on Main Street. Luke, of course, had a valid permit for each of his handguns, and he clearly had been acting in self-defense when he shot and killed Fate Porch, so there was no doubt that his use of deadly force was justified. Joe Rob Campbell was a different story. Batty was still grilling the boy in the back room where the office supplies and assorted junk were stored on metal shelves, and Luke figured the boy was sweating bullets after more than a full hour in the hot seat. Batty could be a bear when he wanted to be.

"Okay if I use your phone?" Luke asked Keller.

"Knock yourself out," Keller said with a weary-eyed wink.

Luke thumbed through the city phone book, found Ree Tyler's home number and hit the digits. Ree answered after the third ring. "Hey, this is Luke," he said softly. "Something's come up and I don't think I'll be able to make it tonight."

Her voice seemed a little tight. "You're breaking our date?"

"Uh, no, just postponing it. How about a rain-check?"

"What's going on, Luke? You're not getting cold feet, are you?"

"No, nothing like that. I'm helping out down at the station. Police business."

After a brief pause, she said, "Then I'll hold dinner. That's no problem. You'll find that I can be a very patient person, given the right circumstances."

"You sure? That's it's all right, I mean?"

"Yes, I'm sure. If you still want to come, I don't mind waiting for you."

"I do." He was a little surprised at how much he did want to be with her tonight. Then again, the thought of being home tonight with no one but his dog for company was not very appealing. He had just killed a man and seen two others lying dead in the dirt; he knew he would be replaying that bloody scene over and over in his head as soon as he was alone, with time on his hands. "It might be another hour or two. When I finish up here, I'll need to go home and clean up. I'll call you before I leave home."

"I'll be here," she said. "Are you okay? You sound . . . a little tense."

"Yeah. I'll tell you about it when I get there. Thanks for being so patient with me."

"No problem. We'll have a nice dinner, a little wine, and see if we can't get you loosened up."

"Sounds good. I'll see you in a little while."

He hung up, and Keller said, "There's no need for you to hang around, Luke. Batty's done with you, the bodies are on the way to the medical examiner, suspect's in custody. I've just got this damned paperwork."

"I know. But I want to see how it turns out with Joe Rob. He almost bolted on me before you got there, and I had to tell him he probably wouldn't get locked up to keep him from panicking. I guess I feel sort of responsible for him." Luke rubbed his eyes, then added, "I had to lie to him to get him to give up his guns. I told him he wouldn't go to jail, but hell, they'll have no choice but to prosecute. As unpopular as that will be."

Mookie Vedders appeared in the doorway. "Evening, gents," he said. "I understand you've got my client here. Joe Rob Campbell?"

"Mookie," Luke nodded.

"The boy didn't ask for a lawyer," said Keller, dropping his ballpoint pen on the blotter and standing up.

"James Partain's footing the bill," said the short, hatchet-faced lawyer. "He wants to make sure the lad who saved his boy's life is afforded due process."

"He will be," said Keller, defensive. "They're in the back room."

Mookie followed Keller to the unmarked door, then turned back to Luke and said, "I'm glad you're okay, Luke. Off the record, you did a great public service in getting rid of Fate Porch."

"Thanks," Luke said.

Keller knocked on the door, opened it and said, "Joe Rob's lawyer is here."

Joe Rob looked up and saw Mookie Vedders walk into the room like a bantam rooster, cocky and self-assured. For a little man, the guy walked like he had a humongous pair of balls—like the cock-of-the-walk lawyer he was.

Batty the homicide dick tried to keep the surprise off his face, but Joe Rob could see he was thrown off his game.

"Hello, Brian," Vedders said to Batty. "How's the family?"

"Fine," Batty said without getting out of his chair.

"Joe Rob, I've been hired to give you legal representation," the lawyer said, "and as of right now, I don't want you to answer any more questions. Has Mr. Batty explained your rights?"

"Yeah, I think so."

"Brian, I'd like some time alone with my client, if you don't mind."

With a sigh, detective Batty stood and said, "You got it." He left the room and shut the door softly.

Mookie sat in the chair across the green table from Joe Rob. "What have you told him so far?"

"Pretty much the whole story. He had me going back over parts of it, looking for holes, I guess. Who's paying you for this?"

"James Partain."

Joe Rob nodded. It didn't surprise him that Skeeter's old man would foot the bill, not after he'd saved Skeeter's bacon. And Mr. Partain could afford it. Everybody knew undertakers made a killing, money-wise.

"Okay," Vedders said, "I want you to tell me what you told him, word for word if you can do that."

"Man, I'm already bored with this. It was wild while it was happening, but this shit's getting old. All this talking about it."

"Joe Rob, I'm trying to keep you out prison. Now, based on what I've already been told, I think I can do that, but you have to cooperate with me. No matter how boring it is. All right?"

He nodded. He knew the man was right, but he was coming down off the speed and coke, and he was getting more and more irritable and short-tempered. He wished he had some dope to smoke or booze to drink to mellow him out and cushion the crash, but that was out of the question for the moment.

"Good," said Vedders. "Now go ahead and tell me what you told him."

Joe Rob scratched an itch behind his ear, then said, "First thing I said was those motherfuckers had it coming. They thought they were gonna kill my friend and me, but this time they fucked with the wrong hombre. That was the word I used, *hombre*. Pretty good, huh? Just popped in my head, probably from an old western."

"Yeah, that's pretty good, son. Go on."

Joe Rob grinned and went on with his story.

*   *   *

Charlotte Claymore was taking the night off. She was in no mood for turning tricks, not tonight. Her bumhole was still sore from having that punk-ass prick ram his cock up her rear. And the worst part was, it had played holy hell with her hemorrhoids and started them bleeding. She had a Tuck's medicated pad back there now, but it didn't stop the pain. That little fucker was going to pay through the nose for what he did to her. Better yet, he was going to pay through his goddamn prick. Charlotte didn't just want him killed—she wanted him tortured, *then* killed. And Carl knew just the man for the job.

She smashed out the butt of one smoke in the full ashtray, then lit another. Poured herself another shot of vodka and tossed it back. It burned good going down, and she had a nice buzz on when the knock rattled the back door.

She answered it without turning on the back porch light, just as Carl had instructed her. This was one visitor she didn't want the neighbors to know anything about. When Carl had told her that the hit man was coming to her house, she had protested. "I don't want him here," she'd said. "Why don't you handle it?" Because that's the way the dude does business, he'd told her. Then he got this weird smile on his face and said, "Don't worry, nobody'll see him. This guys sticks to the shadows. Hell, he *is* a fucking shadow." She wondered if he meant the guy was a nigger, but she didn't pursue it. She didn't care if he was black as the ace of spades, as long as he got the job done.

She pulled the back door open. The light from the laundry room showed her a tall, thin man with a navy-blue ski mask over his head. His eyes were green, the flesh around them wrinkled and pink. Pale, thin lips poked through the mouth hole, a fever blister slathered with some kind of ointment dotting the upper lip.

"Jesus Christ," she said. "What the hell is this, trick or treat?"

"Step outside," the man said with a rumbling drawl. "And shut the door."

"Carl sent you, right?" Charlotte wanted to be sure this was the right guy before she set foot out of her house. Of course, that was stupid, because if he wasn't the guy, she was already fucked, standing here in her robe, an arm's-length from the masked man.

"No, Mickey fucking Mouse sent me," he snarled. He grabbed her arm and yanked her outside, shutting the door behind her so that they were in darkness.

"Hey! Keep your hands off me, you—"

He clamped a big hand over her mouth. "Ssshh. Not so loud. Okay?"

Charlotte nodded. He removed his hand.

"Your friend said you want a guy done," he said softly.

"Damn right, I do," she said in a loud whisper. "I want him to suffer before you kill him."

The masked man shook his head. "That's a whole different proposition."

"You mean more expensive, right?"

"Right. More risk, more money."

"I don't care. I want the sonofabitch tortured. I'll pay the extra. And I want you to tell him it's from me. When he dies, I want his last thought to be about me. Can you handle that?"

"For three hundred bucks."

"Shit," said Charlotte, "is that the lowest you'll go?"

"Bottom line. Three hundred up front."

She thought about it for a moment, then said, "Okay, three hundred. On one condition. You take a couple of Polaroid shots for me. Like before and after. I'll give you one-fifty right now, and when I get the photos, I pay you the rest."

In the dim moonlight she saw his lips part in a reptilian smile. "With one stipulation," he said.

She smiled back. For a hit man, the guy had an interesting vocabulary. "What stipulation?"

"When I bring the photos, I want a freebie. I like to get my rocks off after a job. But I don't like paying for it. Call it professional courtesy."

After a long pause, she said, "Deal. Hang on, I'll get the cash."

As she went to the bedroom to dig out her stash of cash, the burning pain in her bumhole seemed to lessen. She wondered if the medicated pad was doing its job, or if it was some kind of psychological relief from knowing that her hit man would be doing *his* job.

CHAPTER 21
NIGHT MOVES

All spiffed up with a hot date to boot, thought Luke as he drove into town. The night had turned out cool for this time of the year, and for that he was grateful. It wouldn't do to show up at Ree's door sweating like a funky field hand. He hit the eject button, pulled out the old Allman Brothers CD and replaced it with The Best of Sade. Her sultry, soft-jazz style hit the right notes for the mood he wanted, but the mood eluded him, and he couldn't get the afternoon's carnage out of his mind. Maybe he needed to talk about it. He knew Ree was a good listener, but did he really want to mar their first date with such unseemly talk? No. He didn't even want Ree Tyler to know that he had killed a man, but in a town the size of Vinewood, there was no way she wouldn't find out. Better that she heard it from him. Tell her. Downplay it. Express regret, but don't whine about it. "I hate that I had to do it," he said aloud, sound-checking it. "But I had no choice. He was going to shotgun me and Joe Rob." Yeah. Sounded all right. And it was true. *But damn, I hate that it had to happen today, of all days. I should've postponed our date. But she was so insistent. Ah, stop it. Stop debating yourself. You're worse than a moony schoolboy.*

He turned up the volume and hummed along with the music. Then he was turning into her driveway and parking behind her Toyota. Sade was singing "Smooth Operator," and Luke chuckled to himself at the irony. A smooth operator he was not.

Ree came to the door of her modest brick house, a big smile on her lips and a red drink in her hand.

"I made it," said Luke, already wincing at his dumb remark. *Of course I made it, or I wouldn't be standing here saying something so dumb.* "I mean, you know, I didn't know if I was going to. Make it."

She laughed, took his hand and pulled him inside, then put the drink in his hand. "Here, I think you need this more than I do."

"Thanks," he muttered. He brought the cold glass to his lips and took a sip. "That's good. What is that?"

"Strawberry margarita, with a double-shot of tequila."

"Oh." He took another sip.

She smiled up at him.

"Tasty," he said.

She winked.

"Kinda sweet," he said.

She gave him a sweet smile.

"Say something, Shorty. I can't carry this conversation by myself."

She narrowed her eyes in mock anger. "I'm gonna let that one slide, but if you call me that again . . ."

"It's an affectionate thing," he said. "You know, a term of endearment."

"Nice try."

"Really. I mean it."

Ree suddenly leaned into him, taking his free hand in both of hers. His arm found its way between her breasts. "I know you do," she said. "Come on into the den and get comfortable."

She led him into the pine-paneled den furnished with restored antiques and a loveseat with plush upholstery, wine-colored and patterned with pink roses. "Have a seat," she said. "I'll be right back."

Luke settled in, sipping his margarita and staring at the dark screen of an old console TV. He was feeling better already. The tequila was rushing to his head, relaxing him and dulling the residue of emotion left by the shootout at the Jenkins place. Even when Ree was out of the room, he could feel the warmth of her presence. He let go and immersed himself in it. By the time she came back into the den, he had finished his drink and his mood had turned almost as rosy as the loveseat's upholstery. He watched her walking toward him, drinking in the graceful movement of her supple body and the tantalizing bounce of her abundant bosom.

"You look great," he said, shaking his head as if in awe.

"I wish." She sat beside him, holding her own drink in both hands.

"You do," he said. He rattled the ice cubes in his glass.

"I'm glad you think so. You need a refill. After one more of those, I'll probably *really* look good to you."

"You always look good," he said. "The booze just loosens my tongue enough so I can tell you."

"You're sweet," she said, then amended: "Sweet in a manly way."

"What's that wonderful smell coming from the kitchen?" he asked, deflecting attention from himself.

"Poppy seed chicken. It's my grandmother's recipe. I think you'll love it."

"My mouth's already watering."

"Give me your glass and I'll mix you another drink."

"Are you trying to get me drunk, young lady?"

"What if I am? You afraid I'll take advantage of you?"

He laughed. "No. I'm afraid you won't."

She took his glass. Gave him a look. "Have no fear."

Luke watched the provocative play of her buttocks beneath her thin cotton slacks as she walked back to the kitchen. For the first time since losing his wife, he found himself feeling real desire for a woman. That he felt it for a woman he really liked and respected only deepened the desire, adding the emotional dimension that could easily transform desire to love. He didn't know if he was ready for love, but right now he was in no mood for self-inventory. He was content to bask in Ree Tyler's sunny presence. And to let the proverbial chips fall where they would.

When they sat down to eat in the candlelit dining room, Ree was obviously as tipsy as he was, and her mood equally rosy. They drank white wine with the poppy seed chicken, cranberries, tossed salad and buttered crescent rolls, and by the end of the meal, the wine bottle was empty and they were both pretty soused. They had kept up the suggestive banter and playful innuendo, and Luke's desire was turning into out-and-out lust. He sensed that she was feeling the same thing.

She put a cigarette between her lips, leaned forward and drew fire from the candle flame. She inhaled deeply, then blew a stream of white smoke toward the ceiling. Luke's eyes were on her pursed lips and on her tongue that flicked out to moisten them. His long-dormant penis awakened, twisting slightly against his thigh.

"You never told me what you were doing at the police station," Ree said.

If she had thrown cold water on his crotch, it would've had the same effect on his fledgling arousal. "Ah, I don't want to get into that now. It's a definite downer. And I'm feeling too good."

"Oh, okay. We'll let that sleeping dog lie. But I do want you to feel like you can talk to me, you know, about *any*thing."

"Okay. Just not now."

She nodded. Took another puff on her smoke. "I have something I want *you* to know. It's not a downer, not really. But it's something I've never told anybody, and I feel like I should tell you so you'll know what you're getting yourself into . . . with me. I hope you won't think I'm crazy, but . . ."

"What?"

143

"Maybe I shouldn't."

"Don't tease."

"No, I just . . . Well, okay. But trust me, I'm not a nutcase."

"No, you're not."

Ree took another sip of wine and a draw on her cigarette, then said, "I have a guardian angel."

Luke looked at her with a blank face, waiting for her to elaborate.

"Do you believe in guardian angels?" She smiled self-consciously.

"I dunno. I never thought about it."

"I hadn't either, till one came to me."

Luke smiled.

"You're laughing at me," she said.

"No, no, I'm not. I just . . . it just made me smile. You're so cute."

"Cute? I'm trying to be serious here. I knew I shouldn't tell you."

"Come on, Shorty. I want you—"

She jabbed a finger at the air and said, "Ah-ah, don't call me that."

"Sorry. But I do want to hear about your angel. Honest."

She stabbed her cigarette out in the ashtray. "All right, but you'd better not laugh or I'll come over there and slap you silly."

"Fair enough," he said, trying not to smile.

"Okay." A look of displeasure came into her face. "I think I had too much to drink. I hope to God I don't embarrass myself too much."

"You can tell me anything," he said. "It won't change how I feel about you."

She pushed her plate aside, folded her arms across her chest and leaned her elbows on the table. "After Ben died, I got really depressed. So depressed I actually thought about killing myself. I was taking a lot of tranquilizers, but they didn't do anything but make me feel out of it all the time. It was like I was in a deep, dark hole and couldn't get out. I started thinking how good it would be just to take the whole bottle of pills and go to sleep forever. I knew suicide was a mortal sin—at least according to the Catholics—but I was so pissed off at God for taking Ben away from me, I just didn't give a damn. It was like, *screw God*, you know? I was really messed up. Then I decided to do it. To end it all. I closed the shop for what I thought would be the last time. It was just getting dark outside. I shut off the lights in the shop and headed for the door, and that's when he appeared. At first I thought I was seeing things, like my eyes playing tricks and all. But when I got closer to the mirror, he didn't go away."

Luke folded his fingers under his chin, listening closely but showing no reaction to her tale.

"He always appears in the mirror of the same antique vanity. The wood's so old, it's almost black. I had several offers, but I never could bring myself to sell that piece. Now I know why. When he started talking to me, I realized I'd always known he would show up. Like I'd been expecting him. See, we were lovers in a previous life. That's what he told me. He was killed in the Civil War. Anyway, Beau—that's his name—told me to stop taking the tranquilizers and to stop feeling sorry for myself. I knew he was right. That I would be okay if I followed his advice."

"And you don't think it was some kind of hallucination?"

"I really didn't think so, but I wasn't sure. Not until Beau saved my life again by telling me not to step in front of a car. I guess I was preoccupied that day, 'cause I didn't even see it coming as I stepped off the curb. But there was Beau—just his voice that time, I never see him except in the mirror in the shop. How can I not believe he's real, after he saved my life two times?"

"That's . . . really something," said Luke.

"You believe me? You don't think I'm out of my mind?"

"No. You're about the most down-to-earth person I know."

Ree reached for the brown sack containing her smokes, fished one out and lit it in the dancing flame of the candle. "There's more," she said, exhaling smoke. "It gets freakier. This is the part I'm sort of afraid to tell you."

"You don't need to be afraid. Not of what I may or may not think. You obviously want to tell me, or you wouldn't have brought it up. So go ahead. I can handle it."

"It gets weirder. And more personal. For you, I mean. For us."

He gave her a puzzled look. "Go on."

"Beau appeared again this afternoon. He said, 'Darkness is gathering,' and that I must be careful where you're concerned because the darkness may *gather* you. And me if I get too close to you."

Luke shook his head. "I don't get it. Your angel was talking about me?" She nodded.

"What does that mean? *Gather* me?"

"That's what I don't know. That's the way Beau talks, like an educated Southern gentleman of the eighteen hundreds. I asked him if he was trying to tell me I should stop seeing you, and he said he couldn't tell me that, that I should follow my heart."

He stared into her eyes, unsure of what to say. So he said nothing.

Ree said, "There's more. He said the darkness has made 'inroads' and that there is one who would open floodgates."

Luke shrugged. "That mean anything to you?"

145

"*No.* Not specifically. I suppose he's talking about evil. But I don't know. And when I asked him what he expected me to do, he said I should give up tobacco."

"*What?*"

"That's what he said. Then he faded away, like always. Maybe I *am* a nutcase. Hearing myself say all this out loud, I know I sound crazy as a loon. You're probably wondering how you can get the hell out of here before it rubs off on you."

Luke stared at his empty wine crystal, then said, "I had to kill a man today."

"Oh, my God."

"Fate Porch. He was going to shoot me with a shotgun. That's what I didn't want to talk about."

"Oh, Luke." Concern deepened the lines of her face.

"There was a shootout at the old Jenkins place."

"The haunted house?"

"When I got there, Joe Rob Campbell had already killed two of Fate's sons. Porch and his boys had kidnapped Skeeter Partain, cut his finger off and had him strung up on a chain in the barn. They used Skeeter to lure Joe Rob out there so they could kill him. Because Joe Rob had killed Odell Porch several days before."

"Holy . . ."

"I never killed a man before. I . . . I can't get it out of my mind. Well, I couldn't until tonight. With you, and the booze and all."

"But you had to do it," she said. "He would've killed you."

"I know. But it still makes me sick."

She reached across the table and held his hand. "Maybe this is what Beau was trying to tell me. Fate Porch could be the one who opened the floodgates."

"I don't know about that. But it's all over now. Porch and his boys are all dead. There's nobody left but the old lady. Fate's mother. And she's in the hospital."

"I'm so sorry, Luke. I can't even imagine how you must feel. But you shouldn't be too hard on yourself. You didn't do anything wrong. You're not in trouble with the law, are you?"

"No. I was working with the police. Keller knew I was trying to stop the whole thing from happening. We were just too late. That damn sinkhole on Main Street had Keller's people tied up. Almost like fate had a hand in it. Not Fate Porch. *Fate.* Like it was meant to happen the way it did."

"Maybe it was."

"Maybe. I don't know. But when you were telling me what your guardian angel said, about getting too close to me . . . and the darkness, it sort of clicked. Like it made sense in a way."

"What are you saying?"

"I dunno. That maybe you should stay away from me. That I'm not good for you." He shrugged, freed his hand from her grasp and leaned back in his chair. "You're too good . . . too pure to be with somebody with blood on his hands. You deserve better."

"That's crazy. I'm a long way from pure. I'm just your average sinner who happens to have an overprotective guardian angel. I'm *certainly not* too good for you, Luke Chaney. If anything, you're too good for me. I'm a middle-aged whack-o who sees ghosts in old mirrors. But you, you were the chief of police, an upstanding citizen. You risked your life trying to stop men from killing each other. I don't want to hear any more of this 'you're too good for me' crap. You hear?"

He tried to smile. "I hear. But I do feel . . . tainted. I don't want it to rub off on you. If darkness 'gathers' me, you might better keep your distance."

Ree stood up, glided around the table and wrapped her arms around his head and shoulders and crushed Luke's face to her bosom. "I'll do the gathering around here," she said. "And if Beau doesn't like it, he can stay the hell away from me."

Luke closed his eyes and gave himself to the comforting pillows of her breasts. He slipped his arms around her hips and rested his hands on her firm buttocks. She kissed the top of his head.

"I think I'm falling in love with you," she whispered. "Darkness be damned."

*   *   *

Agnes Porch set the vase of flowers down on the over-the-bed table and looked up at the chunky young man standing over her bed. Without her glasses, she couldn't make out the features of his face, but she knew him by his whining voice and his adenoidal breathing. Judy's boy, Delbert Hicks. Her only grandson still living. "I cain't stay but a minute," he said. "It's after visiting hours."

"Del, I need you to do something for me," she said. "Something real important."

"Name it, Granny," he said. "I'll do whatever you say."

"Shut that door."

Delbert crossed the room and closed the heavy door of her hospital room.

"Come close," she told him. "No other ears can hear this."

"Ain't nobody here but you and me."

"Mind me, Delbert."

"Yes ma'am." He came to the side of the bed and waited.

Agnes could smell his sweat-soured clothes and hear his noisy breathing. She took a shallow breath, then said, "You can't ever tell nobody any of this. You understand?"

"Yes'm."

"I want you to go out to our . . . to my place and get a shovel out of the barn. Then go out to the old well behind the house. You remember where that is. Then go about forty paces toward the woods and you'll come upon a willow tree sapling. About knee high. Dig it up. Keep digging till you find a gunnysack. Take the sack to the kitchen and get the biggest pot you can find and fill it with water and set it to boil. Here's where you'll need a strong stomach, Delbert. In the gunny sack you'll find a man's head."

"A *head*?"

"Damn you, boy. Not so loud. We can go to jail for this."

"Shit fire, Granny. I don't know if I—"

"Hush up and listen. Take the head and put it in the boiling water. Boil it till the skull is clean. If you have to do any scraping, take care you don't damage the skull. Put some bay leaves and garlic in the pot to make it smell like food's cooking."

"It's Monroe Shockley's head, ain't it?" Delbert said in an excited whisper. "God almighty."

"'Course it is. That's why you can't tell nobody about it. Not even your momma. You hear?"

"I hear."

"When you get it all cleaned up, put it in a clean pillow slip and hide it under my bed."

"You mean bring it *here*?"

"No, you ninny. Not here. My bed at home."

"Oh, yeah. All right."

"Whatever's left in the pot where you boiled it, dump it in the hole where you dug it up and cover it up good. Can you remember all that?"

"Yes ma'am. I don't reckon I could forget it now if I wanted to."

"Good boy. Now go on. I'm going home tomorrow, and I want it to be ready for me. You can do it early in the morning."

"What you gonna do with it?"

148

"I will have my vengeance," she said. Talking made the pain in her head worse, but the words had to come out. "I lost a son and three grandsons. You lost your grandpa and three cousins. You think them who did it don't have to pay restitution?" She licked her dry lips. "They'll pay in blood and suffering. The whole damn town will pay for the way they treated us. Mark my words, boy."

*   *   *

Corny slipped out the back door of the boarding house, the loose sole of his shoe slapping time to his shuffling gait. He always went out the back way at night because he didn't want anybody asking him where he was going. He didn't like it when people asked him questions. Questions made him feel dumb. Questions were supposed to have answers, but there just wasn't enough room in his head for answers to all those things people like to ask him about, things he didn't usually care about anyway. Questions were for people with normal brains, for thinkers and scholars. Not for somebody like Corny, whose brain was like a train running out there where the tracks didn't go. Where he was going now was to the Vinewood train yard, where the tracks all went somewhere.

He loved trains. Even before his accident he had loved them. Boxcars, flatcars, cabooses, the great and powerful engines—he loved them all. But those awesome locomotives were the best and the most mysterious. They had the power of dragons. *They pulled the train.* The engineers thought the power was theirs, but it was the big, sleek dragons that did the magic and made the trains fly all over the land. And sometimes the dragons broke free and really did fly. It was a flying dragon that killed Corny's dad. Big Bill Weehunt had been a railroad man all his working life, a brakeman with cinders in his blood and diesel fumes in his lungs. He'd once told his son that he had the best job in the world because they paid him to do what he loved most—ride the rails. Then on a cold night in December of '88, Big Bill was killed when the dragon flew off the rails and took the train down the side of a mountain. They called it a tragic derailment, but Corny knew it was the mechanical dragon trying to fly that killed his dad, and that Big Bill wouldn't have wanted to die any other way.

He shuffled across quiet streets where street lights were starting to come on, cut through yards without dogs, ducked through a hole in a chain-link fence, went up the back alley and gave wide berth to the sinkhole in Main Street. No way was he getting close to that hole again and to that hungry darkness. He rounded the corner where City Drugs flashed its electric signs, then crossed the gravel parking lot behind the line of stores on Main Street and followed the footpath down the rocky embankment to the train yard.

Otis Dellums was waiting for him at the edge of the yard. He was crouched like a toad, watching a switch-engine coupling a string of boxcars and digging his fingers into a small can of Vienna sausages and fishing one out and shoving the whole thing in his mouth.

"Don't ya ever get tired of them thangs?" asked Corny as he hunkered down beside his friend and scratched an itch in his armpit.

"Naw," said Otis, chewing with his mouth open and licking his fingers.

Corny reach over and pushed Otis's dirty ball cap down over his eyes.

"Don't you get tired of doing that?" Otis took off his hat and swatted Corny's knee with it.

"Naw," said Corny, grinning.

They both laughed. After a while, Corny said, "Be great to hop in one of them boxcars and go somewheres."

"Why don't cha?"

"You come with me?"

"Naw, I ain't goin' nowhere."

"Why not?"

Otis shook his large head. "Don't know where they goin'. Might be to a bad place. Might get caught, too."

"Somewhere where they ain't got them sausages."

"Hah." Otis ate the last one, then tossed the can away. "You ain't goin' nowhere. You just talk."

"Lots of men ride the rails. I could do it too."

"You ain't no hobo."

"No, but I could be."

Otis lifted one cheek and farted. Corny fanned his face. They both laughed. Corny said, "Wisht I *could* leave this town."

"Why's 'at?"

He shrugged. "Just wanna get away. Too many spooky thangs goin' on."

"You scared of that hole, ain't ya?"

"Not just that. Other thangs too."

"Like what?"

"Witches and such."

"What witches?"

"Aw, forgit it. I ain't hoppin' no train."

"Just talkin' out your hat," Otis said with a big, lopsided grin.

"You're fartin' out of yours."

150

They laughed, then started grappling with each other like playful pups. Though Otis was the bigger of the two, he was less coordinated, and Corny easily pinned him to the ground. Otis was no longer laughing. His eyes were big with fear. "Don't hurt me, Corny. I give."

"I ain't gone hurt you."

"Sometimes you do."

Corny got off him and fell back on the weedy ground. "That's different. This ain't like that. You ain't got to be scared of me."

"You busted my lip that time. Looky here." Otis pinched his lower lip to show the scar marking the place where Corny had kicked the can of sausages against his mouth. "Seeth?"

"Ain't gone let me forgit it, are ya?"

"Cain't forgit it. You did it, Corny."

"Ain't sayin' I didn't. I couldn't help it, though. Sometimes somethin' comes over me and makes me do bad things."

"'Cause o' you fallin' on your head?"

"That's right. Doctor said lots of people with head injuries fly into rages for no reason."

"Razors?"

"No. Rages. Like when you get real mad and hurt somebody. But I take medicine for it now, so you ain't got to worry."

"That's good."

A distant train whistle came out of the night and sent a chill up Corny's back. He stood, dusting off the seat of his britches, and said, "Here comes one. Let's get closer so we can get a good look at it when it pulls in."

Otis Dellums stood and followed his friend onto the train-yard grounds.

The train whistle sounded again, and its sad call was answered by incoherent whispering inside Corny's head. Whisperer was awake, but wasn't making any sense.

Corny, with Otis in tow, walked as close to the tracks as he dared. The ground shuddered with the approach of the train. He tried to tune out the confused whispers buzzing in his head like a nest of hornets. But Whisperer wouldn't shut up.

*   *   *

Joe Rob stretched out on the bunk, put his hands behind his head, stared up at the ceiling tiles and started counting the little holes in them. "I'm a fucking jailbird," he said to himself, then laughed. The laugh rang shrilly against the cinderblock walls of his cell, then escaped through the iron bars and echoed down the short hall to the main room of the station house, where the night-shift cop sat behind his desk. "Mookie fucking Vedders," Joe Rob said softly. "If he's such a hot-shit lawyer, how come I'm locked up in here?" Joe Rob wasn't in the habit of talking aloud to himself, but he was still wound up from the drugs and the adrenaline rush of the shootout. Besides, there was no one else to talk to in this cramped cell.

He couldn't really blame his lawyer, though. The county homicide cop had talked to the County D.A. and the D.A. had said, "Hold him overnight. I'll get back to you tomorrow." Vedders had explained that the D.A. was just doing his job, and that he had to give his investigators time to verify the facts of the case. "There's a good chance they could charge you with murder," the lawyer explained. "But I'm confident no jury would convict you, once the facts are know. You killed Odell Porch in self-defense while trying to prevent the rape of an escaped mental patient. You killed Odell's brothers in self-defense while you were trying to rescue Skeeter Partain. The physical evidence supports your story. We have the severed finger and the threatening note directing you to the scene of the shootout. You didn't go to the police because you feared Skeeter would be killed if you did. Your admitted drug use at the time of the shooting could be a problem. The lab results will show, as you said, that you were under the influence of cocaine and amphetamine, and that could go against you. It tarnishes your hero persona. People, juries in particular, like their heroes squeaky clean. So we'll have to try to turn the drug use to our advantage. I want to go ahead and try to get you into a drug treatment program. I think I can pull a few strings and get you into Browner's Hospital. It beats the hell out of the state facility and you'll be close to home."

Mookie Vedders was sharp, no doubt about it. Joe Rob liked the man's supreme confidence and self-assured manner. No, he couldn't really blame the lawyer for his incarceration. But that son of a bitch Luke Chaney had lied about not doing any jail time just to get Joe Rob to surrender his guns. The lying pussy. Washed-up cop. He did blow Fate Porch's shit away, though, so you couldn't call him chickenshit. *But I wanted to kill the old man myself. Except for Chaney, I would've pitched a perfect game and taken them all out myself. The dude spoiled my average.*

He closed his eyes so he wouldn't start counting the holes in the ceiling tiles again. Even though the caged light bulb in the ceiling washed the cell in harsh yellow light, Joe Rob felt himself surrounded by deep darkness.

And the darkness was soothing, nourishing.

In that fertile darkness, he began to plot his escape.

Ree snuggled against him and draped one leg over his thigh. Her breast flattened pleasantly against his chest, and he could feel the hard nipple poking him. The ceiling fan hummed softly above the bed, and the air moved languidly over their naked bodies. She moved her fingernails lightly over his belly, trailing them down, down toward his groin. His penis stirred against her gentle touch.

"Mmmm, I think it likes me," she said, wrapping her fingers around the semi-flaccid shaft and stroking its weeping head with her thumb.

"Didn't raise no fool," Luke said, then kissed her forehead.

She giggled. "Certainly not. And I think it's raising its cute little head again."

"I'm not surprised."

"Oh, Luke, this is even better than I dreamed it would be. Please tell me it doesn't have to end."

"It doesn't have to end."

"You're not just saying that so you can keep me in the sack?"

"No. I don't want it to end. Unless some jealous ghost comes between us, we can just go on and on."

"You mean Beau? No chance. That was in another life. I like my men flesh and blood." She squeezed his swelling penis for emphasis. "I don't think a guardian angel's duties extend to the bedroom."

Luke was thinking of Jenny as a jealous ghost, but he didn't voice his thought. Now was not the time to bring up his deceased wife. Ree gave him another squeeze, and Jenny left his thoughts like smoke on a stiff breeze.

She climbed on top of him, straddling his loins with her thighs, then arched her back and guided him into her. They were both still slick from the first bout of lovemaking, and he went in with ease. He caressed her breasts while she rode him, slowly at first, then faster and faster. She threw her head back and braced her hands behind her on his knees without disturbing the rhythm of her ride.

Luke lay still as she glided up and down his shaft, savoring the glove-tight fit of their genitals and thinking he didn't deserve such ecstasy. It was too good to be true. How could something so wonderful exist in a world of pain, sorrow, violence and degradation? Unbidden images of bleeding gunshot wounds and dead flesh jarred him and he started to lose his erection. He shook his head as if to dispel the grisly images. He opened his eyes and watched Ree's fevered movements as she rode him. Light from a single candle illuminated her jiggling breasts and the ecstatic expression on her face. Forgetting himself, he concentrated on his partner. Her unrestrained passion rekindled sympathetic passions within him, and his erection reasserted itself. He began to move with her, thrusting upward each time she came down. Their pace became frenzied, and Luke could feel her building to climax. She threw herself forward, crushing her breasts against his chest and hugging him tightly as her pelvis pumped and thrust against him, taking him still deeper. He let himself go and completely gave in to the moment. They came together, crying out in harsh harmony. Unlike their first time, this orgasm went on and on, extended in time and rich in blissful release.

When she caught her breath and could speak again, Ree said, "Praise God, that was good."

Luke, chuckling, said, "Tell the truth and shame the devil."

After a while, Ree rolled off him and fell asleep by his side. He drifted into sleep with the sound of her feathery breathing in his ear.

He slept the night through.

CHAPTER 22
BLEAK MORNING

S keeter was finishing his breakfast when the detective came to question him. The man's name was Batty, and he seemed easy-going for a homicide cop. His hair was gray at the temples but the rest of his buzz-cut hair was black. "How do you like hospital food?" Batty asked, pulling the chair up to the edge of the bed and sitting down.

"It's not too bad. I guess I was pretty hungry."

The detective smiled. "When I was your age, I'd eat anything they put in front of me, then ask for seconds."

Skeeter laughed, being polite. The windows were glowing with the gray light of a dismal morning. The weatherman on the TV was predicting a stormy afternoon.

"Mind turning that off?" Batty said, nodding toward the TV.

Skeeter used the remote and killed the picture.

"Your friend Joe Rob has told me his side of things, and now it's your turn. Now I like things told from the beginning, so I can see what comes later in light of what went before. Things generally make more sense that way. So I want you to start with what happened out at the dump the day Odell Porch was killed. I want to know what you heard and what you saw. The truth and nothing but. Now I know you and the Campbell boy had time to get your stories straight, but if you lie to me, you could find yourself in serious trouble. You understand me?"

"Yes sir." Skeeter scratched at the bandage on his thigh. "Where's Joe Rob now?"

"He's in custody for the time being. That's not your worry right now. You just concentrate on telling me the truth of what happened." Batty pulled out a black notebook and clicked his ballpoint pen. "Shoot," he said.

Skeeter told him. He started with their encounter with Odell, and ended thirty minutes later with the confrontation between Joe Rob and Luke Chaney, after the Porch men were all dead. He told the truth, making sure the detective understood that Fate Porch and his boys were bent on killing him and Joe Rob. "I guess we should've gone to the police after Odell was killed," he concluded, "but we knew the Porches would come after us when they found out what happened. That's the kind of people they are. *Were*. We knew they'd try to kill us."

Batty flipped his notebook shut and stuffed it in his pocket. "All right, son. You did good."

"Am I in trouble?"

"That's not up to me. The District Attorney will go over all the facts, then decide whether or not to prosecute. But based on what you told me, I don't think you're in deep do-do. Maybe just in up to your knees."

"Whew," said Skeeter, "that's good to hear. What about Joe Rob?"

"I'd say he's in up to his neck. But he's got a good lawyer, and he'll likely have public opinion in his favor. After all, he risked his life to save his friend. Even if he did go about it the wrong way."

"Wasn't for him, I wouldn't be here now," said Skeeter.

Detective Batty stood. "When they gonna turn you loose?"

"Later today. I think they want to give me some more IV antibiotics."

Batty nodded, moving toward the door. "Take care of yourself. And stay out of trouble. We'll be in touch."

"Yes sir, I will."

Skeeter turned the TV back on and caught the morning news from a Savannah station. The blond newswoman said, "In a Wild-West style shootout near Vinewood, Georgia, three men were shot and killed yesterday, and another man was injured. One man is in custody. No names have been released yet."

"Holy shit," Skeeter said. "We're gonna be famous."

*   *   *

Luke stopped at the nurses' station and asked what room Agnes Porch was in. Though visiting hours didn't begin till noon, the nurse allowed Luke to visit. Being the former police chief had its perks. He knocked on the door of room 106, then entered.

Agnes Porch was sitting up in bed, pinning her braided hair on top of her head in concentric circles that resembled a lusterless gray crown. "Who's there?" she said. She was without glasses and obviously couldn't see well.

"It's Luke Chaney, Miz Porch." He stepped closer to the bed. "I just wanted to come by and tell you how sorry I am things turned out the way they did. I tried to stop it, but I got there too late."

"Cain't *un*sour milk, Luke Chaney."

"No ma'am."

"It was you found me, wasn't it?"

"That's right."

"Seemed like a dream. Bumped my head purdy good. Broke my glasses too."

"They told you . . . what happened?"

"They finally got around to telling me my boys are all dead. That one what killed 'em must be a sure-fire hellion."

"The Campbell boy didn't kill Fate," Luke said. His voice sounded hollow in his ears.

"Who did?" she snapped.

"I did."

"They Lord, you did."

"Yes ma'am. He didn't give me a choice. He was coming at me with a shotgun. He would've killed us both. I told him to throw down his gun, but he wouldn't. He was already wounded. I think maybe he wanted to die."

The old woman stared at him with weak, murky eyes.

"I'm sorry it had to happen that way. If there's anything I can do to help you in some way . . ."

"Ain't nothing you can do for me," she spat. "Ain't nothing nobody in this goddamn town can do for me. We take care of our own. I reckon things will be set right directly."

Luke had nothing to say to this. His hangover from last night's wine and tequila suddenly spawned a throbbing pain behind his eyes, and he felt a twinge of nausea.

"You best make your peace with the Lord, Luke Chaney," the old woman said. "And leave me the hell alone."

He left the room and closed the door softly behind him. He hadn't expected to feel so much guilt for killing a man out of necessity, a man who had *needed* killing, but he did feel the weight of it, and it conferred upon him a raw sympathy for Agnes Porch.

He left the hospital and walked out into the dreary morning. The trees in front of the building were dead still in the breathless, humid air. He glanced up at the overcast sky, then climbed into his truck and started the engine. He had to see Ree again. He would go to her shop and offer to take her across the street for coffee in the Vinewood Cafe. He wanted reassurance that last night had been more than a wonderful dream.

His headache backed off as soon as he pulled away from the hospital.

Even though he was slightly hungover, he felt remarkably good. After the vigorous lovemaking, he'd slept the night through, not waking till Ree's clock radio came on playing a country & western song. He smiled to himself, marveling at his discovery of a cure for his insomnia. He could've slept longer, and in fact, he had been reluctant to leave her bed at all, but she had to get up and get downtown to open the shop. She did her best business on Saturdays and couldn't afford to be late. Luke had declined her offer of breakfast, and had gone home to take a shower and change clothes before his visit to the hospital.

He drove into town, found a parking space close to Ree's antique shop and was climbing out of the truck when he saw the "Closed" sign hanging in the shop's glass door. Had he gotten to the shop before her? Or had Ree simply forgotten to turn the sign around? She'd had as much to drink last night as he had, so it wouldn't be surprising if her own hangover had left her a little muddle-minded and forgetful. He stepped onto the sidewalk and approached the shop's door. He tried the knob. The door was locked. A glance at his watch told him it was quarter past ten. She usually opened the shop at nine on Saturday mornings.

He rapped his knuckles on the glass door, then peered inside. All he saw was assorted pieces of antique furniture and various housewares and knick-knacks from bygone eras. Looking at an old vanity's cloudy mirror, he remembered her guardian angel, Beau, and wondered if the ghost had done something to her in a fit of jealousy, then immediately chastised himself for thinking something so ridiculous. He didn't even believe in ghosts. If Ree needed to believe she had a guardian angel on her shoulder, that was her business and he had no right to try and talk her out of the notion, but why was *he* suddenly thinking along those same superstitious lines? Luke thought: *Lord forbid. Last thing we need are ghosts hanging around, mucking up things for the living.* He shook his head at the thought of being haunted by Fate Porch, then he saw the haggard face of Fate's mother leering at him and telling him to get right with God. Even if, as some said, Agnes Porch was a witch or some sort of voodoo queen, she couldn't have any power over Luke, because he didn't believe in any of that nonsense. As long as you didn't believe it, it couldn't touch you. But if you were foolish enough to fall for such bull hockey, then all bets were off.

Luke looked around, noting the sparse traffic and dearth of pedestrians. Unusual for a Saturday, but then folks were probably afraid to come downtown because of the damned sinkhole. And who could blame them. Keller had told him last night that Mr. Peters had arranged for an engineering geologist from Atlanta to come and find out just how extensive the sinkhole actually was. Until they knew, everyone downtown would be wondering just how firm the ground under their feet was, and Main Street merchants would lose customers to the area malls and outlying businesses.

Luke walked down the street and around the corner to City Drugs. He craved a second cup of coffee, and Doc Taggert was not one to refuse an impromptu coffee break and an opportunity to chew the fat with an old friend.

Doc was in his elevated glass cage, counting pills. He acknowledged Luke with a nod and an arched brow, finished his count, then exited his exalted lair through its side door and joined Luke in their usual booth near the lunch counter. The smell of frying bacon and pancakes on the griddle made Luke's stomach growl, though he didn't feel up to solid food just yet. A couple of people were seated at the counter and two other booths were occupied with diners whose hunger was apparently stronger than their fear of being swallowed by the sinkhole.

Looking officiously debonair in his starched blue smock, Doc caught Betty Lee's attention and held up two fingers, signaling that he wanted two coffees post-haste.

"So you finally got him," Doc said. His voice and inflection reminded Luke of Walter Cronkite reporting the news.

Luke said, "Yeah. But not the way I wanted to get him."

"He was really going to shoot you, huh?"

"No doubt about it. It was him or me. He was already wounded and I think he was ready to die, but he was hoping to take me with him."

"That sounds like the Fate Porch we all knew and loved," Doc said with a nod.

"Yeah. I just came from the hospital. I had to tell Agnes Porch it's was me who killed her son."

"Ah, and was the confession good for your soul?"

"No. I didn't expect it would be. It was just something I had to do. I wanted her to hear it from me. I was trying to stop the whole damn thing from happening, but I was too late. She knows that. Not that it makes a damn bit of difference to her."

"No, of course not."

Luke looked down at the table. "I think she's probably gonna do some backwoods voodoo on me."

"What?"

"She said things would be set right directly and told me I'd best make my peace with the Lord."

Doc shook his head. "She's a senile old woman. Surely you aren't really worried about a voodoo curse."

"No, I'm not. But she's not senile. She's too full of hate to be feebleminded. I hope I'm as sharp as she is if I make it to *my* nineties."

Betty Lee set two mugs of coffee down in front of them. "There ya go, gentlemen," she said with a lipstick smile. "Drink it in good health."

"Thanks, Betty," said Luke.

She breezed away to tend to one of the other booths. Luke watched her rounded backside moving against her close-fitting blue skirt and thought of Ree's sweet, supple cheeks. He pictured her above him, her breasts inches from his face, nipples erect and aureoles as big as silver dollars.

"Tell me about the Campbell boy," said Doc, bringing Luke out of his brief sexual reverie. "They say he was hell on wheels."

"Our law officers shouldn't be saying a damn thing about it. I shouldn't either. But he was something, all right. When I got there, he had a gun in each fist, blasting away at Luther Porch, who was already down. He was like a mad-dog gunslinger out of the Old West. He'd already shot and killed the younger brother and wounded Fate with a shotgun. How he came out of it unscathed, I don't know."

"You think they'll file charges against the boy?"

"Hell, Doc, I don't see how they have a choice. Joe Rob went there armed to the teeth with the intention of killing them. He told me that himself before he went out there. Called me at home to tell me."

"But he saved Skeeter Partain. People are already saying he's a hero."

"And Mookie Vedders is representing him. Ol' Mookie'll have the jury recommending the boy for a medal."

"Wouldn't surprise me," said Doc, sipping coffee, then wiping some from his mustache. "Hell, I'm not sure myself he shouldn't get one. Boy's got guts."

"Something about the boy spooks me. I'm not sure he's right in the head."

"How do you mean?"

Luke shrugged. "He's not the All-American clean-cut football jock he used to be—if he ever was. There's something dark in him. Something hiding in the darkness. I can't explain it, really. But when you look into his eyes, you're not sure what's in there looking out at you. But you know you don't want it to come out."

"Interesting." Doc steepled his hands in front of his face. "You doing okay, Luke? With what you had to do?"

"Killing Fate? I wish I hadn't had to do it, but I did. You play the hand you're dealt, you know? No sense in dwelling on it. It bothers the hell out of me now, but I guess I'll get over it."

"You do that, Luke. I mean it. I know how you take things to heart sometimes. And believe me, this is not anything you want to take to heart. The quicker you put it behind you, the better off you'll be."

"You know," Luke said with a smile, "I really do think you missed your calling. You shoulda been a headshrinker. You would've made a damn good one."

"No way. I couldn't stand to listen to other peoples' problems all day, every day. I get enough of that just hearing the complaints of patients getting their prescriptions filled. Lord God, but folks love to talk about their ailments. Just about runs me crazy as it is."

"Just the same, I thank you for dispensing sound advice. You're a true friend."

"Don't you get maudlin on me," Doc said, feigning irritation.

"Hell, Doc, I don't even know the meaning of the word." Luke grinned.

Doc chuckled, his eyes twinkling with devilment. "It means lachrymose, mawkish"

"Uh huh." Luke deadpanned him.

"Sentimental, mushy."

"Every so often you just have to whip it out and dust it off, don't you? That highfalutin vocabulary of yours."

"Use it or lose it," said Doc.

Luke couldn't keep the big smile from his face as he once again remembered last night's romp with Ree. "Amen to that," he said.

"Luke, you old devil, are you trying to tell me you—"

He held up his hand like a traffic cop stopping traffic. "A gentleman doesn't discuss such things."

"Well, I'll be damned. You *are* human after all."

"More or less."

"Maybe now you'll be a little less ornery." Doc fiddled with his mustache like a sideshow barker.

"Don't count on it."

They finished their coffee. Doc returned to his post, and Luke headed back to the antique shop, his mood considerably brighter than the gloomy morning. Ree's shop was still closed. Where the hell was she? With growing apprehension, he got into his truck and headed for her house.

* * *

"Cornelius? You sick, son?" Aunt Mattie's shrill voice was like an ice pick hammered into his skull. "It's nearly ten o'clock and you're still in bed."

Corny pushed the pillow off his head and opened his eyes. The curtained window of his room was glowing with weak, gray light. "I ain't sick," he mumbled, blinking his eyes at the pale glare.

"Well, don't forget you've got to clean out the gutters today. You sure you're all right?"

"Yes ma'am. I'm just tired is all. Durn nightmares kept me awake."

"If you were having nightmares, you couldn't have been awake."

He didn't feel like arguing with her, telling her that, yes, he *could* have wide-awake nightmares. He just didn't have the energy to set her straight. He yawned, making his ears pop.

"You missed breakfast," his aunt said, "but you can have a bowl of cereal before you get started on the gutters. Weatherman says we're in for some hard rain this afternoon, so you've got to get the gutters done before the deluge."

"Day-looj," Corny echoed. It was one of those words Aunt Mattie got from the Bible, he was pretty sure. One that would stick in his head all day and repeat itself over and over, no matter how sick of hearing it he might get. And if Whisperer took a liking to it and started repeating it, he would be deluged to death by the end of the day—not *really* dead but worn out with the word. Some words were like that.

She picked up a pair of jeans off the floor, folded them and draped them over the back of a chair. "I've got to do my grocery shopping," she told him, "so I won't be here when you get up on the roof, but Mr. Jones said he'll keep an eye on you. You just let him know when you're fixing to go up the ladder."

"Yes ma'am." He knew his aunt always worried about him whenever he had to climb a ladder, but Corny didn't see that there was any reason to worry. Just because he'd fallen off a ladder that one time didn't mean he would fall again. The parts of his brain that were damaged affected some of his thinking and his memory, but there was nothing wrong with his sense of balance. He'd been up on ladders dozens of times since the accident and he'd never fallen again. If he wasn't scared, why should his aunt be? He liked climbing. Always had. He'd been climbing trees for almost as long as he'd been walking. His dad had said he was a natural-born climber. And he especially liked getting up on the roof of the two-story boarding house. From up there you could see things you couldn't see when you were down on the ground. Everything looked different when you were way up there, looking down. Cars passing on the street looked like big wind-up toys, and the other houses on the block didn't seem so big or fancy. A lot of folks looked down on Corny and treated him like a retard, but when he was up on the roof or high in a tree, *he* was the one looking down, seeing things in a way other folks didn't. And when he was way up high, nobody could look down on him. If it sometimes got a little scary being up there, it was worth it.

Aunt Mattie left the room and Corny rolled out of bed and got dressed. He put on his oldest pair of jeans and a faded blue T-shirt, then he slipped his feet into his good pair of sneakers because you needed good traction when you were up on the slanting roof.

While he ate a bowl of corn flakes at the kitchen table, he tried to remember the nightmares that had disturbed his sleep last night. All he could remember was moving through thick darkness, trying to find his way home. He thought something had been chasing him through the dark, but he wasn't sure. All he knew for sure was that he'd been afraid something bad was going to catch him. If Whisperer knew what the dream was about, Whisperer wasn't saying. He hadn't heard a peep out of Whisperer since last night at the train yard.

"Good morning, Cornelius." The deep voice startled him and he dropped his spoon and looked up at the tall, thin man with the piercing blue eyes.

"Morning," he said to Rufus Tilley, the book writer from Atlanta.

"You know where your aunt keeps the coffee?"

Corny pointed at the cupboard containing the big canister of coffee.

"Thanks," said Mr. Tilley. "I've got my own coffee machine, but I ran out of coffee. I have to have my caffeine to get anything written, I'm afraid."

Corny was naturally curious about this man who kept to himself and never had much to say to others. He asked, "You really writing a book?"

"Yes, I really am." The man smiled. Corny didn't get the feeling that Rufus Tilley was looking down on him or seeing a retard with those smart blue eyes.

"What's it about?" he asked, hoping he wasn't being too nosy.

"Well, it's about murder in Graves County. It's fiction, but it has a lot of truth in it. You understand that?"

Corny nodded. "I met a writer one time. Over in Manchester. He was signing his books for people. I got one up in my room. It's a history book about railroads, but it's got lots of good pictures of trains in it. You wanna see it?"

"Maybe later. I'm pretty busy with my writing right now." Tilley opened the canister of coffee and poured some of the fresh grounds into a cup.

"You like trains, do you?"

"Yessir, I love trains. My daddy was a railroad man. Till he got killed. I was gonna work for the railroad too, but I had that accident and they didn't want me after that."

"That's too bad. But you're still a railroad man in your heart, aren't you?"

Corny thought about that for a moment, then grinned and said, "I reckon I am."

"What matters is what a man is in his heart," said Rufus Tilley. "That's more important than what he does for money. It's what he is that counts."

Corny nodded. His eyes watered a little at the truth of what the man had said. He wiped a tear from the corner of his left eye and looked down at his soggy corn flakes.

"Well, I'll see you later, Cornelius. Tell your aunt I'll replace the coffee I borrowed."

"Okay. Uh, what's the name of your book?"

"I'm calling it *Bloody Graves*. Because the county has a long history of violence."

Way in the back of Corny's head, Whisperer hissed: *Bloody Graves.*

Corny shuddered as though a window had been thrown open upon a winter day. The room darkened around its edges.

*   *   *

The doctor wrote the discharge order after seeing her early that morning, and Agnes was on her way home by ten-thirty. Delbert was driving her in his rattletrap old Ford, and judging by the way the boy smelled, he'd already worked up a good sweat this morning.

"You do what I told you?" she asked him.

"Yes ma'am. I was boiling the water when Momma called me at your place and told me to come get you."

"Humph. Your momma was too drunk to come get me herself. She thinks I don't know but I do. I could hear it in her voice. Don't you ever start drinking or you'll end up just like her."

"No ma'am. I won't."

"You put the head on to boil before you left?"

"I sure did. I don't think I'll be able to eat for a week after that. Just about made me sick."

"Won't hurt you none to miss a few meals."

He lit a cigarette, then turned on the radio and found a Willie Nelson song.

"Turn that off," she said. "I cain't have my head cluttered up with such as that. I have to be clearheaded to do what I'm gonna do."

"What *are* you gonna do, Grandma?"

"Never you mind about that. But when I start, you best be gone. I never done it before and I ain't sure how it will go. They's a chance it could blow back on me, and on you if you're close by."

"You gonna do some hoodoo, ain't ya?"

She scowled at him, but his eyes were on the road ahead.

Delbert was in a talkative mood. He said, "I tell you what's the truth, I don't get how that one peckerwood got the drop on Fate and them. I woulda said he was ate up with the dumbass to even try it. How in the world—"

"Two," she said sharply. "They was two of 'em. Luke Chaney's the one killed Fate. Told me so hisself."

"That sumbitch . . ."

"Said he tried to stop it, but everybody knows he's been looking to get Fate for the longest. He'll reap what he sowed. No two ways about it."

"I sure hope so. I'll kill him my own self, come to that."

"No. You stay out of this." She sighed, touching the knot on her forehead. "Now hush up and let me meditate. Plenty of time for jaw-jacking later."

Delbert was quiet for the rest of the ride but when his grandmother's house came into view, he said, "Damn! Oh shit!"

Unable to see much without her glasses, Agnes said, "What is it?"

"Police car's parked in front of the house. What if they find the head cooking? Oh, Jesus, what do we do now?"

"Just go on about your business. They won't find it. And if they do, we don't know nothing about it. We ain't even been here. You hear?"

"Yes'm. But when they see the water boiling, they'll know somebody's been here today."

"Let me do the talking. You just keep your mouth shut. Where are they? You see 'em?"

"Two of 'em just sitting in the car. Like they're waiting for us."

"Good. Then maybe they ain't seen nothing yet. You just pull up in front of the house and help me up the steps. And keep quiet."

Before she was even out of the car, the two policemen approached her, one of them saying, "How do, Miz Porch. Sorry to trouble you at a time like this, but—"

"Then don't," she snapped, getting to her feet and staring at the blurred khaki-colored shapes in front of her. "Doctor says I'm not to be disturbed. And here you are already disturbing me before I can even get to my front door."

"Sorry, ma'am, but we're still looking for . . . Odell. His remains."

"Odell ain't lost."

"You know where he is?" The lawman's voice was deep, yet gentle.

"Yes, I do. He's laid out in his bed. We was going to have a ceremony for him today. But since y'all killed the rest of my family, I reckon there won't be no ceremony."

"No ma'am, we didn't kill anybody. What we'll have to do is get the coroner out here to collect the body, then he'll turn the remains over to whichever funeral home you want and the family can make the arrangements for a proper funeral."

"Too late for that. My boy Fate already embalmed him. He used to be a mortician and he used that old embalming rig he hung onto." In truth, Fate hadn't been a mortician, but he'd worked in a funeral home and learned how to flush out the blood with the preserving fluid. But the cops didn't need to know that.

"Is that right?" said the lawman with the deep voice.

Delbert was at her elbow, breathing heavily but supporting her weight. "Do what you got to," she said. "Then get off my land. You ain't welcome here. And don't go snooping around 'less you got a search warrant. This family's been violated enough by you town folks."

Del escorted her upstairs to her bedroom where she found her extra pair of glasses and put them on. It was good to be able to see again, though the bifocals put pressure on the bruised bridge of her nose. She sat on the edge of her bed. "Nothing to do now but wait till they get Odell and clear out of here," she said. "Then you can go home and I can get down to business."

"What you want me to do in the meantime?" asked Delbert.

"Nothing. Just stay here with me and keep quiet. If them cops find that head a' boiling, we'll be in a real bad fix. Without the head of a conquered foe, I cain't do my conjurin'."

* * *

Joe Rob couldn't get his mind straight. When he tried to hold a thought in his head, it seemed to swirl away like windblown smoke. He was groggy and he wondered if his jailors had slipped drugs in his food or drink. The cement walls and iron bars of his cell oppressed him, mocked him with harsh yellow light. It wasn't supposed to be like this. Somehow he'd lost something of himself in the dark chamber of sleep. He was a soulless zombie in the waking world, and the core of his being was still back there, lost in the darkness, lying dormant. The confinement was slowly killing him. He had to get out, but his plan for escape hadn't jelled. He was at the mercy of his captors and that galled him.

He'd only picked at the scrambled eggs, greasy bacon and burnt toast they'd served him and passed on the coffee. If they were going to drug him some more, they'd have to come out in the open with it.

His lawyer visited him mid-morning. Mookie Vedders told him that the county prosecutor was going to file charges against him. Two counts of murder in the first degree. "As of now, it looks like they aren't going to charge you with a capital crime in the death of Odell Porch," said Vedders. "Skeeter backed up your claim of self-defense, so we can concentrate on defending against the two murder counts. All in all, I think we're in pretty good shape. I'm working on having you transferred to Browner's for emergency treatment of drug abuse and for a complete psych evaluation. The hospital will be a lot better than languishing in jail."

Joe Rob stared at the floor.

"You hear what I just said?"

He nodded.

"Are you all right, Joe Rob?"

"I don't know. I don't feel right. Guess I crashed pretty hard last night."

"You want me to get a doctor to see you?"

He shrugged. "I don't think it's anything a doctor can fix."

"I'm going to have Dr. Jackson see you. That all right with you?"

He leaned his back against the wall behind the bunk. "Don't matter."

*   *   *

Ree Tyler came to the door and tried to smile when she saw Luke, but the tears in her eyes betrayed her inner turmoil.

"What's wrong?" he asked, stepping through the front door of her house.

"I don't know. I . . . I saw something . . ."

"Saw what?"

"Oh, it's probably nothing. Just a case of the middle-age crazies."

"What are you talking about?"

"Come on in the kitchen. I'll make some more coffee."

He followed her to the kitchen. "I went by the shop and you weren't there," he said. "I thought maybe something was wrong."

She busied herself with the coffeemaker. "Would it scare you off if I told you I sometimes have visions?"

"You couldn't beat me off with a stick."

She forced a laugh. "It's true. It's only happened once before, and it scared the hell out of me then, too."

He sat at the kitchen table. "What did you see?"

She sat opposite him. The coffee machine began to make gurgling sounds.

"The first time was six years ago. I was wide awake, so I know it wasn't a dream. Ben was at work and I stayed home that day with a bad cold and a fever. I was sitting in the den, drinking hot tea and all of a sudden these horrible images started coming to me. At first I thought I was hallucinating because of the fever, even though my temperature was just barely over a hundred. I closed my eyes and waited for the images to go away, but they didn't. They got more . . . intense. And more frightening. I saw a man with a knife lurking in some bushes and he was watching a woman in a green jogging suit running toward him. I knew he meant to kill her. And there was nothing I could do to stop it. I was just an observer. I was there but not really *there*. Like watching a movie. But I knew this was no movie. I had to watch as he jumped out of the bushes and took her down and stabbed her over and over. All the blood. The terror in the poor girl's face. It was so intense! He killed her and I watched her die. Then he ripped off her clothes and raped her. And I knew that's why he killed her. So he could have sex with her after she was dead. When he was done, he cut off her nipples and I saw the tattoo on the back of his hand. A devil's head in blue ink. Then the images faded away. I couldn't stop shaking for an hour. I didn't know what to make of it. Nothing like that had ever happened to me before. But I couldn't get rid of the feeling that it hadn't happened yet, that it was going to happen in the near future. I told Ben about it when he got home that evening, and he just pooh-poohed it and said it must've been like a fever dream or something. I'd just about convinced myself he was right till I saw on the news the next week that a woman jogger had been stabbed to death on a jogging trail near Kennesaw, Georgia."

"Jesus," said Luke. "That's spooky as hell."

"That's not all. It gets spookier. Against Ben's wishes, I called the Cobb County Police and told a detective what I'd seen in my vision and described the tattoo and the knife—it was a big buck knife—and he thanked me very much and blew me off. Then the following week, he called me back and told me they had a suspect in custody that had just confessed to the murder and *that he had a blue-devil tattoo on his right hand*. The detective said he'd never put much stock in psychic phenomena before but that I'd made a believer out of him."

Luke felt goose bumps crawl up the back of his neck. "Okay. That was six years ago. What happened this morning?"

Ree took a cigarette from her little brown bag and lit it with a green lighter. She blew a bluish cloud of smoke toward the ceiling. "I was putting on my makeup and having a second cup of coffee when it happened again. This time, I recognized the location." She trembled and looked at Luke with pleading eyes. "My shop. I saw myself . . . hacked with a machete." She covered her face with her hands and shook, sobbing soundlessly.

"Easy now," Luke said as gently as he knew how. "We won't let anything happen to you." He took the cigarette from between her fingers and set it in the ashtray, then watched the smoke curling up as Ree cried herself out.

She removed her hands from her face and said, "I'm sorry. I didn't mean to put on such a show."

"You needed to get it out. Did you see who it was?"

She shook her head. "I couldn't see his face. It was like I was looking over his shoulder while he was attacking me. He was naked. He seemed familiar, but I can't say who it was. It was eerie as hell. Like I was out of my body, watching what was happening to me. I couldn't feel the knife blade going in, not physically, but . . . I don't know . . . it was like I could feel it in my soul. It was horrible."

Luke remembered her guardian angel's warning to her that darkness would *gather* him, and her too, if she got too close. His imagination supplied an unwanted image of himself with a blade, attacking Ree. Preposterous, he told himself. No way in the world could that ever happen. But then why did he just now picture it?

"What?" she asked when she noted his expression. "What are you thinking?"

"Nothing, really. I was just remembering Beau's warning about me."

"Don't even think it. It wasn't you, silly. You couldn't . . ."

"No, I couldn't. But if I had enemies who wanted to get at me through you . . ."

"Do you have enemies? Who would go that far to hurt you?"

"Not that I know of. No one but old lady Porch, and I can't see her going at somebody with a machete. She's got relatives in Vidalia, but none with *cojones* that big. And anyway, nobody knows about us."

"Not yet. But they will."

"Maybe we shouldn't see each other. For a while."

"Luke, I'm not going to stop seeing you because of a stupid vision. I'll stop going to the shop before I do that."

"Could you afford to close up shop for a few weeks?"

She picked up the cigarette and took a puff. "Not really. I don't make a lot of profit, but without the income, I couldn't afford the overhead."

"Is there somebody you could get to run it for you for a while? At minimum wage?"

"No one I can think of." She ground out her smoke. "We shouldn't overreact to this. I'll just have to be—"

"I could do it. Run the shop for you. Why not? I'm retired, remember? An old fart with time on his hands."

"You would do that for me?" Her eyes softened, shining with emotion.

"I'd do most anything for you, Shorty."

"I love you, Luke." She reached across the kitchen table and took both his hands in hers. "I really do."

"Me too," he said.

She made a sound that could've been either a laugh or a sob. She stood and leaned across the table and kissed his lips. "I didn't know I could be this happy ever again."

"Me either," he said.

"Nothing can hurt me when I'm with you. We could work together in the shop. I'll teach you all about the antique business. It'll be fun."

"Fun," Luke said, smiling. He was touched by her childlike enthusiasm and was glad to see her suddenly so happy, but something—his innate pessimism?—told him that fun was not in the cards.

Thunder rolled and tumbled in from the west. A sixth sense of his own intimated that the immediate future was going to be as bleak as the dreary sky he saw through the kitchen window.

CHAPTER 23
INVOCATION

The thunderclap rattled the aluminum ladder Corny was standing on and made his heart leap for his throat. He grabbed hold of the rung in front of his face and held tight until the dizzying fear of falling passed.

"Lord, don't let me get struck by lightning," he petitioned the great bearded Father who ruled heaven and earth and tossed down lightning bolts the way kids chucked rocks. "I got to finish cleaning out these gutters or Aunt Mattie'll skin me for sure."

With a wary glance to the cloud-dark sky, he continued his climb and stopped when he reached the corrugated gutter running the length of the side of the house. He'd already cleaned the pine straw, dirt and leaves from the other gutters affixed to the eaves of the roof, and he knew he couldn't quit until the job was done. He still remembered the two Golden Rules his father had drilled into him as a boy: "A place for everything, and everything in its place," and "If you do a job, do it right. A half-assed job ain't no job atall." Corny didn't know if it was true that the dead watched over the living, the way some folks said, but if Big Bill Weehunt *was* keeping an eye on him, he didn't want to disappoint the old railroad man, so he had to clean out this last stretch of gutter before the storm hit.

"Hey, Cornelius?" a voice called from a window below and to his right, and just for a piece of a second he thought Whisperer was actually calling his name, but then he realized it was Mr. Jones calling out to him from his bedroom window, so Corny answered, "Yeah, it's me, Mr. Jones."

"Better get down off'n that ladder 'fore you get lightnin'-struck."

"I will. I just got this last gutter to do."

"Your aunt told me to watch out for you and I'll not have her chewin' on my hind end 'cause of you gettin' kilt by lightnin'."

"No, sir, you ain't gotta worry 'bout that. The storm's still a ways off thataway," he pointed toward the black thunderheads in the western sky, "and I'll be done before it gets here."

"Don't say I didn't warn ya," Mr. Jones grumbled, then slammed shut his window.

"Won't be sayin' nothin' if lightnin' hits me," he mumbled, then dug his fingers into the gutter and pulled out a clump of damp pine straw interlaced with dead leaves, dropped it to the ground below, then reached in for another handful of the mulchy crud. A sharp pain shot through the base of his thumb and he yowled like a whipped dog as he jerked his hand out of the gutter. A big wasp was curled about his thumb, its antennae twitching on its black head and its red body hanging on by the stinger still embedded in his flesh. "Yeooow!" he cried and swatted the wasp with his other hand. When he let go of the ladder to swat the wasp, he leaned back and away from the ladder and the gutter in an instinctive reaction to get away from the stinging pain, and now his shins were no longer braced against the ladder, leaving him standing upright on the lower rung, teetering for balance. In the time it took for his brain to receive the message that his body was losing its equilibrium, the sensation of standing in mid-air made him forget all about the wasp, and he windmilled his arms and grappled for the nearest ladder rung even as he began to fall backward. A bright flash of light and another clap of thunder accompanied his fall. And as he fell, he remembered clearly the long-ago fall that had damaged his head and changed his life, and in an odd way, the falling was comforting in its familiarity.

* * *

The police car followed the coroner's vehicle down the drive and onto the road. Agnes Porch sat in the old armchair by the cold radiator, and Delbert stood at the window, his thick forehead pressed to the glass.

"There goes the meat wagon," he said. "And the cops, too."

Agnes grunted and continued to finger the juju beads presented to her so long ago by Red Queen Rose.

He ambled toward the bedroom door.

"Now you can tend to that head," she said. "I want it clean, Del."

"Wisht you'd tell me what you're gonna do with it."

"You don't need to know."

He shrugged and walked out.

Agnes got up and moved slowly to her cherrywood vanity and sat in front of the mirror. She removed the pins from her braided crown of hair and uncoiled the long, rope-like tail of white, then she set to work unbraiding it with her gnarled fingers, ignoring the arthritic pain in the joints of her knuckles. It took a while to get it done, but that was all right. She used the time to center herself, and the practiced activity became a meditation. When Del came back upstairs she was still brushing out the dry fall of hair.

"I'm done," he said, holding up the white pillowslip containing the skull. "Gave me a case of the willies, but here the damn thing is."

"Thank you, Del. Just set it under the bed and you can go."

He did as told, then came over and kissed her on the cheek. "Want me to come by later? Momma says you can stay with us till you're back on your feet."

"Humph. Next time I leave here they'll be carrying me out feet-first."

"Aw, don't talk like that, Granny. You still 'bout as spry as a spring chicken. And twice as feisty."

She didn't tell him that this was likely the last time he would see her alive. She didn't want to start him blubbering all over her or to go home to tell Judy that she was fixing to die. That wouldn't do at all. She watched him lumber out of the room like an awkward baby bear, and she stifled a brief impulse to shed a tear—not just for Del, but for her whole family. The time for sentimentality was past. Now it was time to use those darkest secrets whispered to her on that moonless night so long ago by Red Queen Rose, the most powerful witch the Louisiana bayous had ever spawned.

She got up, went to the four-poster and retrieved the pillowslip from under the bed. She reached in and pulled out the skull and held it in front of her eyes. "All right, Monroe Shockley," she addressed the head of bone, "one more task, then your soul can rest forever."

The house shuddered under a boom of thunder, and the lights flickered once, then went out. The afternoon had grown as dark as night.

*   *   *

Alvin Snow ran a hand through his sandy hair and ogled Holly Stimson's backside as she bent over to get something out of the filing cabinet. She had a nice ass for somebody who spent most of the day sitting on it, he thought. Nice and tight and not spreading out with age or with a dispatcher's physical inactivity. He hitched up his gun belt and turned away before she could turn around to catch him leering at her. He decided she probably worked out during her off hours. Had to, to maintain that shape.

"Alvin, did you check on the prisoner?" Holly asked him when she saw him standing there with his hands on his hips.

"Last time I looked, he was still sawing logs."

"What?"

173

"You know, *sleeping*."

"He has to be checked every thirty minutes, you know."

Snow glanced at his Timex. "Why you busting my balls, Holly?"

She cut her eyes at him. "Why do you have a need to bring your genitalia into every conversation? Could it be some sexual inadequacy you feel?"

"Jeez, now you're really busting my balls." He grinned at her, then winked.

"You're hopeless."

"No ma'am. I'm still hoping. Hoping you'll see the errors of your ways and let me take you out."

She slapped the folder down on the desk and sat down, smoothing her skirt. "Go check the prisoner," she said sternly.

"Ooh, I love it when you boss me around. I can picture you with a whip, all dressed in black leather."

"Officer Snow," said Holly, reddening, "can you say *sexual harassment*?"

"Okay, okay, Just kidding. Don't have hissy fit." He turned and walked down the short hallway leading to the cell occupied by Joe Rob Campbell. Midway down the hall, Boots Birdwell was wringing out his mop in an old metal bucket and humming a gospel-sounding tune. The old black man looked up and said, "How do, Officer Al?"

"Hey, Boots. What's that tune you're humming?"

"Didn't know I was." He flashed a smile that made his eyes shine with warmth.

Boots was a retired railroad man who stayed busy with part-time janitorial work and with his occasional evangelical preaching at various black churches in Graves County. It was said that he could electrify a congregation with his hellfire-and-brimstone rants and fill a collection plate faster than any white preacher in the entire state. Snow knew from past conversations with Boots Birdwell that the old man was as sharp as a well-stropped razor and much too intelligent to waste his time with menial labor, but Boots always said he enjoyed cleaning things up and making them shine like a new silver dollar.

"How's our boy?" Snow nodded toward the only occupied cell.

Boots's smile disappeared, and dark lids hooded his eyes. "I'm afraid that boy's lost in the wilderness."

"Why do you say that?"

Boots leaned on his mop and lowered his voice. "I can see it. Like a black cloud all around him. The boy's a troubled soul. And he ain't by hisself."

"How's that?"

"Well, it's what some folks over on my side of town call bad juju. You

174

know what that is?"

Snow, remembering an old blues song, smiled and said, "I reckon that's like when your mojo ain't working."

"Something like that," said Boots. "A juju's a good luck charm for warding off evil and bad luck. If you got a juju that don't work, then you got no protection and bad luck will find you, so when folks speak of bad juju, they generally mean evil's crowding in and there ain't much to stop it. That's bad juju. Like what the hippies used to call bad vibes. Folks on my side of town are saying there's a whole lot of bad juju hereabouts."

"Is that what you think?"

"I know there's evil in the world. Always has been. Demons, elementals, dark gods and such. Nowadays, folks put it all off on Satan, but Satan's just a fallen angel who rebelled against God. There's things worse than the devil, and older too, meaning they been around long enough to sink deep roots. Being a Christian, I have to believe that faith in the Lord is the only true salvation. But I know there's older religions with different outlooks on things. My great aunt was a healer, a root doctor, and when she became a Christian she didn't give up all her old pagan ways, no sir. She prayed in Christ's name and used her healing herbs in His name. But the old magic never died out. That's the way folks are. They say they believe one way but they stick with what they know and what works for them. Plenty of good Christians still knock wood for good luck or throw spilled salt over their shoulder. You see what I'm saying?"

"Yeah, I think so," said Snow.

"I'm saying the old ways are still with us, even in these days of cell phones and computers. And so are the old gods and elemental forces. Sometimes those ancient evils reach out and touch us and remind us that we're all just children in the wilderness. Frail lights in the darkness. And I think maybe that boy there's been touched by that dark, and now he's lost in it."

Snow felt a chill. "That's sure nuff some scary stuff, Boots. You 'bout convinced me to go to church in the morning."

The old man smiled. "May the Lord bless you and keep you, Officer Al."

A loud peal of thunder made Snow flinch. He shook his head, then said, "Thank you, Boots. I reckon I need all the blessing I can get."

Boots Birdwell nodded and rolled his bucket of soapy water down the hall. Snow went the other way to check on the young man in the last cell.

"Joe Rob?" he called.

Joe Rob didn't respond. He was stretched out on the bunk, eyes closed and hands folded across his belly in the posture of a man in a coffin. Snow

175

called out again, louder. Still no response. He leaned close to the iron bars and looked closely to see if the boy's chest was moving. *Christ, is he breathing?* "Hey!" he shouted. Nothing. He moved quickly down the hall, slipped on the wet floor but kept his balance with a quick-step shuffle, then went to the office to get the key to the cell from the dispatcher's desk drawer.

"What's wrong?" Holly asked him.

"He's unresponsive. I wanna see if he's playing possum or if something's really wrong with him."

"I'll come with you," she said. It was standard procedure for there to be no fewer than two officers present whenever an occupied cell was opened, and Alvin and Holly were the only staffers at the station just then.

"Watch your step," Snow said as he led the way down the hall. "Floor's wet."

He jammed the key into the lock, turned it and pulled the cell door open, then entered the cramped space. Holly stood behind him, holding the baton she'd grabbed off a hook in the office. She had been trained to subdue a prisoner with the non-lethal use of the baton, but she'd never had to use it on a real-life prisoner or detainee.

"Lock it back," she blurted.

"What?"

"Your gun."

"Oh. Shit." Snow slammed the cell door and locked it. He'd forgotten to remove his weapon before entering the cell. Chief Keller would have his ass if he found out one of his troops broke *that* cardinal rule. He hustled down the hall to the office, put his pistol in a drawer, then dashed back to the cell, where Holly stood with her baton at the ready. He reopened the cell door and stepped inside.

"Joe Rob?" he said, standing over the prisoner's bunk. The boy didn't respond. Not even a flutter of eyelids. He reached down on shook the boy's shoulder.

"Is he breathing?" asked Holly, edging through the cell's doorway.

"Yeah. But real shallow. I think something's wrong with the kid."

"His lawyer said Dr. Jackson's coming to see him this afternoon. Maybe we better call him now."

"Yeah. Good idea." Snow delivered a couple of light slaps to the boy's face with the flat of his hand. "Didn't even flinch. The dude's out of it."

"Maybe he had some drugs hidden on him that they missed in the strip search," she suggested. "Could've OD'ed."

Snow turned away from the bunk. "Maybe." He was looking at Holly and was suddenly puzzled by the strange expression that jumped into her face. He was about to ask her what was wrong when he was hit from behind and knocked forward into her lower legs. Holly let out a whoop as she fell backward, her baton clattering on the tile floor.

Joe Rob crawled over his back, mashing Snow's face into the floor, and sprang to his feet with the nightstick in his hand. Snow pushed himself up to his hands and knees and watched the Campbell kid jerk Holly Stimson to her feet and shove her into the cell.

"Don't make me hurt you," the escapee warned. Then he shut the cell door and turned the key. "Anybody else out there?" He pointed the baton toward the offices.

Snow shook his head in defeat. He knew Boots Birdwell had left for the day and was probably already cleaning floors at City Drugs. "No. But you know they'll catch you."

"You don't want to do this, Joe Rob," Holly told him.

Joe Rob laughed. "You have no idea what I want, darlin'."

"She's right, man," Snow agreed. "This just makes it worse for you."

"Save your breath, Bozo. It's done. Now have a seat on that bunk, both of you. If I hear any yelling, I'll have to come back and shoot you."

Snow and Holly sat side-by-side on the bunk and watched their former prisoner disappear down the hallway. A thunderclap rattled the door's iron bars. "We sure fucked that up royally," he said, hanging his head.

"No shit, Sipowicz," she said in reference to an old cop show Snow never shut up about.

* * *

She went down the wooden steps to the root cellar, toting the head in the silk pillowslip in one hand and holding the storm lantern in the other. The lantern's wick burned with a white flame and its glass bell took the light and cast it in refracted ripples about the walls and dirt floor of the cellar. The walls were lined with wooden shelves, and the shelves bore countless jars and tin canisters containing her assortment of roots, herbs and medicinal tinctures. The musty smell of damp earth mixed with the variety of odors leaking from the containers, producing an earthy bouquet of bitter sweetness. It was an aroma Agnes had grown over the years to love. Even though her sense of smell had been considerably dulled by age, she was nevertheless able to distinguish many of the individual scents that went into the heady, aromatic mix, and each one kindled a particular memory from her life of nearly one hundred years.

Rooted in the center of the dirt floor was the stump of the oak tree Fate had felled before the house was built. Agnes had insisted that the stump be left intact and the foundation laid around it, explaining to her bewildered son that the wide stump retained special power she needed for her esoteric doings. Fate had put up a weak argument, citing an infestation of termites as a reason for removing the stump, but in the end Agnes had prevailed and the stump became the heart of the farmhouse. Fate had made the mistake of calling her "stump witch" one time when he was in his cups, and she had cuffed him upside the head with a rolling pin. He never called her that again. But in truth, Agnes reckoned that *stump witch* came closer than any of the other titles folks used to describe what she was. She thought it was a name Rose would've liked. The regal Creole woman always was one to laugh at a good joke or a perverse twist of wit. Without Rose—whose given name was Simone—Agnes would've led a completely different life. It was Rose who recognized the extent of Agnes's inborn talent for seeing into the darkness. "We all come from de dark, cher," she'd said one sweltering evening as they sat on Rose's front porch with their feet hanging in the black bayou waters. "But dere are few wid de power to talk to de t'ings dat live in it. I'm talkin' 'bout de Yawahoos, Aggie. Elementals. De oldest gods in de world." That was the day Rose had explained that there were forces in the world able to take on the characteristics and personalities concocted by mortals with the need to believe in godly entities. "Dese elemental forces fill de man-made molds an' de people call dem gods, but dey are much more dan what people t'ink or can conceive. Dey are more dan gods, cher. An' dere are ways to work wid dem and' use dere powers. I can teach you, but it is very dangerous. One does not trifle wid de Yawahoos."

So Agnes had spent three years under the tutelage of Red Queen Rose, learning the tricks of the old witch's trade. She didn't call herself a witch, but to Agnes, that was what she was—and what Agnes herself became at the end of the three years. Rose was dead now, but Agnes was sometimes able to communicate with the Creole woman's spirit. She did this with the aid of a talisman Rose had presented to her at their last parting, back in 1946. It was a finger bone attached to a strip of rawhide—the index finger from Rose's left hand, severed by her own right hand in a ceremony to mark their separation by binding them together forever in the world of the spirit. Rose had explained that in birth there is pain, blood and sacrifice, and that she had given birth to the "new" Agnes in accordance with those same natural laws. Agnes had been deeply touched by her mentor's macabre gift, and had kept it ever since, locked away in a small wooden box fashioned by her own hands.

But now, as she stood before the varnished surface of the sacred stump, the talisman of bone hung from her neck by the strip of rawhide. She knew that her powers alone would not be enough to complete the dangerous ritual. She would need Rose's help in summoning the elementals from the darkness and directing their awesome power to her own human ends. If the elementals saw this as trifling, then she and Rose could be lost to the darkness for eternity—a fate far worse than any ever imagined by Christian or visionary poet. But Agnes felt that she had no choice. She was willing to sacrifice her life in the name of vengeance and to risk her soul for the opportunity to exact retribution from those who had condemned her blood kin and snuffed out their lives.

She set the lantern on the dirt floor of the cellar, then disrobed, letting the housecoat fall away. Now she was naked, except for her glasses and the rawhide necklace with its suspended bone. She picked up the lantern and went to a row of shelves, squinting up at the mason jars and dark vials of liquids, all hand-labeled with yellowed strips of paper. She found a jar marked only with a black X, and took it down, unscrewed the lid, dipped her fingers into the jar and pinched off a thumb-sized piece of dried root. She stuck the crumbling piece under her tongue and left it there as she went to another shelve on the opposite wall and found an old lard can labeled: ANOINTMENT. Setting the lantern on the shelve, she removed the can's lid and stuck her hand into the lard-like substance which smelled of pine tar, cedar and jasmine, then began to smear the greasy stuff on her shriveled teats, over her rounded belly and down to the sparsely thatched mound of her pubis. As her skin absorbed the goop, her flesh began to feel more pliant and as supple as the skin of a woman fifty years younger. Another dip of her fingers into the can, then onto her wrinkled face. The smell was nearly overpowering so close to her nose, but she kept rubbing it in until it was adequately absorbed and her face felt smooth to her touch. She caught her lantern-lit reflection in the glass of a big jar and she saw her face shining with a youthful, oily sheen. She smiled at her mirror image, her face now as it was when she was young and vital, with tides of lust surging through her shapely body. She was moving back in time, recapturing feelings long since lost to ravages of age and relentless decrepitude. She was suddenly dizzied by the sensation of flying. She reeled over to the stump and plopped down on it, her thin rump making a raw slapping sound as she did so. She closed her eyes and rested her head in her ointment-greased hands.

"Mercy," she muttered.

After an indeterminate length of time, her head stopped swimming and she did her best to collect her scattered thoughts. The bit of root she'd placed beneath her tongue had long since dissolved, leaving a bitter aftertaste that was nevertheless agreeable to her—a little like the bitter brown slivers of a pecan's inner shell. She saw herself as a child, sitting under a pecan tree and eating pecans picked up off the ground, her mother's head poking through a window and scolding her for spoiling her supper. *No, I ain't, Momma*, she shouted back.

"No, I ain't, Momma," her voice rang sharply in the close confines of the cellar. She giggled. It was a girlish sound, young and vibrant, out of place in the gloomy root cellar. "All right now, Agnes," she scolded herself. "Enough Tomfoolery. Time to get serious."

She straightened her spine and sat stiffly upright on the stump. Her fingers closed around the bone hanging from her neck, then she began the pidgin-Creole chant Rose had taught her many years ago. She closed her eyes and called up an image of Rose's coffee-colored face. Her chanting grew louder and the visualized image of Red Queen Rose became more distinct.

Bonjou, cher, whispered Rose.

Agnes opened her eyes and saw the sorceress floating in front of her in the shadow-streaked lantern light. Her dark eyes sparkled with a light of their own as she smiled at her old apprentice.

"I need your help," she said. "I want to call up the elementals."

The smiled died on the apparition's luminous face. *Pronga to*, she said.

"Be careful?" Agnes translated the warning. "I'm past care. I *have* to do this, Rose. The line's drawn. But I'm not sure I can do it without you."

Mo pa konmprann. Rose's image wavered, then darkened.

"Yes, you do understand. You know what they done to my family. To me. If you won't help me, just say so. With or without you, I'm gonna do it."

The sorceress smiled again. She was as young and beautiful as she had been in the old photos she'd shown Agnes years ago. *You are old, Aggie, but your spirit is fearless. I always admired dat in you.*

"*Mersi*," Agnes thanked her grudgingly.

And stubborn as a mired-up mule.

Agnes nodded her head, the cascade of brittle, white hair shifting like dying moss over her bare shoulders.

You know what you must sacrifice. Your blood, your life. To konmprann?

"Yes, I know that," she snapped.

All right, my little bird. I will help you. Rose began to whirl around, spinning faster and faster. *Welcome de serpent!*

Agnes watched with slack jaw as the sorcerer's apparition spun itself into a thin twist of light, then suddenly winked out. On the dirt floor a small black snake uncoiled itself and crawled toward her, its tongue flicking rhythmically.

Agnes took a deep breath, then opened her legs to receive the reptile. It slithered up the side of the stump, paused at the mossy lips of her sex, then darted inside, its slip of a tail disappearing into the anointed lips.

Agnes gasped at the cold sensation. She groaned and pressed her hands between her legs. Severe cramps gave way to a pleasant tingling that was almost sexual.

Then she felt the unmistakable presence of Rose deep inside her, and she knew she was ready. She stood and walked on strong legs to the shelf where her ritual knife waited within a teakwood box, removed the knife and returned to the stump. She extracted the skull of Monroe Shockley from the pillowslip, set it on the stump, then used a kitchen match to light a black ceremonial candle and set it on top of the skull. She hawked up a meager wad of sputum and spat it into the skull's left eye socket. Then she tied three little knots in a black thread and burned the knotted string in the candle's flame as she mouthed words of an ancient curse. When the thread was burned to ash, she knelt at the stump, laid her left arm across the varnished surface and opened a vein from the crook of her elbow to her wrist. Blood flowed freely, pouring from her arm and pooling on the tabletop of the stump.

She chanted words she had never heard before, and she knew the sorceress was moving her tongue for her, singing sounds older than any of the world's spoken languages—word-like sounds that had spawned all languages and shaped the minds of humanity's ancient ancestors. Words of real magic, echoing all the way back to the beginning of time. Growing weak with the loss of so much blood, she kept up the chant in a trance-like state. Thunder shook the house to its foundations, but she hardly felt it. Rain lashed the house and pounded the roof with thousands of watery drumsticks, but she was well beyond the reach of the rain and the impending flood. An image of the town of Vinewood came into her mind, and a flood of darkness swept over the streets and houses and stores until there was nothing left but the fathomless darkness.

The electricity came back on, the naked bulb hanging from the cellar's ceiling suddenly washing the dank place in yellow light. Agnes saw dark shapes coming through the cellar walls, moving toward her from all sides. With another thunderclap the light went out once more. The flaming wick of the kerosene lantern flared, then dimmed to an ember-like glow. The rain on the roof sounded like voodoo drums.

The dirt floor rippled like dark pond water, as if the soil had all at once come alive.

Dey here, cher, Rose whispered inside her head. *De Yawahoos!*

"Yessss," Agnes rasped, knowing her blood had drawn them. She slumped over the blood-slick stump and slid to the ground. The swarthy dirt began to swarm over her bleeding arm like an army of bugs. A swirling dust devil arose from the floor and danced over her, grains of dirt stinging her naked skin and stealing beneath her eyelids. She saw things no human could've ever imagined, visions of luminous creatures in a world without light. They were communing with her, reading her most closely held wishes and divining the deepest secrets of her soul. They were *feeding* on her. The pain was ecstatic. When she opened her mouth to scream, the animated dirt filled the fleshy cavity and silenced her forever.

CHAPTER 24
RAYS OF DARKNESS

When Corny came to, Mr. Jones and Mr. Tilley were looking down at him, their faces lumpy with concern. Behind their heads, the stormy sky was all churned up like water in a mud puddle when you stir up the bottom dirt with a stick.

"Cornelius? Are you all right?" asked Mr. Tilley.

"Told him to be careful," Mr. Jones said, then spat on the ground as if he had something distasteful in his mouth and couldn't get rid of it.

"I reckon I fell," Corny said, sitting up.

Rufus Tilley put his writer's hand on Corny's shoulder and said, "Don't stand up too fast. Go easy now."

"What the hell happened, boy?" Mr. Johnson demanded.

"Wasp stung me," he said, rubbing his aching hand. "Think the stinger's still in there. S'like a hot needle stickin' me."

"Didn't break anything, did you?" Mr. Tilley squatted beside him.

"Don't think so. Just a little bummed up."

"Good thing you got a hard head," Mr. Jones said.

Rufus Tilley shot the man a hard look, then said, "Stand up real slow now."

Corny got to his feet. Rolling thunder pounded the sky. "They're rollin' pumpkins down the stairs in heaven," he said with a crooked smile. "That's what my daddy used to say when it thundered like that."

"How do you feel?" asked Mr. Tilley. "Dizzy?"

"No suh. Well, maybe just a little."

Big drops of rain began to fall on the lawn, the biggest Corny had ever seen, though they were spaced far apart.

"Comin' up a real frog choker," Mr. Jones said, glancing up at the turbulent sky. "Better get inside 'fore we all get struck by a thunderbolt."

"Aunt Mattie's gone kill me," said Corny. "I's spoze to have them gutters cleaned out before it rains."

"Your aunt will be so thankful you weren't seriously hurt, I don't think she'll go too hard on you," the writer said with a wink. "Let's get inside."

He followed the men into the house, wondering what the weird feeling he was having was all about. Something was . . . not exactly wrong, but different. He couldn't shake off the feeling that he'd lost something or left something behind. It was right there in the back of his mind. If he could just concentrate hard enough then he could see what it was. It was right there, right in . . .

"You ort to put some tobacco on that sting to draw the venom out," said Mr. Jones. "Best thing you can do for it."

Then it was gone, like a door in his head had slammed shut and sealed off whatever it was he was trying to get to. *Damn that Mr. Jones. Always running his mouth like he knows it all.* Corny immediately felt bad for thinking so ill of the old man. The old guy was only trying to be helpful.

Corny thanked the two men for seeing about him, then stopped off at the fridge for a glass of iced tea and took it to his room. He kicked off his sneakers and fell back onto his bed.

For some reason, he felt an overwhelming sense of loneliness, as if someone close to him had just died. He laid an arm over his eyes and cried tears of real grief—though he had no idea why he should be grieving so.

* * *

Luke stood in front of the vanity, gazing into a looking glass clouded with years of exposure to whatever it was in the air that caused mirrors to cloud up. Probably oxidation, he thought. Then a crazy idea flitted into his mind—the idea that the mirror was cloudy because it had kept a little part of every reflection it had ever held. He looked at his own hazy reflection and shook his head. Such fairytale notions were foreign to him, and he chastised himself for entertaining the thought. *Ree's haunted-mirror tale must be getting to me.*

Ree crept up behind him and stood on tiptoe so she could rest her chin on his left shoulder. "See anything interesting?"

"Uh-huh. You."

She nibbled at his ear lobe.

"You're not afraid Beau will get jealous?"

"No, silly. I told you, that was in another lifetime. Now he's nothing more than my guardian."

The bell over the shop's door tinkled, gaily announcing the arrival of a customer braving the inclement weather. Ree disengaged from Luke, smoothed the front of her blouse and walked into the front room to greet the patron. Luke stared into the mirror a moment longer, then combed his hair with his fingers, lamenting the fact that his hair was thinning on top. When he felt the urge to speak to the alleged man in the mirror, he spun on his heels and walked away. Then, in uncharacteristic behavior, he turned back to the vanity and whispered, "She's mine, now, Beau. Keep your dead paws off her."

"Luke?" Ree called from the other room. There was an edge of anxiety in her voice, and he moved quickly to see what was wrong.

Wearing a yellow rain slicker, Chief Keller was standing with her by the door, his face a mask of worry. Through the glass display windows, Luke saw a hard, slanting rain beating down on the street and on the squad car parked in front of the shop.

"You ain't gone believe this," said Keller when he saw Luke.

"Believe what?"

"Joe Rob Campbell escaped."

"Nah."

"Yep. Walked right out the front door. I wasn't there at the time, but hell, it's still on me."

"Jesus, Bill, how'd he get out of the cell?"

"Played sick. Like he was out cold. Then got the jump on Snow and Holly and locked them in the cell. He took off with Snow's pistol, too. You seem to know a lot about the boy. You got any idea where he might go?"

Luke shrugged. "Not really. If he doesn't wanna get caught, I guess he'd leave the county."

"His car's impounded, so if he didn't steal some wheels, he's on foot. I figured I'd better let you know, since you're the one who took him into custody. I don't think he'd be bent on revenge, but you never can tell with a boy like that. He ain't quite right in the head, what with all that crazy stuff he said about seeing dark things everywhere."

"Well, thanks for alerting me. Let me know if I can be of help."

The chief nodded. "I just saw your truck out front and figured I'd give you the bad news. Y'all have a good one." He touched his fingers to the brim of his hat, then went out the door, the bell above it ringing with a mocking peal.

"I'll be damned," Luke said. "That boy's not helping his case with this stunt."

Ree moved close to him and put a hand on his chest. "I know what you're thinking. If you want to look for him, I'll be fine by myself. I'd rather you didn't because it could be dangerous for you, but I just want you to know that you don't have to stay here to baby-sit me. I'm not as spooked as I was by my . . . vision. I just want us to get off on the right foot, you know? The last thing I want to do is smother you."

He smiled. "You can smother me any time, babe."

"You know what I mean."

"Yeah. And I really do appreciate it. You're too good to be true."

She hugged him. "I'll be true to you. As long as you're true to me."

"Count on it." He kissed her parted lips. He tasted her wintergreen mint. He drew back and said, "I think I'll just stay right here. Chief Keller can do his job without my help. I'm just a private citizen now. A regular Joe Blow."

"Mmmm, you're giving me wicked ideas, Mr. Blow," she said with a vampish look.

"But I thought you were going to teach me the antique business."

"Oh, I am. But that's not all I have to teach you. I was just thinking up a wicked homework assignment for you."

"As long as you're there to help me with the, uh, blow-by-blow."

They laughed together, both blushing.

A crack of thunder rang the bell over the door.

*   *   *

Joe Rob slogged through the piney woods, his shoulders hunched against the heavy rainfall. Mud sucked at his shoes, and his socks were already soaked through-and-through, clinging to his feet like an extra layer of clammy skin. The .38 he'd found in the desk drawer at the police station was stuck in the waist of his jeans. He would've taken one of the shotguns racked on the wall, but a civilian walking out of the station house with a shotgun would've attracted unwanted attention.

He knew the smart thing to do now was to get the hell out of Vinewood and out of Georgia, but something he couldn't identify seemed to be holding him here—some vague sense of unfinished business. It would be good to see Skeeter before he lit out—perhaps to Florida—but that was too risky. The cops would probably be expecting him to contact his best friend and would be keeping close tabs on Skeeter, so he had no plans for seeing him in person. He would try to catch him with a phone call. The same was true for his grandmother. No way could he sneak home for a farewell visit to the old lady. He regretted that he'd sullied the family name (he knew that was how *she* would see things) and that he couldn't thank her in person for taking him in and seeing him through high school. His grandmother and Skeeter were the only real ties he had to Vinewood now, but he was more than ready to sever those ties. So what was it that was still holding him to this place? He had no clue. All he had was the sense that invisible ties as strong as thick vines were binding him to the land. And he didn't like it at all.

His immediate course of action was hiking to Candyman's trailer for something to eat, some ready cash and some clean clothes. Then if he decided to hit the road, he would take Candy's old Harley—if they could get the vintage hog up and running. Candy would balk at the idea of letting him ride off on his chopper, but if Joe Rob decided to go, the fat fuck wasn't about to stand in his way.

A deafening crash of thunder startled him, and he slipped on muddy pine straw and went down hard. As he was getting to his feet, a blinding bolt of lightning struck a tall pine less than ten yards in front of him, the concussion of the strike knocking him back on his ass. A ball of red-and-blue fire ran down the trunk of the tree and hit the ground, where it broke apart like a giant drop of water and spread little rivulets of flame in all directions. One tiny tributary of fire darted over the earth and touched the toe of his left boot. A tingling sensation ran through him like a weak electric current, and he tried to crawl backward to get away from the freakish fire, slipping in the mud and falling flat on his back. The tingling stopped, leaving his muscles so relaxed that he couldn't move, so he lay there with the heavy rain hitting his face, blurring his vision and making him gag on the water pouring into his nostrils and down the back of his throat. Just when he thought he might actually be drowned by rainfall, he coughed and sputtered and sat up, his motor control returning.

He heard music. Someone was strumming steel strings of a guitar. A bluesy progression of chords.

He wiped water from his eyes and saw his father sitting cross-legged on the ground, his back braced against the lightning-struck pine tree.

"Dad?" he said, his voice waterlogged and hoarse.

Billy Joe Campbell looked up from his fingerwork on the frets and grinned at his son. Then he started humming along with the guitar, and the humming became a musical moan. It was the blackest blues Joe Rob had ever heard. It was a sound too sad for human ears, an eerie tune not born of this earth. He knew this instinctively—and with great certainty.

"Devil's fucking Valley," Billy Joe sang.

Then Joe Rob saw the blood-caked crater in the side of his father's head, and he knew his old man was dead.

187

"You're a fu-fucking ghost," he stammered.

Billy Joe winked a dead eye at his son and played on.

*   *   *

The sound of the rain beating on the roof and windows of his old pickup gave Boots Birdwell goose bumps and made him shiver. It was not the pleasant sort of shiver he sometimes got from a thunderstorm. He was cozy and dry, sitting here behind the wheel of his old Ford, but *this* case of the shivers was the kind you get when somebody walks over your grave or when you hear the lonesome hoot of an owl in the middle of the night and you know it's foretelling the death of someone close to you.

Something bad was coming.

Could be it was already here. Coming down all around like the rain, seeking its lowest levels and seeping into the darkest nooks and crannies of the human heart to foul the mortal soul.

Boots had seen it before. Evil conjured by hate and set against folks who had no idea of its power in this world and never saw it coming till it was too late to get out of the way. He had seen it only once, a long time ago, but he remembered it as clearly as if it had happened last week. He'd been living in Florida then, in a little settlement of colored folks on the edge of the Everglades swamp. The place was never on any map and never had a legal name, though folks in the area called it Holy Crossing. That was back in his rambling days, before he settled down to a steady job with the railroad. He was a wild buck back then, drinking shine, carousing with fast women and committing just about every sin there was—including killing. He'd got into a fight with a rowdy young bull at a juke house, and when the man went at him with a knife, Boots had flicked out his straight razor and opened up the poor bastard's throat. He would never forget the bug-eyed look of surprise on the dying man's face as his blood spurted three feet in front of him and fell on the sawdust floor like red rain. He'd often wondered if that killing had anything to do with the black evil that fell on Holy Crossing a few months later. He knew he hadn't been a specific target of the old conjure woman who called up the darkness, but still he wondered if the killing hadn't contributed to the general atmosphere of wickedness that hung over the swampland community like dirty fog. He was certainly not without sin—not back then.

But now he was a different man. Since he'd been called to preach the Gospel, he did his best to keep his sins small and his heart open. But there was danger in that, too. When a man opens his heart to his fellow men, there is always the danger of something evil slipping in and taking over. That's where the Lord comes in. If a man sets his heart and soul on God, he stands a better chance of being untainted by evil when it comes.

He gazed through the rain-streaked window at the railroad yard below the gravel parking lot behind Main Street. Boxcars sat motionless on a sidetrack. A man was climbing into an old sedan parked outside the squat office building. A black dog ducked beneath a trailer set on cinderblocks, seeking shelter from the rain.

Boots shuddered again, harder this time. He was tired from his afternoon of sweeping, mopping, and cleaning sinks and toilets, but he felt a bone-deep weariness that he couldn't put off on his janitorial labors.

"Lord," he said as he gripped the steering wheel, "give me strength to stand against the darkness and to do *Your* bidding. I ask this in the name of Jesus the Savior, amen."

He cranked the engine, turned on the windshield wipers and drove slowly homeward.

* * *

"You need to eat something, Cornelius," his aunt said from the door of his room.

"Ain't hungry."

"Your sure you're all right?"

"Yes ma'am. Just ain't hungry."

"Well, then I reckon you won't get to meet our new boarder. And he's such an interesting man."

"Who's that?"

"Mr. Goolsby. He's the geological engineer who's to go down in that sinkhole and see how big it might get and tell us what's to be done about it. He'll only be with us a day or two. The town's paying for his room and board for as long as he needs to be here. He didn't come right out and say so, but he let on that there could be a whole network of caverns under the town. A scary thought, I tell you what's the truth."

Corny sat up in the middle of his bed. "He's gone go down in that hole?"

"Sure is. Him and his crew. That's the only way to see what's really down under there. You ought to come on down and hear him talk. He's scaring stew out of everybody and he don't even know it. I reckon it's just an everyday thing to him. But goodness gracious, it's our *town*."

"I might be down directly."

She came into the room and stood over his bed. "I'm so glad you weren't hurt when you fell off that ladder today. I never would've been able to forgive myself. Now, Corny, I don't want you cleaning the gutters no more. I'll hire it done from now on. It's just too dangerous for you."

"Aw, Aunt Mattie, it wouldn't na happened 'cept for that dadgum wasp stingin' me. I wisht you wouldn't treat me like a retard."

"You know better than that," she chided. "I just don't want you up on ladders any more. Now there's the end to it. My final word. You hear?"

Corny sighed. "I hear."

When she was gone, he rolled on his side and rested his head on the worn-flat pillow and stared at the framed photos of trains. His feeling of profound loss was still with him, and he wondered if he was longing for his dead father. The bedroom window was partially open to the rainy evening, and the rainfall drowned out the usual house-filtered sounds of the TV down the hall in Kirby Cone's room and the buzzing conversation of the boarders gathered around the supper table downstairs. Beneath the droning rain there was an unaccustomed silence deeper than any silence he could remember. Then it came to him why he was feeling such a sad emptiness. Whisperer was gone! It wasn't just that Whisperer was being quiet. His long-time secret companion was simply not there. He could *feel* the absence—just as sure as you can feel a hole in your gum after you lose a tooth. Whisperer had abandoned him.

He sat up in bed and gasped for breath. He was scared, nearly as scared as he'd been the time he got separated from his mother in a department store when he was four years old. Lost, alone and scared.

He stumbled out of bed and grabbed his old engineer's cap off his hat rack and jammed it on his head. The cap his father had given him made him feel a little better, for engineers were fearless men, and when he was wearing the cap he believed he could be almost as brave as those manly train drivers. At least he could breathe a little easier.

"Musta been the fall," he whispered to himself. Sure, that had to be it. When he hit the ground, it knocked Whisperer right out of his head. It made sense, didn't it? Whisperer came to him after that first fall that damaged his brain, and now this second fall had knocked the whispering companion loose. He wasn't sure how he should feel about it. There had been plenty of times when Whisperer seemed like a curse, a troublemaking voice in his head telling him to do bad things, but there were those other times when he was glad to have Whisperer warning him of things he wouldn't have otherwise noticed. Blessing or curse, Whisperer was gone now, and Corny was saddened by the loss.

He walked over to the window and threw it all the way up and pressed his nose to the rusty screen. Though it was too early in the evening to be dark outside, the stormy weather had turned the day to deep dusk. Lightning flashed silently off to the east. The late-summer rain smelled faintly of river water and bottom rot, and he wondered if the Ohoopee River had flooded its banks.

"I reckon it's just me now," he said. "Whisperer's gone and I'm on my own. Huh. Can always talk to myself, cain't I? Dadgum right I can. Ain't gotta whisper either."

A sudden gust of wind blew rain through the wire mesh of the screen, and he drew back from the window.

"Something's out there," he said, warning himself in Whisperer's stead. "Something bad."

He felt it rushing toward him, but before his brain had time to process his terror, it was upon him, smothering him in darkness, flooding him with sensations so alien that he no longer knew who he was. He tumbled backward to the hardwood floor, lost in molasses-thick darkness.

Within the bone-chamber of his skull, it whispered to him with a thousand slithery tongues. It whispered and whispered, sharing its darkest secrets and not ceasing till he was filled with feelings he couldn't have named even if he'd he been able to speak.

*   *   *

Over his mother's objection, Skeeter Partain drove his truck to his father's funeral home. She had strongly advised him to stay home and rest up, but he'd argued that he'd had more rest than he could stand during his hospital stay and that he was okay to drive downtown to see his father. "He'll be home in a little while," she'd said, "why not just wait? What's so important that you have to go right this minute? And in this weather?" But Skeeter had to get out of the house. The walls had started closing in on him, and the storm seemed to be calling him out. He hadn't tried to explain to his mother that being cooped up was too much like being strung up on that chain in the barn loft. He had to have freedom to move, to *go* when he wanted to go. He'd told her that he wanted to talk to his dad about Joe Rob's legal situation, but that wasn't really the reason. He just had to be on the go and out and about in the night. He felt most free when he was driving his truck, and that's what he did. He stopped at the Quickie Mart for a can of Skoal and a root beer, then he circumnavigated Vinewood just for the joy of feeling the tires humming over the wet streets. He rolled down the window and tossed out the empty root beer can, then put a pinch of his Skoal between his cheek and gum. He drove around until he got a little buzz from the smokeless tobacco, then he went on to the funeral home. He parked in the rear and got out of the truck slowly so as not to aggravate his bandaged wounds. The prescription codeine was numbing some of the soreness, but if he moved a certain way the pain would flare up and he could almost feel the knife blade going in again and see that Porch son of a bitch leering at him with those beady eyes.

By the time he'd hobbled up the back steps and ducked inside out of the rain, he was pretty well soaked with chilling rainwater. He took off his cap and slapped it against his uninjured thigh to knock some of the rain off. He shut the door softly and started down the hall, trying to be *as quiet as a church mouse*, as his father used to tell him when he was a child. Skeeter had never actually seen a mouse in church, but he'd always understood the need for being quiet and reverent inside a funeral home. Grieving relatives of the recently deceased didn't care to have their mourning disturbed by a bratty undertaker's kid acting like he was in a playhouse or raising Cain the way he would in a big rumpus room.

He heard the muffled voice of his father from the office up front. Hearing no other voice, he figured his dad was on the phone. Rather than stand and wait for the phone conversation to end, Skeeter decided to have a seat behind his dad's desk in the back office. As he turned and started back down the hallway, he heard a thud behind the door of the embalming room. He thought it must be Charlie Taylor, a.k.a., The Silver Fox, who was his father's senior mortician on staff. Skeeter liked Charlie because he reminded him of that old comedian, Jonathan Winters, and Charlie was just as funny—if not funnier. A good sense of humor in the funeral business was a definite asset. Smiling in anticipation of Charlie's first one-liner, Skeeter opened the door and entered the embalming room.

Charlie wasn't there. There was no body laid out on the stainless-steel table. Wondering what had made the thudding sound, Skeeter was about to turn off the goose-neck floor lamp and leave the room when he saw the naked woman standing in the shadowy corner with her back to him. Her flesh was shockingly pale, but a patch of skin just above the cleft of her buttocks was discolored a bluish yellow. Her auburn hair hung in wild tangles halfway down her back.

Skeeter knew who she was before she turned around. *This can't be real. She's dead and buried in Vidalia.*

Then she did turn to face him. Her breasts youthfully firm, her abdomen only slightly rounded above her auburn thatch of pubic hair, Jessica Lowell fixed her dead eyes on him and twisted up her mouth in the same lunatic expression she had exhibited at the city dump and said, "It wants you." She raised her arm and pointed her finger at him, then cackled with insane laughter.

Skeeter shook his head in profound disbelief. "No," he croaked. He'd last seen this same woman laid out on this very table, dead of snakebite poisoning. She could not be standing here before him now, pointing that accusatory finger at his heart. He reeled backward into the wall, the jolt setting off pain in his wounds. He was suddenly dizzy, and though he wanted more than anything to run out of the room, his vigor and powers of movement had deserted him, and he slid down the wall and onto his sparse haunches.

The dead woman walked toward him, her bare feet softly slapping the tile floor.

Trembling involuntarily, he wanted to call out to his father, but he couldn't find his voice.

"It wants you," she repeated, but this time it wasn't the voice of Jessica A. Lowell he heard. The sound issuing from her mouth was a deep, cavernous croon. It was, Skeeter knew, the voice of his doom.

*   *   *

James Partain hung up the phone, locked the front door, and then started down the hallway to get his raincoat from his office, which was across the hall from the prep room. Above the sound of the steady rainfall, he heard another sound and immediately identified it. Somehow the aspirator had come on. The motorized device used for suctioning the contents of the abdominal and chest cavities of the deceased was whining like a high-powered vacuum cleaner—which was exactly what the aspirator was. He thought the lightning must've sent a surge of electricity through the wiring strong enough to override the power switch and turn the thing on. But as he drew nearer, he heard the wet, gurgling sound the aspirator makes when the sharp point of the trocar is inserted in the body and is sucking out the contents of the stomach, the intestines and the kidneys.

"What the hell?" he said as he strode toward the closed door of the prep room. "Charlie? Is that you?"

But he knew it couldn't be Charlie Taylor. Charlie was on a fishing trip to Florida. And there was no one in extremis, awaiting embalming. There were no bodies at all today.

He turned the doorknob, flung open the door and froze when he saw his son stretched out on the table, his shirt pulled up over his belly and the trocar inserted in his abdomen. He watched in horror as Skeeter's insides were sucked through the long, rubber tube that emptied in the sink at the foot of the table. The familiar stench was all the more overwhelming because he knew it was coming from his son's innards.

"Skeeter!" he cried, rushing to the table to grab the unattended aspirator and pull it out of Skeeter's obscenely shrunken abdomen. The stainless-steel trocar came out with a sickening, wet whine. He shut off the motor and dropped the blood-streaked instrument to the floor, its attached rubber hose giving one final snake-like twist, then falling flaccid. Though he already knew no living person could survive the grisly aspiration, the terror-stricken expression frozen on his son's face confirmed that Skeeter was indeed dead. "My God, *why?*"

He closed his son's eyes, then draped himself over the supine body and sobbed.

A short time later, James Partain picked up the phone and called the police. "This is James Partain," he said, trying to steady his voice. "My son is dead. We're across the street at the funeral home. I . . . I think he killed himself."

*   *   *

The rain began to slack off after nine o'clock that night, but Charlotte Claymore paid no heed to the rainfall; she was embroiled in her own stormy emotions, stirred up by news concerning her plot to have Joe Rob Campbell killed. First, she heard that the boy had been jailed for murder, then a few hours later she was told by one of her policeman clients that Campbell had escaped and was on the lam. Hearing the latter, she got on the phone to Carl and bemoaned the loss of her down payment to the masked hit man. "How can he do the job if the bastard is on the run? Do you think he'll give me my money back?"

"Don't count him out just yet," Carl said. "The man has his ways of getting the job done. It's goddamn spooky the way he knows things."

"He's spooky all right," Charlotte said. "He wants a freebie as part of the deal. I almost hope he can't find the little bastard. The thought of doing him turns my stomach. I hope he keeps that mask on his head. I don't think I want to see his frigging face."

Carl said, "I'll page him and see what I can find out. I'll get back to you soon as I know something."

She hung up and poured herself another shot of booze and fired up a cigarette. She used the remote to turn on the TV and caught a weather bulletin warning that flash flooding was expected for parts of the county and detailing some of the damage already done by severe thunderstorms. "That's all I need," she muttered, "a fucking flood." Her back yard lay in the flood plain of Willow Creek, and the last time the creek overflowed its banks, the water had come up to the back-door stoop. She went through the kitchen, opened the back door and looked out at the rainy darkness. She shivered, though the night air wasn't really cool. She turned on the porch light and saw no sign of flooding in her small yard. Nevertheless, as she gazed out into the darkness beyond the reach of electric light, she grew anxious with a feeling that something very bad was going to happen.

*   *   *

Joe Rob pounded on the door of Candyman's trailer and hurled a barrage of curses at the fat bastard when he opened his door.

"Jeez, man, what's eating you?" Candy asked as he stood in the doorway with his bare belly hanging over the waist of his cut-off jeans.

Joe Rob pushed past him to get out of the rain. "What the hell you think? I like feeling like a drowned rat?"

Candy's woman was lying on the couch with her head on a pile of pillows. With her fleshy tits hanging most of the way out of her red halter-top, she raised her head and looked at Joe Rob with bleary eyes. "Hey, there, honey," she said. "What brings you out on such a dark and stormy night?"

"Y'all ain't heard? I'm a fucking fugitive. Busted out of jail a few hours ago."

"Bullshit," Candy said, his eyes falling on the pistol sticking out of Joe Rob's jeans.

"Don't you ever watch the news on that thing?" Joe Rob nodded at the television, which was playing an old horror movie.

"Hell, no. Not since we got the DVD player. Only thing we watch on regular TV is Marilyn's cartoons."

"I'm a toon-head," she admitted with a giggle. "I can't help it."

"What's this shit about being a fugitive?" Candy asked.

"I killed Fate Porch and his three asshole boys. It was self-defense but the damn prosecutor's charging me with murder. Mookie Vedders says he can get me off in a jury trial, but fuck that shit, I ain't waiting around in jail while they try to hang me for shit I didn't do. I killed 'em all right, but I didn't murder the motherfuckers."

"You're serious, aren't you? You really did it. Holy shit." Candy went to the fridge and snagged two bottles of beer, then tossed one to Joe Rob. "What're you gone do now?"

Joe Rob twisted off the cap and threw it at the garbage can, then took a big swallow. He cut loose with a rolling belch. "Get the hell out of Dodge. I need your bike. And some cash."

Candy started to protest, but the look in his friend's face stopped him. "Yeah, sure, man. I can let you have a couple of Ben Franklins."

"You got more than that, the way you been dealing."

"Yeah, but I got expenses, man. I have to pay for the shit, too, ya know."

"You can front me five. And throw in some coke. I got a lot of road ahead of me."

"You actually killed those in-bred rednecks?" Marilyn was sitting up now, exposing more bosom. "Hell, they oughta give you the key to the city. I'm surprised nobody killed 'em before now."

"Nobody else ever had the balls," Joe Rob bragged. He was doing his best to keep his mind off the ghostly vision of his father, but the image of Billy Joe's mortally-wounded head remained as an after-image burned upon the back walls of his eyeballs. "I'm hungry. What ya got to eat?"

"You can have some left-over Sloppy Joe," said Marilyn. She giggled again. "Sloppy Joe for Joe Rob. Sloppy Joe Rob . . ."

"She's fucked up," Candy said, shaking his head and rolling his eyes.

"So?" she said. "You are too, Candy-ass."

"Watch it, bitch."

"Hey, cool it, will ya," Joe Rob raised his voice. "I ain't in the mood for a fucking lovers' spat."

"You tell him, honey," Marilyn said.

"He's talking to you, cunt."

Joe Rob was about to draw back his fist and pop Candy a good one on the arm when the front door flew open to reveal a man in a black ski mask with a gun in his fist. "Nobody move!" the man shouted.

"Who the fuck're you?" Candy demanded.

The masked man took a step forward and hammered Candy's nose with his fisted pistol butt. Candy staggered backward, then dropped to the floor. The trailer shook with the weight of his fall. Marilyn squealed, clutching a pillow to her breasts.

Joe Rob made a quick decision. Even as he reached for the pistol in his pants he knew the decision was a bad one. The silencer affixed to the barrel of the man's gun was the tip-off that the dude was a pro, but it was already too late; Joe Rob had made his move. As he freed his pistol from his rain-soaked jeans, the masked man's gun made a sharp spitting sound and the slug tore through Joe Rob's right shoulder. The stolen gun slipped from his numbed fingers and clattered to the floor, and he grabbed at his wounded shoulder with his left hand. Warm blood wetted his fingers. A wave of dizziness roared through his head.

The tall man in the mask pointed his silenced pistol at Marilyn and said, "We were never here. You tell anybody different, I'll come back and kill you and your fat fuck here." He waved his weapon down at Candy, who was crying and holding both hands to his bleeding nose. "Say it!"

Marilyn stammered, "You wu-were never here. You'll ku-kill us if we say different." "Remember that. I'm a man of my word."

She nodded. Her face had gone milk-white to match her fleshy jugs.

The shooter put the muzzle of his gun an inch from Joe Rob's face and said, "Let's go, hero."

"Where?" Joe Rob asked. He should have been shit-scared but he was remarkably calm, considering he'd just been shot and was about to be abducted.

"You'll see."

The gunman pushed him out the door and into the drizzling rain. Once they were outside the cone of light slanting down from the pole in front of the small trailer park, Joe Rob's eyes adjusted quickly to the darkness, and he began to see dark shapes lurking about, following them through the night.

*   *   *

Luke leaned back in his chair and patted his full belly. "Well? How did you like your first meal from Luke's Kitchen?"

Ree exhaled smoke from her after-supper cigarette and said, "That was really very good. I'm impressed. Almost as good as my own chicken and dumplings."

"Thank you, I think." He gave her a look of mock bewilderment, then said, "Talk about your left-handed compliment."

"It *was* good. But in all modesty, mine's better. I really am a good cook, you know."

"You can drop the sales pitch, Shorty. I'm already sold."

She cut her eyes at him, but didn't attempt to kick him under the table. Holding her cigarette between two fingers and pointing both fingers at him, Ree said, "I guess I don't mind so much that you persist in calling me that. So long as that's not the only thing you call me."

197

"Like I said, it's an affectionate term. I'm not much for saying things like 'honey' or 'sweetheart,' I guess because everybody else does it. Besides, 'Shorty' is more personalized."

"That makes sense," she said, "in a Luke Chaney sort of way."

All at once Hondo commenced a ferocious barking on the front porch.

"Goodness," said Ree, stabbing out her smoke. "What's got him so riled?"

Luke rose from the table and crossed the dining room in three big strides. "I better check it out." He went to the den, unlocked the gun cabinet and chose his Rossi .357, checked the load, then headed for the front porch with the magnum held close to his leg. He turned off the living-room light before he went through the doorway, so as not to make himself a backlit target. He stepped onto the front porch and went into a squat. "Hondo, what're you barking at?"

The dog didn't acknowledge him, but went on barking at whatever had set him off. Luke recognized the bark as the one Hondo used whenever he felt threatened. Peering out into the rainy darkness, Luke could see nothing out of the ordinary, but he knew his eyesight and his night vision weren't as sharp as they had been in his younger years. "Hondo, hush now," he commanded.

"What is it?" asked Ree from behind the screen door.

"Get out of the doorway," he whispered to her. "Just in case there is a bad guy out there."

She came out onto the porch and crouched beside him. "You think it's Joe Rob Campbell?"

"I doubt it. But I don't know. *Something's* sure got him worked up, barking like that."

"You see anything?"

"Nope."

"Maybe it's just a 'possum or a coon."

"Maybe."

Hondo's barking racket began to subside. After a little half-hearted growling, he whined and turned to Luke and licked his offered hand. Luke patted the dog's rump. "Okay, boy. Good job. You scared 'em away. Whatever the hell it was."

Ree patted Luke's rump and said, "Bet you can't scare me away, big boy."

He relaxed his grip on the pistol, stood and slipped his arm around her tiny waist. "Now why would I want to do something as foolish as that?"

She slipped into her Scarlet O'Hara voice and lilted, "Why, Mistuh Chaney, suh, when a lady sees a big hairy monster staring her in the face, she's just liable to turn tail and run off screamin'."

He chuckled. "You're bad."

"Fiddle-dee-dee. I'd never believe anything any ol' man told me."

"Frankly, my dear . . ."

"Come inside," she said, batting her long lashes, "and I'll make you give a damn."

"Yes ma'am," he said, casting one more glance in the direction of the front yard and the drizzly darkness beyond.

* * *

Boots Birdwell shut his Bible, stood up and put on his plastic raincoat.

"Where you going, Granddaddy?" asked Eartha, looking up from her magazine.

"Got to pay a visit to an old friend," he answered.

"On a night like this?" she said, trying to sound older than her sixteen years.

"Cain't put off the Lord's work on account of a little rain."

"You been nervous as a cat all evening. What's going on?"

"Nothin' you need to worry about, precious. Now stop doggin' an old man."

Eartha laughed. "All right then, old man. You just be careful driving on those wet roads."

He came over to her armchair and gently touched her smooth cheek. "You look more your momma ever day," he said. "Shame she ain't here to see you grow up. She'd be so proud."

She smiled. "She sees me. She watches me from Heaven."

He bent down and kissed her forehead. "That's right, baby. Don't wait up for me. I might be late."

He went outside, climbed into his truck and drove to the outskirts of Vinewood's Southside. The rainfall was finally fizzling out, and the night air was turning cooler as a cold front crept in. Patches of fog appeared on the lowland road, blunting the old Ford's headlight beams. Ghostly shapes capered within the foggy patches, but Boots knew he was seeing ghosts created by light and fog and imagination. He suspected that real haints were relentlessly advancing.

"Lord, I hope I'm wrong," he mumbled to himself as he turned onto a muddy dirt road behind an old churchyard. "Please, let me be wrong."

His tires lost traction in the muddy slush and the truck hydroplaned, turning sideways on the road. He lightly tapped the brake pedal, then righted the vehicle and proceeded with greater caution. The road dead-ended in a cul-de-sac lined with big pussy willow trees. Nearly invisible behind the trees, a modest cottage with a single lighted window lay in repose, reminding Boots of a house in a fairy tale. He parked under drooping limbs and rain-laden leaves, got out and slogged through the wet muck to the front door of the fairytale cottage. He rapped on the door with a weathered brass knocker in the shape of a ram's head.

The rumbling voice of an old woman answered his knock: "You come on in, Brother Birdwell."

He went inside. Odessa Nell greeted him with a wan smile. A Persian cat lay curled in her ample lap. Satiny yellow light softened by an old lacy lampshade bathed her brown face. "I's wonderin' when you'd come," she said.

"Is that right?" Boots grinned, showing her most of his fine white dentures.

Odessa Nell nodded. "'Less you was already passed on to the next world, I knew you'd come callin'."

"You always was one for knowing things like that, Miz Odessa." He shucked his plastic raincoat, hung it on a tall hat rack, and sat on the worn but comfortable sofa.

"Go on and ask it," she told him. Her dark eyes seemed to gleam with an inner light.

Boots nodded. "It's happening again, ain't it? Just like it did down in Holy Crossing a whole lotta years ago."

"Umm-hmm," she rumbled. "It is, Brother Birdwell. It sho is."

"Can we stop it?"

She laughed a joyless laugh. "Us old coots? Lawd, have mercy. You know we cain't do nothin' like that. Look at us! We too old and used up."

He shook his head. "Ain't nothing we can do?"

"I wish you'd tell me what. That time in Florida I was still young and full of the power, and even then it liked to killed me. You was there. You saw how it was."

"But there must be somebody younger who can do something. Somebody with some of the knowledge, at least."

"Ain't nobody like that now. I tried to pass what I know on to my grandbaby, but she ain't got time for such nonsense. Folks today are soft, Brother Birdwell. They ignorant, and they don't want to hear about the real evil things in this world. They think they see evil every day on the news and in the streets. They don't know most of that's just outright meanness. They got no idea what pure evil is. But I reckon some of 'em is about to find out."

Boots sat and digested her words in silence. Odessa Nell stroked the cat on her lap. The grandfather clock in the corner chimed the hour. After the tenth and final chime, Boots said, "Who you reckon's done it?"

"That I *don't* know. But it's got to be somebody powerful, somebody who knew what they was doin'. If these old bones ain't lyin' to me, I'd say whoever called it up is most likely already dead. The Yawahoos don't be comin' without somebody dyin' in they own blood, by they own hand. Somebody wanted this real bad." She shook her head slowly from side to side. The cat stirred and began a loud purring. "And *real bad* is zackly what we gone get."

"It don't seem right, Miz Odessa. Don't seem right at all. What if a good man . . . or woman, was to give his own life for the sake of others, like Jesus did? Wouldn't that count for something? I cain't believe a sacrifice in the name of evil carries more weight than a sacrifice for good. That goes against everything I been preaching all these long years."

"You talkin' 'bout you and me? Lawd, we so old and we ain't hardly got no life to give up. We got two feet in the grave already, you and me together. We ain't got power enough to fight what's comin'. I tell you, this thing was done by a conjure woman the likes of which ain't been seen for years. Ain't no man coulda done it. I'm talkin' 'bout a conjure woman from the other side of the grave. *I feel it.* Never been but one woman like that I ever knowed of. And she been dead a long time. Lived and died in bayou country. But somebody round here knowed how to call her up. Sure as we sittin' here, that's what did it. Best we can do is pray to the Almighty and ask that our own sins be forgiven. Then hold tight and wait for the axe to come down."

"Still don't seem right," said Boots. "I got to believe somebody hereabouts can find a way to stop it."

"'Less you know more than I do, that ain't gone happen."

"I don't know much, but I got to have faith. If I give that up, I may as well go on and hand over my soul to Satan."

Odessa Nell made a hissing noise. "Satan ain't nothin'. It's the Yawahoos you got to worry 'bout. And they ain't interested in your tired old soul. All they be wantin' is to spread their evil darkness and feed on our fear and sufferin'."

"God be with us," he said softly. The hollow sound of his weary voice fell flat and seemed to die on the floor.

"Amen," said Odessa Nell.

The cat lifted its head and looked around expectantly.

CHAPTER 25
IN EXTREMIS

Cornelius Weehunt waded through the boggy back yard to the tool shed. The rain had stopped, and the night was filling up with fog. His head was filled with fog, too, but the voices in that skull-fog were making everything very clear to him. He'd never heard such voices! As sharp and clear as the sound from the best CD player in the world, laser-sharp and irresistible. Like the voice of God spoken with a thousand mouths. Even when the voices were saying different things at the same time, he was able to hear them all and understand them all. The presence of the Godlike voices somehow gave him the special power of hearing them all at once and sorting them out and taking them to heart. Corny understood that he was the instrument, the special tool, of the ones behind those magic voices, that he would do—must do—whatever they told him.

And now they were telling him to go the tool shed and get the machete he sometimes used for cutting vines off the dogwood trees in the front yard or chopping a path through the small patch of woods beside the house just for the fun of doing it. They hadn't yet told him what they wanted him to do with the machete, but he knew they would when the time came. Corny always kept his tools in good condition, just the way his father had taught him; he was especially proud of the way he had honed the machete's blade to the sharpest edge possible, *razor* sharp and free of nicks. He could chop most anything with it. It was the same with the axe, but he was partial to the machete. Whenever he used it, he imagined that he was in some thick jungle, chopping his way through the undergrowth, on his way to save a beautiful woman whose clothes had been ripped to shreds by a wild beast. He pictured her now in his raucous mind and sprouted an erection. He fondled his hard-on through his jeans, then opened the door, stepped into the little hut and pulled the chain on the naked bulb hanging from the center beam of the shed. They were all there, his tools neatly put away in their proper places and shining in the 60-watt glare. The voices sang. They harmonized so sweetly! Like a chorus of angels. The many voices became one, and that one overwhelming voice told him to take the machete in his hand and test its blade against his own flesh. He obeyed, drawing the length of the blade across his wrist. A line of blood rose from the cut to kiss the moving blade. The mouth of the shallow wound joined the chorus, and Corny realized with wonder that his blood was singing. The voices were in his blood!

The night fog was billowing into the shed now, hazing the edges of things and misting Corny's eyes. His vision blurred, but the voices remained as sharp and clear as heavenly bells, ringing, ringing, ringing . . .

He reached up, found the hanging chain and turned off the light. The thick fog brightened the darkness as he left the shed and quietly shut the door. The voices softened their song to a melodic whispering, and in those insistent whispers Corny clearly heard his instructions. Now he knew what they wanted him to do. It was not something he ever would've thought of himself. It was like something you would see in one of those old slasher movies on cable TV, only much worse.

"I cain't do that," he whispered back. But then the whispering in his skull-fog got loud again, so loud that his head felt like it might explode, and Corny knew he *could* do it. He *had* to do it. There was no disobeying *these* whisperers.

Cloaked in lush fog, he sat down on the boggy lawn and waited for the people in the boarding house to shut off their lights and go to sleep.

The whispering voices altogether bewitched him.

* * *

The masked man shoved Joe Rob through the doorless doorway of the tumbledown house, and a rat scurried into shadows thrown by the hostage-taker's flashlight. Joe Rob stumbled over a loose board in the floor and went to his knees. A pair of handcuffs clattered to the floor in front of him. "Cuff yourself to that radiator."

With reluctance, Joe Rob snapped one of the steel bracelets around his left wrist, then closed the other one around the iron pipe coming out of the floor at the radiator's foot. He glanced up at the dark sky visible through the jagged opening where part of the roof had collapsed. "How'd you find me?" he asked.

"Does it matter?" the man said in a voice burned raw by years of tobacco and alcohol use.

"Yeah. I wanna know."

203

"When I accept a contract, I learn all I can about the target's social strata, his circle of associates. It's easy in a town this small. Your grandmother was most helpful. When I heard of your escape, I figured you'd show up at that trailer."

"Who the fuck *are* you, man?"

"I'm the angel of death."

"You're a hit man."

"If you wish to use that cheap term."

"Who's paying you?" Joe Rob lean his back against the radiator's ribs.

"One Charlotte Claymore. Affectionately known as Charlotte the Harlot, I believe."

"You're shitting me. Why would she want me killed? All I did was . . ."

"Yes?" The man's thin lips formed an ugly smile in the mouth-slit of the ski mask.

"Fuck her up the ass."

"Over her protestations, I presume."

"You don't talk like a hit man."

"Oh? And how does a hit man talk?"

"I dunno. You're the first one I've ever met."

The man shrugged his narrow shoulders as he shone his light about the ruins of the room. Jewels of raindrops shimmered within the intricate patterns of a spider web in the corner. The room smelled of mildew and rotting wood.

"How much she paying you?" Joe Rob asked.

"That's immaterial."

"Huh?"

"It doesn't matter. What matters is that she wants you tortured before I deliver the *coup de grace*."

"That bitch!"

"Aren't they all? But sometimes very serviceable, eh?"

"You're gonna torture me?"

"Afraid so."

"Fuck, man, why don't—" Joe Rob broke off his words when he saw the shapes moving through darkness in the adjoining room. Three, four, maybe more. He smiled at his captor. "I think they want you."

"What's that?" The hit man licked his lips, his tongue a startling red within the black mask.

Joe Rob nodded his head in the direction of the other room. "Those things moving around in the dark. I think you're the one they want now."

The man turned and shone the light in the adjoining room. Seeing nothing but empty space and discolored walls, he turned back and put the beam of light in Joe Rob's face. "I don't know what drugs you're on, but I'm afraid they won't dull the pain you're about to experience. Don't go away. I'll be right back."

The hit man went outside to his car, presumably to get his instruments of torture, and Joe Rob sat in the dark, watching the shapes slither along the walls and over the floor.

"It's not so bad, son," said Billy Joe Campbell. He was sitting in the open window, strumming his guitar. His face was a phosphorescent green. "It's some ways better being dead. You might like it."

Joe Rob was anxious to talk to his father before he disappeared again, like he'd done in the woods. "Did you kill yourself, Pop?"

"Hell no. Sumbitch shot me out back of this ol' honky-tonk in Mississippi."

Joe Rob strained his eyes for a better look into the eyes of his dead father. "Why are you here now? How come I'm seeing you?"

"Devil's Valley, Joey," said the ghost. "Devil's Fucking Valley. Ain't no way out of it." Billy Joe slid his guitar strap around so that he was wearing the instrument on his back, then jumped out of the window and disappeared in the thick fog.

"Pop, wait!" Joe Rob tried to get up, but the handcuffs didn't allow it. The gunshot wound in his right shoulder started throbbing with deep pain. "Cain't you help me out me out here? This sumbitch's gone kill me!"

His executioner was back, chuckling to himself as he set a battery-powered lantern on the floor. He was wearing a blue-vinyl butcher's apron. "Do your hallucinations talk back to you?"

Joe Rob glared at the masked man. "Ain't hallucinatin'. It's a ghost."

"Really." The man held up a chain saw. "Shall we begin the fun?"

"Whoa, motherfucker, you ain't—"

The silenced pistol in the man's right hand spit two times as he fired one round into each of Joe Rob's kneecaps. Joe Rob screamed and grabbed at his right knee with his free hand.

"That's to keep you from kicking me when I start separating you from your limbs." He holstered the pistol, then yanked the starter-cord and the chainsaw came to life with a sputtering whine.

The psychic shock of knowing what was about to be done to him was greater than the physical shock of the pain in his knees. He knew now that the lurking shadows were not there to help him. More likely, they were there to harvest his soul. Soon he would join his father as a soulless ghost in a hell called Devil's Valley. The crazy girl who had started the unlikely chain of events leading up to this terrible moment had been right all along when she said the dark thing wanted him. Sure as hell, it was about to have him.

The man stood over him, leaned down and guided the racing chain of teeth into the flesh just above Joe Rob's left knee. The sawteeth bit all the way to the bone, slinging shredded flesh, denim and strings of blood into the air. The pain was unimaginably ferocious and Joe Rob screamed. He saw his lower leg fall away from the bloody stump of his thigh. Seeing the lifeless limb there on the floor, he couldn't believe it had actually been a part of him. When the chainsaw started on his other leg, his mind slipped into darkness.

A vial of ammonia broken under his nose brought him back to consciousness, but it was a consciousness of altered perception, of a mind fogged by physical trauma and great loss of blood. He was dying. The abyss had opened to receive him, and its great yawning maw was about to swallow him up. He looked down at the stumps of both legs, then he saw his severed right arm lying across his blood-soaked lap. With detached wonder, he noted that his right arm was still a part of him, still cuffed to the radiator.

"Smile for the camera," said the masked man, and then snapped Joe Rob's picture with a Polaroid camera. The flash seemed to set off the dark shapes surrounding them, and they capered wildly about the room. After two more flashes from the camera, the hit man drew his pistol, aimed at Joe Rob's face, and said, "Nothing personal, Bubba. Rest in peace."

The madly circling shadows closed in on Joe Rob, and as they entered him, he felt an unearthly coldness.

When the killing shot blew a hole between his eyes and ripped into his brain, Joe Rob was thinking: *Rest in peace, my ass.*

* * *

The man in the ski mask pressed his fingers to his victim's throat to confirm that the young man was dead. He was. The man took two close-up shots of the corpse's face, taking care to center the shot on the bullet-hole between the half-open eyes. "The cunt will cream in her jeans when she sees these shots," he said. "And that's when I'll have her."

He was hot and sweaty beneath the woolen mask, but it was his practice never to remove it until he had disposed of the body and was well away from the scene of the execution. His routine had served him well for a long time and he was not about to change it now. His clients knew him only as

Mort, and none ever saw his face. He was known as a cold-blooded killer, but he was just the opposite; he was passionate in his work. He wasn't in it for the money. He killed for the joy of killing. The pay simply made his nomadic way of life possible. Whenever there was a shortage of clients, Mort found victims of his own to satiate his bloodlust.

He got a sheet of plastic from the trunk of his car and took it into the house and spread it out on the floor as close to the corpse as he could without getting the bottom-side of the plastic bloody. Then he unlocked the cuffs, dropped them in his apron pocket, and bent down to pick up the mutilated body. The boy had been big boned and muscular, but with both legs and one arm gone, he wasn't too heavy to lift. Mort slid both arms under the boy's trunk and lifted him off the killing floor. The corpse's head lolled backward, and a hiss of air escaped from lungs that had breathed their last. The remaining arm dangled toward the floor and brushed against Mort's left thigh. As he stepped toward the plastic drop-sheet, the dangling arm and the lolling head came to life. The arm swung up and wrapped itself around Mort's head, and the head swiveled up to allow the dead boy's teeth to tear into Mort's throat. He tried to free himself from the deadly, biting vice, but the arm and the jaws were too powerful.

Mort fell to the floor with the corpse firmly attached. He tried to scream but the dead boy's teeth had already ripped out his throat and were now burrowing into the side of his neck, chomping and snarling relentlessly, severing Mort's jugular and gnawing all the way to the vertebrae at the base of his skull.

Mort died with his mask on.

*   *   *

Luke Chaney came awake with a start, and tried to brush away the hand that was jostling his bare shoulder.

"It's me," Ree Tyler whispered. "You were mumbling in your sleep and thrashing around like a wild man."

"Umm, nightmare," he said with a foul taste in his mouth.

"Must've been a dilly," she snuggled against him, their bodies naked beneath the sheets.

"Yeah."

"Tell me."

"I don't remember much. Just that . . . somebody was going after you with a big, bloody blade."

"Like my vision." Ree shuddered. "Was I in the shop?"

"Don't know. You know how dreams are. I guess you were in dreamland."

"Well, did he get me?"

"No, you woke me up before he could. What time is it?"

She looked across his chest at the red numerals on the clock on the bedside table. "One-forty-four." She kissed his shoulder and draped her leg over him so that her inner thigh rested lightly on his genitals.

"Let's get out of town for a few days," he said. "Take a little vacation. You can close the shop for a couple of days, can't you?"

"Well . . ."

"Go down to Florida. St. Augustine. I love that place. You ever been there?"

"No, Ben and I used to always go to Panama City."

"Too crowded. Too many drunk, horny kids. St. Augustine is quieter. A place where you can touch history."

Ree slipped her hand between her thigh and his belly and caressed his semi-flaccid penis. "I'd rather touch this."

"Damn, Shorty, you trying to send me to an early grave?"

"No! Don't say that." She withdrew her hand, but Luke caught it and drew it back to this groin.

"Just kidding," he said. "I'm just about too old for an early grave, anyway. Go ahead and do your worst—I mean your best."

She gave his stiffening member a playful yank. He rolled over on top of her, and they made love once more. A short while later, he fell asleep and resumed the dream of someone with a bloody machete stalking Ree.

* * *

The fog was so thick he couldn't see the house. But he saw the last light go off in the writer's window. What was the name of that book he was writing? Corny couldn't think of it. He caressed the cool blade laid across his lap and tried not to think about what the voices had told him to do. The pool of water he was sitting in no longer felt so cold on his butt, but the coolness of the ground seemed to find its way up through his bumhole and into his belly, twisting and turning through his intestines, rising into his stomach and streaming into his chest. He hoped those little hookworms they'd warned him about in school weren't crawling up inside him with the cold. Those things did bad things to you once they got inside you. He didn't remember what exactly, but he knew it was bad. The voices that were inside him didn't seem bad, though they wanted him to do very bad things. But things weren't always how they seemed. His mother used to say that when she was still alive, and he figured that was the case with what the voices told him he had to do. He'd always been a little afraid of Whisperer, but these new voices didn't make him afraid. They made him feel strong and sure. Like he could do no wrong as long as he did what they said. They were pretty quiet now; so quiet he could hardly hear them over the noisy singing of the tree frogs and the crickets and whatever else was out there in the woods making all that racket. A snake crawled out of the fog in front of him. It was impossible to tell what color it was in the dark and the fog, but he thought it was black. And it was slithering right for him with its head raised out of the wet grass. He raised the machete and was about to bring the blade down on the little serpent's neck when the voices stopped him and told him it was their snake and that he couldn't kill it. They even told him the snake's name. It sounded something like Simon or Seemon, like a foreign name, but he wasn't sure. He just knew he wasn't to hurt it. The snake paused at his crooked knee and lifted its flared head over his jeans, flicking out its tongue, then it slithered over his leg and into his lap. Corny moved his hand out of the creature's way, and it darted its head into the waist of his jeans. He didn't like this one little bit, but the bossy voices told him to hold still and let the snake have its way. It was cold and icky against his belly as it disappeared into his pants. It slithered down past his dick and balls and up the crack of his butt. He gasped as it entered him, but the voices wouldn't let him move to stop it. His anus tingled as the snake's muscles propelled it deeper inside him, but he couldn't even squeeze his asshole tight to stop it.

"Holy crap, I got a durn snake up my butt," he said, or thought he said, but probably just thought it real loud. It didn't feel bad, not really. Actually it felt kind of good, so good he got another hard-on. It was sort of like the time when he was little, lying in bed one night and for no good reason he stuck one of his mother's clothespins up his butt and beat his meat. He thought of beating off now, but the voices told him it was time to go into the house and do what they wanted him to do. He got to his feet and headed for the back door. As he turned the knob and pulled the door open, he suddenly remembered the name of the writer's book and he whispered it out loud: *"Bloody Graves."*

* * *

Boots Birdwell couldn't sleep. He hadn't been afraid of the dark since his childhood in Florida, but now, as he lay abed, the darkness of his room oppressed him and filled him with apprehension. He reached up and turned on his bedside lamp, and the darkness fled into shadowy corners, still there but weakened by the light and not quite as scary.

He got up and crept down the hall to his granddaughter's room and peeked in to make sure she was all right. The nightlight gave a soft illumination, and he could see that Eartha had her head stuffed beneath her pillow, but that she was breathing. Sweet girl, and smart, too. She was going places, better than the places he'd been to, he was sure.

Boots was in the bathroom trying to pee when the phone rang. His prostate had been grieving him a lot lately, and he suspected the worst: cancer. He put himself back in the folds of his pajama bottoms and padded on his bare feet to the phone in the kitchen. "'Lo," he said.

"Brother Birdwell? Somethin' bad's 'bout to happen in town. You got to try an' stop it."

"That you, Miz Odessa?"

"'Course it's me," rumbled the old lady. "Get on over to that boardin' house on Poplar Street. That's where they are."

"*Them?*"

"Yes, Lawd, *them*. The Yawahoos. It come to me in a vision. They found their puppet an' they 'bout to pull his strings."

"You know who it is?" His pulse was thudding and whooshing in his ears.

"I don't know his name, but look for somebody who ain't right in the head. They always seek the lowest level, like foul water flowing into a sump. Get on over there now."

Boots sighed, his windy breath feeding back to him in the phone's earpiece. "But you said there ain't nothin' we can do. We too old, remember?"

"I know what I said, but I had this vision and I think I was wrong about that."

"What did you see?"

"Killin'. Lots of killin'. Ohhh, it hurt my heart to see it. So much innocent blood shed."

"Miz Odessa, how can *I* stop it? I'm just uh ol' worn-out preacher."

"We ain't got time to argue 'bout it," she said, raising her voice. "You an' me are the only ones who seen it before. Now get on! I'll be doin' some spells here that might help. Somethin' will come to you. Now go!"

She hung up. Boots replaced the receiver and stared at the yellowed kitchen wallpaper, noting how much the blue flowers had faded over the years, and it made him feel sad and terribly old.

*　　*　　*

Corny stole up the stairs, wincing each time a stairstep creaked underfoot. He held the machete down by his right leg and he could swear he heard the blade ringing softly in the darkness as if an invisible clapper had struck it. The blade was alive and hungry. It translated its hunger through his hand and all the way up to his gut and head, turning hunger into what felt like lust. The snake in his belly was coiled into a tight spiral of cold-blooded passion, and he knew that the snake was directing him as much as the voices were, commanding his actions and overcoming his resistance. When he reached the top of the stairs, he crept softly down the hallway to his aunt's room. The single nightlight plugged into the outlet halfway down the hall threw strange shadows, splotchy and somehow cold. His own distorted shadow moved along the floor and the lower wall like a slithering serpent, and Corny knew in his heart that his shadow was not merely his own—the things inside him were casting their shadows with his. He reached out, turned the heavy glass doorknob and gently pushed the door inward. He stepped into his aunt's room and moved soundlessly to the brass bed where she lay sleeping. She was on her back, her head resting on a thin pillow. Even in the dim light from the hallway he could see the white flesh of Aunt Mattie's throat, and he knew this was the place to strike. He raised the machete over his shoulder. The blade sang softly to him, and the chorus of voices in his head sang along in delirious harmony.

Cut the vine, they sang. *Cut the vine and free the soul.*

A familiar voice cut through the din of voices inside his skull: "Corny, no. Don't do it. It's murder."

He looked up and saw his dead father standing on the other side of his aunt's bed. Big Bill Weehunt stood tall and proud in the faint light, just as he'd always stood when he was alive. His father's eyes were alive with sadness and pleading.

"Daddy?" whispered Corny.

"I taught you better than this," said his father. "Didn't I?"

The voices in his head grew louder, hissing and chanting their commands. Corny's unnatural shadow came off the bed and the wall and leapt upon the ghost of his father, obscuring the fragile spirit-body, and Corny knew they were eating his daddy's soul. A tear ran down his cheek as his father was lost to him forever. The serpent in his belly began to uncoil, setting off horrible cramps in his gut. His churning intestines threatened to foul his shorts.

Cut the vine, the shadow-voices screamed. *Cut the vine and free the soul.*

* * *

211

Luke grabbed the phone before the third ring. "Yeah," he said hoarsely.

"Mistuh Chief? This is Boots Birdwell. Now I know you ain't chief no more, but I can't call Chief Keller 'cause he thinks I'm just a crazy old nigra. So you got to call 'em and tell 'em to get over to Miz Weehunt's boardin' house quick. Something bad's gone happen there. May be it already has. Somebody got to get over there."

"Boots, what the hell are you talking about? Have you been drinking?"

"No, suh, I ain't been drinking. Now you got to get somebody over there fast. Maybe they can stop him before he kills too many."

"Stop *who*?"

"I ain't sure, but I think it's probably that Weehunt boy whose head ain't right. He's the only one I can think of who'd make a good puppet."

"You know how crazy you sound?"

"Cain't help that. Just get over there. You'll see what I'm saying. I got to go. I don't know if I can stop it, but I got to try."

The line went dead. Luke hung up the phone.

"What was that all about?" asked Ree, touching his shoulder.

"Damned if I know. It was ol' Boots Birdwell, the black preacher who does janitor work for the department. He says something's going on at Mattie Weehunt's boarding house and that I've got to do something about it before people get killed."

"My goodness. *Did* he sound drunk?"

"No. He's never done anything like this before. He's a devout Christian, and smart as a whip. This isn't like him at all. I don't know how he knows, but if he says something's going on there, then it probably is."

Luke picked up the phone and called the station. Alvin Snow answered, and Luke told him that he'd had a tip that something was happening at the boarding house and suggested that Snow send a squad car over there to check things out. Snow said he would. Then Luke got up, found the phone book and called the listed number for Matilda Weehunt. He hated to wake her up in the middle of the night for nothing, but his gut told him that this was no false alarm.

After the tenth unanswered ring, he cradled the phone and started getting dressed. "I'm going over there. I think something really is wrong."

"Are you forgetting you aren't a cop anymore?" Ree asked, sitting up and hugging the sheet to her breasts.

"Hell, Shorty, I'll always be a cop. I guess I've got donut jelly in my blood."

He pulled his boots on, stood and kissed her lips.

"Be careful," she said with arched brows. "You better come back to me in one piece."

* * *

The phone stopped ringing just before Corny ripped its cord from the wall. He avoided looking at the bloody thing in his aunt's bed. It wasn't Aunt Mattie anymore, not really, but he didn't want to see it again. He didn't understand how the things inside him could make him see so clearly in the dark, but somehow they did, and he'd seen all too clearly the way the machete's blade had hacked into the old woman's fat neck and opened up her throat like the pale belly of a skinned rabbit. The blood had gushed out like oil from a well, making him think of that theme song from *The Beverley Hillbillies*, and the song started running through his head. The "bubbling crude" from his aunt's throat looked oily, darker than blood was supposed to look, and Corny knew then that the things inside him craved blood and that they were feeding on it, even though he couldn't see them doing it. They robbed the blood of its redness and turned it dark like oil. If he cut himself now, would his blood be black, too? The snake undulated in his belly, and warm liquid squirted out of his bumhole, fouling his shorts. The stench drove him from the room, but that was stupid, he realized, because the source of the stench was in his pants. The voices told him to go to the next room, where the soul of Kirby Cone waited to be freed by Corny's magic blade.

* * *

Ree Tyler wiped herself with Luke's harsh bathroom tissue, then got up and flushed the john. She went to the sink, filled her cupped hands with water from the cold-water tap and washed her face in it. As she daubed her face with a hand towel, she watched her reflection in the mirror over the sink. Her hair was mussed from their sweaty bedroom activities, and she noted that her graying roots were showing again. *Time for another dye job.* She replaced the towel and studied her face in the mirror. Wrinkles around her eyes and in her forehead were more pronounced, and she wondered if her smoking really did cause extra wrinkles. Maybe now was a good time to give up tobacco—now that she had Luke. After Ben died, she had smoked more, using tobacco as a way of coping with the stress of being left alone in the world. With Luke in her life, that particular stress would be eliminated; so, she reasoned, now she should be able to kick the habit once and for all. *As soon as I finish my last pack, that's it. I'll quit cold-turkey.*

She lowered her gaze to her breasts. In the mirror they looked heavy and unusually voluptuous on her small frame, but they didn't sag too much, considering that she was well into middle age. Luke surely appreciated them. Hell, he practically worshiped them, she thought with a smile. His wife Jenny hadn't been big in the boob department, she recalled, so Luke was probably getting his first real taste of a big set of knockers. Ree cupped her breasts and lifted them a little. *Still got a few years before they start drooping toward my navel. Then I'll get a boob-job.*

She turned away from the mirror and had her hand on the light switch by the bathroom door when she heard the whisper. She froze, then turned toward the mirror. Beau was there; the outline of his face was blurry, but it was Beau, beyond a doubt. But why was he appearing in Luke's bathroom mirror? She'd only ever seen him in the antique mirror at the shop. "Beau?" she whispered, modestly covering her breasts with her hands.

A look of profound distress showed in his face as his image grew more distinct. His deep-blue eyes were filled with pleading, and she knew he was trying desperately to tell her something, but she couldn't make sense of the buzzing whispers in her head. He raised his hands and began to motion wildly. His dark cloak billowed as if blown by a stormy wind.

"Beau, what is it?" she asked the ghost in the mirror.

His ageless, princely face darkened, and Ree suddenly went cold. She shivered, hugging herself against the otherworldly chill as Beau began to age right before her wide eyes. Deep lines appeared in his face, the flesh beneath his eyes became puffy and sagged like loose bags of bruised tissue, and his eyelids grew droopy, hooding his murky eyes. His thick, dark hair went gray and thin, and his whole aspect seemed to be shrinking.

But the wildly accelerated aging didn't stop there.

She watched with growing horror as her guardian angel began to decay and molder like a corpse in some hideous time-lapse video. His desiccated skin blackened, then crumbled and flaked away from his skull. The whites of his eyes turned yellow and the eyeballs shriveled like dried blue berries, then tumbled from their sockets. His cloak slipped off his once-proud shoulders to reveal bones covered with patches of leathered skin. Finally, his skull collapsed inward upon itself, and the mirror filled with an inky fog.

She stared helplessly into the mirror at the swirling black mist and knew that Beau had been taken from her forever, that whatever had taken him was wholly evil. And whatever it was, it was still here with her.

* * *

Odessa Nell anointed her hair with sandalwood-scented oil as she sat naked on the floor before the four white candles burning three inches apart on the altar in her sanctified devotional room. Protected by the magic circle painted in red within the rectangular confines of the room, she called upon the Archangel Michael for his protection as well.

She had known for years that this night was coming, and now that it had finally arrived, she didn't know if she was strong enough to fight the evil. She longed for the youthful strength and energy she'd had as spiritual leader of the brothers and sisters of Holy Crossing, but no amount of longing was going to return her to the state-of-grace and seat-of-power position she'd held in the little community on the edge of the Everglades. Time had changed everything. Attitudes had changed with each new generation, and not for the better. Nowadays folks didn't believe a woman could be a strong spiritual leader. They didn't understand that a woman was naturally closer to the world of the spirit than a man could ever be. Just as a woman could bring a new spirit into the world by giving birth, a woman of true wisdom could deliver her people into the world of the spirit. But the old days were gone and the old ways were all but gone with them. The secret knowledge passed down from Odessa's great-great grandmother the slave was going to die with Odessa—not because she was unwilling to pass the secrets on, but because she had found no one willing to accept the teachings. The magic of science and technology had all but replaced the spiritual magic. Folks still went to church and prayed in the name of Jesus Christ, but most of them worshiped material goods and reserved their wonder for the high-tech gadgets and conveniences that made their lives easier. It was a crying shame, but she knew crying wouldn't help.

Odessa had known for years that something dark and wicked inhabited the crust of the earth here in Vinewood. Why it was so, she didn't know. Some places made better homes for evil than others; whether it had to do with electromagnetic power grids as some speculated, or whether it had to do with the kind of people who lived on the land, it didn't matter now. All that mattered was that the Yawahoos not be allowed to tap into that dark power and use it for their destructive purposes. If the elementals wedded their sinister designs to that ungodly darkness, then the marriage made in the cellar of Hell could give birth to something the world had never seen before. Something that could spread well beyond the tainted ground of Vinewood. She clasped her hands together and prayed aloud until she lost her voice to hoarseness.

*   *   *

215

Corny went from room to room, methodically hacking each occupant to death and leaving them in their bloodied beds, their souls cut loose from their vile bodies. He moved in a daze, his mind fogged, blinded to the horror of his deeds. The voices urged him on; they stroked him, soothed him, baby-talked him, and showed him the rightness of his actions.

It is written. Written in blood. Cut the vines! Free the souls! They sang. They chanted, they crooned, they demanded.

And Corny obeyed. *Good boy!*

When he tried the door of the writer's room, he found it locked. "What do I do now?" he whispered. The voices told him to go on to the next room and to come back for the writer after all the others were freed. He slipped soundlessly into John Henry Jackson's room, stood over his sleeping form and raised the blade. The old man sat up with a start. "Cornelius? What in hell are you doing, son?"

Corny gripped the machete's handle with both hands and swung the blade as if he were swinging a bat at a fastball, going for a homer. The blade chopped into the old man's upthrust arm and he yelped in pain and surprise.

Silence him!

Corny grabbed a pillow and crammed it over Jackson's face, pushing him back down on the mattress. Straddling the man's thin frame, he held the pillow in place until the muffled sounds ceased and the old man quit struggling. Then he cut the vine and John Henry's head fell away from his scrawny neck. The voices instructed him to pick up the severed head and take it with him to the landing at the top of the stairs. Looking down the steep stairway he grew dizzy and afraid that he might tumble down the stairs. Still, he complied with the voices' wishes and tossed the head down the steps like a bowling ball with teeth and hair. It bounced and thudded to the bottom, coming to rest against the front door of the house. Ignoring his dizziness, he followed it down to the first floor and proceeded down the shadowy hallway to Elsie Royal's room back by the kitchen. As the sole female boarder, the widowed Mrs. Royal had the only rented room on the first floor because, as Aunt Mattie had explained to him, it would be improper for a lady to be sleeping upstairs where all the male boarders lived. Down here on the first floor she had her own private bathroom and shower. Corny thought she must be in her middle fifties because her hair was mostly gray, but she had a good figure for a woman of that age, and he sometimes fantasized about watching her undress for a bath in the old-timey tub with the claw-feet, soaping those big tits and washing between her legs. As he tried her door, his erection pushed against his zipper in pulsing anticipation of seeing her in her nightgown or maybe even her birthday suit. The door was locked. He didn't wait for the voices to tell him what to do this time. He knew he couldn't break the solid door open by throwing his body against it like cops do on TV, so he crept to the kitchen, got the screwdriver from the tool drawer and went back to the door and began to unscrew the bolts holding the doorknob and locking mechanism to the wood. He thought he was being quiet but Mrs. Royal gave him a start when she cried, "Who's there?" He removed the last screw and the knob and lock fell to the floor with a thump. "Who is it?" the woman shouted.

He pushed the door open. Elsie Royal was sitting up in bed, staring at him with eyes as big as hen eggs. The lamp on her bedside table was on and he could see her nipples poking the thin cloth of her pink gown. Then he saw the gun in her hand. It was a small pistol, but he didn't doubt that it was real and that it could hurt him real bad if she shot him with it.

"Cornelius, what—" Her eyes got even bigger when she saw the machete in his hand and his blood-spattered clothes. "Oh, my Jesus!" she shrieked. "Get away from me! I'll shoot you!"

At the same instant a loud knock rattled the front door and somebody shouted, "Police! Open up!"

Corny turned and ran out of the woman's room, cut through the kitchen and went out the back door. The things making the voices in his head were angry now. They didn't like not having their way, and they took it out on him by having the snake writhe wildly in his belly. Warm liquid began to ooze from his rectum, and he was sure there would be blood mixed with his runny shit. He ran through the foggy night, the bloodied machete swinging with his right arm as though it had become a part of him. "Where do I go?" he asked, panting and driving forward on his strong legs.

The hole, the voices chorused.

The hole? Corny slowed his pace, unsure of what they meant. Then they flashed a picture in his mind of the big sinkhole in Main Street, and suddenly everything made sense. He ran across the street, cut through dark yards, setting every dog in the neighborhood to barking, and then he ran for the sinkhole, finally unafraid of what awaited him there in the unnatural darkness in the bosom of the earth.

*   *   *

Luke parked beside the squad car with its rack of roof lights flashing, jumped out of his truck and raced to the front door of the boarding house. Boots Birdwell was standing just inside the door, much of the color gone from his nut-brown face. He looked old and deflated, as if his many years on earth had all at once caught up with him and sucked out the last remnant of his lost youth. "We too late," said the old man. "Boy killed four of 'em and run off before they could catch him."

The Luke saw the decapitated head on the floor to the right of the door. It was resting on its left cheek, a small patch of blood pooled beneath its smooth-cut neck. "Jesus Christ! That's . . . Is that John Henry Jackson?"

Boots avoided looking at the head. "I don't rightly know."

"Jesus."

Voices drifted from a room in the rear of the house: the shrill, excited voice of a woman, and the clipped baritone of a male. Luke looked at Boots Birdwell. "Corny Weehunt did this?"

Boots nodded. "I know that boy. He got a bad brain but a good heart. Wasn't his fault. They made him do it."

"What do you mean? Who made him do it?"

The old man arched his hoary brows. "Evil spirits. Elementals. We call 'em by their African name. The Yawahoos. That's how they do. Find a weak spot and burrow in like ticks on a dog. Boy never would done this on his own. Wasn't in him to do it."

Luke put his hand on the old man's bony shoulder. "How'd you know about this, Boots?"

"Odessa Nell called me up and said she saw it in a vision. You know her, don't you? Lives in that gingerbread house out past the Southside cemetery. She's old now, but there was a time when she was a powerful spiritual leader. The Lord truly touched her, Mistuh Chief. She still has the sight, but there ain't much fight left in her. Same as me."

"I know of her," Luke said. "But I don't understand all this stuff about evil spirits and Yahoos or whatever you called 'em. You're saying Corny's possessed, right? That he's not responsible for his actions?"

Boots nodded, sneaking another look at the severed head. "He's not responsible for *their* actions. Which is what this terrible thing was."

The sound of an approaching siren filtered in from outside. Rufus Tilley came out of the back of the house in a shuffling trot and dashed into the bathroom to throw up.

"Ain't but two left alive," said Boots, inclining his head toward the bathroom. "Him and the lady back there with Officer Snow. Boy even killed his own aunt."

Two ambulance attendants came up the front steps bearing a stretcher. Alvin Snow came up to meet them and told them that all the victims were dead and awaiting the coroner. He told them to stand by in case they were needed to transport the bodies. Then he nodded to Luke and went back to Elsie Royal's room to finish taking her statement.

Boots slumped against the wall.

"You all right?" asked Luke.

"I'm just . . ." He shook his head, unable for the moment to find the right words.

"Any idea where Corny went?"

"No suh. Lady back there pulled a gun on him and the police came, so he run off. Wherever the Yawahoos told him to go, that's where he is. They ain't done with him yet. They just be getting started. Things gone get a whole lot worse before it's all over."

Another siren wailed outside. Luke looked out the door and saw the squad car lurch to a stop. The flashing emergency lights painted the night's thick fog red and blue. Chief Keller wrenched his big frame out of the blue-&-white and came quickly across the front lawn. He touched a finger to his hat when he saw Luke in the doorway.

"I cain't believe this shit," he said as he stomped onto the front porch. "Has the whole fucking town gone nuts?" Then he saw Boots Birdwell and said, "Excuse my fucking French, Reverend."

Boots smiled, sheepish.

Keller saw the head on the floor and jumped back in surprise. "God *damn*. That's old John Henry, ain't it?"

"'Fraid so," said Luke. He waited a long moment for Keller's shock to wear off some, then he said, "What's the plan, Bill?"

"We use Ev Tatum's bloodhounds to find the crazy sumbitch and we lock his ass up tight and put him in a straight jacket. My God, what ever possessed the boy to do something like this?"

Luke and Boots exchanged glances. "Well," said Luke, "he sure ain't in his right mind."

"Hell, I always knew that boy was trouble," Keller said. "He shoulda been put away a long time ago. This never shoulda happened."

"You already talked to Tatum?"

"Yeah. He's rounding up his dogs. He'll be here directly. How the hell did you get wind of this so fast, Luke?"

"You wouldn't believe it if I told you."

"I'll believe anything after this shit."

"You tell him, Boots," Luke said. "I don't believe it my own damn self."

"Never mind," said Keller. "I ain't got time for tall tales right now. Bad as I hate to, I got to go see the rest of the victims. Is that Snow back there?"

"Yeah. He's talking to Elsie Royal and that writer from Atlanta." Luke could smell the blood-scent of the upstairs slaughter. The odor mixed with the floured-biscuit-and-cold-grease smell wafting up from the kitchen and the resultant aroma nearly turned his stomach.

"What about that geologist who's here about the sinkhole? He dead too?"

"I don't know anything about that," said Luke.

"God A'mighty, I bet Snow ain't checked all the rooms. The city's put him up here, room and board, while he checks out the sinkhole. I was told he arrived this afternoon. Goolsby, that's his name."

Luke glanced out the front door. "Maybe that's him," he said with a nod toward the tall man coming up the front steps.

Keller met the man in the doorway. "Mr. Goolsby?"

"Yes?" Goolsby's balding pate wrinkled with expressive concern.

"I'm Chief Keller. And you're one lucky son of a buck. If you'd been here a little earlier, you'd be dead."

"Pardon?"

"Have a seat out there on the porch. We got a multiple homicide here and we'll need to question you before the night's over."

"My God," said Goolsby. "I was at the hotel talking to my crew chief. He came down early so we could get things set up for tomorrow. He can verify my—"

"You're not a suspect," Keller told him. "We know who did it. Just have a seat out there."

The geologist nodded and walked as if in a stupor to a rocking chair on the porch and sat down.

Keller turned to Luke and said, "Don't you want your old job back? I'm not sure I'm up to it anymore."

"No thanks. But I'll help out any way I can in my auxiliary capacity."

The chief nodded gravely, then started up the stairs. He stopped and looked back at Luke. "You hear about Skeeter Partain?"

Luke shook his head. His stomach clenched.

"He's dead. Somebody sucked his guts out with an embalming tool. James was there when it happened, down the hall when he heard the racket. He says the boy must've killed himself, but I'm damned if I see how anybody could do something like that. Boy'd have to be slap out of his mind. Skeeter was a mite strange maybe, but not that crazy. You reckon the Campbell kid coulda done it?"

"I don't know why he would. They were best buddies."

Keller shrugged his big shoulders. "I ain't buying suicide just yet." He continued up the stairs, mumbling something that sounded like "Lord, give me strength."

"Reckon it'd be okay for me to go home now?" asked Boots. His eyes were bloodshot and rheumy.

"Yeah, go on," said Luke. "They know where to find you if they need you. If your friend Odessa gets any more visions or anything like that, let us know."

"I will," Boots said, weary with more than just his advanced age.

The gruesome death of Skeeter Partain was more than Luke could handle now, with the blood-and-death scent of the upstairs slaughter still clinging to him, so he pushed it from his mind and went out on the porch and sat in the rocker next to the geologist. "So you're here about our sinkhole," he said.

"Yeah," Goolsby affirmed. "Are you a policeman?"

"Not any more. Retired. I just help out when they need extra help."

"What the hell happened here?"

"Old boy with a head injury went on a rampage and killed some of the boarders. His aunt was the owner. Mattie Weehunt?"

"Yes. I just met her this afternoon. God, that's awful."

"Did you meet Cornelius?"

"No, I don't think so. Is he the one who did it?"

"That's what they're saying. He fell off a ladder years ago and it damaged his thinker. I think they finally had to put some kind of shunt in his brain. Never had any serious behavior problems before. I always thought he was a pretty good old boy."

"I guess you never really know."

"Guess not." Luke rocked slowly. The creaking of the chair was somehow comforting, and it helped to settle his nerves a little. He stared ahead into the night fog and remembered the last time he'd seen Corny Weehunt. Corny had stumbled into the street, right in front of Luke's truck, running away from the sinkhole. Said he thought he'd seen something coming out of the hole. Something chasing him. Luke had given him a ride home. What had Corny been doing by the hole in the middle of the night? He'd said he was keeping watch on the hole because something told him he ought to. Was he hearing voices that night? Boots Birdwell said the evil spirits were telling Corny to do things. Luke didn't believe in evil spirits, but he knew mentally disturbed people sometimes heard voices and that sometimes those voices told them to do things. Corny could've been hearing voices that night. Voices telling him to watch the sinkhole. That would explain why he was shagging ass away from the big hole in the street.

Goolsby interrupted Luke's musings. "Do they know where Cornelius is?"

"Nope. They're bringing in bloodhounds to track him." Luke abruptly stopped rocking. "You have caving equipment with you, Mr. Goolsby? Headlamps and such?"

"Yeah. My personal equipment's in my van. My crew will be bringing theirs in the morning, along with the drilling equipment."

"How about your crew chief in the hotel? He got his?"

"Yeah. Why?"

"How would you like to get an early start on that hole?"

"What do you mean?" Goolsby's forehead wrinkled up again.

"I mean you and me go into that sinkhole right now. I'll borrow your crew chief's headlamp. I got a notion Corny just might be hiding down in that hole."

"I . . . I'm not . . . I mean—"

"If he's there, I can handle him. I just need you to stand by and advise me, in case there are tunnels or caves under there. I understand some of these things can be pretty extensive, and I wouldn't want to get lost down there."

"That's right, but—"

"I want to find that boy before the search party does. Some of them old boys might get caught up in the spirit of the hunt and shoot on sight. I'd hate for that to happen."

"What makes you think he's in the hole?"

"Just a wild-ass hunch. But I've been right before. What do you say? You game? We might save the young man's life."

"I don't know. It sounds awfully dangerous. Vinewood's not paying me to catch a fugitive. A mass killer."

"Just let me use your headlamp. I'll go by myself."

"Sure. You're welcome to." Goolsby was obviously relieved that he wouldn't have to go into the pit in search of a killer. "I'll get it. My van's parked on the street."

Luke followed Goolsby to the street. The fog was beginning to thin a bit as night inched closer to dawn. Luke went to his truck to get his pistol and holster from his glove box. As he strapped the gun on his hip, he sent up a silent prayer to a God he wasn't sure he believed in. *Lord, please don't make me have to shoot Corny Weehunt.*

* * *

Shaken by the vision in the bathroom mirror, Ree reached out her hand

and tried to rub the blackened glass clean, but the think murk would not rub off. It was as if the inky mist had permanently clouded the *other* side of the glass—the darkside portal to the world of the dead. Her guardian angel was gone, destroyed, and she was vulnerable, naked and unprotected. She walked out of the bathroom and shut the door, then she went to Luke's closet, pulled one of his flannel shirts off the hanger and put it on. She went downstairs to the kitchen and sat at the table to smoke a cigarette. Her fingers shook as she brought the filter to her lips. She sucked the smoke deep, taking small comfort from the taste of tobacco and from the familiar feeling of smoke tickling her lungs.

She tried to make sense of what she had seen in the mirror, but logic was a poor tool for dissecting supernatural phenomena. She had to use her instincts and intuition. She exhaled a cloud of smoke and watched it drift toward the ceiling. She relaxed a little and drifted with it. She replayed her bathroom encounter with Beau and opened herself to its ghostly nuances. Doing her best to keep her sense of horror in check, she saw it through to its grisly end. Had Beau been trying to warn her of some danger, or had he simply been horrified by his own demise. Her recent psychic vision of the attacker with a blade had clearly been a warning. Had Beau sensed or seen the same thing? Was he destroyed because he was trying to warn her? She had felt the presence of evil, she was sure, but what was the intelligence behind that evil? The Christian concept of Satan didn't seem to fit what she'd felt. *Okay. Go with impressions. Free-associate: Evil, black, billowing, whispering, soul-killing, hungry, nebulous, spreading like a virus, like vines, wild runners slithering, reaching, entwining, shroud-weaving, winding sheets for binding the dead . . .*

The cigarette slipped from the V of her fingers and dropped in her lap. She snatched it up before it burned her bare thigh. She jabbed the butt out in the ashtray, venting her frustration in the small act of violence.

"Come home, Luke," she said aloud. "I need you."

She got up, went to the fridge and poured herself a small glass of milk. *Comfort food. Mother's milk, Mother's breast. Mother dead and buried, same as husband Ben.*

A dog barked. Hondo on the front porch, barking. Was Luke coming up the drive? Milk slopped over the rim of the glass and dribbled over her knuckles.

She could feel it coming. Something bad.

She was suddenly four years old, seized by an impulse to hide in a closet and bury herself beneath the rough fabric of her father's overcoat.

CHAPTER 26
SACRIFICE

Corny sat in the darkness and hugged the blood-greased blade of the machete to his heart. The voices were silent for now, but he knew they hadn't deserted him. The little snake was coiled up in a nook of his intestines, waiting—waiting for what? He was glad he hadn't killed Elsie Royal or Mr. Tilley, but he didn't want the things behind the voices to know it. That would make them mad and they would punish him. It was bad enough he had to sit down here in this infernal darkness smelling the blood and the foul stuff in his shorts. He could smell the wet darkness too. And the dirt and asphalt and the motor oil on it, and the tiny bits of tire tread flaked off all those tires rolling down Main Street, rain or shine, night and day. Corny was at the heart of his town now. Its heartbeat was his heartbeat and his heartbeat was thumping really loud and echoing off the dirt walls of the pit and making the thick syrupy darkness beat in time to his pulse. He could see it beating. The darkness was *alive*. He'd been right all along. It was alive and it could think, probably better than he could think, since his brain was broken and not much good for hard thinking anymore. Well, that was all right. He didn't have to do the thinking now. He only had to do what they told him to do. Like he'd done back at the house. Chopping all those people-vines, vine-people. Aunt Mattie, Mr. Jackson, Mr. Cone, Mr. Jones. They were free now, weren't they? Wasn't that the whole idea? Free the souls. But why had the shadows of the things behind the voices eaten Daddy's soul? That did happen, didn't it? I saw it. I'm sorry, Daddy, I didn't know. I just did what they said. But you said you taught me better than that. Are those things really—

Hush! The voices chorused so loud it made his head hurt and his ears ring deep inside his head.

"I'm sorry," he squealed, holding both hands to his head.

The snake uncoiled in his gut, sending a new squirt of hot liquid into his shorts. The smell was awful. His eyes watered.

Get up.

He obeyed and got to his feet. The nasty liquid dribbled down the back of his leg. The voices told him to go behind the slanting slab of asphalt. He didn't understand how he was supposed to do that, but he didn't ask because he didn't want to make them any madder. He ducked into the cramped space behind the big hunk of street, and though it was dark down there he could see a cave-like opening below the place where the top of the slab rested against the side of the hole. He reckoned the voice-things gave him the power to see in the dark, or maybe it was the black snake that did it. He got on his hands and knees and crawled into the mouth of the little cave, his hand still holding tight to the machete's handle and dragging it in the mud. He could see in the dark like a cat and what he saw scared another squirt of nasty liquid out of him.

*   *   *

Luke put the hard hat with attached headlamp on his head and clicked it on. A beam of light sprang from his head and illuminated the fog in front of him and splashed on the broken rim of the sinkhole.

"We'll use heavy equipment to haul those slabs out of there," said Goolsby, "then my drilling crew will drop down and start looking for tunnels or caves. From the looks of things so far, I'd say there's a good chance we'll find some. It's just a question of how far they extend under there. I found a system of caverns in South Carolina one time that ran on for nearly a mile. Fortunately, there was no town sitting on top of it."

Luke nodded. His headlamp beam moved up and down in front of him. "Can't see anything from here. I want to have a look behind that second piece of pavement. When you get a hunch, you've got to play it. Especially when that's all you've got."

"Right," said Goolsby, though his face expressed uncertainty.

Luke climbed down onto the twenty-foot-long chunk of asphalt and walked backward down its sharp incline, bracing his hands on it as he descended into the hole. His light played on the yellow centerline in front of his face and he wondered how many times he'd driven over this hunk of Main Street. He had never been troubled by heights and had never even considered that he might have a touch of vertigo, but as he crab-walked backward down the asphalt, he experienced a light-headed disorientation. His perception played tricks with his memory. He was a kid again, playing some childish daredevil game in the middle of the street, walking backwards on all fours, vulnerable to unseen threats from behind. Darkness seemed to eat up his bobbing light; it closed around him like dark water and all at once he grew afraid of drowning in the unnaturally thick darkness. Nevertheless, he pressed on. His foot slipped and he fell forward onto the slab and slid down to the bottom of the hole. His hard hat was knocked askew, its light beaming off to the side. His feet splashed in the pool of rainwater.

"You all right?" Goolsby called.

"Yeah." Luke stood erect and straightened the hat. The dizziness had passed.

The geologist tossed down a length of robe. "It's tied to a parking meter," he said. "For when you're ready to climb out."

"Thanks." Luke moved to the uneven wall of the hole behind the slab of fallen street. "There's an opening here," he said. "Looks big enough to crawl into."

"Maybe you should wait for my crew to get that out of there. If that falls on you—"

"Yeah, I know. I'm a greasy spot *under* the road. Nah, I'll just go a little ways, see what I can see. If he's in there, I'll see him."

"Watch yourself down there. If you do find a tunnel, don't go far into it."

Luke looked up at Goolsby, his headlamp's beam shining in the man's face and making him shield his eyes. "If I'm not back in ten minutes, go get the cops." Then Luke got on his hands and knees and crawled into the small opening behind the leaning tons of asphalt and into the manhole-sized mouth of what appeared to be a tunnel. He inched forward, sweat burning his eyes and clouding his vision. He smelled the wet, loamy scent of broken earth and a hint of the fresh-blood odor he'd smelled at the boarding house. Corny was here—somewhere ahead in the dark tunnel snaking deeper into the earth.

He crawled on. The light hit what appeared to be a dead-end, but as he moved farther ahead, he saw that the little tunnel branched off to the left. He crawled toward the branch. The blood-scent grew stronger.

"Corny?" he called. His voice sang with a peculiar echo. "It's Luke Chaney. I'm here to help you, Cornelius. I'm not going to hurt you."

He stopped moving and listened for a response.

"Talk to me, son. Answer me if you can."

Silence.

"I'm coming in, Corny. I just want to talk to you." he reached the place where the tunnel branched to the left and followed it. As he rounded the turn, the narrow passage opened into a small cavern roughly the size of a pup tent. His shaft of light seemed to burn into the limestone wall in front

226

of him. He shifted his head to his right. The light's beam swept right and came to rest on Corny Weehunt's pale face.

"You gone shoot me?" Corny asked him. He was sitting with his back against the cavern's wall, a machete in one hand and something that looked like a big hunk of bone resting on his lap.

"No, I'm not gonna shoot you. I want to make sure nobody else shoots you. I want you to come with me now. That's the way it has to be."

"I don't think they'll let me."

Luke looked more closely at the thing on Corny's lap. It was the skull of an animal he couldn't name. It was larger than a cow's skull; the top of the smooth cranium swept back from thick ridges above close-set eye sockets and its wide jaws were lined with teeth as big as a gator's. Its overall shape made him think of a giant snake or even a fairytale dragon. He shifted his gaze to Corny's face. "Who won't let you?"

"Them. The ones talking to me."

"Did they tell you to kill those people?" Luke sat back on his haunches, freeing his hand in case he had to draw his pistol.

"Yeah." His clothes were covered with the blood of his victims, as was the handle of the machete. Its blade was encrusted with clots of dirt.

"You know it was wrong, don't you? Killing your aunt and the others?"

"I reckon. But they don't think so. They said I was freeing souls."

"They lied. You can't believe what they say. You understand me?"

"Yes suh." Corny licked his lips, capturing a speck of gore.

"What's that thing in your lap?"

"Skull. They told me where it was." He pointed with the machete at a hole in the cavern's floor. "See? I dug it up."

"What for?"

Corny shrugged. "They said to."

"All right. Here's what I want you to do. Put down the machete, leave the skull and come out of here with me. I'll take you to a safe place where nothing can hurt you."

Corny stared at him. His eyes gave away nothing.

"Right now. Men are coming with bloodhounds and guns. If you don't come with me, they'll probably kill you. Now I'm backing out of here and I want you to follow me. Don't listen to the voices. Trust me, not them. Let's go now."

Luke began to crawl backward out of the narrow tunnel, keeping his eyes on Corny. Weehunt let go of the machete, lifted the alien skull off his lap and raised it over his head. Luke froze, then reached for his gun. He thought Corny was going to attack him with the hunk of bone, but what he did was pull it down over his head so that he was wearing it like a bizarre Halloween mask, his big eyes looking out over the lower row of teeth. Then he got on his hands and knees and began to crawl toward Luke, watching him through the skull's big eyeholes.

Luke didn't pull his pistol. Corny followed him out without resistance; that was the main thing. He'd deal with the skull-mask later. Right now he was thankful he hadn't had to shoot the crazy kid.

*   *   *

When he put the skull over his head, the magic happened. The darkness inside the skull swarmed all through his body like a million ants tickling his insides. It was like something out of a comic book, the way it made him feel. It made him strong like a superhero. Powerful. Fearless. *Invincible*—that was the word. Luke Chaney had scared him with his talk of bloodhounds and men with guns, but now Corny knew nothing could hurt him. The voices *hadn't* lied to him. Chaney was the liar. Chaney was trying to trick him. When he'd first crawled into the tunnel where the skull was buried, Corny had seen the blob of darkness quivering there over its grave and it had scared him half to death. But then the voices told him not to be afraid. The darkness didn't want to hurt him. It wanted to help him. It wanted to give him a gift. All he had to do was dig it up. So he used the machete to dig up the skull, but just when he was about to put it on his head, Chaney had come in calling his name and talking his bullshit, and at first Corny had almost believed the man. But now he knew better. Now he knew they wanted Luke Chaney dead because Chaney was a bad man, a murderer. And they wanted Corny to do the killing. He knew he could do it. Killing was easy. He knew that now. It was easy and in some ways fun. It felt good, sort of like beating off, but better. Spanking the monkey, choking the chicken, pounding the pud—you had to do that under the covers, but killing people you did out in the open. You didn't have to hide to do it. People didn't like what you were doing but you killed them. Tough shit. Who were they gonna tell? Nobody when they were dead.

The skull slipped, blocking his vision while he was crawling out of the tunnel. He reached up and adjusted it so he could see again. There was Chaney, out of the tunnel now, standing by the edge of the asphalt with his hand resting on the butt of his gun, watching him. Yeah, Chaney was afraid. He didn't understand what was happening inside the magic skull. Corny didn't understand all of it, but he knew the dark stuff had lived inside the skull a long time ago, back when men still lived in caves and worshiped gods nobody remembered now. Back when the things men called dragons lived in the earth and men wore animal skins and furs for warmth. Corny was seeing pictures in his brain of that long-ago time. The skull was showing him things nobody alive now had ever seen. Things ordinary folks wouldn't believe. It was almost more than he could hold in his mind, but because his brain was like nobody else's brain, he was able to see it all and understand some of it. He understood that the living darkness moved easily through the earth like water passing through a giant sponge. It traveled under ground, covering miles in a matter of seconds, going wherever it wanted to go and nobody even knew it was down here. But he had known. He'd known it before the voices came into him, before Seemoan the snake had crawled inside him. He was special. That was why the voices had chosen him, why the old, old darkness had jumped into him to show him its secrets. Like God the Bearded Father had chosen Jesus as his Son, the dark thing had picked Corny as its human kin. He was connected to it now. He could feel it flying through the ground, going a lot of different places all at the same time, reaching up like big huge fingers to touch anybody it wanted to use. It made him dizzy to think about it, but he had to think about it because he was *feeling* it. He was there. In all those places the dark thing was. He was there in the house with the dog barking on the porch. Bark, bark, bark, rroof, rooooff. The dog didn't like the dark fingers that were coming out of the ground to grab him. Neither did the old naked black woman sitting in the circle with her candles and her prayers. She was so scared she shit all over herself when the black fingers came up through the floor to reach in and grab her old heart and crush it. There was no limit to what the dark thing could do. It had already scared up a lot of ghosts and made the dead walk its earth. Corny didn't like seeing the ghosts, not since he'd seen those shadows eat the ghost of his daddy, but he knew they were there and that they were as real as he was.

"Corny? Why don't you take that thing off your head?"

He emerged from the tight tunnel and stood up straight. Chief Chaney—no, he wasn't chief anymore—was looking funny at him. Did he suspect what was happening to him under the magic skull? Did he have any idea he was about to die?

*   *   *

Ree was hiding in the downstairs closet when the German Shepard's barking became a yelping whine. It was the sound a dog makes when it's been suddenly hurt. *Yip, yip, yip.* Then silence.

Hondo's obvious distress spurred her to action. How could she explain to Luke that she'd been hiding in the closet like a frightened child while his faithful dog was being done in? She threw open the closet door, grabbed the scarred baseball bat from the corner and crept out of her hidey-hole, the bat poised over her right shoulder, ready to strike. Being naked beneath Luke's flannel shirt, she felt more vulnerable than she otherwise would have in these strange circumstances, but she nevertheless pressed on, creeping up the hallway toward the front door and the porch where the barking and yipping had originated.

"Hondo? What is it, boy?" she called in a shaky voice.

She found the wall switch and flicked on the front-porch light, and then opened the door and peered out through the screen.

The wet gray wood of the porch gleamed in the yellow light. Tendrils of fog hung in the air like misty vines.

"Hondo, come here, boy. Where are you?" she tried to whistle but her mouth and lips had gone dry.

She heard him before she saw him. His nails ticked against the wood as he came toward the screen door. Ree felt the deep rumble of his low-throated growling. Then she saw him advancing warily toward her, his ears laid back, his teeth bared and dripping saliva. His wide eyes held the reflection of the porch-light and shone a malevolent yellow. He wasn't foaming at the mouth, but he certainly was acting like a mad dog.

She put down the bat and squatted by the screen door and spoke to the snarling beast in a soft, non-threatening voice: "Hondo, it's me. What's wrong, boy?" It was difficult to keep the fear out of her voice. She tried to cover it by cooing in singsong tones. "What's the matter, baby? Did something scare you?"

Hondo stared through the screen at her, his fierce eyes locked onto hers. She remembered that it wasn't good to maintain eye contact with angry animals because they took it as a threat, so she looked down at his big paws. "I'm your friend, remember? Be a good boy."

With no further warning the dog leapt at the belly of the screen. The thin door banged against the doorframe, Hondo's weight keeping it firmly shut. Ree fell back on her rear, then grabbed the bat and scrambled to her feet. The rusted screen was ripped where he'd hit it with his head and paws. She slammed the front door and threw the bolt. The dog barked savagely, frustrated as well as angry now. She knew he would rip her apart if he could get at her, and getting at her was apparently foremost in his canine mind.

She considered calling the boarding house to ask for Luke, but nixed the idea. If there really was trouble there, she didn't want to bother Luke or the police with a barking-dog complaint—which was probably what it would sound like to them. She was safe, after all. Hondo couldn't open the door and come in after her. Just the same, she would feel better if she had a better weapon than a baseball bat. She went into the den and tried to open the gun cabinet, but it was locked and she had no idea where Luke kept the key. She could break the glass to get a gun, but that seemed a little extreme. She didn't want Luke to think of her as a woman who easily panicked. Armed with the ball bat, she started up the stairs. She would shut herself safely in the bedroom and wait for Luke there. But what would happen when Luke got home? If something really was wrong with Hondo, he might attack an unsuspecting Luke as he got out of his truck. Maybe she *should* try to call and warn him.

She was halfway up the stairs when the dog crashed through the living-room window amid a hail of broken glass. The window screen hit the floor a second before Hondo did. The dog slipped on it and rolled over once, then sprang to his feet, growling and slinging saliva. The beast's eyes found her and he charged the stairs.

Having played for years on the women's softball team, Ree knew how to handle a bat, how to keep her eye on the ball and connect with it at just the right time; those skills kicked in now and she substituted the dog's head for a ball. She cocked the bat over her shoulder and waited for Hondo to come into range. He bounded up the steps and lunged at her bare legs. She swung hard and brought the bat down on top of his head. The bat glanced off the dog's skull and hit the stairs, but the blow was enough to stop his first assault. Hondo's forelegs buckled and his snout thumped against the edge of the stairstep.

She cocked the bat again and brought it straight down off her shoulder as the dog was regaining his footing. The thickest part of the bat struck the flat of Hondo's skull. The muffled *crack* was not the sound of the bat breaking; it was the sound of a skull fracturing beneath the fur and skin. Hondo went down with his legs splayed awkwardly on the steps. Blood leaked from his snout and ears, and his eyes remained open and quickly glazed over.

A sick feeling gnawed at the pit of her stomach and she thought she was going to vomit, but she held it down.

I have to get him outside. I can't have Luke come home to find his dog dead on the stairs.

But she wasn't entirely sure Hondo was dead. He *should* be dead, but if not, it would be dangerous to try to move him. How did you check a dog's pulse? Feel his throat? That in itself could be a dangerous chore, putting your hand that close to the animal's mouth. But it had to be done.

She saw no sign that the dog was breathing, so she reached slowly with her left hand and slipped it underneath the dog's throat. She pressed her fingers into the fur and felt for a pulse. She detected no heartbeat. Hondo's glazed eyes remained open, seeing nothing. Satisfied he was dead, she sat on a step and leaned the bat against the wall. She propped her arms on her bent knees, rested her forehead on her arms and cried. She had never deliberately killed an animal before, and she didn't like the way it made her feel. The fact that she had done it in self-defense didn't lessen her anguish. She lifted her head and looked once again at the bright blood on Hondo's white fur and sobbed so hard her nose started dripping. She wiped her nose on the shirtsleeve and put her head back down on the bridge of her arms.

A whisper of movement. A soft sigh of air.

She looked up as the dog was getting to its feet. She threw her arms behind her and tried to climb backwards up the steps and out of Hondo's reach. Then she remembered the bat and made a grab for it. The dog made no sound as it sprang at her. His teeth sank into her outstretched forearm, and the bat fell over and slid down the stairs. Her arm was trapped in the vise of the dog's powerful jaws. She buried her bare feet in his belly and kicked out, lifting him into the air. His teeth tore a chunk of flesh from her arm as the dog went airborne, bounced against the staircase and tumbled to the foot of the stairs.

Ignoring the searing pain, Ree turned and ran up the steps, her eyes on the door to the bedroom on the right at the top of the stairs. She glanced back over her shoulder and saw him charging after her, already halfway to the landing.

She stumbled through the bedroom doorway, turned on her side and tried to kick the door shut as the beast leapt at her, his dead eyes shining in the dim light.

* * *

Luke decided not to force the issue. Corny obviously did not want to remove the skull from his head, and the thing would likely slow him down if he bolted, so Luke pointed at the rope lying like a thick vine on the length of the asphalt and told Corny to grab hold and climb out of the sinkhole.

Goolsby watched with a bewildered expression as Corny pulled himself hand-over-hand up the rope and out of the hole. Luke imagined that the big-city geologist was wondering just what the hell he'd gotten himself into with this job in a hick town where a mass killer wore a freakish skull on his head.

"Stay right there, Corny," Luke said as he grabbed the rope and began to walk up the asphalt incline.

Corny began to pace about the rim of the hole, clearly agitated now. Goolsby stepped away from him, but Corny suddenly shot out an arm and seized the man's shirtfront. Street light glinted on something in Corny's other hand. Luke recognized it as a knife blade. Holding onto the rope with one hand, Luke drew his pistol. "No!" he shouted as Corny jabbed the knife at Goolsby's abdomen.

Luke squeezed the trigger. The sinkhole trapped the concussion and amplified the pistol's report. His ears rang with sharp pain.

*   *   *

The voices told him to kill the stranger. Corny's buzzing brain made the connection that the stranger was the sinkhole-expert his aunt had mentioned and that the dark thing didn't want the man poking around in the warren of tunnels and caves. Obedient, he pulled the bone-handle hunting knife from its hiding place under his shirttail and stabbed at the man's belly. The man was too quick and the tip of the blade caught nothing but shirt. At the same time there was a loud bang and Corny felt like he'd been kicked in the stomach. He wobbled on rubbery legs and almost fell back into the hole. He lifted his shirt and saw blood pouring out of the hole in the left side of his belly. The voices jabbered like a flock of blue jays, and Seemoan the snake shrieked hisses as she writhed inside him, and he knew she was dying. It was odd, but he didn't feel any pain. He knew he'd just been shot, but all he felt was a wet, numb feeling where the bullet hole was, and his legs felt a little weak. He looked down at Chaney who was still hanging on the rope and pointing the gun at him. He didn't want to get shot again, so he threw down the knife. With the crazy voices making all kinds of racket inside his skull-within-a-skull, something *clicked* in Corny's brain. It was like somebody had actually flipped a switch in there, and all at once he saw everything in a different light—a light the dark thing didn't like at all. He saw the terrible things he'd done back at the house, saw himself hacking Aunt Mattie and the others to death with his machete and he was sickened by what they had made him do. Chaney was right! The voices had lied to him. They used him. Instead of being the town hero, they had turned him

233

into a monster. A killer. A psycho retard. But now he *knew* what they were and what they really wanted. When he heard the distant train whistle, he knew he had one last chance to be a hero. The train was calling him. He *was* a railroad man at heart—just like that writer had said—and the train was showing him the way. He was going to be a hero, but nobody would ever know it. But that was all right. It was like his daddy always told him: "A good man does the right thing even when there's nobody around to see him do it." Well, they would see it but they wouldn't really understand it. He would be the best kind of hero—the *unsung* hero. He remembered that word from some movie and he understood its meaning for the first time. Nobody would sing songs of his heroic deed, but God would know, and that would be good enough. He looked out over the row of dragon teeth at Chaney climbing out of the hole, then he turned and ran down the street and cut through the narrow alley that would shoot him toward the train yard and to his heroic destiny.

*   *   *

Ree shoved the heavy cedar chest against the bedroom door. She didn't think the dog would be able to knock down the door to get at her, but this was no ordinary dog. This was some kind of demon dog who had come back from the dead to attack her. When the beast had leapt at her the last time, she had kicked the door shut on its head, and because this was an old house with doors of solid wood, the door had saved her from being ripped apart by teeth and claws.

It was scratching and pawing at the door now. Ree grabbed the cordless phone off its base on the bedside table and took it into the adjoining bathroom and shut herself inside. Then she sat on the toilet seat and called the Vinewood Police Department. When the man answered, she said, "This is Ree Tyler. A mad dog has me trapped in an upstairs room at Luke Chaney's house. It bit me once, and it won't go away. It wants to kill me."

The officer said he would send help as soon as possible. She thanked him, then broke the connection. For the moment she wasn't the least concerned with the gossip her call was certain to generate. Her only concern was the living-dead dog that wanted to tear her to pieces.

*   *   *

After making sure that Goolsby wasn't hurt, Luke went after Cornelius Weehunt. He jogged into the alleyway between the Economy Hardware Store and Robert's TV Repair. The alley was dark. His foot kicked a piece of wood and something skittered over the toe of his boot. In the distance a dome of glowing fog hung over the railroad yard, and he saw Corny start down the embankment to the yard, the ridiculous skull bouncing on the boy's shoulders. He ran across the parking lot behind the row of Main Street shops, his boots crunching gravel as he made for the spot where Corny had dropped out of sight.

The wail of a distant train whistle gave Luke the idea that Corny intended to hop a freight and ride the rails out of town. Luke couldn't let that happen. He was thankful the gunshot he'd inflicted on the boy hadn't been fatal—not yet—but if he had to shoot him again to stop him, he would; this time he would bring him down with a shot to the legs.

Behind him he heard the braying of bloodhounds. Ev Tatum's dogs had the scent and were on the hunt. As soon as he started down the embankment, he slipped in the mud, fell and rolled halfway to the bottom. He got to his feet and saw the train approaching, the locomotive's headlight carving a pearly shaft in the fog. Corny shambled alongside the track, running to meet the train.

*   *   *

The ground trembled with the approach of the train, and the locomotive's single headlight was shooting out rays of glowing fog. Corny saw it as the magical eye of a flying dragon, the same sort of dragon that had flown his father to the Promised Land. The engine roared. The boxcars and flatcars rattled over the crossties, sounding like a marching band's rhythm section gone wild. The voices were wild as well, shouting curses in a language he'd never heard before, yet he somehow understood that he was being cursed like no human had ever been cursed before. The hole in his belly was beginning to hurt now, and the front of his pants was soaked with blood, his own and the nasty-smelling stuff the dying snake was bleeding. His legs went out from under him and he tumbled to the ground beside the track. The big skull was knocked sideways on his head and he couldn't see. It felt good to be lying down and he wanted to stay there and rest a minute, but he knew he had to get up before the train passed him by. This was his only chance. If he didn't do it now, the dark thing might take him over again and make him its slave. He couldn't be a hero if that happened. He got to his knees and straightened the skull so that he could see out of its mouth-hole, then he looked up at the charging train, which was about twenty yards away now. He looked back and saw Chaney running toward him, but he was too far behind to get here in time. Corny waved at Chaney to let him know he wasn't mad about getting shot and to show him that he wasn't a crazy retard. He *knew* what he was doing. Still on his knees, Corny fell forward across the track like he was going to do pushups. The train was so loud now that he couldn't hear the voices. He turned his head and watched the locomotive bearing down on him. The engineer had seen him and started blowing his whistle like crazy.

Corny smiled within the haunted head of bone.

The ground quaked as the train rushed to meet him.

The earth rocked him in its big arms.

He laughed like a little kid on a roller coaster.

It was the wildest ride of his life.

*   *   *

When he saw what the boy meant to do, Luke stopped running, bent over and rested his hands on his knees to catch his breath. There was no point in yelling to Corny because the roar and rattle of the train drowned out all other sound, and he was too far away to reach him before the train did. All he could do was bear witness to the boy's suicide.

The engineer saw Corny stretched out across the track and sounded his horn continuously. There was no way he could slow down in time to avoid running over him. Though it was traveling only ten or twelve miles an hour through the yard, Luke knew those moving tons would easily cut Corny in half.

He could not look away as the steel wheels sucked Corny up like meat through a grinder. His legs twisted and flopped as his torso disappeared beneath the front of the locomotive. He wasn't sure, but he thought he saw blood splash up from the wheels.

The train rattled past, its brakes shrieking. Luke felt a sick emptiness. Someone touched his shoulder. He turned and Chief Keller was there, shouting above the din. "That him?"

Luke nodded.

"Jesus God."

Ev Tatum was there too, reining in his hounds.

Keller cupped his hand to Luke's ear and said, "Call just came in. Ree Tyler says a rabid dog has her cornered in an upstairs room of your house."

Luke didn't believe he'd heard right and asked Keller to repeat what he'd just said. Keller repeated his words.

"I'm on the way," Luke said and started running back to where his truck was parked.

*   *   *

"Thank God," she said when she heard his truck rumble up in front of the house. She parted the curtains and looked out to see him leap from the cab of the pickup and disappear beneath the roof of the porch. The house had been quiet for the last ten or so minutes and she had no idea where the demon dog was—or if it was still "alive." She pushed the cedar chest out of the way and cracked the door a few inches to look out. She saw blood on the floor but no sign of the dog.

"Luke, be careful," she called when she heard him coming up the stairs. "He's still out there somewhere."

"Is it Hondo?"

"Yes." She opened the door wide and stepped out of the room to meet him.

There was a pistol in his hand and he was looking about for the dog. "Stay in the bedroom while I look around," he told her.

They saw him at the same time. Hondo was stretched out on the floor at the end of the hallway. His white fur was stained with drying blood. He wasn't moving. Luke stepped lightly down the hall, softly calling his dog's name.

"I killed him," Ree said from the doorway. "I'm sorry. I had to."

Luke knelt down and touched his hand to Hondo's chest. "He's gone."

"I killed him and he came alive again and attacked me. I know it's crazy, but that's the way it happened." She took a few tentative steps toward Luke.

He flashed a wan smile. "He's dead now. Looks like you cracked him pretty good. I saw the bat. Is that what you hit him with?"

"Yeah. But he was dead. I felt for his pulse. He didn't have one. He wasn't breathing. He was dead. Then he came at me again."

"Was he foaming at the mouth?"

"No."

"What the hell could've gotten into him? He's never done anything like this before."

"I don't know. He was barking out front again and when I went to see what he was barking at, he tried to get at me through the front door. Then he came crashing through the window."

Luke saw the hand towel wrapped around her forearm. "He bite you?"

She nodded. A tear slid down her cheek.

He holstered his pistol, then took her arm and unwrapped the blood-stained towel to examine the bite. She had washed it with soap and water and poured alcohol from the medicine cabinet on the wound. The towel

237

had stopped the bleeding, but it still ached like the devil.

"Get dressed," he said. "We're going to the hospital. That needs stitches."

"I'm so sorry I killed your dog," she said.

"Hey, you had to. I'm sorry he did that to you. I just don't understand it."

"It was like he was possessed. I've never seen a dog go so wild and vicious for no reason."

Luke gently pulled her to him and kissed the top of her head. "I'm just glad you're okay," he said. "It's been a night from hell."

"Yeah, tell me about it." She tried to laugh, but what came out sounded more like a whine.

CHAPTER 27
THE UNFORESEEN

Agnes Porch was no longer her tired, old self. Her useless body was twisted down there on the cellar floor, a lifeless lump of frail flesh and bone. She hadn't liked dying one damned little bit. Choking on that dark dirt had been the worst experience of her life, but what came after death was like nothing she could've imagined. She drifted now on unseen currents with luminous darkness flowing through her, the darkness connecting her to the fierce intelligence of the Yawahoos. The darkness itself was alive with a will of its own and that was what scared her. She sensed that it could snuff out her soul if it so desired and that it was a natural enemy to humanity, living or dead. The elemental Yawahoos seemed somehow to be drawing energy from that pulsing dark thing the way earthly life draws energy from the sun.

Red Queen Rose had been with her at the moment of death, but then she abandoned her to direct the Yawahoos to the feeble-minded boy who was to be the instrument of Agnes' vengeance. Without leaving the physical confines of the root cellar, Agnes was able to see what Rose saw, rode the darkness with her, entered the good-hearted boy with her and helped make the boy do horrible things. The boy (he was a man in years but his mind was the mind of a boy) was an innocent and it was a shame that he had to be used in such a way, but it had to be done. The town and Luke Chaney had to be made to suffer. To die. The odd thing—the really unexpected thing—was that Agnes was losing her taste for vengeance and its accompanying violence. Now that she was no longer connected to her wasted body, she (her spiritual essence) was too overwhelmed with the wonders of the afterlife to give much thought to such a trivial thing as vengeance. Now she could see that Fate and his boys were doomed to cling for a time to the earth they had lived and died on, that their souls were not ready to pass on to other levels of spiritual existence.

She believed she was ready. But to ascend to the next tier she would have

239

to give up her desire for vengeance, and she didn't know if Rose and the Yawahoos would allow that. Once set in motion, their unholy machinations seemed unstoppable, and Agnes didn't know how to dissociate herself from them—or if they would allow it.

Then Rose got herself trapped in the dying body of a snake, and Agnes could almost feel Simone's spiritual anguish as the little serpent twisted and writhed within the belly of the wounded boy. It seemed that the plan for vengeance was falling apart, going to hell in the boy's breadbasket, and that was perfectly all right with Agnes, but when the Weehunt boy threw himself in front the train, Simone's snake died and her soul was whip-shot through the luminous darkness and Agnes could feel her screaming agony. The Yawahoos were angry, but the immense dark thing was furious that the skull it had once inhabited was crushed beneath the wheels of the train. Agnes didn't know exactly what the dark thing was. It was well beyond her comprehension. She only knew that it had changed over the aeons, evolved from a flesh-and-bone creature that tunneled through the earth into something that no longer needed to be housed in a physical frame. Whatever it now was, the amorphous thing of darkness was unfettered by physical boundaries and it could travel through the earth or above the earth with ease and astounding quickness. She knew, too, that Simone was afraid of it.

Agnes was aware that her link to the earthly plane was weakening. With this awareness came the realization that she could have been so much more in life if she hadn't been slavishly bound by blood and familial tradition to the backwoods Porch clan. The blood-for-blood legacy and the primitive lust for revenge had brought her low, kept her down, destroyed her family, and now it was holding her fast to the base existence she wanted to leave behind forever. Was this her punishment? Were the dark gods holding her accountable for her human failings? Simone couldn't help her out of this spiritual predicament; she was too caught up with being Red Queen Rose the Conjure Woman, and she didn't want to give up her power. Couldn't she see that her hunger for that power held her back from higher planes of spiritual existence?

Aggie, help me. Rose's disembodied voice was a ghostly echo.

No. I don't want this now. I want to go from here.

Rose was enraged. *You started this but you can't stop it. They will destroy us if you try.*

A dark energy surged through Agnes and she saw with her soul's eye what the dark thing meant to do next, saw it reaching out for the remains of her loved ones even as she reached for Heaven. *I've damned us all. God, forgive me!*

Opposing forces ripped her soul asunder.

* * *

Craig Hemphill saw the light in the window of the tumbledown house, turned his cruiser around and drove back to investigate. He knew no one had lived in the old house for years, so the light in the window was very much out of the ordinary and called for a closer look. The soupy fog in this predawn hour was already playing on his nerves; he kept imagining things lurking inside the ghostly mists, but he figured it was due to his fatigue. The chief had called him in on what should've been his day off, and Craig hadn't had much sleep since his last tour of duty on the graveyard shift. Hell, the chief had called *everybody* in because of the boarding house massacre and the suicide-by-train of the killer, so Craig knew he couldn't complain. And on top of all that, there had been the bizarre funeral-home death of Skeeter Partain. The chief was going to be inundated with paperwork and would probably have to call in the county homicide unit for assistance with the hinky death of the Partain kid. God, what a way to go! Having your guts sucked out with an embalming tool!

Hemphill rolled up in front of the abandoned house and turned on his flashing lights, then he got out and walked to the front door with a flashlight in one hand and his other hand on the grip of his holstered pistol. When he went through the doorway the odor of carnage hit him full-force and set off his gag reflex. He drew his gun and crept through the empty living room toward the adjoining room bathed in a pale white light. Thumbing back the hammer of his .38, he advanced through the second doorway.

The bloody thing on the floor didn't look real. It looked like a special-effects dummy in a horror movie. Both legs had been severed above the knees and one arm had been amputated at the shoulder. The bloody pallet of plastic on which the body rested only added to the unreality of the ghastly scene—as if the corpse had made his bed only to die in it. The light Hemphill had seen in the window was from the electric lantern on the floor by the blood-streaked chainsaw. The lantern's batteries were apparently low; its anemic light was dying in the palpable gloom of the murder room.

Hemphill flashed his light around the room to make sure the person who had committed this heinous crime was not lying in wait for another victim, then he shone the light in the face of the victim of this real-life chainsaw massacre. What looked like a chunk of raw meat hung from the victim's mouth, and there appeared to be a bullet hole in the center of his forehead. Hemphill recognized the dead man: Joe Rob Campbell, former high-school football jock and fugitive from the city jail. Being careful not to step in spilled blood, he checked the other rooms, then ran to the cruiser to call it in. The chief was going to blow a fuse when he heard about this. Hemphill was close to blowing a fuse himself. He knew he would never be able to erase the stark picture of this atrocity from his memory. It would stay with him, vividly painted in blood-red, and even if he lived a hundred years he would carry it to his grave.

*   *   *

The slow, steady pounding snatched Charlotte from her sleep. She sat up and looked at the clock. A dull ache behind her eyes reminded her that she'd had too much vodka last night. It took a long moment for the numbers on the digital clock to register meaning in her booze-fuzzed mind. 4:59. The little dot of light that signaled PM was unlit, so it had to be 4:59 in the frigging morning. Who the hell was pounding on the door at this fucking hour? Whoever it was, she was going to give them what-for and more. The son of a bitch.

She crawled out of bed, slipped into her housecoat and went toward the steady hammering sound.

The back door. Bad news. Nobody came to the back door—nobody except that creepy hit man. Had he done the deed? Was he here to collect what he was owed? She surmised that this would be his style—to show up at five o'clock in the fucking morning with a hit man's hard-on and that stupid mask over his head. *God, why did I say I'd give him a freebie?*

And that knocking! *Thump . . . thump . . . thump*, on and on with no let-up, no break in the beat, like some mindless mechanical man who will keep on knocking until his winding mechanism winds down.

"Jesus, all right," she called. "I'm coming. Hold your goddamn horses."

Thump . . . thump . . . thump . . .

She went through the kitchen and stepped down onto the cool laundry-room tile. She hadn't bothered to tidy herself, figuring that if she looked bad enough, the bastard wouldn't want to fuck her.

Thump . . . thump . . . thump . . . thump . . .

Her hand touched the doorknob and she froze. Something, some inaudible voice deep within, advised her not to open the door. She drew back her hand.

Thump . . . thump . . .

The pounding ceased. The sudden silence roared in her ears.

Charlotte stopped breathing. She backed away from the door, holding her breath.

The door came crashing inward with a bang. The masked freak came in with it. His dark clothes were shiny with blood. His head was tilted at an odd angle and his beady eyes were glazed, unblinking. A sickening stench came off him and assaulted Charlotte's sense of smell.

Then she saw the gaping wound in his throat and the white of his vertebrae within the ruined flesh. How could he be standing here after suffering such a grievous wound? More repulsed by the sight of him than frightened by the violence of his forced entry, Charlotte turned to run back into the house but the man grabbed her shoulders and rode her to the floor.

Just before the masked killer began to chew her face off, Charlotte Claymore realized instinctively—at a deep and long-dormant animalistic level of awareness—that a dead man was ravaging her with a rigor mortis dick.

*   *   *

On the way home from the emergency room, they swapped horror stories. Luke told her about the boarding house slaughter and Cornelius Weehunt's subsequent death on the railroad tracks, and she told him about the visions she'd seen in his bathroom mirror and about her battle-to-the-death with Hondo.

Dense fog muted the dawn's light, and Luke had the feeling that he was driving through an alien landscape. Ree held her bandaged arm in her lap as if it were some extraneous part of herself she wasn't sure she wanted to keep. She had thirty stitches and untold milligrams of local anesthetic in her arm, but she looked remarkably beautiful in a little-girl-lost sort of way.

"I need a cigarette," she said, shattering the little-girl image.

"We're almost home," said Luke, and he realized then that he wanted his house to be her home—*their* home. "Your smokes are there, right?"

"Yeah." She sighed. "You don't believe me, do you? About Hondo coming back to life."

He measured his response before he spoke. He placed a hand on her knee. "You were pumped full of adrenalin. That affected the way you saw things. Hell, you did good just defending yourself. Hondo could've torn you to pieces but you got the best of him. That's what amazes me. You're a little bundle of dynamite."

"I knew you didn't believe me."

"Come on, Shorty. Dead dogs don't come back to life. You stunned him with the first blow and you couldn't find his pulse, but that doesn't mean he was out-and-out dead. Why make a big thing out of it? He's dead now. And you're all right. That's all that matters."

"No, that's not all that matters. Something's happening here, something nobody understands. Don't you get it? It's all connected somehow. All the killings, my visions, what happened to Beau . . ."

"Ol' Boots Birdwell says Corny was possessed by evil spirits," he admitted. "Yahoos or something like that. Hell, I can almost believe it. And that damned petrified skull Corny had on his head. I've never seen anything like it. It wasn't the skull of any creature I've ever seen. But I just can't buy all this supernatural stuff. I'm sorry, but I can't. I've never seen a ghost or an angel and I don't expect I ever will."

"I know. I used to feel the same way before Beau came along. But now I *can* see that there's another world right here with us, one most people can't see—or don't want to see. But the fact is, I know it's there. And I know something *is* going on below the surface. And whatever it is, it scares the hell out of me. That black fog I saw in your mirror was real. I didn't hallucinate it, I swear to God. I could *feel* it. It was evil. And it destroyed Beau. Just ate him away like . . . I don't know . . . like a soul-eating cancer."

"How can ghost die? It's already dead, by definition."

"I didn't say I understood it. Maybe it just destroyed his connection to me. I want to believe his soul is at rest in Heaven now. But I just don't know. I only know he was good and that black stuff is evil. And I think it's what brought Hondo back from the dead. It wanted to kill me."

"Okay." Luke saw his mailbox appear out of the fog and he slowed down and turned into the driveway. He parked under the pecan tree and killed the engine. He touched his fingers to her cheek. "Know this. Nothing is going to get to you without going through me first."

Ree tried to smile. "I know. And I love you for it. But that just makes it worse. You're one more thing it can take away from me before it destroys me."

"You make it sound like it's a personal thing. Like this evil has set its sights on you, like a personal vendetta."

"That's the way it feels. But maybe it wants all of us. It's already taken a hell of a toll, hasn't it? Maybe those folks at the boarding house saw it and felt the same way just before they died. We'll never know, will we?"

Luke opened his door and told Ree to wait in the truck.

"Where are you going?" she asked.

"I'm going to take that mirror off the wall, bring it out here and smash it to smithereens. And get Hondo out of the house. Then we're going to bed and sleep all day. And when we get up, things are going to look a whole lot better."

She attempted another smile, but something in her eyes told him she expected things to get a lot worse.

*   *   *

Boots Birdwell wasn't sure if he'd slept. He didn't feel at all rested. He remembered rolling and tumbling in bed most of the night, but he must have slept some because he remembered the nightmare. It had been a bad one, but not as bad as what he'd seen at the boarding house on Poplar Street. Nothing his mind dreamed up (*nightmared* up) could touch the terrible sights he'd seen in the waking world. The severed head, the hacked-up bodies in bloody beds—the aftermath of the Weehunt boy's rampage put any nightmare to shame.

He rolled out of bed, went to the bathroom for his usual torturous urination, and then called Odessa Nell again. He'd called her last night after he got back from the boarding house, but all he got was a busy signal; he guessed she'd taken the phone off the hook so as not to be disturbed while she was performing her evil-banishing rituals. But now it was the same thing: a busy signal. Maybe she'd forgotten to hang up the phone. He hoped that was it, but he feared the worst. Boots knew enough about the Yawahoos to know they didn't go down without a fight. He didn't think Odessa was strong enough to win a face-off with them now. She was old and tired, same as he was. Her spirit was strong, but the body housing the spirit was worn out and used up by the years. Odessa's body couldn't survive a direct confrontation with the elementals.

He got dressed and drove to her house, fearful of what he would find there.

When he entered the gingerbread house, he knew she was dead. He'd had the same icy-fingers-on-the-back-of-the-neck feeling when he entered the boarding house. Death houses were always the same. Death came, did its work and left a piece of itself within the walls like an echo that won't stop repeating itself. It gets fainter and fainter until finally you don't hear it anymore, but you know it's still there just below the range of your hearing. Death leaves its shadow behind and it takes a long time to fade out.

He found her on the floor. Cold. Naked. Dead. A few candles were still burning. One of her eyes was half-open, dead as a cat's-eye marble, glassy and dull in the weak light.

Boots dropped to his knees and held her cold hand. "You rest now, sweetheart," he said softly. "Your earthly trials are done. You go on home to Jesus."

Tears rolled down his cheeks but he hardly felt them. All his senses seemed to be concentrated in the hand that held the hand of Odessa Nell. It was scaly, cold, and rubbery like a dead fish, but Boots felt something else, something below the surface of dead flesh and bone, and it was warm and full of life. "Odessa Nell?"

I waited for you, said the voice in his head. Odessa's spirit's voice. *They're scattered, the Yawahoos. And that dark thing is losing its hold. The boy smashed its old skull and that weakened it. But be careful. It's like a wounded animal. Wild and dangerous. Out of control. You can beat it if you keep your faith, Brother Birdwell.*

And then she was gone.

*   *   *

Where the hell *was* he?

Ree could hardly see the house through the thick fog. She wiped her side of the truck's windshield with her hand, but it did nothing to improve visibility. She rolled her window down and called: "Luke?"

What was taking him so long? He knew she was dying for a cigarette, didn't he? Besides, smashing the bathroom mirror wouldn't do any good. Evil wasn't evicted that easily. Not the evil she'd seen and felt when Beau fell to rot in front of her eyes.

Then she heard the music. It came out of the fog from above—from the pecan tree?—and the haunting ringing of the steel strings raised gooseflesh on her arms. When a man's voice began to sing along with the guitar's bluesy chord progression, Ree knew it was live, not recorded. "Who's there?" she called.

The hoarse voice sang:

She say you don't see why, ooh
that I will dog her 'round
It must be that old evil spirit
so deep down in the ground

She opened the door and stepped out of the truck and peered through the fog at the pecan tree. "Who are you?" she shouted.

You may bury my body
down by the highway side
so my old evil spirit
can catch a Greyhound bus and ride

She bravely walked closer to the tree. She could just make out the dark shape of a man sitting on a thick lower limb. He was hunched over a guitar, and he gave no sign that he even knew she was there. She found a small rock on the ground, picked it up and lobbed it. It should have hit the man or his guitar and bounced back to the ground, but it went *through* him and thumped to the ground on the other side of the tree. As she was turning to run to the house, the music stopped and the man spoke: "Devil's Fuckin' Valley, darlin'. It's Devil's Valley all over again. You cain't ever leave it and it never leaves you. Livin' or dead, it's all the same."

He dropped to the ground, swung his guitar onto his back and rambled off into the fog, alternately laughing and humming to himself.

"Luke!" she yelled at the top of her lungs.

*   *   *

Luke heard Ree call his name, but he couldn't move. His dead wife was jumping up and down on the bed, chanting a child's rhyme: "Called for the doctor and the doctor said, 'That's what you get for jumpin' on the bed.' Ah root! Ah root!"

"Jenny . . ." Luke moved to the edge of the bed, looking up at Jenny's naked form. Her small breasts jiggled and her hair billowed each time her feet came down on the mattress. She stopped jumping and looked down at him. "You took that whore to our bed, Luke Chaney. You think I'll let you get away with that? Hah!"

Luke wanted to reach up and touch her to see if what he was seeing and hearing was real, but he couldn't bring himself to actually do it. Real or not, it could not be good that she was here before him. Either way, he was in deep trouble.

"Tell me, big man," she said, her sallow face contorted with anger, "was your little whore a good fuck? You can tell me. I'm your goddamn *wife*."

"But you're dead," he said. "You can't—"

"I ought to fuck you to death myself. You think I can't? I could do it right here and now." Jenny jumped off the bed and landed on the floor without making a sound.

"You're not real," Luke said, backing away.

247

"Ah, what's the matter, stud? Don't you want to know how the dead do it?"

Through the open bedroom door, he heard Ree running up the stairs, breathlessly calling his name.

Jenny flashed him a wicked smile. "Ah, perfect! A three-way. I could fuck you both to death. How about it? A murderous *ménage à trois*."

Ree came through the doorway and skidded to a halt when she saw Luke's dead wife. Her mouth flew open but no sound came out.

"Just in time, you little slut," said Jenny. "Now we'll see how good you really are."

Luke grabbed Ree's hand and pulled her out of the room. "Run," he told her.

They ran down the stairs and out the front door with Jenny shouting obscenities after them.

"You saw her, right?" Luke asked as he opened the pickup's passenger door for Ree.

"Yes, I saw her," Ree answered as she hopped onto the seat. "Jenny Chaney. Two years dead and mad as hell."

Luke raced around to the driver's side, jumped behind the wheel and started the engine. "She wanted to kill me," he said, bewildered. "Wanted to kill both of us."

"I got that."

He shifted into reverse, backed up and turned the truck around. "That wasn't Jenny. It looked like her, but she's not like that. Sure, she could be jealous, but she was never that . . . vicious."

"Maybe now you believe me. Something evil is making this stuff happen, making us see horrible things. Making people *do* horrible things. While you were in the house, I saw a freaking ghost sitting in the pecan tree, playing guitar and singing. I don't know who it was, but he said something about Devil's Valley. He called me *darlin'*. I don't know who the hell he was."

He gunned the truck toward the road. He shook his head as if trying to dispel what he'd seen in the bedroom. "I can't believe this shit. It can't be real."

"You better believe it. Whatever it is, it gets people killed."

They drove through the fog. They were both quiet for a while. Then Ree said, "Where are we going?"

"To see Boots Birdwell. He seems to know more about what's going on than anybody else. Maybe he knows what the hell we can do to get rid of these ghosts—or whatever they are."

"God, I hope I don't see Ben's ghost. I don't think I could handle it."

"We're going to handle it," he said. "Whatever the hell it is, whatever it throws at us next, we're going to handle it."

She looked over and saw grim determination on his face.

"Right?"

"Damn right," she said, trying to make herself believe they could. "But right now I need a smoke. I'm sorry, but could you stop at the Quick Mart before we go see Mr. Birdwell?"

"You bet. I could use one myself."

* * *

Ron Gentry stopped at the Vinewood BP station to gas up the hearse. He didn't like the idea of gassing up with two bodies in the back; it seemed undignified and disrespectful of the dead he was ferrying on a sea of fog to the funeral home in Vidalia, but the tank was on empty so he had no choice. As he slid the cold nozzle into the mouth of the hearse's tank, he told himself that this particular duo of dead passengers didn't really deserve much respect. Lem and Luther Porch were low-life white-trash rednecks, shot and killed in a shootout after torturing that Partain kid. How much respect could they deserve? Hell, it would've been all right with Ron if they had piled the bodies of Old Man Porch and the third dead son on top of the two in the back, but since they hadn't, he was going to have to make another trip to the Coroner's Office after dropping these two at the funeral home, and the round trips would eat up most of the morning. But what the hell? He was getting paid good money. The surviving relatives wanted the dead Porches buried in Vidalia, though they had lived and died on the outskirts of Vinewood. It seemed like a lucky break for Ron's employer—as long as the Porches had good death insurance or enough personal funds to pay the bills. But that wasn't Ron's worry. He was just the hired help, and he would get paid no matter what.

When the tank was full, he replaced the nozzle on the pump and went inside to pay with the company credit card. The old guy working the register looked like he was three breaths away from being a corpse himself, but when he spoke he seemed to come to life with an abundance of animation for a cadaverous old dude. "Gave me a start when you pulled up in that thing," he said. "Seeing it come out of the fog like that, I thought the Grim Reaper was coming for me sho nuff."

"No, sir, I'm not him," Ron said with a fake laugh. "I don't guess the Reaper ever has to stop for gas."

"Reckon not, haw, haw, hee-hee-hee." When the man laughed, his toothless gums showed, and Ron pictured the old guy dead on the embalming table. Then he laughed for real.

He stuck the receipt in his pocket and walked back to the hearse. The fog was so thick he couldn't see much of anything beyond the gas station's three islands of pumps and the surrounding pavement glowing in hazed light. Ron rattled his keys in his pocket as he reached for the door handle and froze when he saw that someone was sitting in the hearse's passenger seat. The next thing he noticed was that the man was naked.

"Hey! What the hell . . .?" Ron said, pulling the door open.

The naked man slowly turned his head and looked over at him. The man's one eye was only partially open, hooded by a flaccid lid. Where the other eye should have been was an empty socket. Ron got the impression that the man wasn't really seeing him standing there. Then he saw the bluish holes in the strange man's shoulder and torso, and it dawned on him that he was looking at a corpse. His mind rebelled at the thought. This had to be a joke his co-workers were playing on him. No way could a corpse be sitting in there, looking at him with a dead eye. No way in hell. Nevertheless, he backed away from the naked man, repulsed by the sight of him. He backed into someone standing behind him and almost said "Excuse me" as he turned to see who was there, but a thick arm slipping around his neck and a hand grasping his hip stopped his turning.

He smelled the familiar odor of dead flesh. The hand on his hip slid into his pants pocket. Ron struggled to get free of the cold grasp of the one holding him but the man was too strong. *He wants my keys*, he suddenly realized. Then the groping hand came out with the keys and Ron was shoved to the pavement.

The man with his keys was also completely naked, his torso split open in the Y-shaped incision of an autopsy, his ribs showing beneath the flaps of flayed skin and his trunk empty of internal organs. The man was completely bald, his head shining in the amber light filtering through the fog. Ron recognized him: Lem Porch, also known as Cowboy.

"No fucking way," Ron said from the pavement.

Moving awkwardly, Lem Porch slid his naked body into the driver's seat and tried to stick the key into the ignition switch.

Ron couldn't move. He wanted to get up and run, but his ass seemed frozen to the pavement, and he wasn't sure he could make his legs work well enough to stand up, much less run. All he ended up doing was shouting: "Hey! Hey! "

The dead man behind the wheel finally succeeded in getting the key into the switch, but apparently couldn't remember which way to turn it to crank the engine. Finally the engine started and the hearse lurched forward with its driver's door still open.

Ron Gentry managed to get to his feet and started running toward the toothless old man coming out of the station. "Call the cops!" Ron shouted. "They stole my fuckin' ride! Jesus, did you see that?"

∗   ∗   ∗

Ree used the lighter from the dash to light her cigarette.

Luke said, "Let me have one of those."

"I thought you were joking," she said. She pulled one out of the pack, lit it with the ember of hers and handed it to him.

He took a drag, inhaled too deeply and coughed. "Whoa, that's nasty. Not like I remembered at all. Can't believe I used to smoke a pack a day."

"I think they taste better after you kill off a few taste buds and smoke enough to get the nicotine monkey on your back. Makes all the difference."

"I guess."

He took another drag, then tossed his smoke out the window.

Ree said, "I was thinking . . . maybe what I saw in your bathroom mirror wasn't really Beau. He only used to appear in the antique vanity mirror, so why would he all of a sudden show up in your bathroom?"

"You got me."

"Because it wasn't really Beau. Like that wasn't really Jenny . . . or her ghost we saw in your bedroom. You said so yourself. It was an illusion, created by whatever's behind all the other bad things that have been happening. The evil spirits. I know people can be possessed by demons, but I didn't know a whole town could be. But that's what seems to be happening."

"If you'd said that to me yesterday, I'd think you were out of your mind."

"But now?"

"I've seen enough to know better," he said. "That or we're *both* crazy as hell."

She blew smoke out the crack in her window. "I want to go to the shop and see if Beau will come to me in the vanity mirror. If he hasn't been destroyed, he may have some more information we can use."

"If he does, I hope it's a little more helpful than *give up tobacco.*"

Ree took one more pull from her cigarette, then tossed it out the window. "Easier said than done."

Luke slowed down and started looking through the fog for Birdwell's little house on Sycamore Street. "Can't see shit in this fog," he said. "This is like you'd expect to see in London."

"Yeah. With Jack the Ripper lurking in it."

"Shit, Shorty, get your mind out of the spook house, will ya? We're jumpy enough already."

"Sorry."

"I think that's it." He nodded toward a modest house with an old pickup parked at an odd angle in the narrow driveway. "That looks like his truck."

"The lights are on. Somebody must be home."

Luke parked behind the old Ford and killed the engine. "Well, let's see what he can tell us about our spooks."

*   *   *

Delbert Hicks crept down the steps to his grandmother's root cellar. The electricity was out, so he was using the flashlight he'd found in the kitchen. The old woman hadn't been answering her phone, so Del's mother had insisted that he drive over from Vidalia and check on her and tell her that the bodies of her menfolk had been released to Cox Funeral Home. He hadn't wanted to come. He didn't want to see that boiled skull again, or smell the awful smell it gave off while it was boiling in the big pot, but sure enough, the smell still hung in the kitchen like the odor of rancid meat cooking. He loved his grandmother, he supposed, but some of her witchy doings scared the hell out of him.

He was scared now. He'd searched the whole house and the barn and hadn't found her. The only place left to look was down here in the root cellar. In the dark. With a flashlight with weak batteries. And with the rotten-meat smell of Monroe Shockley's boiled head still in his nose.

He didn't really expect to find her down here in the dark. Not alive, anyway. But he knew her special stump was down here and that this was probably where she would've done her conjuring or spell casting or whatever the hell it was she did.

He went down the steps slowly, reluctantly. He stopped halfway down and put the beam of weak light on the stump in the center of the cellar. The skull rested on the stump. What looked like melted candle wax coated the top of the skull and hung like dark icicles from one of the eye sockets.

"Granny?" he called.

He moved the light over the dirt floor. His breath caught in his throat when he saw the thing on the floor by the thick stump.

"What the hell *is* that?" he asked aloud.

It looked like somebody had made a body out of dirt the way kids on a beach make a castle out of sand. His natural curiosity pulled him to the bottom of the steps, but when his feet touched down on the cellar's dirt floor, he stopped cold. He smelled death. Delbert was well acquainted with the smell of death. You didn't grow up in this part of the country without smelling plenty of dead critters in the fields, in woods or on the side of roads, and he was familiar with the way a dead human stinks up a house when it (his Aunt Clara) lies undiscovered for several days on the floor of a house in high summer. What he smelled now wasn't as strong as poor Aunt Clara's stench had been, but there was no mistaking what it was. Or where it was coming from.

The dirt-covered shape by the stump was Grandma Porch.

He made himself walk toward her, keeping the beam of light on what would be her head. The way she was covered with blackish dirt reminded Del of the tar baby in that Uncle Remus story he'd loved as a kid.

He didn't want to touch her (when you touched the tar baby, you got your hands stuck fast in black tar) but he knew he had to see her face so that he could tell his mother that he was sure this thing on the floor was Granny Porch. He pulled his soiled handkerchief from his back pocket, squatted down and wiped some of the dirt off her face. Pale, wrinkled skin glowed in the Rayovac's light. There was no doubt who this was, but he couldn't just leave the old lady with dirt on her face, could he? He started wiping her face clean but stopped when he saw that her slack mouth was crammed full of that dark dirt. His stomach seemed to do a back flip and he almost hurled his grits-and-biscuit breakfast. He stood, turned around and was about to run up the stairs and out of the house, but froze when he saw strange shadows rippling all around him. These shadows didn't seem to have anything to do with the light from the Rayovac. These shadows were not cast by anything in this world.

These shadows were alive.

When he regained control of his legs, he bounded up the steps and ran as hard as he could to get away from those shadow-things he was sure Granny Porch had conjured. She had conjured them up and they had killed her, sure as sin.

CHAPTER 28
DARKNESS AMOK

"Mistuh Chief," Boots said with a weary nod. "Ma'am. Y'all come on in."

He stood aside and Ree entered the old man's cozy little house. Luke followed, thinking that Boots had been expecting them.

"I got some coffee on," said Boots. "Be ready in a minute."

"Sounds good," Luke said. He noted that Boots looked every bit the old man he was, as if his characteristic spark of eternal youth had finally flamed out.

"Y'all have a seat."

Luke and Ree sat on the sofa, and Boots sank back into his old easy chair.

"Odessa Nell's dead," Boots said. "I just now came from her house. They were taking away her body when I left."

"What happened?" Luke asked.

"She died fightin' the evil. Before her soul departed, she told me the dark thing's wounded. And dangerous like a wounded animal."

"The Yahoo things?"

"Yawahoos," Boots corrected. "She said *they're* scattered. But this something else. She called it 'the dark thing' and said something about that boy smashing its skull and that wounded it. I don't know what that was about."

"Cornelius Weehunt dug up this weird skull down in the sinkhole on Main Street and was wearing it over his head. When he lay down in front of the train, he was wearing it. I don't know what kind of animal that skull was from. It was like nothing I've ever seen. Like something out of a monster movie."

"I reckon that's what Miz Odessa was talking about then."

"But how could smashing an old skull have any effect on this 'dark thing'? Whatever it is."

"I don't rightly know," said Boots. "All I know is that the laws of nature don't always work the same as the laws of the supernatural. How did Jesus raise the dead and come back from death Himself? There's powers we don't know nothing about."

"That's so true," Ree said. "God did raise Jesus from the dead, but we don't know *how* He did it. Which is why so many educated people *don't* believe it."

Luke rubbed the rough stubble on his chin. "Damnedest thing," he said, "when Corny turned and waved to me just before he stretched out on the track, I got the feeling that he was telling me . . . that he'd come to his senses and was trying to tell me that he knew exactly what he was doing and that it was . . . all right, and that even though I'd just shot him, he understood why I'd done it. I don't know. Maybe that's just how I want to interpret it. Maybe he waved 'cause he was completely out of his mind."

"Maybe you have to trust your first feeling about it," suggested Boots. "Could be the boy *did* know what he was doing. Maybe the Lord was guiding him to do it. But what matters is that he hurt it and now it's out of control. That's what Miz Odessa said. She said I . . . we can beat it if we keep our faith."

"I saw it," Ree said. "I saw this black boiling cloud in the mirror and I could *feel* the evil coming off it. It destroyed my guardian angel." She laughed; it was a mirthless, near-hysterical laugh. "I'm sorry. I know how psychotic that sounds, but that's what I saw with my own damn eyes."

"I believe you, Miz Tyler. I've seen things in my time that you wouldn't want to believe."

"I saw a dead dog come back to life and try to kill me."

"You got me beat there," Boots said with a little twist of a smile on his lips. "I never saw the dead walk. But I know they can."

Luke said, "We both saw my dead wife. She spoke to us. But I don't think it was really her. It was an imitation. A damn good one."

"Evil, like Satan, is Lord of Lies. It can take a true thing and twist it all around just to confuse you or make you despair. I think that's why it killed those folks at the boardinghouse. Not because it wanted to kill 'em, but to make the living despair."

"Like terrorists," Ree said. "Like those evil bastards who took down the World Trade Center Towers."

"That's right." Boots leaned forward in his chair, propping his thin arms on his knees. "But this is different. When the author of evil is wounded and out of control, I don't know we can expect."

"The author of evil . . ." Ree repeated.

Boots flashed a self-conscious smile and shrugged. "I am a preacher, you know."

"No, it makes sense," she said.

"Miz Odessa said we can beat it by keeping our faith strong."

"That's all well and good, Boots," said Luke, "but I need specific details. I have no idea how to fight whatever the hell this thing is. How can we fight a black cloud?"

"I doubt it's really a cloud," he said. "If it's anything like the Yawahoos, we'll never really see it. Its shadow maybe, and we already seen its effects, but I don't think human eyes are made to see something like this."

Luke sighed in frustration. "If I have to rely on my faith in God, I'm in trouble."

"Mistuh Chief, folks find God in different ways. You start where you are, where you live. Have faith in yourself and those you love. That's where you'll find the Lord. Might be he'll find you first."

"Nice sentiment, but I don't think we have time for spiritual discovery. And stop calling me 'Mistuh Chief.' *Luke* will do just fine."

"Luke it is."

Luke shifted his hips on the sofa so that his pistol's butt stopped digging in his side. "All right. If this thing possessed Corny and made him do what he did, then it'll be needing a new pawn to move around the board. Who would be its next likely target? Did it choose Corny because he wasn't right in the head? Will it go after the next mental defective it can find?"

Ree said, "It's like we're playing some kind of souped-up Dungeons and Dragons game. Is there some game master or wizard we should consult? I'm sorry, but I don't see how this is going to help us."

"Odessa Nell was the closest thing to a wizard we had," said Boots. "Now we just got ourselves. And the Lord."

Luke wanted to tell the old man to stop preaching, but he held his tongue and reeled in his frustration.

"And," Boots went on, "according to what she said, the Yawahoos are scattered, so I don't think we have to worry about them now. They're elemental spirits, probably conjured up by a witch with bad intentions. If they're scattered, then whoever called 'em up is most likely out of the picture now. They can't really be controlled for long anyhow. When you call on them, you're playing with fire. This other thing I don't know nothing about. All I know is Miz Odessa believed we could beat it 'cause it's hurt."

"And out of control like a wounded animal," Ree added.

"And it can make us think we see ghosts and it can raise the dead," Luke said, scarcely believing his own words. But how could he not believe them? Hadn't he seen Jenny jumping on his bed and heard her venomous curses?

"Boots, can these ghosts actually hurt us? Physically?"

"I don't know. I never heard of ghosts hurting the living. And I know lots of folks who say they've seen ghosts. It's usually demons that do the hurting."

"But what we saw might not have been real ghosts," said Ree. "You said that wasn't really Jenny we saw."

"So maybe it was some sort of hallucination, drawn from my own mind and turned against me."

"But I saw her too," Ree reminded him. "And the man I saw in the tree I'd never seen before. He didn't come from my mind."

Luke shrugged. "We're not getting anywhere trying to make sense of all this. Boots is right, we dealing with things that don't obey natural laws. One thing I do know: Agnes Porch vowed revenge on me and the town. If somebody conjured up evil spirits, she's the prime suspect. I think I'll pay her a visit. She's as good a place as any to start."

"But this other thing, this dark thing," said Boots, "I doubt she'll know anything about. And that's the thing we got to worry about now. Besides, if this lady you're talking about *did* conjure the Yawahoos, then she's probably already gone. Dead or turned into a turnip."

Ree looked askance at the old man.

Boots caught her look and said, "*Mentally* like a turnip. Not physically." He smiled at her. "I ain't *that* crazy."

"Well, what do *you* propose we do?" Luke asked him.

"Reckon I'll get myself ready for church. I'm preaching over at the Church of the Holy Savior. After that, I don't know. I'll have to pray about it. Wouldn't hurt for you to ask for the Lord's guidance either."

Luke blew out a big breath.

Boots Birdwell sat up straight and said, "I'm reminded of a Bible quote."

"Uh-oh," Luke muttered.

Ree elbowed him.

Boots quoted: "'Behold, I give unto you power to tread on serpents and scorpions, and over all the power of the enemy and nothing shall by any means hurt you.' Luke 10:19."

Ree said, "How about this one? 'For these be the days of vengeance, that all things which are written may be fulfilled.' Luke 21:22."

Luke looked at Ree, then at Boots and shook his head. "How about this? 'Whatever *can* go wrong, *will* go wrong.' Murphy's Law, chapter one, verse one."

* * *

After he turned onto the blacktop, Craig Hemphill saw the hearse weaving from one shoulder of the road to the other and turned on his flashing lights. He tapped the siren to send up a single whoop as he accelerated and closed on the vehicle in front of him. The fog was still pea-soup thick and visibility was poor, but that didn't explain the erratic driving of the vehicle's operator. Nobody but a drunk would be weaving up the road like this. A drunk or a driver who'd just suffered a stroke.

The hearse didn't slow down or alter its erratic course, so Hemphill cut loose with the siren. Unless the drunk driver was stone-deaf, he would get the high-decibel message this time.

The dark hearse rolled on its merry way. It didn't speed up, didn't slow down. The driver seemed totally oblivious to the fact that a police car was in pursuit. Hemphill was pissed off now. The driver was heading for downtown Vinewood, where the streets would be busy with vehicles en route to local churches for Sunday school meetings. Vehicles with kids in them. Whole families on their way to worship.

Hemphill waited for the hearse to weave to the right, then he floored the accelerator and shot forward, coming abreast of the meandering hearse. He looked to the right to see who was driving the dead-meat wagon. Craig was cranky and tired, still bummed out by the bloody scene he'd happened upon a few hours ago in the abandoned house, and his usual patience was in very short supply. The drunk son of a bitch behind the wheel of the hearse was begging for a taste of roadside justice, and Craig was in a mood to oblige. He couldn't make out the driver's features through the thick fog—except for the fact he was bald as a bowling ball. The chrome-domed jerk was either ignoring an officer of the law or he was so drunk he didn't even know Craig was there beside him with lights flashing and siren wailing.

He goosed the gas pedal and shot ahead of the hearse, then swerved sharply to the right and pulled in front of the offending vehicle. The hearse's front bumper clipped the right rear door of the cruiser. He slowed his speed and attempted to force the hearse off the road and into the ditch. He was gambling that the driver wouldn't step on it and spin the cruiser around and into the ditch, but given the apparent degree of the driver's inebriation, he figured such a maneuver was beyond the drunk's present capability. If he was wrong, he was screwed.

Hemphill wasn't wrong. The hearse's snout pushed against the side of the cruiser like a living creature—a great black shark came to mind—before finally slowing down and stopping on the soft shoulder of the road. Relieved and thankful that his dangerous gamble had paid off, Hemphill stepped out of his squad car and unbuttoned the snap over the butt of his pistol as he came around the rear of his vehicle, fully prepared to use force if the perp offered the least bit of resistance. With enough adrenaline surging through his bloodstream to charge a dead battery (chemically impossible, but that was how he felt), Craig grinned when the bald-headed asshole started climbing out of the hearse. When you're stopped by a cop, you don't get out of your vehicle unless and until the cop tells you to; otherwise, your actions could be interpreted as resistance—which was exactly how Craig Hemphill wanted to interpret this bozo's stepping out of the vehicle. His stepfather had been a drunk and had bullied and beat him until Craig was big enough and pissed-off enough to fight back, and on that memorable day, young Hemphill had administered a beating the redneck stepfather never got over. Till the day he died of cirrhosis of the liver, old Bubba Oates couldn't breath through his crooked beak without whistling like guinea pig. And that was precisely the sort of beating he wanted to give this drunk-ass peckerwood. But when the driver came out from behind the driver's door of the hearse, Hemphill suddenly lost his desire to give the guy a bloody thrashing.

"What the fuck . . .?" Craig said when he saw the naked abomination zombie-walking toward him. The fact that the guy looked exactly like Lem "Cowboy" Porch was not so startling as the fact that his chest and rib cage were split wide open. It looked as if his innards had been scooped out with a giant spoon.

Hemphill's mind balked. The repulsive visual image his brain was transmitting had to be a fluke. Some wires had crossed somewhere, short-circuiting the whole cerebral shebang. That, or he was having some delayed shock reaction to the grisly scene earlier this morning. One or the other, because this thing his brain was telling him he saw *could not be real.*

He blinked his eyes and tried to clear his optic circuits of this hideous vision.

But the walking dead man didn't go away. He was coming closer with each clumsy step.

Craig drew his .38 Police Special and aimed it at the man's empty chest, then he remembered Hollywood's lore of the living dead and raised his aim to the thing's head. "Freeze!" he shouted.

But the chrome-domed zombie came on with outstretched arms and fingers like fat overblown worms.

Hemphill thumbed back the hammer. His mind was a jumble of mixed messages: *Lem Porch is dead; he's been autopsied; he's walking toward me with bad intentions; dead men can't walk; dead men can't drive a hearse; shoot him in the head, that's how you kill 'em; but his brain's been removed, and anyway this is not real.*

The pop of his pistol shut down his inner dialogue (he had pulled the trigger without conscious decision) but it didn't shut down the shambling advance of Lem Porch's nakedly obscene and gutted body.

Craig fired again and saw the slug impact the dead man's bald head, but the walking abomination still came on. He stepped back, holstered his useless gun and popped his baton off his belt. If he couldn't kill it, he sure as hell could beat it into submission; even dead bodies have to yield to the laws of physics.

He cocked the baton over his shoulder and snapped it forward, landing a solid blow upside the ghoul's head, staggering him. Craig swung again, this time striking the outstretched left arm. The arm buckled and he heard the bone snap.

But the ghoul wasn't stopping.

Craig gripped the handle of his baton with both hands and delivered a roundhouse blow to the thing's left leg. Again the sound of breaking bone. The corpse listed to its left, but hobbled forward.

From the corner of his eye, Hemphill saw a second naked man coming toward him. Luther-fucking-Porch! Sure as shit, and why not? Butthole brothers gotta stick together, right? *Come on, motherfucker, I got some for you too.* Craig was beyond freaked-out now; he was in the *zone*, the never-say-die zone, and he was hell-bent on putting these dead-but-won't-lie-down zombie sumbitches down for good, just the way God planned it. If he was seeing this shit because he was in the middle of a psychotic break with reality, well, he would just deal with that later, but right now he was not going to be bested by two dead redneck refugees from a funeral home, no fucking way.

He took the attack to the walking corpse of Luther Porch. Hemphill went wild with his nightstick, pounding, pounding, pounding, and trying to drive the ugly bastard into the ground, making ground-meat hair pie of the face and head.

But nothing seemed to stop the ghoul. He was so intent on hammering Luther that he failed to see Lem coming up behind him, and when Lem's cold hands closed on Craig's neck, it was too late. Then both dead men were on him, taking him to the ground.

Hemphill knew he was dying. The hands at his throat were too strong to pry off, and he figured he had only a minute or two left before choking to death. When the ghoul began to rip away the flesh of his face with its teeth, Craig Hemphill drew his pistol, put the muzzle to his own temple and squeezed the trigger.

He was dead before the last blasted bit of his brain hit the road.

*   *   *

Otis Delums dug his grubby fingers into his little can of Vienna sausages and fished one out. He sucked the juice off it, then popped the whole thing into his mouth and chewed it with great gusto. He wasn't really hungry, but eating the sausages gave him something to do while he waited for Corny to show up here at the train yard. Otis liked all the fog. Fog was fun. You could see things in it the way you could see faces and things in clouds. He was seeing something now, but he didn't think it was real. If it was real, Otis would be scared, but since he didn't feel scared, he thought it couldn't be real. So he just sat on his haunches and watched the thing move around in the fog sort of like that thing in that movie he and Corny had watched a bunch of times—what was the name of it?—and laughed because it wasn't scary at all. Who could be scared of something that looked like a giant blob of Jell-O? *The Blob!* That was the name of that movie. And Corny had said if he ever saw the blob, he'd get a spoon and eat the thing to death. That was funny. But this thing he was seeing now wasn't red like cherry Jell-O. It was sort of black or purple-gray. And it wasn't oozing on the ground. It was floating, sort of. Maybe it was some of that pollution stuff people sometimes talked about. Sure, that was it. It was just a cloud of dirty air floating in the fog. Nothing to worry about.

Otis looked at his wristwatch and tried to make sense of the numbers and the little black arrows called hands. The short hand was pointing close to the 10 and the long one was on the 2. He chewed his lower lip and tried to remember how to figure out the time from those numbers. Was it almost 10 o'clock or was it already after 10? He wished his daddy had given him one of those watches without hands that just came right out and told you what time it was, but his daddy was always saying it would be good for him to think things through and figure them out his own self. Maybe so, but if you had to know the time real quick, wouldn't it be better to have a watch without hands?

When he looked up from the watch face he saw something that did scare him. It scared him so much he peed in his britches. The dark stuff in the fog was changing, turning into the shape of a man. Not like a snowman shape but like a real-life man. Otis wanted to jump up and run but he couldn't move. The only thing moving was the pee running over his lap and the dark stuff making a man right in front of him.

"C-Corny?" he said when he saw that the man-shape had Corny's face. "You ain't gone hurt me, are you? It's me. Otis."

The dark thing with Corny's face moved toward him and suddenly he *could* move. He dropped his can of Vienna sausages, jumped up and ran up the embankment to get away from it. Otis didn't know what the thing was, but he knew it wasn't really Corny. He knew it wanted to do bad things to him.

*   *   *

There were times when George Taggert wished he'd chosen a different career path, and this was definitely one of those times. A small-town druggist is frequently called upon to leave the comfort of his home and go to his place of business to fill a prescription for a customer outside of regular business hours. George didn't really mind doing it if the customers were truly in need, but nine times out of ten they weren't. Millie Peak's husband Ralph had called George at home this morning and said Millie was in "a bad way" and needed a refill on her Prozac. Ever the faithful pharmacist, George said he would be glad to oblige and told Ralph to meet him at the store in half an hour, though the truth was, George didn't believe Prozac was what Millie needed. If the sour old biddy needed anything, it was a swift kick in the ass and an ultimatum from her husband that she straighten up and fly right—or else. With these unprofessional thoughts running through his head, George Taggert got out of his Pontiac, walked up to the front door of City Drugs and stuck his key in the lock. The fog seemed to cling to him and it chilled him to the bone. Damned odd fog it was. Something otherworldly about it, he thought, almost as if it had rolled in by magic from some remote and exotic corner of the world. George was not accustomed to such fanciful thoughts, and he wondered if this mental tug backward into the magical thinking of childhood was a sign of getting old. The proverbial second childhood. The tip-off that your brain wasn't firing on all the right cylinders and that memories embedded long ago were suddenly flaring up and burning brightly enough to color your sober-adult perceptions.

He shrugged off the thought and keyed the lock.

"Ai-yi-yi-yi-yi-yi . . ."

George turned toward the source of the strange childlike cry. He saw Otis Delums running out of the fog near the sinkhole. What on earth had gotten into the boy? He was moving with a stumbling gait along the edge of the hole, and George was afraid the poor kid was going to fall in. "Hey! Get away from that hole!" George shouted.

But Otis didn't get away from the sinkhole. Instead, he began to shamble around its jagged rim, as if he were playing some retarded version of ring-around-the-rosy.

"Merciful Heaven," George said, borrowing a phrase his mother had been fond of using when he was a kid. (Second childhood?) He dropped his keys back into his pocket and hurried to rescue the boy from his dangerous game. He ducked under the yellow tape and stood at the hole's edge to wait for Otis to come around again. If Otis was aware of George's presence, he gave no sign of it. He came on in his sad, lumbering run, his eyes bugging out of his large head, his mouth O-ed and still making that run-jarred "Ai-yi-yi-yi" noise.

George squared and braced himself to intercept the boy. "Otis!" he shouted again. George spent most of every working day on his feet, and he had kept himself in pretty good physical shape since his days as a Naval officer patrolling rivers in Vietnam, so when Otis Delums crashed into him, he was able to stop the boy (*The Catcher In The Rye?*) and wrap him up in his arms.

"What hell are you doing, son?" he asked the bugged-eyed, babbling boy.

"Aiiiiiiiiiii . . ." Otis kept up his haunting, nerve-wracking yammering. He didn't seem to even see George. If he was seeing anything, it was nothing in this world.

George held him at arm's length and shook his shoulders. Otis' big feet were still stabbing the pavement, running in place.

"Otis!" George yelled right in his face.

Otis ran, going nowhere.

"Aw hell," said George. It was clear Otis wasn't going to stop until he dropped from exhaustion—or dropped into the hole. Keeping a firm grip on him, George tried to walk him to the sidewalk, but Otis wouldn't budge from the rim of the sinkhole. The poor kid didn't look that strong, but he was more than George Taggert could handle for any length of time, and there was no one else on the street to help him. He released Otis and ran inside the drugstore to call 911. With any luck, Otis wouldn't fall into the hole and break his fool neck before the EMTs arrived to strap him to a stretcher and zip him off to the ER.

Luke wanted to return to his house to see if the "ghost" of his wife was still there in the bedroom, and Ree wanted to go to her shop to see if her guardian angel would appear in her special mirror, so after as rational a discussion as they could muster, given the bizarre circumstances, they agreed to first go to Luke's.

"What if she *is* there?" she asked as they rode up in front of his house. "What if she *can* hurt us?"

"It's not a *she*," he said. "And it sure as hell ain't Jenny. You heard what Boots said. He's never heard of a ghost hurting anybody."

"I know, but if it's not Jenny, then it's not a ghost, and we don't know what the hell it is. It sure did affect your dog. What's to say it can't do the same to one of us? *Both* of us?"

"You should wait here. Whatever it is, I don't want you near it."

"No, sir, I'm not letting you go in there by yourself. We have to look out for each other. One for all, all for one."

"No. It's too dangerous." Luke opened his door.

Ree opened her door. "You can't stop me."

"Goddammit, Shorty . . ."

"Ah-ah," she scolded. "You don't wanna piss off the Lord now. We need Him on our side."

"Sorry. Come on, then. But you stay behind me when we get inside."

"Okay." He got out of the pickup and shut his door softly.

Ree walked beside him, holding his hand. She spoke quietly: "If she . . . *it* . . . is still there, what are we going to do?"

"See if it bleeds," he said, patting the butt of his pistol.

* * *

Paul Goolsby assembled his crew of six men in the middle of Main Street, twenty yards away from the sinkhole. They all wore yellow hard hats and navy-blue jumpsuits, and they all listened as Goolsby briefed them on their initial plan of approach. "As soon as they get that crazy kid off the site, John will crane the loose slabs of asphalt out of there and then we'll go down with the portable drills and see what we've got. The east rim should be stable enough for the crane, because that's the spot they used to haul up the dump truck that went down. We already know there's a tunnel running off to the west, so that's where we'll start. There was a heavy rainfall yesterday, so it's going to be wet down there and possibly unstable.

At the first sign of a cave-in, sing out and get out. Questions?"

Stroking his bushy beard, Bear said, "What the hell's wrong with that kid?"

"He's retarded, mentally challenged, whatever they're calling it these days," Goolsby said, turning to watch the boy loping around the hole. "The pharmacist has already called for an ambulance."

"Here come the cops," said John, nodding toward the squad car coming down the street with its blue lights flashing in the fog. "They'll take care of the retard. I'll go ahead and get into position."

Goolsby kept his eyes on the young man circling the sinkhole and did his best to conceal his anxiety. He wanted his crew alert, but he didn't want to spook them or infect them with the uneasy feelings churning inside him. A psycho killer had almost stabbed him, so of course he was still upset, but that didn't explain his feeling that the damned sinkhole wanted to kill them all. As a geologist, Goolsby knew that a sinkhole was the result of long-term underground erosion, a perfectly natural geological phenomenon, so why was he entertaining the superstitious idea that the hole wanted them dead? It was ridiculous. It was unworthy of a man of modern science. Theirs was a dangerous job, and it was natural to feel a certain amount of fear in doing the job. The thing was, you couldn't give in to fear or cower in the face of a dubious premonition springing from that fear.

"Okay, you all know what to do," he said, turning to his men and rubbing his palms together as though he couldn't wait to get started. "Be careful down there."

He thought of his wife and children, and wished he were home with them right now.

*　　*　　*

Luke crept up the stairs. Ree followed.

"L-u-k-e . . ." came the voice from the bedroom. It was an excellent imitation of Jenny's voice, he thought, right down to the extra little emphasis on the *k* she'd used whenever she was emotionally wrought.

"God be with us," whispered Ree.

They reached the second-story landing. Luke moved into the bedroom doorway and stopped. Ree bumped into him. "Sorry," she whispered.

Jenny was lying naked in the middle of the bed with her knees bent and her feet flat on the mattress. She was rubbing her hideously distended belly with her hands and humming a lullaby. She turned her head and fixed her dark eyes on Luke. "I've got something for you, honey," she said. "I carried it such a long way just to get it here. You're going to love it."

"You . . . are . . . not . . . my . . . wife," he said, slowly and deliberately.

"Don't be ridiculous," said the Jenny-thing. "Of course I'm your wife. And this is your son." She cupped her hands over the huge mound of her abdomen.

"My wife couldn't have babies." Luke's voice trembled with anger. "Whatever the hell you are, I want you out of my house. Right now!"

"Oh, I think it's time," said the imitation wife. She began to twist and writhe on the bed. "Yes, it's coming! It's for you, Luke. It's coming for you."

"Stop it!" he shouted.

Ree pushed around him to see what was happening. "Oh, my God," she said when she saw the thing that looked like a hugely pregnant Jenny Chaney with her thighs spread wide and dark fluid spewing from the pink gash between them. A foul odor filled the room as that pale belly ballooned.

"Here he comes," squealed the gleeful apparition.

"Don't look at this," Ree told him. "It's an abomination before God."

But he couldn't look away. He and Jenny had badly wanted a child, and his greatest regret was that his dear, sweet Jenny had never been allowed to know the joys of motherhood before she was taken from him.

The baby's head crowned amid the matted curls of pubic hair.

But it wasn't the head of a newborn human. It was hairless and pebbled like the skin of a serpent.

The birthing mother groaned, gasped and grunted like a woman in the throes of a great orgasm.

"Luke, *do it*," Ree said sharply.

The thing's head slid all the way out, lubricated by bright red blood and some darker, noxious fluid. Tiny arms popped out and began a paddling motion, as if the infant was swimming into the world with the breaststroke.

"Kill it!" shouted Ree. "It's *evil*."

Luke slowly lifted the pistol from its holster on his hip.

The thing being born slithered free of its mother's birth canal, kicking its webbed feet and working its lipless mouth as though desperate for air. A long black tongue flicked from its mouth as it rose up on its hands and feet and began to crawl toward the foot of the fouled bed—and toward Luke.

"Luke!" shouted Ree. "Do it!"

He raised the pistol and pointed it at the crawling beast, but he couldn't bring himself to squeeze the trigger. *I can't kill a baby. What if I am its father?* Even as this irrational thought ran through his mind, the humanoid alligator-skinned infant reached the foot of the bed and leapt at him. With a surprisingly strong grip, it latched its little arms around Luke's left thigh and sank fangs into his flesh.

Luke reacted instinctively and hammered the butt of the pistol on top of the baby's blood-slicked head. The creature relinquished its fanged grip on Luke's thigh and emitted a mewling cry as it grappled for a better hold with its tiny talons.

Ree cried out. Luke looked up to see that the obscene replica of his dead wife had pulled Ree onto the bloody, rumpled bed and was climbing on top of her. "Adulterer!" the Jenny-thing bellowed as it opened its mouth impossibly wide, exposing long snake-like fangs.

He delivered another hammer-blow to the baby's head, knocking it off his leg. It hit the floor with an ugly thump and began to wail like a helpless human baby. Luke rushed to the side of the bed, put the pistol's muzzle against the naked woman's temple and fired. The thing shrieked as it dropped to the mattress beside Ree and began to thrash its limbs in apparent agony, its face phasing through a series of inhuman contortions. Black liquid oozed from the bullet hole in the side of its head.

Luke fired a second shot point-blank into the Jenny-thing's forehead, and its thrashing ceased, its unbearable shrieking reduced to hissing whimpers.

Ree rolled off the bed and landed on her feet. She pointed to the floor behind Luke, and he turned to see the hideous infant slithering toward him. Without hesitation, he aimed his gun and shot the thing in the head. The tiny monster twitched and flopped about like a fish on dry land, then convulsed one last time before falling still.

"Jesus Christ, deliver me," said Ree, steadying herself against the wall. "I never . . ."

"Me neither," said Luke.

Then the bodies of the monstrous mother and child began to melt where they lay. Flesh and bone liquefied, converted by some otherworldly alchemical process into a bubbling, tarry substance with a stench so strong it drove Ree and Luke from the room.

They embraced at the top of the stairs. Ree buried her face in his chest. She began to tremble and shake, and Luke thought she was crying till she looked up at him and he saw she was laughing with tears in her eyes.

"Evil bitch messed with the wrong ones that time," she said.

Luke tried to laugh, but what came out of his mouth sounded like a strangled hiccup. "We got 'em, all right," he said, "but I'm not sure it's over yet."

"You think . . .?"

"I think we probably pissed it off real good."

"Tough noogies," she said. "I'm pissed off too. I'm ready for the next round."

"Give 'em hell, Shorty." Now Luke did bark a laugh.

*   *   *

"This is a fucking nightmare," said Chief Keller, leaning his elbows on his desk and resting his forehead on the palms of his big hands. "An evil fucking nightmare."

He was alone in his cramped office, talking to himself, telling himself what he already knew—and what the whole town would soon know. Citizens were dying right and left, dropping like soldiers on a bloody battlefield, and he—the chief of fucking police—was powerless to stop it. Or understand it. What the hell was going on? People were killing each other, people were seeing walking—*driving*—corpses. The whole damn town had flipped its fucking lid. "And I'm supposed to keep the lid on it? Cut me a break. *Jesus.*"

He popped four tabs of aspirin into his mouth and washed them down with cold coffee filmed over with creamy scum. "Ughhh. Holly!" he shouted loud enough to be heard by the dispatcher in the next room. "Did the state police call back yet?"

Holly Stimson appeared in the doorway. "Sorry, Chief," she said. "Not yet."

"Call 'em again and see what the hell's the hold-up. We're dying here."

"Uh, I just got a report of an abandoned squad car with its emergency flashers on, out on the Vidalia highway. And I can't raise Hemphill on the radio."

"Christ!" He slammed his fist onto his desktop. "All right. I'll run out there myself. Nobody else is available. If the state boys call, tell 'em again we've secured the scene of the chainsaw murder and we're waiting on *them.*"

He grabbed his hat and stomped out of the office and went outside to his civilian vehicle, actually his wife's Chevy Malibu, because all the cruisers were already taken. He prayed to God that Craig Hemphill hadn't met with foul play, but in his heart he was afraid that was exactly what had happened.

That was how fucking nightmares always went. From bad to worse.

*   *   *

Luke saw the oncoming vehicle and yanked the wheel to the right to avoid a head-on collision. The black hearse whipped past, riding the road's broken centerline.

"Jesus, who the hell's driving that thing?" he said as he narrowly avoided the ditch on the right side of the blacktop. "Didn't even have their fog lights on."

Ree used the ember of her cigarette to light a new one, then tossed the smoked butt out the window. "Some frigging idiot," she said, exhaling smoke. "Wish this fog would lift. Gives me the willies. You think it could have something to do with . . . this whole mess?"

"I don't know. I'd believe most anything after what we just saw back at the house."

"Me too. There's no telling what's creeping around in that fog. Or anywhere else, for that matter. The damned thing seems able to pop up anywhere it pleases."

"Yeah. I guess we know now what your guardian angel meant when he warned you about darkness gathering me. And we know the dark can bite."

"How *is* your leg?" she asked. "Does it hurt much?"

"Nah. I just hope it's not infected with . . . you know, anything evil."

"Well, you poured enough Clorox on it to burn out any kind of bug."

"I hope so."

Ree looked at her watch. "It's just past eleven. Let's go to church."

Luke looked at her to see if she was serious. "I thought you wanted to go to the shop and look for Beau."

"That can wait. Mr. Birdwell said he was preaching at the Church of the Holy Savior. We can be there in about ten minutes."

"I don't think I can sit through a sermon just now. I'm too wound up to sit still."

"But Birdwell said we need to keep our faith strong. I have a feeling that his sermon today will be especially meaningful. We could use a booster, don't you think?"

"I've got faith in this." He touched the gun on his hip. "This is what saved our asses back there."

"Was it? Who's to say it wouldn't've had any effect if we didn't have faith in good over evil? Please, Luke, I have a strong feeling that we should be there to hear Boots. I can't explain it, but I've learned to trust my intuition when it hits me like a ton of bricks. Like now."

"All right. I guess I'll put my faith in you."

Twelve minutes later Luke took off his pistol and put it in the glove box, then they entered the white-clapboard Church of the Holy Savior to the sound of the choir singing a rousing hymn Luke didn't recognize. The members of the all-black congregation were clapping their hands in time to the up-tempo hymn. Ree pointed to a vacant spot on a back-row pew, and they made their way to it and sat down. Several dark faces greeted them with warm smiles and welcoming nods and didn't seem offended that the white visitors weren't dressed in Sunday-best attire. They smiled back and settled into the hard seat. The hymn ended and a rotund minister got up and made announcements, then introduced Brother Birdwell as the guest evangelical speaker.

Looking dapper in his dark suit and white tie, Boots stood behind the podium, smiled and let his eyes roam over the congregation. When his eyes came to rest on Luke and Ree, they widened a little, and then his smile got bigger. "I thank you all for having me back," he said. "It's such a pleasure to look out on all these beautiful faces and know you're all here because you love the Lord and the Lord loves you. And I want to extend a special welcome to our visitors who've come to join us in worship and Christian fellowship. Thank y'all for being here. God bless."

He paused and seemed to be gathering his thoughts, then he said, "My heart is heavy this morning, brothers and sisters. Heavy with the loss of a lady who gave her life fightin' the forces of darkness. Lotta you knew Sister Odessa Nell."

There were gasps and various exclamations of lament from the congregation.

"That's right," Boots proceeded. "She passed in the wee hours of this morning, and I'm here to tell you that she went out fightin' the way she did her whole life. Her fight is over now, and I know she's with Jesus. We've lost a soldier for the Lord, but for everyone who falls, ten will take their place, following the example of people like Odessa Nell. Our fight goes on. The evil is still among us, and we are not in Heaven with Jesus, not yet. But I promise you this: Jesus is here with *you*."

Cries of "Amen" and "Praise God" rose from the congregation.

In spite of his reluctance in coming here and his innate skepticism concerning organized religion, Luke was getting caught up in the religious fervor. It was very much like a high-school pep rally, except that the opponent was Satan rather than a rival school. And from his conversations with Boots and his own recent experiences with the supernatural, Luke knew Satan was not just a boogeyman used for frightening people into the arms of the Lord but a personification of Evil in all its many forms, including the damned thing that was invading the town of Vinewood.

He reached over, took Ree's hand and held it, his big mitt enveloping her dainty fingers. She place her other hand over his knuckles and squeezed.

He felt a twinge of regret that he had inadvertently involved her in Agnes Porch's vengeance curse—if that was what this was all about—and he swore to himself and to God (if He really *did* exist) that he would not let her be further harmed by this dark, evil thing. He would give his life to protect her, not because he thought of himself as a hero, but because he loved her.

Boots Birdwell went on with his eulogy, using Odessa Nell as an example for all to follow. "I know," Boots said, "that some of you are thinking: How can you be singing praises of an old woman who never came to church? Well, brothers and sisters, Miz Odessa was smart enough to know that the whole world is a church. I knew the woman for more than fifty years, and I'm here to tell you, she was the finest spiritual leader I've known. She saw the Lord in the lowliest sinner and in the wickedest places. She knew that God *is* everywhere."

Outside a siren wailed as an emergency vehicle blew past the church. Luke grew restless, anxious to meet the dark enemy on the next field of battle. He leaned over to tell Ree he thought they should slip out and go, but he saw that she appeared to be sleeping. He leaned his ear close to her head and heard the slow, shallow breathing of a sleeper.

"Shorty," he whispered. She didn't stir. "Shorty," he said a little louder.

She woke with a start, her eyes wide in apparent fright. "The hole!" she said.

People sitting near them looked around, surprised by her sudden outburst.

"What?" Luke said, trying to keep his voice down.

"Oh, my God," she said. "I *saw* it. The whole street fell in. The town's going to be swallowed up!"

Boots paused to look at them, then went on with his sermon.

"We have to warn them," Ree said. She stood up and pulled Luke's hand, urging him to follow. "It's going to take down the whole town."

At that moment a lady sitting close to a window pointed at the panes of glass (none of the windows of this modest church were stained-glass) said, "Look at that! Help me, Jesus! It's *black*!"

Heads turned, and stunned worshipers verified the truth of the lady's words.

Dark finger-like threads of mist pressed against the windows as if trying to get in. The fog had turned gray-black like dirty smoke, but there was no smell of burning. A fungoid fragrance of mildew and river-rot stained the air inside the church.

Luke and Ree dashed out of the church and into the swirling, black mists.

*   *   *

James Partain was alone in his funeral home, waiting for word from
the coroner's office that his son's body was being released. James wanted to
prepare Skeeter's body for burial himself. Usually, when a mortician's close
relative passes, the mortician is not involved in the embalming procedure,
but James was determined that his son's remains be treated with rever-
ence and dignity, and the only way to be sure of that was to do it himself.
He would've trusted Charlie Taylor to do it, but Charlie was still deep-sea
fishing in Florida.

James sat at his desk and paged through the family photo album he'd
brought from home this morning. His wife was sedated and her sister was
there to comfort her, and for that James was thankful. He didn't care for
his sister-in-law, but he just didn't have it within himself to comfort anyone
now. Every time he looked at his wife, he felt like crying; he could handle
his own grief (just barely) but he couldn't handle his and Jean's too. The
loss of an only child is the hardest thing a parent ever has to face, he was
sure. He found a photo of Skeeter, age 3, wearing an Atlanta Braves cap
and flashing a heartbreakingly beautiful smile, so innocent and trusting.
His breath caught in the back of his throat and tears flooded his raw eyes.
"Oh, God," he groaned and looked away from the old photo.

Dad?

James stiffened in his chair. He slowly craned his head, straining his
ears. Had he actually heard his son's voice? Now he heard nothing but the
faint humming of the refrigeration unit in the prep room.

Dad, I'm here.

"Skeeter?" He stood and rushed out of his office and into the long hallway.
"Where are you?" Even as he spoke the words, he knew he hadn't really
heard his son's voice. Such things were not possible. He'd spent thirty years
working with the dead and not once had he ever seen or heard a ghost. His
grieving mind was playing a devious trick. There was no other possible
explanation. Was there?

Here. The voice seemed to be coming from behind the closed door of
the prep room—the room where Skeeter had died.

James crossed the hall, turned the doorknob and opened the door. The
hinges creaked as the door swung wide. He flipped on the wall switch and
the overhead fluorescents flickered and came on. Nothing appeared out of
the ordinary in the glaring light. There was no ghostly figure of ectoplasm,
nor any other sign of spectral life. James sighed. He was disappointed that

his son's spirit wasn't there to communicate with him, to tell him his soul was safe. The last time James had been in this room, his son's corpse had been right there on the stainless steel table, his abdomen horribly sunken and its bloody contents gurgling in the drain of the sink at the foot of the table. He shuddered at the memory and tried to expunge it from his mind.

Dad?

The hollow voice emanated behind him.

He spun on his heels and looked out into the dim hallway. He saw nothing, but he clearly heard his son's voice saying: *Dad, where are you? I can't see.*

"Skeeter, I'm right here. Where are you?"

I don't know. It's too dark here.

"Son . . . I love you."

I love you, too, Dad. Skeeter's voice faded as though he were being pulled away.

The fluorescent lights flickered out.

James stood in the hallway, listening to the dreadful silence.

*   *   *

"This can't be good," said Ree. "Like it's showing us how powerful it is. If it can turn fog black, it probably *can* swallow half the town."

"How do you know it was another vision and not just a bad dream?" Luke asked. He was driving as fast as the poor visibility would allow—40 miles per hour.

"'Cause I wasn't asleep. I was resting my eyes and then I *saw* it. The ground was falling away and the stores were falling into this giant hole like little toys. It was horrible."

"The geological engineer and his crew should be down in the hole now, drilling and looking for tunnels to see just how much of the earth has been hollowed out under there. If they see that it's that bad, I'm sure they'll alert everybody so the town can be evacuated."

"No. It's going to happen soon. Like *now*."

"But your vision of somebody trying to kill you in the shop didn't happen."

"Not yet. That doesn't mean it won't."

Luke said, "All right, so what the hell are we going to do? Tell everybody they have to stay out of town because you had a vision? Not only would they ignore the warning, but they'd probably try to have you put away. And me too, for believing you."

"We have to make them believe it."

"How?"

"I don't know, Luke. I'm open to suggestions. If you'd try to help me instead of attacking me . . ."

"I'm not attacking you. I'm just saying . . ."

"I know. I'm sorry. This whole thing is so freaking insane, it's . . . I just don't know what the hell to do."

He reached over and put his hand on her thigh. "Easy, Shorty. We'll think of something. We have to. Even if we have to make something up."

"A bomb!"

"Huh?"

"A bomb scare. We'll say somebody's planted a big bomb downtown and they'll have to evacuate the whole area since nobody knows where it's planted."

Luke grinned. "You're not only beautiful, you're brilliant, too."

"No, but I can make up some clever lies when I have to. I just hope we're not too late. Can't you go any faster?"

"Not if we want to stay on the road. I can't see ten feet in front of us in this black shit."

* * *

George Taggert stood on the sidewalk and watched the men in hard hats descend into the sinkhole. Otis Dellums had been taken away in the back of an ambulance, and the heavy-equipment operator had raised the slabs of asphalt out of he hole. George had held his breath until that stage of the operation was done, still harboring the irrational idea that the sinkhole was going to open up like a giant mouth and eat all the stores on Main Street.

As he was about to walk back to his store, he noticed that the fog was turning dark, as if a cloud of pollution had sneaked in while he wasn't looking. He'd seen similar clouds of dirty air on the outskirts of Pittsburgh, back in the 60s, but there was no industrial pollution here in Vinewood. Was this some freak weather phenomenon he didn't know about? It didn't smell like industrial pollution. It smelled foul like floodwater.

Then he saw the hearse careen around the corner and clip a parking meter with its front bumper. "Crazy bastard," he said aloud. "You can't drive like that in this fog."

The hearse swung about and U-turned off Main Street and disappeared in the dark mist. George went inside the drugstore to get out of the foul-smelling fog.

CHAPTER 29
THE DARK AND THE DEAD

Luke drove straight to the police station, left Ree to wait in the truck, and went inside. Holly Stimson was at her post, dabbing tears from her eyes with a tissue while communicating via radio with dispatched mobile units and holding a telephone to her ear. She glanced up at Luke, and he saw the deep hurt in her red-rimmed blue eyes. "Okay, I will," she said, then hung up the phone.

"What is it?" he asked.

"Craig Hemphill's dead," she said. Her shoulders began to shake as she took ragged breaths. "I don't know if I can do this."

Luke walked around her desk and put his hand on her shoulder. There was nothing he could say to make her feel better, so he just squeezed her shoulder and waited for her to regain her usual business-like composure.

"I'm sorry," she said. "I just . . ."

"I know," he said softly. And he *did* know. He knew too well the helplessness you feel when the world around you is rapidly going to hell and there seems to be nothing you can do about it. But more importantly, Luke knew he didn't have time to indulge in that depressing helplessness. "Listen to me, Holly. We've got a job to do. That sinkhole is ready to take down every store on Main Street and we have to keep everybody out of the area. We need all available units to get the job done. Now get on the radio and get them back here ASAP. Where's the chief?"

"He's . . . with Craig. He's not in a radio car, so you'll have to call him on his cell phone."

Holly gave him the number and he called it. Keller answered. His voice was edged with anger.

"What happened to Craig?" Luke asked.

"Something chewed his fucking face off and ripped out his throat. What the hell kind of wild animal could do that? And it looks like he was shot in the head. Jesus Christ, Luke, what the hell's going on? I—"

"Bill, we've got a bigger problem right now. I have reason to believe that sinkhole is bigger than anybody imagined and the downtown area is about to fall in."

"*What?* How the hell—"

"I don't have time to explain. We need all available manpower back here to keep the area clear. I want your okay to have Holly call everybody back in."

"You got it. Thank God it's Sunday morning."

"Thanks, man." Luke hung up and turned to Holly and said, "Do it."

*   *   *

"You're sure about this, right?" Luke asked as he started the truck.

"I *saw* it," said Ree.

He backed onto the street, shifted gears and sped around the corner toward Main. The black fog was beginning to thin a little, and he hoped it was a sign that the dark thing was losing some of its bite.

Goolsby's van was parked ten yards from the sinkhole, and a portable generator was sputtering on the hole's rim. A man in a yellow hard hat stood by the genny.

"I'll be right back," Luke said as he hopped out of the truck. He ducked under the yellow tape and stepped to the edge of the sinkhole. The metallic chatter of a drill rose from the hole and echoed off the storefronts of Main Street. He told the man in the hard hat that there was a bomb threat and that he had to pull his crew out immediately. The man nodded, then descended a rope ladder into the hole to alert his team.

Two minutes later, Goolsby came up the ladder, shut off the generator and turned to Luke. "This bomb threat is for real?" he asked.

"Afraid so," said Luke. "You have to get your men out of there right now and vacate the area. By order of the Chief of Police."

"You guys got a lively little town here," Goolsby said, shaking his head. Then he turned to his co-worker and said, "You heard the man, Bear. Bring 'em up."

Bear went down the rope ladder, moving quickly for a big man.

Luke asked, "What'd you find so far?"

"Initial impression? I hope all these shop owners have good insurance, because there's a good chance they're going to lose their stores. Caverns and tunnels extend west and south. Not sure how far yet, but based on what we've seen so far, the business district is a potential disaster area. I'll probably have to recommend condemning most of it."

Luke noticed Doc Taggert's Pontiac parked in front of the drugstore.

"Shit," he said.

"Pardon?"

"As soon as your guys come up, get 'em way out of town. I've got to clear the drugstore."

Luke jogged back to his truck. Ree rolled down the window to hear him say, "Doc Taggert's in the drugstore. I'll get him out. You go ahead and drive my truck to your house. I'll meet you there after we get the area clear."

"I'm not gonna leave you here," she said.

"Don't argue with me, not now. I want you away from this damn hole."

"What about you? You think I can just—"

"Dammit, Shorty, move your ass. I'm not playing."

She scooted behind the wheel. "Fine! Never mind that I'll worry myself sick about you. My feelings don't count."

"Go. I'll be all right."

Ree started the engine, backed around and laid rubber on the street as she drove off in anger.

Luke ran to the drugstore. The stench of the black fog was getting stronger, though the fog itself was definitely thinning.

Doc was in his glass cage, his fingers tapping the keyboard in front of a computer monitor. He saw Luke and raised a bushy brow.

"You've got to get out of here right now," Luke said. "The whole area's unstable. This place could go down at any moment."

"You're serious, aren't you?"

"Damn right. Let's go."

Doc exited his pill-laden lair. "I had a feeling about that damned hole," he said. "A premonition, I guess you'd call it."

"You're not the only one."

"Like a huge, hungry mouth that—"

"Doc," said Luke as he grabbed his friend's elbow and urged him toward the door, "we can talk about it later. Right now you have to get in your car and go home."

"Those geologists work fast, huh? Hell, they just went into the hole half an hour ago."

"If anybody asks, there's a bomb threat. That's why we're evacuating downtown."

"Bomb threat. What . . .?"

Then they were outside on the sidewalk. Luke pushed him to his car.

"What the hell's *really* going on, Luke? There's something you're not telling me."

"I'll tell you later. Now get going. And don't come back till I give you the okay."

As Doc was sliding under the steering wheel, he looked over Luke's shoulder, his eyes got big, and he said, "*Look* at that. What the hell . . .?"

Luke turned around.

The black fog was moving, though there was no wind. From up and down the street, it was going toward one central locus. Dark tendrils of mist were streaming toward the hole and swirling around it like water circling a giant drain. Something was pulling it into the hole.

"That's not natural," Doc said. "I've never seen anything like it."

Luke turned back to the Pontiac and slapped his hand on its roof. "Go!"

* * *

Ree was halfway to her house when she decided she should turn around and drive to her shop on 3rd Street. Luke wouldn't like it, but he wasn't around to complain. He was busy playing cop. She had to know if Beau was completely lost to her, and the only way she knew to find out was to go to the shop and see if she could call him up in the vanity's mirror. Her vision of the town falling into the earth hadn't included any stores of 3rd Street, so she was reasonably confident that she would be safe from danger there. It was *her* vision, after all, and surely her personal vision would've shown her own shop falling into the hole if that was destined to happen.

She parked Luke's pickup in front of her store, grabbed the little brown bag containing her smokes, and strode to the shop's front door. She dug her keys from her jeans pocket and let herself inside. The familiar smells of the shop were pleasantly soothing, especially after being out in that stinking black fog. She turned the thermostat down to take the damp heat from the air, then went to the back corner where the antique vanity sat in partial shadow. She dragged a rocking chair up in front of the vanity's mirror and sat down.

I look like hell.

She brushed her hair with her fingers and forced a smile onto her lips. She wasn't pleased with the results. The smile collapsed into a frown.

I look like a middle-aged gnome with big tits.

She giggled at the thought. Her face lit up with genuine amusement.

That's a little better. Luke must really love me to stick with me after seeing me at my worst. God bless him.

She wanted another cigarette, but she didn't smoke because she was afraid smoking might keep Beau away—if he still existed.

She set the chair to rocking, hoping it would calm her enough to open her to the mystical plane where angels and spirits dwelled. She closed her eyes. She saw the demon in the shape of Jenny Chaney giving birth to a monster. She opened her eyes to make the ugly vision go away.

Happy thoughts.

Banish all negativity.

She tried again, closing her eyes and slowing her breath. She stopped rocking.

Better. No monsters, no demons, no living-dead dogs.

"Beau?" she said softly. "If you can hear me, make yourself known. I need to see you, to know you're all right."

She opened her eyes and looked into the mirror. Her lonely reflection stared back at her with haunted eyes.

"Please, come to me, Beau. *Please.*"

Something stirred below the murky surface of the glass. It was like something swimming just below the surface of a calm lake, but she couldn't yet make out what it might be. "Beau?"

A vague outline formed within the hazy darkness. Head, shoulders, a face.

"Talk to me, Beau. Help me."

Ree's ears began to ring with a high-pitched whine. A sharp pain bore in behind her eyes. From the ringing whine came a deeper sound, a bassoon-like voice speaking just above a whisper: *Dark fire of the dragon.*

Beau's face appeared as a smear of light in the dark glass.

His disembodied voice spoke again in Ree's head: *Wicked spirits loosed it on the world and now it runs amok. You see the smoke but not the fire.*

"I don't understand," she said. "What does it mean?"

The whiteness of her guardian angel's face flared briefly then faded to utter darkness.

His fading drawl seemed to cross vast space to reach her one final time. *The dragon's fire will burn you but you must not smoke.*

Then he was gone.

And the only sounds were the humming of the air-conditioner and the thumping of her heart.

* * *

As in many small towns, most stores in Vinewood's downtown business district remained closed on Sundays, and this made the evacuation of the area relatively easy. Still, every shop had to be checked to ensure that no one was inside doing inventory, setting up new displays or doing janitorial work. The main problem was that the local churches were just now letting out, and the streets would be crawling with vehicles carrying families home to Sunday dinner or to the few restaurants just opening for business. The police moved quickly to block off streets, check the downtown stores and hustle churchgoers out of the immediate area without starting a panic. Most of the citizens were kept well away from Main Street, so they never saw the black smoke-like mists swirling above the sinkhole before being sucked down into it.

Luke kept a wary eye on the cloud-eating hole as he moved from door to door down Main Street, making sure the stores were indeed empty. He caught himself hoping that the street and its shops would collapse into the earth so that he would not be making a fool out of himself with his claim that the town was about to go down. He chastised himself for this self-ish thought. Better to be called Chicken Little than to see his hometown destroyed, he reasoned. He went on checking shop doors. Fanny Crandle was in her dress shop, putting out a new shipment of fall fashions, and Luke told her she had to get the hell out of there. She balked at first, but when he mentioned a bomb, she vacated the establishment as if the Devil himself were right behind her.

Alvin Snow was working the other side of the street, banging on doors with his baton. He paused, pointed at the black mists spiraling into the sinkhole and called to Luke: "What the hell's making it do that?"

"Damned if I know," Luke answered. "Just hurry up!"

"Ten-four, big buddy."

At that moment the big siren high over the fire station began to sound its warning as it did whenever a tornado had been reported. Though he hated that anxiety-producing wail, Luke was glad someone had thought to activate it. He had the feeling that time was running out, that he was going to be swallowed up when the earth's crust gave way.

He accelerated his pace, virtually running now from door to door, and always keeping an eye on the dark mists swirling into the hole. It occurred to him that when the last of the black fingers of mist were sucked into the hole, the collapse would begin. And once begun, nothing could stop it. Like a Tinkertoy town, all the stores and sidewalks would crack and crumble into the earthen void.

A police cruiser was crawling the streets, its driver (Luke thought it sounded like part-timer Ty Belson) using the vehicle's loudspeaker to announce the immediate evacuation of the downtown area.

When Luke reached the lower part of Main where a residential section intermingled with the business district, he knocked on the doors and urged the residents to get in their cars and drive to the high school auditorium to await the all-clear. Because the Islamic terrorists' attacks on America were still fresh in everyone's minds, no one hesitated. People moved quickly. There was simply no time to panic.

He reached the end of Main Street and began to jog back toward the sinkhole.

He was drawn to it. There was something about the sight of that shadowy mist whirlpooling into the hole that commanded that he watch.

The civil-defense siren atop the pole high over the firehouse died with a final sinking glissando: WHEEEOOOOOOOOOOOOOOooooooooooo . . . .

Luke stopped running and stood still. Listening.

An eerie quiet settled over Main Street.

Spooky silence.

Like the hush of a lonely churchyard.

Luke watched the last vine of dark mist snake into the gaping hole in the street.

He held his breath.

The ominous silence seemed to grow thicker, as if God had hit the *mute* button on His remote control.

Then a low-pitched roar rose from the earth and the ground began to shudder.

This is it, Luke thought.

*   *   *

The pale hands on the steering wheel were his. He knew that much. He knew they were guiding the hearse down the alley. They seemed to know where to go. Lem didn't. He didn't know much. He didn't know how he'd ended up in this broken husk of a body.

He did remember dying.

He remembered leaving his body and floating high above it and feeling wonderfully detached from all earthly cares and concerns. He remembered seeing his brother die in the dirt in front of the barn. And their old man too, dead in the dirt. But it was no big deal.

He recalled thinking that his life had been a bad joke played by a sadistic God. One second you're there, taking it all so seriously, and then God yanks the rug out from under you and you fall out of your body and float up into the spaces between the worlds of the living and the dead. You drift above the hunk of flesh and bone you used to live in, as if you're still attached to it by an invisible umbilical cord. You watch with little interest as your old body is hauled off to the dead place and you're pulled along with it to see the dumb things they do to your corpse. You feel nothing. You aren't yourself. You're an empty shape filled with echoes of memories. You are the ass-end of an electrical discharge, a ghost of a cosmic mistake. A vacuum waiting to be filled . . .

Darkness rushed in to fill the vacuum. He remembered that well enough. Remembered the awesome power of that darkness. After that he remembered nothing until he woke to this nightmare of being back in his ruined body, dead but still walking the earth, riding the streets and now driving down this alley of a familiar place. Luther was sitting beside him. Luther was dead too, but he was still *in there*, inside that messed up body, his face and head like raw, bloodless meat, his one eye taking it all in like he was having the same nightmare.

There was no pain. Not much feeling of any kind. He could feel the vague pressure of the steering wheel against his hands and the slightly cool sensation of the seat against his backside, but that was all.

I'm a ghost having a bad dream.

A ghost dream.

Then the darkness bubbled up inside his confusion and he felt . . . hate. Black hate. Hate stronger than death. This wild, dark thing inside him was driving him, running on the hate that survived his death, pushing him through this world he thought he'd left behind forever.

Lem looked over at his brother. Luther looked back with his dead-fish eyeball.

Lem tried to speak, tried to tell Luther that he understood now, but he couldn't speak. The dark thing didn't need him to say anything, so it hadn't restored his power of speech. It didn't matter. Luther probably already knew what was going on, knew that after they did this one last thing, the dark thing would release them and their souls could finally rest. All he and his brother had to do was ride this inner wave of darkness and hate and do what it directed them to do.

He stopped the hearse in the narrow alley behind the antique store. The front bumper knocked over a garbage can. The clatter it made sounded a world away and was quickly overshadowed by the roaring howl coming from the dark depths of the earth.

*   *   *

She was still sitting in front of the mirror when the warning siren on

282

2nd Street fell silent. Thank God. She needed quiet to digest Beau's last words. Why did he have to speak in riddles? she wondered. Why couldn't he just come out and say what he meant in plain English? She got the part about the "dark fire of the dragon" being loosed by wicked spirits, or at least she thought she got it, and she sure as hell knew that the dark thing was running amok, but what did "the dragon's fire will burn you" mean? Was the dark berserker going to have its way with her? And what the hell did Beau's final warning mean? *You must not smoke.*

She closed her eyes and offered a prayer. *God, if it's Your will, please let me survive whatever's about to happen. And please watch over Luke Chaney.* That was it. Short, sweet, and simple. Ree had never asked much of God; her prayers were generally of worshipful thanksgiving, asking blessings for others rather than for herself. She hoped she wasn't being too selfish in asking now for the Lord's protection.

The air-conditioner clicked off. A pregnant silence filled the shop. The air was charged with ill omen.

The quiet before the storm?

The floor beneath her chair's rockers began to shimmy and shake.

She stared into the mirror. She watched herself watching herself.

A low-pitched moaning drone accompanied the trembling of the building and the ground beneath its foundations.

She felt, rather than saw, a blackness rising from the earth. It sickened her. She felt like throwing up. She swallowed hard. Licked her dry lips.

She knew what it was.

Hate. Raw, virulent, hungry. Hatred in all its many forms: blind, specific, vengeful. Intense hate. A thunderhead of hate, ready to unleash a rain of violence and blackest evil.

This is it, she thought. *The fall of the town.*

She gripped the flat arms of the rocking chair and held tight. Ceramic and glass knick-knacks fell from shelves and shattered. Furniture legs danced on the hardwood floor. The glass display windows of the storefront imploded with a tinkling crash.

The howling grew louder, and Ree saw a vivid mental image of the demonic sinkhole opening like a giant mouth to howl its hate at the Heavens.

*   *   *

The street shook so violently that Luke could hardly stay on his feet. He tried to turn, tried to run, but it was like running on a treadmill gone wild. At one point he was actually moving backward, though he was trying with all his strength to run forward and get the hell out of the street. Main Street had become a carnival funhouse where everything was distorted and every motion was a goofy parody of itself—a perversion of physics.

He ran. He fell. Got up and ran. He ran past the Post Office like a drunken sailor trying to run across the deck of a storm-tossed ship. He hit the corner of Main and Auburn and cut right toward 2nd Street just as the ground opened up and took down a line of stores thirty yards behind him. He looked back over his shoulder to see the hardware store, the feed store and Mookie Vedders' law office disappear into the yawning hole and a great cloud of dust rising like some angry beast to tower over the massive destruction.

He lost his footing again and fell forward onto his hands, the asphalt ripping them raw. He pushed up and ran on.

A powerful explosion rocked the earth and knocked him down again. A gas main, Luke thought. No one had thought to have the gas shut off. *Shit.*

Once more he got to his feet and started running. Hot winds licked the back of his neck and whistled past his ears. Even as he ran for his life, he could feel the evil intelligence behind the destruction. He could feel its hatred, its hunger for human misery and death. And it made him furious.

He was going to destroy this dark beast, no matter what it took.

He would kill it—if it didn't kill him first.

*   *   *

Lem Porch shambled to the back door of Yeardley's Yard & Garden and used the hearse's tire iron to smash the lock and knock the door open. Luther shuffled along behind him, the flaps of his dissected torso hanging open like lapels of a hideous coat.

The ground shuddered beneath the brothers' bare feet, but they ignored the sound and fury of the geological upheaval that was wreaking havoc on Main Street. They were single-minded in their mission (said single-mindedness was remarkable, given the fact that their brains were gone). The dark thing directed them to ignore all else. This they did.

Lem moved among the garden tools and fertilizers, while Luther stood motionless in front of a display of garden hoses. They were oblivious to the shaking of the small building. Lem's cold fingers wrapped around the wood of a long-handle axe. Luther stood inert like the dead weight he was. Dragging the axe on the floor as he shuffled down the aisle, Lem spotted a bushel basket filled with machetes and pulled one out. He walked back to his brother and put the machete in Luther's hand. Luther looked at the wide blade and made a grunting sound in the back of his throat.

The Porch brothers exited through the back door.

*   *   *

Above the din of deep-earth rumbles and the rattling clatter of the various objects in her shop, Ree heard a rhythmic banging coming from the back door. It was a slow, steady pounding, as of something heavy striking wood and metal. Was someone trying to break in through the back door? No, that made no sense. Looters usually waited until after a disaster was over before they started their looting, and who would want to loot an antique shop? Nobody. *Nobody human*, she amended.

She wanted to get up and run, but she couldn't get out of the rocking chair. The bone-jarring vibrations of the quaking earth seemed to have wrung all strength from her leg muscles. It reminded her of a recurring nightmare wherein she sees a deadly coral snake at her feet but she is frozen by fear, her legs as useless as rubber limbs. The only way to escape the snake is to wake up. But there was no waking from this waking nightmare. All she could do was keep her ass in the chair and wait for the quaking to stop.

She kept her eyes glued to the back door. Saw it jump with each banging blow. The upper half of the door began to splinter.

Then she remembered her vision of the man with a blade coming after her here in the shop. *Stupid, stupid, stupid. I should've gone home like Luke told me to. God help me.*

Then the door crashed inward and hung askew by one broken hinge.

A naked man with an axe shuffled through the doorway.

A naked, *gutted* man. His chest cavity was an empty cage of raw ribs.

A second man, naked and similarly gutted, followed him and he too carried a blade—a machete. He looked like a skeleton wearing a meat suit and a fright mask of pulped flesh.

"No," she said, "no fucking way."

She forced herself to stand on rubbery legs. The rocker bumped the backs of her knees. The shop shook and rattled. She took a step but the floor seemed to dodge her foot and she went down on her knees, throwing a hand out to keep from falling on her face.

She looked up as the living-dead abomination raised his axe.

*   *   *

As his feet hit the pavement of 2nd Street, Luke cut left and started running toward the firehouse and the police station next to it. A fire truck was roaring out of the bay with its siren already screaming. It accelerated up the street and was about twenty yards away from the fire/police complex when both buildings shuddered violently and dropped into the ground. The fire truck narrowly escaped the fate of the buildings.

The street cracked open like a giant egg, and Luke drew up just short of the jagged fissure in the asphalt. He fought to keep his balance, then spun and darted across the street toward the funeral home. He had the idea that the massive cave-in had a personal interest in taking him down, and given what he knew of the dark orchestrator of this disaster, the idea didn't seem that far-fetched. He glanced over his shoulder and saw the slanting roof of the firehouse just above ground level; he saw no sign of the police station. He wanted to know if anyone in either building had survived the cave-in, but he knew he had to get himself clear of danger and wait till it was over before he could go back to help. His priority now was survival.

He ran. He cut across the funeral home's lawn and emerged in the unpaved alley between 2nd and 3rd Streets. The rumbling and quaking seemed to be subsiding. Luke stood in the middle of the alley and tried to catch his breath.

Then he saw the hearse behind Yeardley's Yard & Garden, and through the gap between the garden shop and Ree's antique shop he saw his truck parked in front of Ree's shop.

Why in hell did she come to the shop? I told her to go home.

He knew the answer, of course. She had come in search of her guardian angel.

As he started toward the front of the antique shop, he noted that the doors of the empty hearse were hanging open, suggesting that its occupants had bailed out in a hurry, but in his haste to reach Ree and get her out of the downtown area, he gave the abandoned hearse no further thought.

Until he saw the shop's back door standing open, its upper half splintered like balsa wood.

He juked around the front of the hearse and went through the broken door of Ree's shop.

*　　*　　*

Ree tried to get up off her knees before the axe came down, but a powerful shock wave bounced her off the floor and she came down on her face. The same aftershock threw off the axe-wielder's aim and the axe blade chopped into the floor two feet from Ree's head. Ignoring the eye-watering pain in her bloodied nose, she rolled away from her attacker and scrambled to her feet.

The man with the mutilated face swung his machete side-arm style, and the blade sliced into Ree's left hip, hindered only a little by the thickness of her jeans. The force of the blow knocked her into the wall, but this time she didn't lose her footing. She looked around in desperation for something to use as a weapon—or a shield.

The axe man was struggling to free his blade from the hardwood floor.

Ree picked up a small end table and threw it at the monster with the machete. It struck him squarely in the face, momentarily stunning him, and she made a break for the front door. As she ran past a tall mirror, she saw the blurred reflection of the man raising his axe over his shoulder, saw it fly from his hands as he hurled it at her.

The axe-head hit her between the shoulder blades and knocked her off her feet. Her head banged into an antebellum chest of drawers and she was out cold.

*　*　*

Luke tried to make sense of what he was seeing, but the scene was too bizarre for rational explanation. He saw the backsides of two naked men going after Ree with an axe and a machete. There was no time to make sense of it. There was no time to stop the man from throwing his axe at Ree's retreating back. It struck her upper back and knocked her down. On reflex Luke reached down to his right hip for his pistol, but it wasn't there; he'd left it in the glove box of his truck.

The man with the machete moved toward Ree's sprawled body, and the realization that this was her vision coming true flashed through Luke's mind. He shot forward on the balls of his feet and tackled naked man with the wide blade. As he came down on the man's bare legs and butt, he knew this was no ordinary man. The cold, rigid flesh, the raw-meat smell and the vague hint of a chemical odor informed his instincts that he'd tackled something less than human—something that was not even alive. He remembered Ree's insistence that Hondo had come back from the dead to attack her, and now that idea seemed perfectly plausible.

He crawled up the man's back and grabbed the wrist of the hand holding the machete. The man's head turned stiffly on his neck, and Luke recognized the battered profile. *Luther Porch.* It wasn't possible, but here he was, a dead man with a machete, apparently bent on killing the woman Luke loved.

Luke dug his knees into Luther's back and wrested the machete away from him, then he raised the blade and brought it down across the dead man's neck. He sprang to his feet and spun around to face the second man, who was bending down to pick up the axe. As the second man straightened up, Luke swung the machete at his head. The blade chopped the side of his face with a hollow thump. A blank expression on his face, Lem "Cowboy" Porch looked at Luke with dull eyes, then raised the axe over his right shoulder, preparing to counter attack.

Luke charged him with a body check and knocked Cowboy off balance before he had time to swing the axe. He dropped the machete and grabbed the axe handle with both hands and tried to wrench it out of Cowboy's cold hands. The raw flaps of the dead man's opened torso slapped against Luke's chest as they struggled in an absurd parody of a World Wrestling Federation death match. Raw-meat Zombie vs. Bozo Cop. Luke might've laughed if he weren't fighting for his life—and Ree's.

He shoved Cowboy into the wall and at the same time yanked and twisted the axe from the dead man's grip. He stepped back, cocked the axe and swung it with all his might. The blow struck side of Cowboy's neck and went through it like an axe blade through rotten wood. Cowboy's head came off, hit the floor and rolled to a stop against the leg of an old Singer sewing machine. The headless body flapped its arms as though trying to fly, then staggered forward a few steps and fell over.

Luke turned back to Luther, who was shambling toward him with the machete.

The slow-moving brother was an easy target. Luke swung the axe and took off Luther's head. Luther's body kept coming. Luke stepped out of the way and let him go by. Headless Luther bumped into the wall and started hacking at it with the machete.

Luke braced his feet on the floor and started chopping down the middle of Luther's shoulders. He struck again and again, until the dead man's back began to split open like a hollow log and his body crumpled to the floor.

Satisfied that the corpses were no longer a threat, Luke dropped the axe and knelt beside Ree's unconscious body. The axe thrown at her back had hit with the dull part of the axe-head, so she wasn't cut, but she was still out cold from crashing headfirst into the chest of drawers. He carefully rolled her onto her back, mindful that she might have a serious neck injury.

The rumbling and shaking of the earth had ceased during his fight with the Porch brothers. The destruction he'd witnessed left him with a profound sense of sadness and futility. He'd seen much of Main Street's stores fall into the earth, and parts of 2nd Street too, including the firehouse and the police station. How many were killed? Injured? He couldn't worry about that right now. His main concern was with Ree. She was his responsibility.

Her scalp was bleeding profusely, but he knew scalp wounds often appeared worse than they were because of their tendency to bleed so freely. He pulled off his shirt and used it to stanch the bleeding.

"Shorty?" he said softly. "Wake up. Open your eyes for me. Can you hear me?"

Her eyelids fluttered.

"That's it. Come on, open your eyes for me."

She opened her eyes.

Two pitch-black orbs quivered, then fixed him with a look of black hate.

*   *   *

She was floating on a sea of darkness when it found her.

She tried to resist it, but it was too powerful. It opened her up and entered her with a violence that was somehow sexual. The heat of its passion for conquest scorched her. The coldness of its contempt for all that was human gnawed at her with frigid hatred. The dark thing was trying to turn her inside-out. Her mind screamed in terror. Her soul sought mercy. Found none. The thing inside her was unmaking her in order to remake her in its own vile image—or so she thought, thinking being of utmost difficulty during this psychic rape.

Then came a great ripping sound, as if a giant piece of flimsy fabric were being torn apart. She felt it even as she heard it, and the psychic pain was exquisite.

The bag of skin containing her physical form was peeled away and turned inside-out just the way she'd once seen a rabbit's pelt skinned from its body.

Her inner nature was mercilessly revealed to her. She was a slug-like thing, a grotesque human maggot sent to crawl through the carrion flesh of the earth, a small-brained worm burrowing through rotting muck and the raw meat of humanity. A thing with a pathetic soul.

She was suddenly catapulted from her repulsive body. Her spirit soared toward the stars, and reaching the zenith of its arc, it held there, suspended for a brief moment of eternity, then began a descent into darkness.

The arc of descent carried her back through time, back to an age when the dark thing still inhabited its own physical form and traveled below the earth and lived in dank caverns. Indigenous tribes of primitives huddled round fires and snuggled in animal furs worshiped the great serpentine beast. The beast had many names. Great powers were attributed to it. It could fly above the earth. It could breathe fire. It could make the sun rise or fall. It could bring storms or summon endless days of darkness. Men who worshiped other gods railed at it, challenged it, and some even fought it. Many a brave warrior died in battle against it, while others waged war in its name, its fierce likeness painted on their shields to evoke terror in their enemies.

When the great serpentine worm grew old and finally died, those who revered it kept its spirit bound to the earth from whence it had sprung by their stubborn devotion. The great worm's magic increased with the number of its worshipers.

Then, following cataclysmic geological upheavals, the great worm's spirit fell dormant and slept for aeons in the earth. Other gods arose from the minds of men to be worshiped, and the great worm was forgotten by all but a few acolytes and mystics, who prayed for its awakening.

Then came subtle but significant changes in the earth's electromagnetic fields, and the spirit of the old one was roused from its long slumber. It woke in darkness, drew power from darkness and *remade* itself out of darkness.

It waited in its earthen lair to be worshiped by those who lived above ground, drawing power from dark deeds committed in its vicinity. It influenced beings susceptible to darker desires and impulses even as it fed on them. No worshipers called its name. It grew to hate the frail mortals living on the earth's crust. It longed to vent its anger upon them and to make them fearful of its dark power.

Sensing the time was right, the dark thing gathered itself from the ripe darkness and finally surfaced to proclaim its supremacy and make the human maggots feel its wrath.

Ree saw all this in a momentary flash of light—the light burning just on the other side of her eyelids.

She opened her eyes to the glaring light.

She saw the man hovering over her and she was filled with unrelenting hatred for him and his kind. The dark thing twisted inside her, coiling itself into a knot of burgeoning violence.

"Are you all right?" he asked, his voice thick with pitiful, raw emotion. His face became a mask of uncertainty. This man was an enemy of the dark power. He had to be killed.

But there were other dangers as well.

A fire burned nearby, above and below the earth. Fossil fumes flamed round about, threatening to devour the dark thing's energy and send it back into dormancy. It had compressed itself and had taken refuge in her body and soul, and now it was going to act through her to achieve its aims and ensure the survival of its consciousness.

Yes, it whispered to her.

"Yesss," she spoke its word.

"We should get out of here," said Luke. "What's left of the town is burning."

She looked around. Saw the beheaded corpses twitching on the floor.

"Think you can walk?" Luke asked.

"I can fly if I damn well please," she said, expressing the dark god's angry sentiment.

"Come on," said Luke as he pulled her to her feet. "I'll walk you to my truck. You have the keys?"

Keys? The dark thing accessed her memories. She patted the hard bulge in her jeans pocket. She nodded at the man called Luke.

Luke.

She (a part of her not yet under control of the entity inhabiting her) seized Luke's hand and looked into his eyes. She had to warn him. Warn him that he was in the presence of evil. "Luke . . ."

He gave her a questioning look.

"Luke, I . . . you . . . ."

"We have to go now," he insisted. He slipped his arm around her and ushered her out of the shop.

As he boosted her into the truck's cab, she said, "It's in me."

"What?" he said as she settled onto the seat.

Then the dark thing dropped a black veil over her mind and silenced her. She stared blankly into space.

CHAPTER 30
DARK DEMISE

When he pulled up in her driveway and shut off the pickup's engine, Ree was still staring blankly ahead and remained unresponsive to his gentle overtures, but at least her nose had stopped dripping blood. He picked her up and carried her into the house. He took her to the bedroom, laid her on the bed and stripped off her clothes. With soap and water, and then rubbing alcohol, he cleaned the gash on her hip and bandaged it with gauze and surgical tape he'd found in her medicine cabinet. Her eyes remained open, staring at the ceiling—or at nothing.

He found a lightweight blanket in the closet and covered her, thinking that she might be going into shock. He elevated her feet with two pillows, then kissed her forehead. He wanted to stay with her till she came around, but his sense of duty and his years as a civil servant demanded that he return to the site of the devastation and help with the rescue work. "You rest," he said. "I'll come back as quick as I can."

Her eyelids fluttered and her lips twitched as though she was trying to speak, but no words came out. He kissed her lips, then put on his blood-stained shirt and left her in the cool haven of her bedroom. As he hurried to his truck, he had the feeling that he was forgetting something—or that he'd overlooked something important. It nagged at him with the annoying persistence of a South Georgia gnat trying to get at his eye. Was it the venomous look of hate Ree had given him? Or was it something she had mumbled under her breath that he hadn't quite understood? She'd said something when he was helping her into the truck, something that sounded like *send me*. Send her where? The hospital? And why would she look at him with such raw hatred? He'd given her no reason to hate him or to be angry with him. Had he?

As he yanked open the pickup's door, the thing nagging at his memory broke through his mental fog, and *send me* became *It's in me*. Of course! That had to be it! And that explained those hate-filled eyes, eyes clouded with unnatural darkness. The dark thing had entered her while she was unconscious and vulnerable. But she'd come to her senses just long enough to warn him before it shut her down again. The supernatural entity had entered her—possessed her—just as it had done with Corny Weehunt.

Luke stood for a long moment, holding the door handle of his truck as he weighed the grotesque possibility. His natural skepticism battled his intuition and its notion that a supernatural being might actually be inside the woman he loved. Ordinarily, he wouldn't have seriously considered such a thing, but these were clearly not ordinary times; he had seen with his own eyes the terrible effects of this dark demon and had felt its evil touch as it took down his town. His world had changed over the past few days, and now he had to revise his old beliefs and admit that the world did indeed harbor things never dreamt of in his philosophy.

He slammed the truck's door and ran back to the house.

He didn't know what he could do to rid Ree of the thing inside her, but he knew he couldn't leave her alone with it.

The rescue of any casualties would have to be left to others. Luke's mission was clear: He had to rescue the woman he loved from the clutches of an ancient and evil entity.

*　　*　　*

The moment the man left her alone, the woman kicked off the blanket, rose from the bed and ripped the flimsy bandage off her hip. The dark thing inside her didn't like puny encumbrances of any kind, and it especially hated those that covered wounded mortal flesh. It relished the pain and the bleeding of its host—so long as the wounds were not severe enough to interfere with its control of the pitiful mortal.

Ree was deep inside a dark cave, watching her other self walk across the familiar room and pull open the drawer in which she kept the loaded pistol. Even as her bare feet moved her over the floor and through the bedroom doorway, she struggled in vain to drag her heels and retard the dark thing's progress toward its desired end.

Pain throbbed deep inside her skull. The more she tried to resist, the greater the pain became. The dark beast was enjoying her pain, and her feelings and sensations were becoming increasingly intermingled with the alien feelings of the thing inside her. Soon she would be altogether lost to it, and her sense of self would be forever obliterated. The dark thing was assimilating her soul. She grew very cold. Her teeth chattered.

It intended to make her shoot Luke to death with her pistol, and she was helpless to stop it.

＊　＊　＊

Luke charged through the front door and stumbled to a stop when he saw Ree standing in the middle of the living room with a pistol in her hand. She looked very small, almost childlike in her nakedness, and the gun looked outrageously large in her small hand. Her eyes were unusually big, unnaturally dark. Luke knew without doubt that she intended to shoot him.

"Ree, don't do it," he said. "Listen to me. You have to fight it. *You* don't want to shoot me. *It* wants you to kill me, but you don't have to. Be strong. Fight it!"

She cocked the hammer. Pointed the muzzle at his chest.

He held up his palms. "I love you, Ree. Please . . ."

＊　＊　＊

Her thumb clicked back the hammer of the pistol.

No, her mind shouted, but her weakened will found no connection to her body's movements. The thing inside her had total physical control.

Time seemed to slow down. Seconds lengthened like bands of elastic stretched to the breaking point. Each interminable millisecond bore incredible emotional weight, and the dark gravity at the center of her soul was pulling her into a black hole of despair. A slender, shining thread of love was the only thing keeping her self-awareness alive and connected to the familiar world, the world in which Luke Chaney stood awaiting his execution by the woman he loved—and who loved him.

She felt the dark thing's contempt for human emotion. Love, to its way of thinking, was nothing more than a deceptive emotion caused by biochemical interactions, an illusion, a passing of emotional gas. Pathetic human beings were not capable of seeing the world as it really was; they lived their lives in futility, cutting themselves off from the natural world with their mechanical gadgets and diverting toys, and pretending they were something more than glorified monkeys with pitiful souls. They were hardly worthy of worshiping this dark god. But they were too stupid to see that.

Losing her desperate hold on that thin thread of love, Ree struggled to maintain the last bit of her presence of mind and mount a last offensive against the dark monster.

Love.

Love is more than an emotion.

Love is a thing of the spirit.

God is love.

Love is God.

I love Luke.

Her eyes found him in a dark fog and she focused on his face, his eyes.

God help me.

Then she heard Luke's faraway voice saying, "I love you, Ree. Please . . ."

And her finger involuntarily began to squeeze the trigger.

She sensed desperation in the dark thing.

It was afraid!

It was not omnipotent. And that meant it could be defeated. *Didn't it?*

Emboldened by this revelation, she plunged into the black center of the beast, seeking the heart of its fear. Even as her finger exerted more pressure on the trigger, she found what it feared.

The bone-cave—the skull—it had inhabited when it was still flesh and blood had been destroyed and now it feared it couldn't survive without it except by inhabiting the physical being of another life form. The explosions and the gas fires burning in downtown Vinewood had somehow wounded it and made it realize it was not immortal. The thing *could* die!

And it had no place to hide.

I've got you, you bastard.

The hammer fell and the pistol fired, but Ree jerked her hand and the slug thumped into the wall behind Luke.

"I've got you now," she said aloud. "You're no god. You're just an over-grown worm who's dead and won't lie down."

Then she turned the gun on herself.

*   *   *

Luke flinched when the pistol went off, and the bullet zinged past his ear and hit the wall. His ears were ringing from the report, so he didn't understand the words Ree spoke, but when he saw her raise the pistol and place the muzzle against her temple, he shouted: "No!"

She smiled at him and said, "'Greater love hath no man than this, that a man lay down his life for his friends.'"

He threw himself at her and made contact just as the gun went off.

Her blood splattered his cheek. He fell on top of her, his head resting between her bare breasts.

*   *   *

"No, no, no," he muttered as he brushed back her hair with his fingers and examined the gunshot wound on the side of her head. There was a raw horizontal crease above her right ear but no bullet hole. When he'd thrown himself into her he'd caused the shot to go awry. "Thank God," he said.

Her eyes were shut and she remained unconscious and unresponsive to his attempts to rouse her. He ran to the bathroom, grabbed a towel and wrapped it around her head to cover the still-bleeding wound. Then he wrestled her into a bathrobe he'd found in her closet and carried her to the truck, secured her in the shoulder harness and sped off to the hospital.

He'd expected the hospital to be swamped with people injured in the sinkhole disaster, but when he drove up near the ER entrance, he saw only one ambulance backed up to the automatic doors. He hoped this was a sign that there were few casualties, rather than an indication that most victims hadn't yet been pulled from the ruins of collapsed buildings. He was confident that the shops on Main Street had been empty when the sinkhole opened up and swallowed half the downtown area, but 2nd Street was a different story. There were certain to be victims in the firehouse/police complex.

He unbuckled the harness, picked Ree up and ran through the entrance to the ER. The towel tied round her head was already soaked through with blood, and his own shirt was bloodied from her first scalp wound, so he wasn't surprised when the nurse looked at them with unabashed shock.

"Gunshot wound to the head," he explained as he brushed past the nurse and laid Ree on a bare gurney. "No penetration, but she's unconscious. Also a scalp wound here where she hit her head on a table."

"Who shot her?" the obese nurse asked as she wrapped a blood-pressure cuff around Ree's upper arm.

"She did. Accidentally." The lie was better than trying to explain the bizarre circumstances that had led Ree to try to sacrifice herself. He knew why she'd done it. She thought she could kill the thing inside her by killing herself. What he didn't know—had no way of knowing—was what Ree's rendering herself unconscious had done to the entity. Was it also unconscious? Was it awake and trying to get out of its incapacitated host? Or had it already fled? He stood over her and held Ree's limp hand while the nurse wrote down the blood pressure reading. "How is it?" he asked.

"It's a little low, but not dangerously so," the nurse answered as she began to clean the wound over Ree's ear with a sterile swab. "Dr. Larson will be with her in a minute. Is it really true that part of downtown fell into the sinkhole?"

"Yeah, I'm afraid it is. Half the shops on Main Street are gone. And part of Second Street."

"Thank God it happened on a Sunday."

Luke grunted.

Dr. Greg Larson entered the cubicle. A stethoscope was draped around his bull neck and his thick glasses magnified the dark circles under his eyes. "Hello, Luke," he said. "Is that . . .?"

"Ree Tyler," Luke confirmed. "A .38 slug grazed her head. She's been unconscious since it happened."

"How—"

"Gun went off accidentally." Luke was already tired of the lie. "A graze like that couldn't do any serious brain damage, could it?"

Larson looked closely at the cleaned wound, then said, "I wouldn't think so. Enough of a concussion to render her unconscious, obviously, but she should be coming around soon. We'll do a brain scan to be sure."

"Take care of her, Greg. I've got to get back to town and help with the rescue."

Larson nodded. "We're setting up a triage now. Any idea how many victims?"

"Shouldn't be more than three or four from the firehouse and police station. The last fire truck rolled out just before it happened. Beyond that, I'm not sure."

"Thank God for small favors."

Luke gave Ree's hand a gentle squeeze, then he ran out to his truck and drove back to town. He wanted to stay with her and be there when she woke up, but he knew he would be of more use on 2nd Street.

*　*　*

She awoke in a humming metal tunnel. A dull pain in her head told her that she wasn't dead and that this wasn't a passageway to Heaven or Hell. Then the hard surface she was lying on began to move out of the tunnel, and she was looking up at a young man in a blue smock with a nametag that said his name was Don Smith.

"Welcome back," Don Smith said with a smile. "Do you know where you are?"

"Hospital?" She realized her head was held in place by a cloth strap.

"That's right. Vinewood General. You're a very lucky lady, you know. A bullet creased the side of your head. Another inch or so and it would be a different story. Do you remember what happened?"

"Yes, sort of." She remembered that the dark beast had been inside her and that she had put the gun to her head and pulled the trigger. How had she muffed the shot at that range? Luke must've intervened; she didn't remember that part, but she knew he'd been there with her. Was the thing still in her? She shut her eyes and tried to detect its presence. She sensed no trace of it. Was it really gone, or was it hiding within her? She wasn't sure. Didn't know how to find out.

"This big hunk of expensive equipment that looks like a deluxe washing machine is our brain scanner," Smith said. "We just took some pictures of your brain and the doctor will read them and see if there was any damage to the old gray matter."

"I think I'm thinking okay,' she said. "I don't even have a headache. Just a little soreness is all."

"You're probably fine." He smiled as he removed the strap from her head.

"Don? You haven't seen anything . . . unusual, like shadows or black fog, have you?"

He looked at her with a cocked brow. "No. Why? Have you?"

"No, no. It's . . . never mind."

"You might feel a little foggy for a while, but it should clear up pretty quick."

She attempted a smile. "I'm sure you're right."

But she wasn't sure. She wasn't sure if the dark thing was stunned, in hiding, or completely gone from her. As Don Smith rolled her on a gurney to her room, she watched the ceiling and light fixtures moving overhead and she silently prayed that the evil thing wasn't lurking within her bruised skull, waiting for another chance to hijack her body and soul.

*　　*　　*

Bone-weary and feeling older than his fifty years, Luke Chaney trudged quietly down the hospital corridor toward room 206. The disaster downtown had claimed only two lives, a fireman and Holly Stimson. He was sick about Holly, and telling himself that she had died a hero's death didn't make him feel much better. Given the scale of the catastrophe, only two dead was nothing short of a miracle. The heart of Vinewood was devastated, but the town would rebuild on sturdier ground. He had great faith in his fellow citizens.

He knocked softly on the door, then entered.

Ree Tyler was sitting up in the elevated bed, sipping on a crook-necked straw. When she saw him, she released the straw from her lips and smiled.

"How're you feeling?" he asked as he approached the bed.

"Embarrassed, mostly."

He bent down and kissed her damp lips. "Don't be. It was a brave thing you did—or almost did."

"You saved my life." She took his hand and held it to her breast.

He sat on the edge of the bed. "Is it . . . gone?"

"I think so. I *hope* so. It was awful. I still feel . . . soiled. Unclean. It was *in me*. It tried to make me kill you."

"I know. But you were too strong. The damned thing couldn't beat your basic goodness."

"What if it's still in me? I can't tell if it's gone. Something doesn't feel right. I don't know if it's because I shot myself in the head or if it's because the thing's still here." She clutched his hand more tightly to her chest. "I just don't know."

"Whatever happens, we will deal with it. Together. It can't beat us. Just promise me you won't try to do away with yourself again."

She averted her eyes.

"Promise me."

She looked up with wet eyes. "I promise. You don't have to worry about that. It's different now. I . . ."

"What?"

"I'm pregnant."

"You . . . you're sure?"

"They just told me. The lab work confirmed it. You're going to be a papa."

Luke grinned. "I can't believe it. After all these years . . ."

"You're happy about it, aren't you. Really?"

"Sure I am. I always wanted—" Luke's voice cracked with emotion.

She lifted his hand to her lips and kissed his knuckles. "And I had given up myself. Ben was sterile, but he didn't really want kids anyway. I guess I always resented it."

"You'll make a great mother." Luke slipped off the bed and went to his knees.

"What are you . . . ?"

"Will you marry me?"

She giggled, then quickly regained her composure and said, "Mr. Chaney, I *will* marry you. I love you, Luke."

She pulled him up onto the bed and hugged him. They kissed. Ree's eyes filled with tears. "I never knew I could be this happy," she whispered. "I'm not sure I deserve it."

"You probably deserve better, but I'll do my best to keep you happy. You and the little one."

Her eyes clouded. "You don't think . . . you don't think it could be in the baby, do you?"

"Hush. Don't even think like that. That stuff only happens in horror movies."

"Luke, we've been *living* a horror movie, remember? I was almost killed by walking dead men. I was possessed by the filthy spirit of a giant worm that thought it was a god. We've both seen ghosts. How can I not think like this?"

Luke didn't know what to say, so he said nothing.

"I want to see an exorcist."

"You're not Catholic."

"But I might be possessed. How could they refuse to help me? I'm a good Christian."

"You can't just assume it's still in you. We have to be optimistic. The thing tried to control you but you beat it. Why would it hang around?"

"Because I have a tiny life growing inside me. A helpless fetus. A perfect place for this thing to hide, to sleep, to grow. I *know* what it is. How it works. It was in me and I learned a lot about it." She sobbed. "God help me. And our baby."

He held her. He wanted to protect her, but he didn't know how to shield her from an evil entity that might be hiding inside her, inside the kernel of life they had created. He didn't want to believe it was possible, but he knew she was right. They had seen and experienced too much to discount the fiendish possibility.

She pulled back from him. "Maybe Boots Birdwell knows what we can do. Maybe he knows someone. There *has* to be somebody who can help us."

"If there is, we'll find him. Or her. In the meantime, try not to worry about it. Just focus on taking care of yourself and the baby. Too much worry can't be good."

"You're right." She chewed on her lower lip. "I need a cigarette."

"You shouldn't—"

"I know," she cut him off. "I want one, but as of this moment, I'm a non-smoker. *I quit.*"

"Your guardian angel would be pleased," he said, trying to lighten her dark mood.

She gave him an odd look. "He would, wouldn't he? And that was his answer when I asked him how I could keep the darkness from 'gathering' me. Hmm. Maybe Beau knew exactly what he was talking about."

Luke shrugged.

"Would you do something for me?"

"Name it."

"Get me some chewing gum and some hard candy. Any kind. I'm going into nicotine withdrawal and I want to be damned sure I don't give in and light up. I'll keep candy and gum in my mouth. That should help."

He stood. "There's a vending machine in the lobby. I'll be right back."

He left the room and dug in his pocket for change. He found a quarter and flipped it into the air, playing a silly superstitious game he hadn't played since his childhood. *Heads and everything will be all right. Tails . . .*

It came up tails.

*   *   *

Ree craved a cigarette. She wanted to go through the familiar ritual of placing the filter tip between her lips, holding a flame to the tobacco, and drawing the soothing smoke deep into her lungs where that insidious itch demanded to be scratched. She popped a mint into her mouth and sucked on it with pursed lips. She'd rather be sucking down smoke, but she was determined to be strong in this battle with her addiction. If she wasn't carrying new life in her womb, she probably would've given in already to the craving and driven to the nearest store to buy a pack of smokes, but everything was different now. She had to keep herself healthy for the sake of the unformed child.

If Luke were here, it would be easier to keep the craving in check, but he was with the volunteer cleanup crews, working and sweating to salvage whatever was salvageable from the giant sinkhole, so Ree was alone, left to her own devices and distractions. She had spent all morning cleaning Luke's kitchen, rearranging the cabinets and pantry, scrubbing pots and pans that didn't really need scrubbing. As long as she stayed busy, she could keep her mind off smoking—or so she'd thought. Then the craving—the fiercest yet—had started.

"Maybe I should take up jogging again," she suggested to herself. That would certainly help clear out any residue of smoke, tar, and nicotine, and it might scratch that maddening itch deep in her lungs. But the doctor had advised her to take it easy for a few days and avoid strenuous activity. Her brain-scan reading had been negative, indicating no sign of brain damage, and Dr. Larson had said he wanted to see her again in two days to make sure there was nothing to indicate swelling of the brain. He'd discharged her that same day, and Luke had brought her here to his house and pampered her so much that she'd finally had to tell him to stop babying her.

"Save it for the real baby, honey," she'd said, "you're driving me crazy." The dear, sweet man. He was going to make a wonderful father, she was sure.

She decided that a brisk walk wouldn't jar her brain too much and it might get her mind off the cigarette craving. She put on her sneakers, borrowed one of Luke's old VPD ball caps to shade her eyes from the noon sun, and went out the back door. Luke had cleared a jogging trail through the six-acre wood behind his house, so she set out along the trail at a brisk clip. There was a hint of autumn in the late-summer day; the temperature and humidity were unusually low and sunlight angled to earth with early autumnal brightness. Squirrels chattered, birds chirped, cicadas sang, God was in His Heaven, and all seemed right with the world.

Her feet whispered over the trail as she relaxed into a steady rhythm, swinging her arms and swaying her hips. It was working. She didn't need a smoke. She felt good. Clean. Free.

From a low place inside her the dark thing rushed up to fill her heart with loathing and suffuse her mind with venom. She stumbled, clutching her arms to her chest as if to control the thing inside her, then staggered off the path and bumped into a skinny tree.

"No," she gasped, "not now, damn you. Leave me alone . . ."

But it did not leave. It expanded, and she feared that her skull and rib cage were going to explode. She went to her knees with a whimper.

Feelings entirely alien to her made her fall facedown and writhe in agony. The cap came off her head. She bit the ground and chewed a mouthful of dirt. She was shucking her humanity, shedding it the way a snake sheds its skin, and the thing inside her was making her perform behaviors it had performed when it still had its own physical form.

She fought for control, not willing to give up without a fight. She fought for herself, for Luke, for the baby. For humanity. Just when she thought she was gaining the upper hand, it reasserted itself and sent her crawling along the ground in undulating parody of a serpent, a giant worm with a skeletal structure and a skull sensitive to ground vibrations, a carnivorous creature born to burrow in the dirt and create a maze of tunnels, a creature feared and worshiped by a superstitious race living above ground.

She thrashed about on the trail, crushing her breasts into the ground and painfully wrenching her shoulders as she inched forward in snake-like fashion. She tried to call out to God for help but her mouth was full of dirt and she gagged on it.

Then she realized the thing was in a panic.

It was fighting for its unnatural life. It *was* badly wounded, going down in flames. It was trying to subdue her, not kill her. It was trying to nest in her, to use her as a place for hibernation and recuperation. It had used its old skull as a resting place but now its skull was smashed and it was seeking refuge in a human host. *It's trying to make me its haven.*

Ree fought with renewed vigor, knowing its weakness and sensing that she could win this struggle. She fought with the zeal of an Old Testament hero wrestling with Satan.

Before she realized what was happening, she was on her feet and running headlong into the trunk of a tall pine. She was helpless to stop her forward progress and she crashed into the tree, throwing her arms up at the last instant to protect her head. She hit the rough bark, bounced off and fell backward to the ground, dazed.

When she came to her senses, she had a small, heavy log in her hands and she was hitting her out-stretched legs with it. The pain was excruciating. But she couldn't stop the hammering blows. It wanted to break her legs and incapacitate her. It wanted to strand her out here in the woods where she would grow weak with hunger and lack of water. *Shrewd bastard!* She landed another blow to her lower leg and heard the bone snap. She screamed, choked, spat dirt. She tossed the log aside and grabbed her broken leg, crying. The tears were good. Tears meant she was still human.

But the pain was more than she could bear. Her vision dimmed. Darkened.

Her last thought before passing out was of the unborn baby.

*   *   *

Boots Birdwell entered the empty church and knelt at the altar. Ignoring the pain in his knees, he folded his hands and silently asked God to forgive his sins and to shine his divine light upon those places where darkness was hiding.

When he walked out of the church and into the heat of day, there was no feeling of inner peace to tell him that his prayers would be answered. He climbed into his truck and drove home to be with his beloved Eartha.

*   *   *

Filthy and exhausted from working all day in the sunken ruins of downtown Vinewood, Luke sat in the rocker on the front porch to remove his dirty boots, then entered the house. The screen door slammed behind him with its comforting slap of wood on wood. It was good to be home. Good to come home to the woman he loved.

303

"Ree?" he called.

No answer. The house felt empty. Anxiety edged into his weary awareness. "Where are you, Shorty?"

Still no answer.

He went through the house, checking every room. She was nowhere to be found.

* * *

She crawled through growing darkness, ignoring the pain as best she could. Blood was streaming into her eyes. Her mouth was gritty with a residue of dirt. Her torn shirt was down around her waist, her bra hanging from her left shoulder by a single strap, and her breasts were raw and bleeding. Her bicycle shorts were full of dirt, as was the one remaining sneaker.

Home. It was the one thought still fixed in her mind.

Home.

She lifted her head from the earth and saw the yellow rectangle of light in the distance. A window. In a house.

Home.

A screen door banged shut. A voice called: "Ree!"

Luke. Here. I'm here.

"Shorty?"

"Here . . ." she said aloud, but her voice was too weak to be heard. She didn't have the strength to cry out any louder.

Here . . .

The darkness swallowed her.

* * *

Then she was flying. Bouncing in the air. She blinked her eyes. Saw his face. Then darkness again.

Floating. In warm liquid. In the womb. Stinging pain, somehow pleasurable.

Opened eyes.

"Ah, thank God," he said. "What happened?"

She smiled up at him. She was in a tub full of warm water. He was bathing her with such gentleness and concern she thought her heart would burst with joy.

"I beat it," she said, her voice husky and hoarse. "It's gone."

"I think your leg's broken," he said as he wiped her face with a soapy washcloth. "Get you cleaned up and take you to the hospital."

She looked down at the raw wounds on her buoyant breasts and the ugly bruises on her lower legs. "I'm a mess," she said. "But it's gone. I think it's dead."

He picked her up, wrapped her in his bulky bathrobe, carried her to his truck and sat her in the passenger seat. She shivered in the night air.

"Beau was right," she said as he scooted behind the wheel and started the engine. "I gave up tobacco and my nicotine withdrawal drove it out of me. It tried to nest in me, in the baby, but it couldn't hack the withdrawal." She laughed a little drunkenly.

Luke looked askance at her and said, "I hope the baby's all right. You took a hell of a beating."

Ree opened the robe and placed her hands against the abraded flesh of her belly. "The baby's fine. She's going to be a real daddy's girl. Just you wait and see."

He tried to smile. "And you know this, how?"

"I know a lot of things. You'd be surprised. She'll have raven-black hair and enchanting eyes darker than the darkest night. And a smile to melt your heart. You'll see. She's going to be a real heartbreaker."

Luke gave her a look she couldn't read, then he put the truck in gear and they lurched forward into the dark. She closed her eyes. From a bottomless pool of inner darkness the unborn child reached out for her.

CHAPTER 31
GHOSTS

—I thought you'd be here. You're looking for her, huh? The loony.

—I sure ain't looking for rats.

—Wasting your time. She's not here.

—Time? Time ain't nothing.

—She's gone on.

—I wanted to tell her I was sorry for leaving her out here to die.

—Don't matter now. You know what dying is.

—But she was so . . .

—Forget it. You coming?

—Can't. Not yet.

—But she ain't here.

—My old man might be.

—Don't matter. Devil's Valley, remember?

—You don't know.

—Suit yourself. I'm moving on.

—Later, man. Blood brothers?

—Yeah. Blood brothers.

ACKNOWLEDGMENTS

Bad Juju was first loosed upon the world as a mass-market (in size only) paperback in 2003 by HellBound Walt Hicks who ran the original HellBound Books. Then in 2012 it was brought back into print only as an eBook by Craig Clarke and David T. Wilbanks with their Acid Graves publishing venture. In both cases the book eventually went out of print.

But Bad Juju just doesn't seem to want to stay dead. Now Cheryl Mullenax presents this new Red Room Press edition in trade paperback, eBook and hardback formats. For this current incarnation I gave the novel a tune-up with a few minor changes under the hood so it runs a little smoother—revised for a better ride.

I extend my gratitude to geologist Dr. R.B. Schultz for enlightening me on the subject of sinkholes and geological engineering. Should you, gentle reader, ever need a consultation with a rock doctor, go to www.therockdoctor.com.

I'm happy to acknowledge my old schoolmate and railroad historian Larry Goolsby for allowing me to pick his considerable brain on the subject of trains and train yards.

The blues lyrics Billy Joe's ghost sings in the pecan tree are from "Me and the Devil Blues" by legendary bluesman Robert Johnson. See you down at the crossroads, Robert.

—R.C.

RANDY CHANDLER is the author of the novels *Dime Detective, Daemon of the Dark Wood, HELLz BELLz*, and the fantasy novel *Angel Steel*. He also co-authored *Duet For the Devil* with t. Winter-Damon (God rest his soul). Randy's collection of short stories is *Devils, Death & Dark Wonders*. He is the Associate Editor of Red Room Press and co-editor of *Year's Best Hardcore Horror*.

Randy has been an indie magazine editor/publisher, a freelance book reviewer, a mental health worker, a gas-pump jockey, an ambulance attendant, a soldier in Vietnam, and a funeral home flunky. He often haunts fields of carnage where angels and devils do battle.

YEAR'S BEST
HARDCORE
HORROR
NOT YOUR MAMA'S BEST-OF HORROR ANNUAL
REDROOMPRESS.COM/YEARS-BEST-HARDCORE-HORROR
EDITORS:
RANDY CHANDLER
CHERYL MULLENAX

www.ingramcontent.com/pod-product-compliance
Lightning Source LLC
Chambersburg PA
CBHW070632260626
47161CB00007B/2672